# The Lady By His Side

*A marquess in need of the right bride. An earl's daughter in search of a purpose. A betrayal that ends in murder and balloons into a threat to the realm.*

Sebastian Cynster knows time is running out. If he doesn't choose a wife soon, his female relatives will line up to assist him. Yet the current debutantes do not appeal. Where is he to find the right lady to be his marchioness? Then Drake Varisey, eldest son of the Duke of Wolverstone, asks for Sebastian's aid.

Having assumed his father's mantle in protecting queen and country, Drake must go to Ireland in pursuit of a dangerous plot. But he's received an urgent missive from Lord Ennis, an Irish peer—Ennis has heard something Drake needs to know. Ennis insists Drake attends an upcoming house party at Ennis's Kent estate so Ennis can reveal his information face-to-face.

Sebastian has assisted Drake before and, long ago, had a liaison with Lady Ennis. Drake insists Sebastian is just the man to be Drake's surrogate at the house party—the guests will imagine all manner of possibilities and be blind to Sebastian's true purpose.

Unsurprisingly, Sebastian is reluctant, but Drake's need is real. With only more debutantes on his horizon, Sebastian allows himself to be persuaded.
His first task is to inveigle Antonia Rawlings, a lady he has known all her life, to include him as her escort to the house party. Although he's seen little of Antonia in recent years, Sebastian is confident of gaining her support.

Eldest daughter of the Earl of Chillingworth, Antonia has abandoned the search for a husband and plans to use the week of the house party to decide what to do with her life. There has to be some purpose, some role, she can claim for her own.

Consequently, on hearing Sebastian's request and an explanation of what lies behind it, she seizes on the call to action. Suppressing her senses' idiotic reaction to Sebastian's nearness, she agrees to be his partner-in-intrigue.
But while joining the house party proves easy, the gathering is

thrown into chaos when Lord Ennis is murdered—just before he was to speak with Sebastian. Worse, Ennis's last words, gasped to Sebastian, are: *Gunpowder. Here.*

Gunpowder? And here, where?

With a killer continuing to stalk the halls, side by side, Sebastian and Antonia search for answers and, all the while, the childhood connection that had always existed between them strengthens and blooms...into something so much more.

*First volume in a trilogy. A historical romance with gothic overtones layered over a continuing intrigue. A full length novel of 99,000 words.*

# Praise for the works of Stephanie Laurens

# Other Titles from Stephanie Laurens

# STEPHANIE LAURENS

## The Lady By His Side

### A Cynster Next Generation Novel

Savdek Management Pty. Ltd.

THE LADY BY HIS SIDE
Copyright © 2017 by Savdek Management Proprietary Limited
ISBN: 978-1-925559-01-9


Cover design by Savdek Management Pty. Ltd.
Cover and inside front couple photography and photographic composition by Period Images © 2017

Savdek Management Proprietary Limited, Melbourne, Australia.
www.stephanielaurens.com
Email: admin@stephanielaurens.com

The names Stephanie Laurens, the SL Logo and the Cynsters are registered trademarks of Savdek Management Proprietary Ltd.

# The Lady By His Side

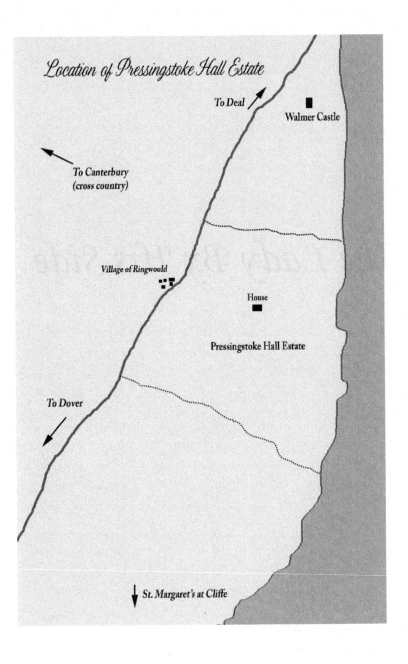

Location of Pressingstoke Hall Estate

To Deal

Walmer Castle

To Canterbury
(cross country)

Village of Ringwould

House

Pressingstoke Hall Estate

To Dover

St. Margaret's at Cliffe

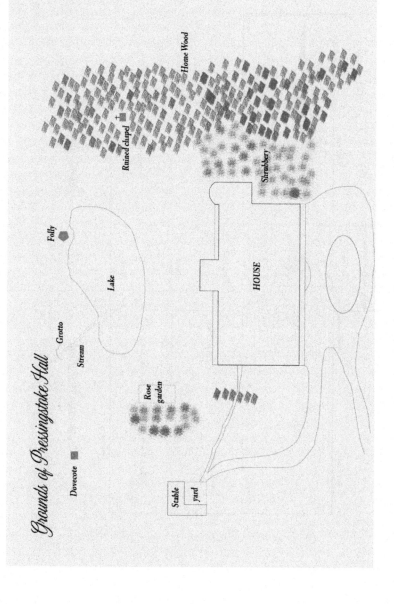

Grounds of Pressingstoke Hall

Dovecote

Folly

Grotto

Stream

Lake

Home Wood

Ruined chapel

Shrubbery

HOUSE

Rose garden

Stable yard

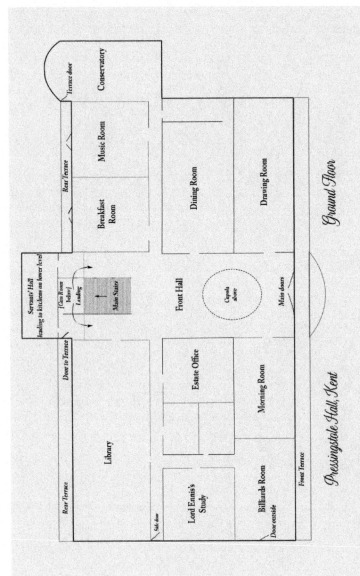

Pressingstoke Hall, Kent

Ground Floor

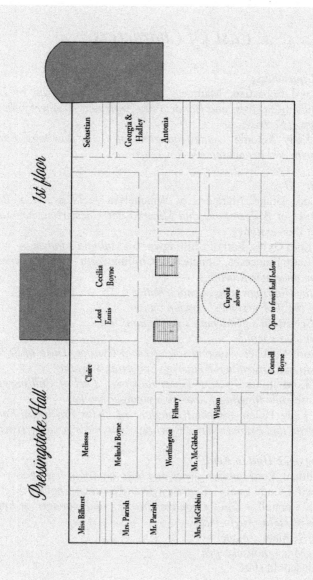

*Pressingstoke Hall*

1st floor

Miss Bilhurst

Mrs. Parrish

Mr. Parrish

Mrs. McGibbin

Melissa

Melinda Boyne

Worthington

Mr. McGibbin

Clare

Filbury

Wilson

Lord Ennis

Cecilia Boyne

Cupola above

Connell Boyne

Open to front hall below

Sebastian

Georgia & Hadley

Antonia

# Cast Of Characters

**Principal Characters:**
Cynster, Lord Sebastian, Marquess of Earith – *eldest son of Devil Cynster, Duke of St. Ives, and Honoria née Anstruther-Wetherby; heir to the dukedom of St. Ives*
Rawlings, Lady Antonia – *eldest daughter of Gyles Rawlings, Earl of Chillingworth, and Francesca née Rawlings*

**In London:**
Varisey, Lord Drake, Marquess of Winchelsea – *eldest son of Royce Varisey, Duke of Wolverstone, and Minerva née Chesterton; heir to the dukedom of Wolverstone*
Rawlings, Lord Gyles, Earl of Chillingworth – *Antonia's father*
Rawlings, Lady Francesca, Countess of Chillingworth – *Gyles's wife and Antonia's mother, née Rawlings*
Withers – *the Chillingworths' London butler*
Hamilton – *the Wolverstones' London butler*
Wilkins – *Sebastian's gentleman's gentleman*
Beccy – *Antonia's maid*
Cynster, Lord Michael – *second son of Devil Cynster, Duke of St. Ives, and Honoria née Anstruther-Wetherby; Sebastian's brother*
Rawlings, Lord Julius – *son of Gyles Rawlings, Earl of Chillingworth, and Francesca née Rawlings; Antonia's younger brother*
Rawlings, Lady Helen – *second daughter of Gyles Rawlings, Earl of Chillingworth, and Francesca née Rawlings; Antonia's younger sister*

**At Pressingstoke Hall in Kent:**
Boyne, William, Lord Ennis – *owner and host, an Anglo-Irish peer*
Boyne, Cecilia, Lady Ennis – *Ennis's wife and hostess; English*
Boyne, Mr. Connell – *Ennis's younger brother and manager of Ennis's Irish estate at Tulla; Anglo-Irish*
Blanchard, William – *butler*
Blanchard, Mrs. – *housekeeper*
Various household staff
Various stablemen and grooms

*Guests at the house party:*
Boyne, Miss Melinda – *cousin of William and Connell, lives in Southampton with her aging mother, invited at the last minute to make up the numbers; Anglo-Irish*

Wainwright, The Hon. Miss Melissa – *viscount's daughter and spinster friend of Antonia, Claire, and Georgia; English*

Savage, The Hon. Miss Claire – *viscount's daughter and spinster friend of Antonia, Melissa, and Georgia*

Featherstonehaugh, The Hon. Mrs. Georgia – *married to Hadley Featherstonehaugh; Antonia's, Claire's, and Melissa's friend; English and distantly connected to Cecilia Boyne*

Featherstonehaugh, The Hon. Mr. Hadley – *Georgia's husband; English*

Parrish, Mr. Samuel – *Ennis's longtime friend; Anglo-Irish landowner*

Parrish, Mrs. Winifred – *Samuel Parrish's wife; English*

Bilhurst, Miss Amelie – *Mrs. Parrish's niece, traveling with the Parrishes; English*

McGibbin, Mr. Harold – *Ennis's longtime friend; Anglo-Irish landowner*

McGibbin, Mrs. Constance – *Harold McGibbin's wife; Anglo-Irish*

Filbury, Mr. Henry – *bachelor friend of Connell and acquaintance of Ennis; Anglo-Irish*

Wilson, Mr. Patrick – *bachelor friend of Connell and acquaintance of Ennis; Anglo-Irish*

Worthington, Mr. Baylor – *bachelor friend of Connell and acquaintance of Ennis; English*

**Others:**
Rattle, Sir Humphrey – *local magistrate*
Crawford, Inspector – *from Scotland Yard*
Crickwell, Sergeant – *of the local constabulary*
Various constables

**At Walmer Castle:**
Wellesley, Lord Arthur, Duke of Wellington – *Lord of the Cinque Ports and Commander-in-Chief of the Army*
Moreton – *Wellington's secretary*

# CHAPTER 1

*Arthur's Gentlemen's Club, St. James, London*
*October 15, 1850*

"*I* need your help."

Lord Sebastian Cynster, Marquess of Earith, sank into the comfort of a leather armchair in the refined quiet of Arthur's and watched as Lord Drake Varisey, Marquess of Winchelsea, settled his elegant length in the armchair facing Sebastian's.

Drake had sent a footman around that morning with a request for this midafternoon meeting. Sebastian had arrived to find Drake waiting in the foyer, and together, they'd ambled through the club. It was too late for the luncheon crowd and too early for the dinner scrum; there'd been few to witness their presence. By unvoiced agreement, they'd made their way to the alcove off the far end of the long, narrow library; from the pair of armchairs slightly angled down the room, they could see at a glance that there was no one near enough to overhear their exchange.

"As I recall," Sebastian murmured, "the last time I helped you, I had to hide my hands from my mother for more than a week." He glanced at one hand, long fingers relaxed on the chair's arm. There was no sign of bruised and scraped knuckles now, but his sharp-eyed mother, the Duchess of St. Ives, had she detected such evidence her firstborn was indulging in fisticuffs, would have evinced far too much interest as to the circumstances for either Sebastian's or Drake's comfort, Sebastian's mother being a bosom-bow of Drake's mother, the Duchess of Wolverstone.

"You enjoyed every minute of it," Drake replied. "And regardless, this is, I'm afraid, a matter of queen and country."

"Ah." Sebastian stilled. "Queen and country" was Drake's way of flagging affairs—more specifically missions—with the potential to impact the security of the realm.

"Besides," Drake said, his dark brows arching, his golden-hazel eyes—eagle's eyes—keen on Sebastian's face, "what other absorbing prospects can you possibly have to fill your hours at this time of year?"

As it happened, Sebastian had a mission of his own that he was currently pursuing, but it wasn't something he had any intention of sharing with anyone, much less Drake.

They were very alike—in many ways and on many planes. Drake was two years Sebastian's senior, and because of the friendship between their families, they'd known each other from their earliest years. As sons of the higher nobility, they'd attended Eton and Oxford, both at Balliol; their paths had, perforce, crossed again and again at both institutions.

Although they would never be mistaken for brothers, the physical similarities were nevertheless striking. Both were tall—several inches over six feet—broad shouldered, long limbed, and lean, and moved with the inherent, somewhat predatory grace of powerful men comfortable in their own skins—men who were confident in their strengths, in their prowess, in their ability to meet whatever challenges the world sent their way.

They were both dark haired, although Sebastian's hair was a true blue-black, while Drake's was sable. Scions of the upper echelon that they were, their hair was fashionably cropped, worn just long enough to brush their collars, and they were elegantly attired, both favoring subdued colors and unobtrusively exceptional tailoring. Sebastian, with his pale green eyes, generally wore some combination of black and tan, while Drake, with his eagle's eyes, habitually wore midnight blue teamed with lighter-hued golds and browns.

Both shared the pale complexions of their Norman ancestors, together with the chiseled facial features and innately autocratic expressions of those progenitors. High cheekbones, wide brows, well-set eyes, and patrician noses, thin, mobile lips, and squared chins completed the picture, yet the impression each projected was quite distinct.

Sebastian appeared hard, shielded—more openly a warrior in civilized garb. Drake, on the other hand, could, when he smiled, seem charming, but behind the façade lurked a ruthlessness that anyone who really looked into his golden predator's eyes could not fail to see.

Drake had, in large part, picked up where his powerful father had left off. When Royce, Duke of Wolverstone, had finally retired from assisting the government and the Crown in dealing with matters that threatened the realm—those matters that required incisive, decisive, and covert action—

many had assumed that, with the wars long over, there would be no real need for the services of such as Wolverstone again.

In that, they'd erred. While no fresh wars had been declared, tensions remained, exacerbated by this action or that, which resulted in plots, clashes, and schemes, some commercial, some political, and many held the potential to destabilize the state and cause havoc in wider society.

When Wolverstone had declined to emerge from retirement, the disgruntled political powers had offered the position to his heir. Drake had inherited most if not all of his father's relevant abilities, including the knack of inspiring other men and building networks of informers; those sterling capabilities had been augmented by some of his mother's traits— such as the ability to charm. Wolverstone had never charmed anyone in his life; Sebastian seriously doubted the duke had ever seen the need.

But Sebastian and Drake lived in a somewhat different world to that of their fathers' heyday. That said, some things remained cast in stone, among them, family honor and loyalty.

Sebastian's father, the Duke of St. Ives, the duke's brother, and his cousins had all fought at Waterloo. The engagement in which their troop was credited with having helped to carry the day had been critical to the battle's outcome—to England's success.

While Sebastian, his brother Michael, and their tribe of Cynster cousins and second cousins no longer had wars in which to serve their country, they still instinctively heeded and responded to duty's call. And Drake had uttered the magic words "queen and country."

There was no point dissembling. Sebastian's personal quest wasn't urgent. More, he knew himself well enough to acknowledge a certain readiness to allow himself to be deflected by a legitimate distraction. He sighed and met Drake's eyes. "What do you need me to do?"

Drake fleetingly grinned, but a second later, all humor drained from his face. "Yesterday afternoon, I received a letter from Lord Ennis." Drake languidly waved one hand. "I believe you and he are acquainted."

"Distantly." Sebastian uttered the word as repressively as he could; his acquaintance was with Ennis's wife, a point he felt sure Drake knew.

"Ennis wrote asking me to call on him at his estate in Kent. Judging by his composition, he was suffering from a degree of agitation. He said he had stumbled on information that he believed I needed to know, but that he was unwilling to commit said information to writing and was unable to travel to London at this time. He and his wife are hosting a house party commencing on the nineteenth—four days from now. Various guests have already arrived. Ennis stressed he needs to see me privately, face-to-face. He suggested I attend the house party as one of the guests. Reading between his lines, I believe Ennis wishes to engineer a situation in which he can speak with me without alerting those about him as to the nature of our exchange."

Sebastian arched his brows. "You turning up at the Ennises' house party…there's no way that won't be noticed and widely commented on."

"Indeed. Which is one reason *I* won't be taking up his lordship's invitation."

Sebastian opened his eyes wide. "*Me* turning up at the Ennises' house party will be every bit as bad. People will speculate wildly."

"But not for the same reason." Drake smiled. "Few know you occasionally sully your noble hands by getting involved in the missions I run."

Sebastian lifted one shoulder. "Few know that you sully your noble hands by running your own missions—society in general imagines you sit in an office in Whitehall and pull strings all day."

Drake's smile turned wry. "Few appreciate that, while in my father's day, our enemies lay over the seas, the realm's current enemies are much nearer to hand."

"It always amazes me that no one seems to notice that, while your father worked under the aegis of the Foreign Office, you report to the Home Secretary."

"In truth, there aren't that many people in the wider population who know of the details of the position I hold, and I would prefer to keep it that way. Which is yet another reason I won't be driving down to Pressingstoke Hall next Saturday." Drake held up a hand to stay Sebastian's protest that him taking Drake's place wouldn't work. "Bear with me—there are reasons I chose you to go in my place."

"Such as?" Sebastian invested all his considerable supercilious arrogance into the words. Futilely; his arrogance bounced off Drake and made no impact at all.

"Quite aside from raising too many eyebrows, along with questions we'd all prefer to avoid, I can't go into Kent to meet Ennis because I'll be leaving tomorrow or the day after for Ireland. My contacts there have turned up information that, if true, is worrisome, to say the least. But at present, the intelligence is fractured. I need to go myself—to show my face—in order to get confirmation from deeper within the insurgents' hierarchy."

Sebastian studied Drake's expression. As usual, it gave little away. "I presume by insurgents you mean the Young Irelanders."

Drake shrugged. "I imagine so, but until I get confirmation, I can't be certain. After their failure in '48, they retreated to lick their wounds, but they haven't gone away. There have been various minor protests, but this is the first whiff I've had of anything potentially serious." He arched a brow. "I have to follow it up."

"Ennis is an Anglo-Irish peer."

"Just so. And there'll be other Anglo-Irish gentlemen at this house party."

Sebastian caught Drake's gaze. "So are the two issues connected—what you're hearing from your Irish contacts and Ennis's sudden wish to speak with you face-to-face?"

"It's tempting to imagine so, but there's no way to tell at this point. I have to go to Ireland and see what I can winkle out, while you, my friend, need to stand in for me at Pressingstoke Hall."

His eyes locked with Drake's, Sebastian considered, then faintly grimaced. "You said there were reasons—plural—why you selected me specifically to take your place. What are the others?"

"Just one, really. Out of all those of our ilk I might call on to attend the Ennises' house party, you are the only one who can do so without appearing entirely out of place." In response to Sebastian's look of disbelief—he was heir to a wealthy and powerful dukedom as much as Drake was—Drake continued, "As you rightly pointed out, either one of us turning up at Pressingstoke Hall without some acceptable reason to excuse our presence is going to attract an inordinate amount of attention, which will fuel gossip and speculation—precisely what Ennis wishes to avoid. But Ennis sent a guest list. As you're no doubt aware, Lady Ennis is something of a social climber—she invited an old friend and encouraged said friend to invite her more exalted circle, which includes Antonia Rawlings, who will be attending."

Drake sat back; raising his interlaced fingers to his chin, he smiled at Sebastian. "I suggest you use your persuasive talents and convince dear Antonia to allow you to accompany her into Kent. The association between your families is widely known. As Antonia's mother will not be accompanying her, no one will be all that surprised to see you acting as Antonia's escort."

Sebastian frowned. He could appreciate the scenario Drake had described. And yes, he suspected he could make it a reality. It would mean gaining Antonia's support and spending more time with her than he had in recent years—indeed, than he ever had—but she came from much the same stock as he and Drake; he didn't doubt that she would help him for the same reason he would help Drake.

After a moment of imagining, he shot a look at Drake. "Ennis is not going to be pleased to see me."

Drake's swift grin surfaced. "Not initially, but he will be. I'll write to him and explain that I won't be coming, but that I'll send someone in my stead. Given Ennis's trepidatiousness, it seems entirely possible someone at the house party is involved in whatever scheme he intends to bring to my attention, so I'm not going to put your name in writing. Instead, I'll tell Ennis that my surrogate will be the very last man he'll want to see."

Sebastian groaned.

"No—think about it. As you're one of his wife's ex-lovers, Ennis won't want you there, and his animosity will show. No one is going to imagine him willingly telling you—trusting you with—anything sensitive. You are the perfect gentleman for the task." Drake's smile returned. "Being Antonia's escort and the hostess's ex-lover...no one will look for any other reason for your attendance at Pressingstoke Hall."

\* \* \*

The following morning at a little before eleven o'clock, Sebastian walked down the steps of St. Ives House in Grosvenor Square. He was correctly attired for a morning visit in coat, waistcoat, and trousers. Idly swinging his cane, he headed for Green Street.

After his meeting with Drake, he'd dined with friends. Rather than join the group in a night on the town—a diversion that was increasingly losing the attraction it once had held—he'd returned to the peaceful quiet of St. Ives House. With his parents still in the country and his sister visiting friends in the Dales, only he and Michael were currently residing in the mansion, and Michael, as usual, was out.

Sebastian had walked into the library, poured himself a brandy, then slumped into an armchair by the cheery fire, sipped, and turned his mind to this morning's endeavor.

At least, that had been his intention, but the pervasive silence of the house—the lack of anyone with whom he might discuss the situation—had impinged and nudged his mind back to his personal project, the one he'd so readily set aside in favor of assisting Drake.

Finding the right wife was no easy task, not for a gentleman—a nobleman—like him or, for that matter, Drake. Sebastian knew Drake was steadfastly avoiding the issue and would for as long as he could—just as his father had. Sebastian, on the other hand, had realized that such a tack was not going to work for him; he had too many female relatives. Various members of that sorority had already started dropping hints. He had, he judged, at most another year—another Season—before they came after him in a concerted way, determined to assist him in doing his duty and ensuring the succession of one of the primary dukedoms in the country.

To date, his mother had held off—and in doing so had kept all the others at bay—but he'd recently turned thirty-one. His father had married at thirty-three. In Sebastian's estimation, his mother's forbearance would almost certainly not extend beyond his next birthday.

He'd decided he needed to attend to the matter himself—within the next year—before his female relatives attempted to take charge.

But finding the right lady to make his marchioness, ultimately his duchess, was proving far more difficult than he'd imagined. Possibly because, until the past few days, he hadn't made any effort to define what qualities that role required. Three very brief excursions into the ballrooms had underscored the conclusion that any of the bright young things—the recent crops of debutantes who circulated in hopeful droves at ton events—would drive him to drink within a week.

He needed someone more mature, someone of his own class with whom he could actually converse. Someone with whom he could share a ducal life.

In that day and age, a ducal life brought with it significant responsibility—politically, socially, and as a landowner and investor. It was a life of assured luxury, but unless one worked at it, satisfaction would not be forthcoming.

He needed a wife who could stand by his side—who had the backbone, talents, and skills to do so.

That much, he now understood. But as to where he might find such a lady, he had absolutely no idea.

Brooding on the matter did no good. Taking a long swallow of brandy, he'd set the vexed issue aside and turned his mind to the more immediate prospect of Drake's mission.

He'd focused on Antonia, calling up all he could remember of her. It was something of a shock to realize that, although he'd known her since birth—hers, as he was two years older—and they'd spent long summers and numerous other holidays running wild as part of the large group of Cynster children of which he'd been the undisputed leader, while he could remember those carefree days—remember her quite clearly as an eager participant in almost any lark—he knew very little of the lady she'd grown to be.

He'd last seen her only months before, in May at his cousin Marcus's wedding in Scotland. He'd recognized her instantly; it wasn't that he hadn't met her over the years, but rather that he hadn't spent any time with her—private time in which he might have learned what she thought about things, how she felt, how she reacted…what sort of lady she'd grown into. All his meetings with her over the past decade had been the same as at Marcus's wedding—in the middle of a large group of his relatives who were as much her friends as his.

Curious, now he thought of it, that on the surface, he knew her well, yet he knew so little about the woman she now was. Too little to feel confident of managing or manipulating her. In order to deal with her, he would either have to learn fast or rely on his persuasive skills.

With that in mind, he'd honed his approach, his arguments. He rehearsed them as he strolled down Green Street, then climbed the steps of Number 17 and plied the knocker.

The butler recognized him. "Good morning, my lord."

"Good morning, Withers. I need to speak with Lady Antonia."
Sebastian arched a languid brow. "I assume she's at home." At that hour
in that season, Antonia was unlikely to be anywhere else.

"Indeed, my lord." Withers stepped back and bowed. "If you will step
inside, I will inquire."

Sebastian walked into the elegant front hall.

Withers shut the door and reached for Sebastian's cane. "The earl is
out at the moment, my lord, but the countess and Lady Antonia have
come downstairs."

Sebastian cooled his heels in the front hall while Withers retreated to
the rear of the house, then returned to escort him to the back parlor—the
room the family used—indicating that the countess, at least, had correctly
deduced that this was not a formal morning call.

Withers opened the door at the end of the corridor and bowed
Sebastian through. He walked in. The parlor overlooked the garden,
possessed an abundance of white-framed windows, and was furnished
with white wickerwork armchairs and sofa upholstered in slub silk. The
silk sported a feathery pattern in white, greens, and blues, creating a light,
airy atmosphere that was the perfect setting for the two very different but
equally vibrant ladies who looked up as he entered. One pair of emerald-
green eyes and another of cool gray regarded him with interest and
expectation.

Chillingworth's countess, Francesca, was perched on the window seat,
while Antonia was sitting in an armchair a little way from and angled to
the window.

Antonia was tall for a female; she'd inherited her height from her
father's side and, like her late paternal grandmother, was slender,
willowy, and effortlessly elegant. Her figure was svelte, lacking
Francesca's abundant curvaceousness, but Antonia's coloring was a more
obvious blending of her father's and mother's—from Francesca came the
lush, gleaming blackness of her long hair, presently up in a fashionable
loose bun, while she'd inherited the fine skin and pale complexion of the
females of her father's family. Her exquisitely shaped ruby lips, finely
arched black brows, and the long black lashes that framed her large eyes
were all Francesca, but those eyes were Chillingworth's silvery gray. The
combination was unexpected and, if come upon unawares, could be
riveting.

In contrast, Francesca was quite short, a pocket Venus in every way.
Despite her matronly status, the countess retained an abundance of energy
along with her bounteous charms.

Sebastian was pleased that none of Antonia's siblings were present, especially her nosy little sister, Helen.

"Sebastian." Francesca had been reading a letter. She set it aside and held out her hand as, with an easy smile curving his lips, he strolled forward.

He took her hand and bowed over her fingers. "Lady Francesca."

Francesca made a rude sound at the formality and flicked her hand, directing him to Antonia.

Her elegant daughter had been embroidering. She laid the frame in her lap and, her fine eyes quizzing him, gave him her hand. "Sebastian."

He grasped her fingers and half bowed. "Antonia."

As he straightened, she arched her brows. "No 'Lady'?"

Those cool gray eyes were laughing at him. He missed only one heartbeat before replying, "You don't need the title."

She smiled, a laughing, radiant smile that lit her face.

Arrested, he stared.

Beside them, Francesca chortled. "An excellent riposte. Who says you young ones know nothing of repartee?"

Antonia glanced at her mother, releasing Sebastian and recalling him to his purpose. He freed her fingers.

Francesca waved him to the chair facing Antonia's across the window seat. "Do sit down, Sebastian—like Gyles and your father, you are far too tall to stand and converse." As soon as he'd subsided into the armchair, Francesca brightly asked, "So what can we do for you? I take it you wish us to assist you with something?"

The countess had spent her formative years in Italy; she had never seen the sense in British reserve, claiming it only wasted time.

Sebastian recalled that now. He glanced at Antonia and saw her lips quirking and her eyes dancing in understanding and empathy. He cleared his throat and returned his gaze to Francesca, who was plainly waiting with mounting impatience. "I've been asked by Winchelsea to assist in a mission that may prove critical to the safety of the realm. However, to successfully conduct the mission, I need your"—Sebastian swung his gaze to Antonia—"or more specifically Antonia's, help."

Antonia widened her eyes at him. "That sounds serious."

"It is." He had Ennis's letter to Drake and a copy of Drake's reply, both of which Drake had sent around that morning, in his pocket to prove that, if need be. He glanced at Francesca, realized she was frowning, and hurriedly added, "There'll be no danger involved. I merely have to act in Drake's stead and speak with someone. Drake is otherwise engaged, but he needs to learn what this person has to tell him."

Francesca looked unconvinced. "Who is this person?"

"Lord Ennis." Sebastian glanced at Antonia.

She blinked, then stared at him. "You want to go to the Ennises' house party?"

He nodded. "But I need a believable reason for attending. Drake suggested that, given our families' long association and"—he looked at Francesca—"that you're not planning to attend, ma'am, then it wouldn't raise eyebrows were we to pretend that I was accompanying Antonia"— he returned his gaze to her—"as her escort."

Antonia's eyes started to narrow, her lips to compress, and her chin to set—all ominous signs.

"Purely pretense." Leaning forward, he clasped his hands between his thighs, fixed his eyes on her face, and spoke directly to her. "*We* would know it was all a sham, but there would be no need to tell anyone else that." He knew how to get Francesca on his side; it was Antonia he needed to convince.

Antonia regarded Sebastian with exceedingly mixed feelings. He had always had the ability to appear entirely sincere—and for all she knew, he might *be* sincere. Might genuinely believe he could pretend to be her escort at a house party and not react in his habitually overprotective— dictatorial and absolute—fashion.

Just the thought of enduring five whole days of him looming at her shoulder was enough to make her nerves cinch tight.

And in the informal atmosphere of a country house party where he wouldn't know anyone else, he might well keep so close that he would rub her nerves—not to mention her senses—raw.

Luckily, he hadn't yet realized that he'd already won over her mother with his comment about Francesca not attending. The Ennises' house party was to be Antonia's first as a spinster—a lady out from under her mother's wing. Her parents had agreed to the arrangement only because three of her friends were also attending, two, like her, as spinsters, along with the fourth member of their small circle, now the highly respectable the Honorable Mrs. Hadley Featherstonehaugh.

Melissa Wainwright and Claire Savage, Antonia's unwed friends, were, like her, expecting to enjoy their first foray free of maternal oversight. It wasn't that any of them expected to engage in any romance but rather the lure of a sort of freedom none of them had ever enjoyed.

For Antonia to then turn up with Sebastian in tow…

She stared at him—nearly glared—and made no effort to hide her dislike of the entire idea. Trust Drake to have thought of it—the man was a menace. "Just how important is this message Lord Ennis has for Drake?"

"Important enough for Drake to not even contemplate putting Ennis off until Drake returns—he's had to go to Ireland."

"Ireland?" Francesca glanced at Antonia, then looked back at Sebastian. "Is there any possibility of some new threat from that direction?"

Sebastian debated for a second; Antonia saw that in his face. But then he evenly replied, "The threat from the Young Irelanders never went away. But these days, they concentrate on protests in Ireland, and whatever Ennis wants to convey, it's all in words—a warning at most, or possibly merely background information. There is no immediate threat involved." Sebastian met Antonia's eyes. "Neither Drake nor I would have contemplated involving you if there was."

While she found that remark comforting on one level, Antonia felt a spurt of irritation at the way gentlemen—noblemen in particular, and she'd always understood the license the rank conferred—invariably shielded women such as her from any possible danger. As if ladies such as she were inherently too weak to stand with them. As if they—the males—were all-powerful, while she and her sisters had nothing to contribute and, more, were something of a liability.

"If there is no danger, why do you need to go at all?" She opened her eyes wide. "Why can't I approach Ennis and get the message for Drake?" She knew the answer, but wanted to make Sebastian say it.

His lips thinned to a line, but when he spoke, his tone remained even—patiently persuasive. "Because, quite aside from us not knowing what action the message might necessitate—such as riding to Whitehall post haste—Ennis is highly unlikely to entrust his message to a lady, no matter how highly placed and well connected."

When Sebastian shut his lips and declined to complete the answer, she added, "And it's possible, even likely, that having a lady sent as go-between instead of a gentleman such as yourself will put Ennis's back up, and he might decline to share his so-important information at all."

Sebastian's fleeting grimace was sign enough that she had that right, too.

Her reaction to what she viewed as a slight was almost intense enough to make her throw caution to the winds and agree to his and Drake's outrageous scheme—she could and would assist them, possibly in ways they hadn't dreamt of—but...when it came to acting as escort for a lady like her, she knew Sebastian. Apparently, better than he knew himself. Rapidly, she considered how best to retain control—of herself, at least. "*If* I agree to this, you need to agree not to actually act as an escort would—that you will not at any time seek to constrain my behavior in any way." *That you will* not *get in my way.*

He understood perfectly, as if he'd heard the words she hadn't said. His lips thinned again, but then he nodded. Curtly. Once. "*If* you agree to our necessary charade, I will give you my word that the only time I might step in is if you are in some degree of imminent danger."

She wasn't going to get better than that. After a second of further consideration, she graciously inclined her head. "Very well."

Sebastian almost sighed with relief. For an instant there, he'd had the feeling he was standing on thin ice—because of what, exactly, he had no real notion—but she'd agreed, and that was enough. Once she'd given her word, she wouldn't renege. "I gather the party starts on Saturday. I'll drive us down. What time should I pick you up?"

"That depends on your horses. How long will it take us to reach Deal? Pressingstoke Hall is on the coast a little south of there."

"Going via the Dover Road will be fastest—we can turn north along the coast road from there." Sebastian rapidly calculated. "It'll take just over six hours."

"We're expected at three in the afternoon."

"Then I'll call here at eight in the morning. We can stop at Faversham for lunch."

"I've been thinking." Francesca addressed her daughter. "You must let the Ennises know that Sebastian will be attending as your escort. I suggest a letter to Lady Ennis, throwing yourself on her mercy and saying that although you had previously gained my permission, when your father heard of your proposed stay, he insisted you have a suitable escort." The countess waved. "No one will be surprised at that—Gyles's overprotectiveness is legendary. And as for the reason Julius isn't with you, as your brother is younger than you, your father refused to accept him as an escort capable of swaying you—which, heaven knows, is true. Consequently, we appealed to Sebastian, and he kindly agreed to act as your escort." Francesca beamed. "There!" Eyes bright, she looked at Sebastian. "And as there is no hostess in England, Scotland, Ireland, or Wales who wouldn't give her eyeteeth to have you attend her house party, Lady Ennis will excuse the late notice—indeed, she'll be in alt."

Lady Ennis, Sebastian feared, would, indeed, be imagining a paradise—a far from innocent and distinctly illicit one. But Francesca's ruse would clear the way for him to attend the house party, and that was his principal aim. He could avoid Cecilia, Lady Ennis, and stick with Antonia on the pretext of taking his escort duties seriously.

If he had, in truth, given the Earl of Chillingworth his word that he would guard the virtue of the earl's precious eldest daughter, then his sticking to her side would be entirely expected.

Slowly, he nodded, then glanced at Antonia. "I second your mother's suggestion. Such a tale will adequately excuse my presence and silence any questions over my turning up more or less unheralded."

Antonia met his eyes. Although nothing showed in her expression, he sensed a certain mutinous reaction. But then she nodded, rather tersely, and he breathed again.

Deciding to quit while he was ahead, he rose. "Thank you both. I must get on, and I daresay you have morning calls to make."

Antonia rose, as did Francesca.

He bowed over Francesca's hand, then turned to Antonia.

She offered her hand, and he grasped her slender fingers. Rather than bow, he pressed her fingers gently and smiled at her. "Thank you for agreeing. I promise you won't regret it."

She stood looking up at him; her face was near expressionless, and he was visited by the odd notion that shutters suddenly screened her eyes. Then her lashes fell, and she looked down. "We'll see."

Cynical skepticism colored the words.

He didn't approve of her lack of faith in him. He'd eased his grip, and she started to draw her fingers from his—he had to clamp down on a sudden urge to tighten his hold again.

He quashed the silly reaction. "Don't bother Withers," he said to Francesca. "I'll see myself out." With a last polite nod and a general smile, he made for the door.

Antonia stood transfixed and watched him go. Even after the door closed on his broad-shouldered figure, she continued to stare, unseeing, at the panel.

She'd always known she reacted to Sebastian in an odd way—in a way somehow different to how she responded to, for instance, his brother, Michael, or his cousins Marcus and Christopher, all of whom were of a similar age. Or indeed, to any other gentleman. She'd put it down to Sebastian being…well, Sebastian—his dominant, not to say domineering, personality, his innate command, his assumption of leadership, and his performance in that role. Or perhaps it was simply because women like her were drawn to strong men. There'd been a plethora of reasonable, conventional excuses, and she hadn't thought more of it—of that shiver of awareness that being close to him provoked—not for years.

She couldn't remember him ever holding her hand before—not in the way he just had, where the gesture was more than just part of a polite greeting.

When he'd squeezed her fingers and smiled at her, something inside her had shifted, and she'd felt as if the bottom had dropped out of her stomach. She'd looked into his face, into his eyes, and without Lucilla or Prudence or any of the others of their group around, had, for the very first time, seen him clearly.

She'd seen him as a man—a man she inexplicably, but utterly undeniably, wanted.

That degree of *want*—sharp, direct, and absolute—had never struck her before.

That it had struck her over him, of all the males in the ton…

"Hmm, my darling daughter…"

Antonia turned to regard her mother, who had sunk onto the window seat once more. Like Antonia, she'd been staring unseeing at the closed door.

As Antonia watched, Francesca's emerald eyes narrowed, then her mother turned her bright gaze full force on her.

"I think, my dear, that you would do well to use this time away from us all to think of what you wish to do with your life." Francesca's expression was serious. "We have never pressed you to marry and will not, now or in the future. All decisions must be your own, but as you are twenty-nine, and with this first excursion on your own, it seems an appropriate time to dwell on what you wish your life to be."

Antonia smiled faintly. "Great minds, Mama—I had planned to do precisely that." And she had. But now...

With a slight shrug, she bent and picked up her embroidery hoop. "With Sebastian going and Drake's mission to deal with, I'll have to see what prospects for contemplation remain."

* * *

Withers had materialized in the front hall and handed Sebastian his cane. He'd taken it with a word of thanks and, once Withers had opened the door, had gone quickly down the steps, walked along to Park Street, and set off for Arthur's, where he had a luncheon appointment with friends.

As he walked, at first, he congratulated himself on successfully negotiating his entrée to the house party. Yet the farther he strode, niggling questions squirmed into his brain and dispelled his smugness. Antonia hadn't been at all thrilled at the prospect of him acting as her escort. They'd known each other forever, so why?

He wasn't a coxcomb, yet there was no question that he ranked among the most highly eligible bachelors in the haut ton. Having him by her side wouldn't hurt her social standing one whit. Why, then, her reluctance?

Was she intending to conduct some illicit romance at Pressingstoke Hall?

The idea stopped him in his tracks—until a gentleman who had been stumping along in his wake poked him in the back, and with a muttered apology, he started off again.

For half a block, the prospect of Antonia, who was twenty-nine and unmarried after all, plotting some seedy affair played havoc with his faculties, but then reality reasserted itself. If she had been planning any such thing, gaining her agreement to having him as her escort would have been much harder.

With that resolved, his wits settled, and his mind moved on to the more important question of why she'd changed her mind—of what in the situation had swayed her to his cause. He always found it helpful to understand the motivations of those he needed to manage.

He revisited her questions and her reactions to his answers and confirmed that, as he'd anticipated, his mention of the "safety of the realm" had paved the way, even though it had taken her a while to admit it, even to herself. She was an earl's daughter; responding to the call of duty came as naturally to her as it did to him.

But there'd been something else, some other strand in her ruminations. Those questions over why she couldn't act as Drake's surrogate herself...she'd known the answers, yet still she'd asked.

Insight bloomed lamp-like in his mind. She intended to actively assist, of course—that was the final lure for her, the prospect of dabbling in intrigue.

He pondered that as he waited to cross Piccadilly.

Once across the busy street and nearing Arthur's, he concluded that, while Antonia attempting to actively help him in what was really a very simple and straightforward mission might prove a trifle annoying, if the prospect of engaging in an intrigue had cleared his way over attending the house party, then dealing with her efforts to involve herself was a small price to pay.

He'd reached the pavement in front of Arthur's when, unbidden, the image of Antonia's face as she'd smiled radiantly up at him filled his mind.

He halted as recollection poured through him.

In that moment...

He stood stock-still on the pavement as understanding dawned.

In that moment, he'd glimpsed the real Antonia—the woman behind the coolly composed social façade.

And to him, to his senses, she'd been *riveting*.

She was, in truth, a blend of her parents—Chillingworth's reserve for her haughtily assured outer shell, but inside...

Inside, she was all Francesca—dramatically passionate and alluring.

Something primitive and predatory in him stirred...but this was Antonia.

Antonia, with whom he had just arranged to spend five entire days, for once free of the buffer of their usually ever-present families.

Sebastian considered the prospect, then slowly climbed the steps to Arthur's door.

Carrying out Drake's simple and straightforward mission might well prove to be more complicated and challenging than he'd thought.

# CHAPTER 2

"*T*here's the entrance."

With his gaze, Sebastian followed Antonia's pointing finger to a pair of gateposts fifty yards farther up the country lane; they'd turned off the road between Dover and Deal half a mile back. Gratitude at the prospect of imminent relief flowed through him as he slowed his matched grays, then turned his phaeton in through a pair of wrought-iron gates obligingly set wide. He set his horses trotting up a tree-lined drive, then cast a sidelong look at the lady beside him.

Her lithe figure sheathed in a carriage dress of fine blue twill, her hair caught in a bun at the back of her head so that it puffed in a sleek frame about her face, with the blue ribbons of her bonnet riffling in the breeze as she looked ahead with evident delight, she might have posed for an illustration for the *Ladies Journal:* Young Lady of the Haut Ton setting out for a Country House Party.

As he watched, she glanced down and consulted a jeweled timepiece pinned to her bodice. "Nearly three o'clock," she observed. "Perfect timing."

He managed not to grunt.

She'd been ready and waiting when he'd drawn his horses to a halt in Green Street at eight o'clock that morning. Her parents had come down in their dressing gowns to wave her away—Francesca with apparent delight, Chillingworth rather less transported. But the earl had said nothing to Sebastian, just grunted a good morning and shaken his hand.

Bright and breezy, Antonia had allowed him to hand her up to the front seat of his phaeton. With their bags in the boot, and her maid, Beccy, and his man, Wilkins, perched behind them on the rear seat, he'd tooled them out of London.

At first, Antonia had preserved an easy silence, allowing him to concentrate on tacking through the traffic. But once he'd gained the clearer stretches of the Dover Road, she'd suggested that she should share with him what she knew of those who would be attending the house party.

He'd agreed with alacrity—anything to take his mind off her. They'd been only an hour into the journey, and he'd already discovered that, presumably courtesy of that eye-opening moment in Green Street three days before, not just his eyes but all his senses appeared to have become…riveted on her.

Aware of her in a way he hadn't previously been—aware in a way he recognized.

Definitely a complication.

He'd encouraged her to describe all the guests she knew and forced himself to pay attention—something that had grown easier the more she'd talked.

The more she'd revealed, he'd realized that what she saw in others, and how she described them, gave him valuable insights into her. Her comments detailing the friendships between her and the other younger ladies, as well as those between other members of the company, also shed light on her—on how she thought, how she felt, on the life she'd been living.

The Dover Road followed the old Roman road of Watling Street and ran wonderfully straight, making for an easy drive. The day remained cool and overcast, but the breeze was gentle, and the clouds weren't so heavy as to threaten rain.

Just before noon, he'd turned off the road at Faversham, and they'd lunched at The Limes. With a fair way yet to go, they hadn't dallied, which had suited him. Spending time alone with Antonia now that his eyes had been opened, and he was so damned aware of her—physically, sexually, and in every other way—was dangerous; even in the dubious privacy of a corner table in the ill-lit dining room, temptation had whispered.

It was continuing to whisper, increasingly stridently and insistently, but he didn't yet know—hadn't yet had time to decide—just what he wanted to do. About her. With her. Not yet.

Completing Drake's mission should come first—he was fairly certain of that.

If the safety of the realm truly was at stake, he couldn't afford to be distracted, and Antonia now figured as a supreme distraction.

The much-anticipated relief flooded him as the trees fell away and the house came into view. A Palladian façade that to eyes accustomed to very old houses appeared relatively new looked out on neatly shaved lawns to the front and the left, while to the right, shrubbery nestled close with the taller trees of woods just beyond. Pressingstoke Hall appeared to be a well-kept, pleasing, but essentially unpretentious gentleman's country house.

Sebastian tooled the phaeton smartly around the sweep of a circular drive and drew the horses to a neat halt in the forecourt before a set of wide steps leading up to a pair of front doors set wide in welcome.

Grooms came running, and footmen hurried from the house.

Sebastian stepped down from the phaeton, handed the reins to a groom, and walked around to assist Antonia down. One footman had brought a set of steps, which he placed beside the carriage. Taking Antonia's hand, grasping her gloved fingers, Sebastian steadied her down from the high seat; as she raised her skirts, he caught a brief glimpse of the half-boots of ivory kid that hugged her ankles.

He had to fight a short battle with his more primitive self before he could make himself release her hand, rather than wind her arm in his. He was there as her escort, not her protector. There was a fine line between the two, and he knew where it lay.

Glancing around, he strolled at Antonia's heels across the gravel and up the steps to the front door.

A tall, white-haired butler bowed them over the threshold. "Welcome to Pressingstoke Hall, Lady Antonia. Lord Earith."

As they moved inside, a cacophony of sound engulfed them. Apparently, a gaggle of guests had arrived just ahead of them, and much of the company had congregated, chatting and exclaiming, in the middle of the long front hall. The interior of the house confirmed Sebastian's assessment that the present structure was most likely less than seventy years old; the lines were simpler, more modern, without the heaviness of earlier ages. A large glazed cupola all but filled the ceiling above the front half of the hall, admitting sufficient illumination to make the hall feel light and airy.

The butler raised his voice to be heard over the din. "I am Blanchard. The housekeeper is Mrs. Blanchard. Please call on us for anything you need."

Antonia bestowed a smile and a "Thank you" and moved down the hall.

Sebastian nodded to the beleaguered butler and followed at her heels.

Now for the moment that might just turn this exercise into a quagmire. He hadn't exchanged more than two words with Cecilia, Lady Ennis, since breaking off their liaison six years ago.

As with all his dalliances, his affair with Cecilia had been exceedingly discreet, at least at the time. Later…he strongly suspected it had been Cecilia herself who had let that particular cat out of its bag. Still, she'd been selective, and not that many people knew of it. Drake did, but then Drake knew everyone's secrets. Ennis certainly did, and some of those at the house party might, but in general, that particular information was not widely known. Sebastian was perfectly certain it hadn't reached the more rarefied circles of the haut ton—those inhabited by his parents and relatives, and Antonia, her parents, and her relatives.

How the next few minutes went would depend very much on Cecilia and how she behaved.

He really had no clue what he was walking into.

As Antonia approached the other guests, the group rearranged itself into several knots, leaving Cecilia Boyne, Lady Ennis—a blonde a few inches shorter than Antonia and considerably more plump—to turn and greet Antonia.

"Welcome, my dear." Cecilia clasped Antonia's fingers, and the pair touched scented cheeks. "I'm so glad you managed to find a suitable escort and could join us."

"Thank you for being so understanding." Retrieving her hand, Antonia gestured to Sebastian, who had halted at her shoulder. "I'm not sure if you've met Earith. Lord Sebastian Cynster—Cecilia, Lady Ennis."

Cecilia's blue eyes lifted to meet Sebastian's, and she smiled. "Indeed, we have met, although it was some years ago. Welcome to Pressingstoke Hall, my lord."

Sebastian took the hand Cecilia offered and half bowed. "It's a pleasure to be here, Lady Ennis."

As he straightened, Cecilia bent a rather searching look on him—one that suggested she was wondering whether his appearance at her home meant anything beyond the obvious.

Pretending obliviousness, he turned and scanned the other guests. Antonia had already drifted away to be greeted by her friends. Until he'd seen her and Cecilia together, it hadn't occurred to him that there was only a year or two between them. Cecilia seemed so much older; a long-established matron, she'd already presented her husband with the requisite two heirs before Sebastian had allowed her to entice him to her bed. Perhaps it was simply experience that made her seem so aged relative to the vivacious, vibrant, untouched passion he now saw whenever he looked at Antonia.

Antonia, who was currently surrounded by young ladies, three of whom were throwing intrigued glances his way.

He looked at the front door, confirming no more guests had arrived. On impulse, he turned to Cecilia. "Are we the last?"

She scanned the heads, then nodded. "I believe you are."

"In that case"—he wasn't sure inviting Cecilia's assistance in even a minor way was wise, but when it came to the other gentlemen present, he needed her insights rather than Antonia's—"perhaps you might introduce me to the gentlemen. I don't see any I know."

Cecilia beamed and linked her arm with his. "Of course."

He endured more than ten minutes of her leaning a little too heavily on his arm, of her pressing a little too definitely against his side. But she did as he'd asked and introduced him to all the men there.

Being the last to arrive was helpful; he was able to put all the men in context—who was a friend of whom.

Ennis's younger brother, Connell Boyne, was about Sebastian's age and had arrived from Ireland over a week ago. Sebastian was given to understand that Connell acted as his brother's agent on the Ennis estate outside Tulla; he was left to infer that Connell's presence in Kent was in relation to the management of said estate.

There were three other bachelors present, all about thirty years old—a Mr. Henry Filbury, a Mr. Patrick Wilson, and a Mr. Baylor Worthington. Filbury and Wilson were Anglo-Irish, family friends of the Boynes and particular friends of Connell's, while Worthington was an Englishman, a friend of Connell's who lived in London.

Two old friends of Ennis's—a Mr. Samuel Parrish and a Mr. Harold McGibbin—were there with their wives. Both men were of an age with Ennis—somewhere around forty years old. The pair appeared to be well-to-do landowners and were Anglo-Irish; by way of a holiday designed to appease their wives, the foursome were making a tour of various spas in southern England. Ennis had invited them to stay as part of their holiday.

Lord Ennis himself wasn't in the hall. Sebastian waited for Cecilia to mention her husband. Had something occurred to send Ennis running? Or…? He longed to ask Cecilia or one of the other men, but didn't wish in any way to signal that he had an interest in Ennis.

Indeed, if any there knew of his affair with Cecilia, him asking after Ennis would be the last thing they would expect him to do.

Eventually, Cecilia towed him to make his bow to the older ladies— Mrs. Parrish and Mrs. McGibbin. Both were thoroughly delighted to make the acquaintance of an English marquess, who, moreover, was a duke's son. To Sebastian's relief, both ladies kept their avid curiosity in check, yet he still felt distinctly hounded, a sensation that only grew when Cecilia drew him across the hall to meet the younger ladies.

Miss Melinda Boyne, a cousin of Ennis's, was a mousy young woman who had been invited to make up the numbers; she blushed furiously as she thanked Sebastian for coming and thus giving her a chance to have a short holiday from Southampton, where she lived with her aging mother.

Miss Amelie Bilhurst was an English miss with bouncing golden curls; she was a cousin of Mrs. Parrish and was making the tour of the spas with the older couple. Sebastian suspected the Parrishes viewed Miss Bilhurst as a fetcher-and-carrier, but she smiled a great deal and seemed genuinely delighted with her lot.

Finally, Cecilia introduced him to Antonia's coterie of friends—the Honorable Miss Melissa Wainwright, the Honorable Miss Claire Savage, both daughters of viscounts, and Mrs. Georgia Featherstonehaugh, a somewhat dashing young matron who was transparently attached to her husband, the Honorable Hadley Featherstonehaugh, grandson of the Earl of Titchworth. The latter greeted Sebastian with patent relief.

Although he gave no sign of it, Sebastian was very aware of the assessing glances Miss Wainwright and Miss Savage directed his way; it seemed Antonia had established his role as unwelcome-escort-foisted-upon-her-by-her-overprotective-father only too well.

Then Cecilia was called away to deal with some query from the housekeeper; as her arm slid from his, and she moved away, he very nearly exhaled in relief. Cecilia had placed herself next to Antonia; now she'd vacated the space, he shifted closer to his supposed charge.

She threw him a quick glance, but said nothing—nor did she edge away.

"They're fussing about rooms," Miss Wainwright said. "I hope they sort things out soon—I'd like to unpack before tea."

"I just want a cup of tea," Georgia Featherstonehaugh said. "We left London in our carriage before six this morning." She turned an inquiring gaze on Antonia and Sebastian. "How did you two get here?"

"Sebastian drove us down in his phaeton," Antonia replied. "It only took us just over six hours, so we left Green Street at the altogether decent hour of eight."

"Lucky you!" Miss Savage smiled at Sebastian. "I came up from the New Forest so had to stop overnight with friends in Brighton."

"Just over six hours…" Hadley Featherstonehaugh looked at Sebastian rather eagerly. "That must mean you used your own horses."

Sebastian nodded. "I babied them along. We stopped at Faversham for lunch, so that gave them time to recover."

"What are they?" Hadley asked.

With a grin, Sebastian settled to discuss horseflesh with Hadley. Predictably, the ladies lost interest and started chattering about projected excursions and events with which they hoped to fill the following days.

Eventually, the topic of carriage horses was exhausted, and Hadley was called to order via a question from his wife. Sebastian raised his head and scanned the company, but other than various staff, no one else had joined the gathering.

Antonia noticed. She put a hand on Sebastian's arm. She'd intended purely to attract his attention, but the muscles under her fingers tensed to steel, and his head whipped around, and his gaze pinned her. Her heart leapt; her pulse spiked. Pretending to be entirely unaware and unaffected, she coolly informed him, "If you're looking for Ennis, Cecilia said he was busy with unexpected estate matters and would join us later."

He stared at her for a second, then his chest rose as he drew in a breath, and he nodded and looked away. After a moment, she remembered and drew her hand from his sleeve.

A second later, he asked, "Is there any event or entertainment scheduled for today?"

She resisted the impulse to blink in surprise. Was his naturally deep voice a touch deeper, rougher? "No. Nothing tonight. Just tea at four o'clock, and then dinner at eight."

"Drawing room at seven?"

She nodded. "The usual."

She'd had plenty of time during the journey into Kent to confirm that her sudden susceptibility to him hadn't faded and, subsequently, to decide how best to cope with—and to hide—her unexpected sensitivity. But if the way he'd tensed and the sheer potency of the look he'd bent on her when she'd entirely innocently laid her hand on his arm was any guide, she wasn't the only one battling a newfound susceptibility.

*That*, she hadn't factored into her deliberations at all.

Indeed, that such a situation might exist had never entered her head!

She needed to rethink, rather desperately, about him and her, but that required time alone, away from him.

Yet she remained determined to participate in his mission and contribute to the outcome as and when she could. She'd wondered if, as soon as he was through the front door, he would quit her side; playing the role of escort at a country house party didn't require him to loom at her shoulder every minute of every day. Yet he'd gravitated back to stand beside her and, even when he might have drifted away, had shown no inclination to do so.

She was in two minds about that. While he was by her side, she could keep abreast of what he was doing vis-à-vis his mission. But if he was by her side, she tensed and remained in a hypersensitive state in which her nerves seemed so taut they quivered, just waiting for a touch, a look, an expression to set them twanging. That seemed to have become her new default state when he was near.

"Everyone!"

They all looked toward the staircase.

Cecilia was standing two steps up, with various footmen and maids behind her and the round figure of the matronly housekeeper beside her. "We have your rooms prepared. If the ladies would like to come forward, we'll have you comfortably settled in good time before tea. Four o'clock, everyone, in the drawing room, which"—Cecilia pointed to her left—"is over there." She looked down and smiled. "Mrs. Parrish. We've put you just along the west wing, with Miss Bilhurst on one side and Mr. Parrish on the other."

Antonia fell in behind the Featherstonehaughs. Somewhat to her surprise, Sebastian maintained his position beside her. They chatted to Hadley and Georgia about the amenities Cecilia had mentioned could be found in the grounds, as others were sent upstairs to their rooms, and the four of them edged closer to the bottom of the stairs.

Finally, Georgia faced Cecilia.

Cecilia smiled on their group. "As it happens, you're all in the east wing—the first three rooms on the eastern side. Your windows look out on the shrubbery and wilderness and over the woods." Cecilia consulted her list. "Antonia, you have the room closest to the gallery, with the Featherstonehaughs next door along." Cecilia paused to allow the housekeeper to organize a footman to lead Georgia and Hadley to their room.

Then Cecilia turned and looked directly at Sebastian.

Antonia nearly blinked. The quality of that look...she felt decidedly *de trop.*

"Given you are Antonia's escort," Cecilia was saying to Sebastian, her tone husky, "I've placed you in the same wing, two doors down, beyond the Featherstonehaughs."

The housekeeper faced Antonia and bobbed a curtsy. "If you'll follow me, my lady, I'll show you to your room. Your maid's already there unpacking your things."

"Thank you." Antonia raised her skirts, and, without looking at Sebastian or Cecilia—*what was going on there?*—she started to follow the housekeeper up the stairs.

She'd taken only one step when Sebastian's long fingers closed like a vise about her elbow.

"As my room is two doors from yours, I'll see you to your door."

Seared by his touch—and equally surprised by his hard tone—she glanced back. His face was set in uncompromising lines. She also saw the hand Cecilia reached out to him that he adroitly sidestepped, leaving Cecilia to turn the surreptitious attempt at a caress into a vague gesture.

Facing forward, Antonia continued up the stairs. Sebastian's grip eased, then his fingers fell away. She gave no sign she'd noticed anything, but once they'd reached the gallery—temporarily deserted—she slowed until the housekeeper was sufficiently far ahead, then halted and looked at Sebastian. "What's between you and Cecilia?"

She'd have to be a ninnyhammer to have missed the implication.

He halted close beside her, but he'd been looking over the gallery balustrade at Cecilia below.

Antonia resisted the impulse to fold her arms and tap her toe and simply waited.

Eventually, his lips twisted in a faint grimace. "We had an affair six years ago. I broke it off. I've barely seen her since."

Antonia blew out a breath; she was rather surprised he'd told her so directly. "Well, *that's* not going to make your mission any easier." Then she realized and frowned. "I assume Drake knew—he always knows everything—so why…?"

She raised her gaze to Sebastian's face in time to see a rueful smile tug at his lips.

"Believe it or not," he murmured, "Drake considered it an advantage." He met her eyes. "He didn't want to write my name to Ennis, to identify me as his surrogate, but the connection—which Ennis knows of—allowed Drake to describe me as 'the man Ennis would least want to see.'"

Antonia made a rude sound. She turned and walked on to where the housekeeper stood not-so-patiently waiting at the archway leading to the east wing. "I've noticed that Drake has a warped sense of humor."

Sebastian said nothing, just followed her to her room. As she passed through the door Mrs. Blanchard had opened, Antonia heard him confirming with the housekeeper that the room he'd been assigned was actually four doors down the wing, there being two dressing rooms in between.

Antonia shut the door and discovered a smile was teasing her lips.

Beccy, her maid, who'd been born on the Rawlings family estate at Lambourn and had been Antonia's maid since Antonia had left the schoolroom, came to bob a curtsy. "Do you want to change for tea, my lady? Or will it be just a wash?"

Antonia handed Beccy the bonnet she'd been carrying by its ribbons. "Just a wash, and I want to redo my hair. I'll wear the gray watered silk for dinner."

"I'll lay it out while you're downstairs." Beccy followed Antonia to the dressing table. After Antonia sat, Beccy started to pull pins from her heavy hair.

"Nice place?" Antonia asked.

"Fair enough," Beccy replied. "They're friendly, and everything seems to be run as it should be. More than one iron, and that's a blessing."

Antonia smiled. Beccy unraveled her long hair, then plied the brush. Antonia closed her eyes, soothed by the regular tugs on her scalp.

She wasn't, she decided, going to worry about Sebastian, not until she had some better idea of what this odd awareness that had sprung up between them presaged. There was nothing gentle about it; her senses responded as if to a spark landing on her skin. The effect was far more marked, far more intense, than anything she'd ever felt with any other man.

Of course, she knew what such sparks normally meant, but this was Sebastian—he was almost like a brother...only she'd never seen him in such a light.

Never. Not ever.

He'd always simply been him—in a class of his own, at least in her eyes.

What his particular class was...that was what she now needed to decide.

Then another thought impinged. He was pretending to be her escort—supposedly there to protect her, to defend her virtue. Yet when Cecilia had approached him, he'd seized *her* arm...as if, in reality, she was protecting him.

Her eyes still closed, Antonia grinned.

* * *

In the room four doors down, Sebastian shrugged out of his coat and handed it to Wilkins. A dapper individual, plain of face and self-effacing in manner, Wilkins was a godsend in many ways. Other servants found him far more approachable than they expected a marquess's man to be—and so they talked, usually more freely than they otherwise would.

"I've laid out a clean shirt, my lord. I gather the second gong will be rung at seven, with dinner at eight."

Sebastian started to undo the links closing his cuffs. "So I heard. See what you can learn about the Anglo-Irish contingent." He glanced at Wilkins. "Have they all brought manservants?"

"Most." Wilkins lovingly brushed the dust from Sebastian's coat. "Mr. Filbury and Mr. Wilson are making do with one of the footmen, and Mr. Connell Boyne is sharing the services of his brother's man, which is causing something of a strain as, apparently, Lord Ennis is very particular about his dress."

Sebastian grimaced. "In that case, concentrate on Parrish and McGibbin, and you may as well see what you can learn about Mr. Worthington, as well."

"Indeed, my lord. I will endeavor."

As he stripped off his shirt and reached for the fresh one Wilkins had laid on the bed, Sebastian found his mind wandering, not to the Anglo-Irish, not to what he might, if he put his mind to it, learn from Cecilia

Boyne, but to the tantalizing conundrum of the lady in the room four doors up the wing.

* * *

Sebastian walked into the drawing room at ten minutes past four o'clock. He was pleased to note that all the other guests were already there, most standing or sitting in groups, holding cups of tea and sipping while they chatted.

His gaze came to rest on Antonia's dark head. She was standing before the windows with Miss Wainwright and Miss Boyne. He accepted a cup and saucer from a little maid who popped up beside him and, before anyone could accost him, strolled across the room to Antonia's side.

A cool glance as he halted beside her was all the reaction she evinced.

He sipped and pretended to listen to Miss Boyne's assertion that there was little by way of society around about while he planned his next move.

When Miss Bilhurst joined them, distracting Miss Wainwright and Miss Boyne, he leaned closer to Antonia, dipped his head, and whispered, "I need to talk with Ennis's friends—the Parrishes and McGibbins. Can you…?" With one hand, he gestured.

She turned her head and met his eyes. "Can I ease your way?"

He nearly got trapped in the silvery gray of her eyes, but managed to nod.

She considered him for a second, then reached out and placed her hand on his sleeve.

This time, he'd anticipated the move and managed to—largely—suppress his instinctive reaction.

She gripped lightly and nudged, steering him back. Over her shoulder, she told the other three ladies, "We'll catch up with you later."

Facing forward, she settled her hand on his arm. With an imperious look, she summoned a hovering footman to relieve her of her empty cup.

Sebastian handed over his as well. Before they moved on—they were in the center of the room and out of earshot of the others—he asked, "Has Ennis put in an appearance yet?"

"No. Apparently, he's still closeted in his study."

He frowned. "I wonder if he's hiding?"

"Cecilia assured us he would join us for dinner." After a moment, Antonia asked, "Why do you want to talk to the Parrishes and McGibbins?"

"Drake realized there would be Anglo-Irish gentlemen here, but I don't think he realized that fully half the guests—the majority of the men—would hail from Ireland."

Antonia met his gaze. "Ennis is Anglo-Irish, and the Anglo-Irish always stick together."

"You know that, I know that, and I'm sure Drake knows that, too, but I don't think it occurred to him that so many Anglo-Irish would be here."

"You mean that some of those here—attending the house party—might be connected with whatever urgent message Ennis wants to convey to Drake?"

"Exactly. And as Ennis appears to be avoiding his guests..."

After a second, she asked, "Does Drake have any idea what Ennis's message is about?"

"No. He had no clue at all."

"So the message might not, in fact, have anything to do with Ireland or the Irish."

He grimaced. "Logically, no."

"But you think it has."

"I think—and Drake thinks—that rumors about fresh plots coming out of Ireland at the same time that Ennis contacts Drake wanting to impart information of a secret and sensitive nature is too difficult to swallow as mere coincidence. Especially given Ennis is an Anglo-Irish peer with an active estate in Ireland, but a preference for living in England, who is married to an English peer's daughter and has his sons being brought up as Englishmen."

Antonia turned to survey the guests; she had to admit Englishmen were in short supply. After a moment, she murmured, "We—you and I—are so obviously English, and upper nobility at that, even if the Anglo-Irish here are discussing such a plot, they're not going to mention it in our hearing."

"No—we'll have to eavesdrop, and even then, it's unlikely they'll let anything fall. But I was thinking more in terms of learning who they are, where they hail from, and so on. I can't see any reason they won't tell us that, and if any of them prove to be involved in whatever plot is being hatched, the more information we have, the better."

"All right." She tightened her grip on his arm. "Follow my lead."

She guided him to where Mrs. McGibbin and Mr. Parrish were now chatting with Melinda Boyne.

Antonia and Sebastian were greeted with interest. It wasn't all that hard to get Mr. Parrish talking about his interests in Ireland—sheep and investments, in that order. When appealed to, Mrs. McGibbin revealed that her husband owned a property in the northwest of the country and augmented his income through underwriting the activities of an increasingly lucrative fishing fleet.

Between them, by subtle degrees, Antonia and Sebastian steered the conversation to comparisons with the Boynes' Irish estate near Tulla—as Mrs. McGibbin, Mr. Parrish, and Miss Boyne had all visited and were familiar with the place, that was a subject on which all three had insights to offer.

Insights, but no startling revelations, yet it was a start.

Tea having been consumed and the cups and saucers surrendered, with the first gong not due to be rung until six o'clock, the company started to drift apart as, in small groups, the guests elected to stroll in the waning light of the mild autumn afternoon.

Some made for the terrace, others for the gardens.

Antonia and Sebastian were joined by Melissa Wainwright and Claire Savage. Together with Miss Boyne and Miss Bilhurst, Antonia's friends were eager to take the path around the ornamental lake to the small folly on the far shore.

Sebastian held aloof from their plans; Antonia assumed he was intending to join—and attempt to extract information from—the other unattached gentlemen.

Then Cecilia Boyne swept up and halted by Sebastian's side. She listened to Amelie Bilhurst's eager outline of their plan and smiled encouragingly. "It is a lovely walk at this time of evening, ladies—I'm sure you'll enjoy it." With that, Cecilia looked at Sebastian, then boldly slid her arm through his. "But I'm sure Lord Earith would prefer to stroll the terrace." To Sebastian, she said, "Perhaps I might show you my new conservatory, my lord."

Antonia didn't think, didn't blink. With an accomplished smile—one she'd learned at her mother's knee and perfected by observation—she leaned forward and, around Sebastian, addressed their hostess. "Oh, but Earith has already agreed to accompany us—and all the other gentlemen have gone off to play billiards, I believe." She turned her smile on Sebastian and allowed the gesture to take on a quite different—more lover-like—warmth. "I know how you feel about me wandering unprotected."

Sebastian seized her lifeline like a drowning man. He turned to Cecilia. "Sadly, Cecilia, as you can see, I'm already committed."

Cecilia shot Antonia a look that was more puzzled than anything else. She eased her arm from Sebastian's, then patted his sleeve. "Later, then." Putting on her hostessly face, she smiled at the other ladies. "Enjoy yourselves, my dears."

Cecilia turned and headed toward Mrs. Parrish and Mrs. McGibbin.

Resuming their artless chatter, Miss Boyne and Miss Bilhurst led the way through the open French doors and onto the terrace. Melissa and Claire followed. Sebastian drew in a breath and offered Antonia his arm. She laid her hand on his sleeve, and they fell in at the rear of the small procession.

Once they were pacing down the lawn toward the lake, he murmured, "Thank you. Clearly, avoiding Cecilia while pursuing her husband is going to be a trifle more complicated than Drake thought."

Antonia made a noncommittal sound.

They walked on in silence, for which she was grateful. She was still coming to terms with the implications of what she'd just done. Sebastian, clearly, assumed her action had been prompted by an urge to help him with the mission.

She knew otherwise.

Cecilia's proprietary assumption had sparked a reaction in Antonia unlike anything she'd ever felt before. Sheer possessiveness had erupted and gripped her. She'd seen her mother react in just such a way toward ladies who presumed to approach her father, thinking to lure him into an affair. Her father found such clashes amusing; he was prone to stand back and watch with an indulgent smile on his lips.

He understood what lay behind her mother's steely rebuffs.

Sebastian didn't possess such insight, an insight born of experience—thank God.

Her head high, her gaze fixed forward, Antonia paced alongside him, her hand resting lightly on his sleeve—gripping only a little; that was all she would allow herself.

Beneath her outwardly composed exterior, she was metaphorically taking in great gulps of air and trying to calm the whirlpool of swirling emotions inside her.

She'd wondered what Sebastian meant to her—how the passionate, fiery woman who lived inside her truly saw him.

Now, she knew.

That woman who was her true self saw Lord Sebastian Cynster, Marquess of Earith, as, quite simply, hers.

# CHAPTER 3

*S*ebastian walked into the drawing room just after the clocks had chimed seven o'clock. The first man he saw, standing before the fireplace and chatting with McGibbin and Parrish, was Lord Ennis.

About forty years old, Ennis was shorter and stockier than Sebastian, and his black hair, gleaming under the gaslight, clustered in thick curls about his pale face.

Unhurriedly, Sebastian crossed the room to the group before the hearth, transparently intent on exchanging greetings with his host, as any guest would. McGibbin and Parrish welcomed him with smiles, but Ennis had stiffened fractionally when he saw Sebastian approaching, and his expression had grown distant and a touch chilly.

His own expression easy and relaxed, after nodding to the other two, Sebastian politely inclined his head to Ennis and offered his hand. "My lord. It's a pleasure to have the opportunity of visiting Pressingstoke Hall."

Ennis briefly gripped his hand. "Earith. Lady Ennis mentioned that you would be here. I hope you find your stay entertaining."

The words were stiff and stilted, contrasting sharply with Sebastian's assured drawl. It was clear Ennis wanted nothing to do with Sebastian, but he'd expected that. And with McGibbin and Parrish hovering, now was not the time to mention a private meeting.

"Actually"—turning, Sebastian scanned the guests—"given I'm here as a favor to the Chillingworths, I expect my appreciation of my stay will largely depend on Lady Antonia."

"Indeed." Ennis's rejoinder was clipped.

Sebastian barely registered it. He'd located Antonia's glossy dark head and discovered that she—and Miss Wainwright and Miss Savage—were surrounded by Connell Boyne, Filbury, Wilson, and Worthington. The four gentlemen were patently putting themselves out to please, although none of the ladies as yet seemed won over.

Worthington laughed and edged closer to Antonia, leaning near as if to whisper something in her ear.

Antonia shifted, easing back.

The impulse to march across and insert himself between Antonia and Worthington was powerful enough to make Sebastian sway...

He wasn't going to accomplish anything with Ennis at the moment.

And if he wanted to keep up the façade of being Antonia's escort...

Adopting a world-weary air, Sebastian turned to Ennis, McGibbin, and Parrish. "If you'll excuse me, gentlemen, I believe my role of escort demands my presence elsewhere."

McGibbin and Parrish were amused. Ennis was relieved.

They parted with nods. His gaze fixing on the group gathered before the long windows overlooking the terrace, Sebastian strolled nonchalantly past the other guests to fetch up beside Antonia.

She saw him coming and readily shifted to make way for him—he sensed with some relief. Worthington looked somewhat taken aback to find Sebastian suddenly beside him, but soldiered gamely on with the story he was telling.

In less than a minute, Sebastian realized that the only threat Worthington posed was that of boring his listeners to madness. But his three friends—Filbury, Wilson, and Connell Boyne—were of quite a different stripe. All three struck Sebastian as minor jackals, gentlemen-scavengers on the lookout for a fortune to make their own. They didn't rank among the more dangerous of the breed, but all three had enough nous to realize that, of the unmarried ladies at Pressingstoke Hall, Antonia was the juiciest plum.

While Worthington rattled on, apparently oblivious to the implications of Sebastian's sudden appearance, the other three eyed him assessingly.

Sebastian stood beside Antonia and, one by one, met Filbury's, then Wilson's, then Boyne's eyes; he didn't actually do anything, just let his threat infuse his gaze, his stance, the very air between them.

All three got his message, loud and clear. They dropped their gazes, and a certain tension—the intentness of hunters assessing prey—that had tightened the atmosphere evaporated.

Antonia exchanged resigned looks with Melissa and Claire; on her part, those looks were also placating. She'd insisted to her friends that Sebastian was merely a family friend sent to fill the role of escort, that he was nothing more to her, and she was nothing more to him. That was what she'd believed at the time. But she and her friends were more than experienced enough to recognize precisely what he had just done, and such heavy-handed intervention didn't fit the script he was supposed to be following.

But her friends' confusion was the least of the problems plaguing her.

The manner in which Sebastian had done what he'd done had set warning bells ringing in her brain.

He'd acted with arrogant, invincible authority, with an air of absolute, inalienable right.

She knew him, knew men like him—she knew the difference between an escort stepping in to protect his charge and...the aura Sebastian had projected, which had been several orders of magnitude more extreme.

There was no way any of the three other gentlemen would approach her now, other than in the most innocent of contexts. Not that she wanted them to approach her in any non-innocent circumstances, but still...

In just a few short minutes, without uttering a single word, Sebastian had declared that she was his.

His—in some way, in whatever way he meant.

He'd behaved as if he owned her, as if she—her time, her consideration—were his by right.

Given her own eye-opening revelation of mere hours before, a revelation from which she was still mentally reeling, him behaving in such a possessive way was only compounding her difficulties.

Apparently satisfied with the result he'd achieved, his expression once more politely mild, he glanced down at her. She caught his eye, narrowed hers fractionally, and with a deceptively sweet smile curving her lips, looped her arm in his and murmured, "Walk with me." She directed her smile around the circle. "If you'll excuse us?"

It wasn't a question. Melissa and Claire inclined their heads with clear relief; they didn't want Sebastian destroying all their fun.

The other gentlemen brightened and replied, "Of course" and "Until later."

Maintaining an expression of unimpaired calm, Antonia steered Sebastian toward an unoccupied corner of the room. He didn't resist; from the look in his eyes, he assumed she had something to impart regarding the mission.

Doing her best not to grit her teeth—could his obliviousness over what he'd just done be any more obvious?—she halted and seized the moment of him turning to face her and her drawing her arm from his to jab a finger into his side. *That* got his undivided attention. She glared into his eyes. "Behave."

His pale green eyes searched hers even as his brows lowered and bafflement overwhelmed his arrogance. "What?"

He truly had no idea. She resisted the urge to wave her arms. "You can't just go around"—she gave in and waved one hand—"*intimidating* people."

His features set—in intimidating lines. "Why not?"

"Because we're here—supposedly—to enjoy ourselves as a group."

"But they were—"

"Behaving exactly as anyone would expect." She couldn't put her hands on her hips. "You appear to have forgotten that I—and Melissa and Claire—are twenty-nine. We knew perfectly well what those three—indeed, even Mr. Worthington, teddy bear though he is—were thinking. For all their belief in their own sophistication, they are boringly predictable and nothing we haven't dealt with before—but they can be entertaining. If you're imagining we're three innocent misses who require a nursemaid, you are a long way off the mark."

"I'm hardly a nursemaid." He stared frowningly down at her for several seconds; she glared belligerently back. Eventually, he grated, "So what am I supposed to do? Just let those jackals sniff about your skirts?"

"Unless I signal otherwise, *yes!*"

Sebastian's jaw clenched even more tightly. He wasn't sure he could do as she asked. Just the thought set his hackles rising. But her eyes were flashing more silver than gray, and she appeared very set on him backing off.

He consulted his inner self and inwardly acknowledged that him backing off wasn't going to happen. But he had to say something to appease her. He forced himself to nod—an exceedingly small nod. "Very well. We'll see how matters progress."

She wasn't convinced she'd got what she wanted. She searched his face, then she appeared to accept she'd done enough for the moment; the passion left her eyes to be replaced with her usual cool hauteur. She shifted to his side and turned to view the gathering. "Have you spoken with Ennis yet?"

"Only to greet him. He's surrounded by others, and this is hardly an appropriate venue." He studied their host, still standing before the fireplace. "I'll need to watch and seize a moment to make it clear that I'm Drake's surrogate. Then he and I will need to meet privately, and I assume he'll want to keep that meeting secret."

"Well, we've a few minutes yet before dinner will be announced." She slipped her hand into the crook of his arm. "Come with me, and let's see if I can engineer your moment."

He let her guide him to the group about Ennis, but although they joined it, there were too many others in the company likewise intent on spending a few moments with their host; despite Antonia's best efforts, no opportunity arose for Sebastian to exchange even a few private words with Ennis.

Blanchard appeared and announced that dinner was served. Courtesy of their ranks, Sebastian and Antonia were separated by the full length of the table; as the highest-ranking lady, she was seated on Ennis's right, while Sebastian, as the highest-ranking male, led Cecilia in to dinner and sat at her right.

As course followed course, Sebastian found his frustration mounting. Not only had he yet to speak with Ennis, but he also had to sit and watch Antonia being made much of by the gentlemen at the other end of the table, while simultaneously keeping his wits about him sufficiently to avoid Cecilia's lures.

Despite all evidence that he was uninterested in reanimating an affair long dead, she continued to eye him with open speculation, as if she remained hopeful that his escorting Antonia was merely a convenient excuse he'd seized in order to return to her—Cecilia's—orbit.

Sebastian was quite sure that, despite his usual perspicacity, Drake hadn't foreseen the mounting complications evolving from what Drake had considered a fortuitous set of circumstances. Not only was Sebastian juggling the mission itself, but he also had to contend with Ennis's understandable reluctance to have anything to do with him, with an unexpected company of Anglo-Irish all around, plus his increasingly unsettling and potentially highly charged interactions with Antonia, and on top of it all, he needed to douse Cecilia's increasingly transparent expectations.

Very much aware that Ennis was directing occasional dark looks down the table at him, Sebastian made every effort to keep the conversation general and otherwise direct his attention to Mrs. Parrish, seated on his right. While at the dinner table, he could do nothing about his mission, or about Antonia, so he devoted his energies to avoiding Cecilia and ignoring her thankfully subtle encouragements.

Nevertheless, he'd rarely been so grateful to see the end of a meal. After Cecilia rose and led the ladies back to the drawing room, the gentlemen moved up the table, and the decanters were passed around. There was no chance whatsoever of speaking privately with Ennis; rather than further aggravate the man, Sebastian kept his distance. He sat beside Hadley Featherstonehaugh and talked of horses and the latest fads in carriages. They were joined by Worthington and McGibbin, and the interlude passed in companionable bonhomie.

Sebastian perked up when, by general consensus, the men decided not to join the ladies but instead to retreat to the billiards room. But he was destined for disappointment; as even Parrish and McGibbin elected to eschew the ladies' company and crowd into the billiards room, there was no chance to approach Ennis, even to simply drop a quiet word in his ear.

It was increasingly obvious that any such word would have to be exchanged in relative privacy at the very least—in a situation where Sebastian could overcome Ennis's unwillingness to interact with him without alerting anyone else to the exchange being in any way notable.

Sebastian played two rounds of billiards—one with Hadley, Wilson, and Filbury, the other with Connell Boyne, Worthington, and Parrish, who, despite his age and girth, proved a dab hand at the game.

Ennis didn't play but circulated among his guests, stopping here and there to chat and replenish the glasses of brandy or whisky most held. Ennis gave Sebastian a wide berth, but not so obviously that any but Sebastian would notice.

Stepping back from the table and ostensibly chalking his cue while he waited for Parrish to line up his shot, Sebastian surreptitiously studied Ennis. He took in the way Ennis moved around the room, the quality of his actions, his stride, listened to his rather forced laugh…

Ennis was nervous—anxious. The longer Sebastian watched, the more he was sure of it.

Ennis *had* been hiding earlier—he'd wanted to limit the time he spent with his guests.

And now Ennis was watching certain of those guests closely…all the Anglo-Irish men and also Worthington…

*Damn!* His lips compressing, Sebastian looked away. Drake had been too clever. Ennis had misinterpreted Drake's message. If Ennis's thoughts were fixated on an Irish plot, then the man Ennis would least want to see…wasn't Sebastian but someone Ennis thought was connected with whatever plot he had word of and was, presumably, planning to betray.

Ennis would never *like* Sebastian, but he wouldn't care that much about a long-ago affair.

But Ennis cared, deeply, about whatever was going on, or he would never have contacted Drake.

Ennis thought Drake's messenger was one of his Anglo-Irish compatriots. He thought Drake had a man buried in the group—and given Drake's reputation, that wasn't any great stretch of the imagination—so Ennis was waiting for that man to give him a sign. But Drake didn't have a contact among this lot—he'd sent Sebastian instead.

Sebastian felt like hanging his head. In the next instant, he was visited by an urge to put down his cue, march across, and put Ennis out of his misery by simply telling him that he—Sebastian—was Drake's surrogate.

But if Ennis was nervous, presumably he had reason to be—presumably at least one of the men there, and more likely more than one, might, at least in Ennis's eyes, have some connection to the plot. Or was Ennis's nervousness due to something else entirely?

Sebastian finished the game, playing largely by rote; he'd been playing billiards since he was tall enough to see over the table. He smiled, laughed, and accepted the congratulations of the others, then handed his cue to the next would-be player.

He glanced around, but Ennis was still circulating; as host, he was unlikely to retire until at least Parrish and McGibbin did, and neither looked ready to call it a night.

Even when they did, Ennis would still avoid Sebastian, and even if he didn't retire with his friends but remained, too many others would still be present for Sebastian to force a confrontation.

"I'm for bed." Hadley Featherstonehaugh halted beside Sebastian. "We have another four days and nights in which to knock balls around."

Sebastian nodded. "I'll go up with you."

They called a general farewell and left the others still playing and talking.

As Sebastian and Hadley climbed the stairs, Sebastian asked, "Have you heard anything of the plans for tomorrow?"

"No. But I'm sure Georgia will know—it always seems it's the ladies who make the plans at this sort of thing."

"Speaking of the ladies"—Sebastian glanced back at the front hall and the now-open door of the drawing room—"it appears they've already retired."

"Ah, well, no excitement for them given we all hid in the billiards room." Hadley grinned.

The clocks struck twelve as they reached the gallery.

Sebastian walked with Hadley into the corridor running down the east wing. Hadley halted at his door, and they exchanged quiet goodnights, then Sebastian ambled on to his room. He opened the door and walked in.

One step—and his gaze fixed on the shadowy figure sitting on his bed, and he froze.

Lust *roared* through him.

Powerful enough—violent enough—to rock him.

He clamped his fingers on the doorknob, gripping hard as he fought to regain his mental feet—to keep his expression utterly closed and not allow any of his searing desire to seep through.

He finally managed to draw in a tight, too shallow breath.

Draped in shadows, she sat on the far side of the bed and watched him, but she made no move, made no sound.

Almost as if she understood the unwisdom of even shifting.

Carefully, he eased his fingers from the doorknob. He forced himself to draw in another breath, step fully inside, and shut the door.

Slowly, he turned and faced her.

Antonia.

His first impulse was to trap the surging compulsions and feelings and push them deep, lock them away.

Deny them.

But even as his gaze passed over her veiled features, he accepted that this—all he felt, all she made him feel—was *real*.

He'd seen her anew—or perhaps for the first time—in Green Street three days ago. The sight had riveted his mind and his senses.

Now, unexpectedly finding her in such a place had provoked...another level of recognition.

Through the dimness, he looked at her and realized—knew—who, exactly, he was looking at.

The exceedingly beautiful, haughty and aloof, elusive and willful, noble-born, socially adept daughter of an earl—who was no blood relation.

His senses, he realized, had always known. Some part of his mind had, too. But for decades, most of his conscious mind had relegated her to the status of an almost-sister.

He didn't truly think of her as a sister, and he never would attempt to again.

He took a step forward, only to realize just how giddy the abrupt, unanticipated revelation had left him. Such a fundamental rearrangement of the landscape of his life...perhaps it was unsurprising that he felt a touch disoriented.

Distantly, he heard the sound of men's voices, of footsteps, and doors closing. The movement in the corridors had masked—excused—his hesitation. As the sounds faded, he drew breath and, still moving slowly—carefully—walked to the tallboy, which stood a window width from the foot of the bed.

No way would he trust himself anywhere near that bed. Not until he'd had time to study his new landscape and decide on his best way forward.

Ravishing her tonight almost certainly wasn't it.

To account for his direction, he drew out his watch and chain, detached the latter, and set them and his purse on the top of the tallboy.

She finally broke the silence. "Did you succeed in speaking with Ennis?"

She'd kept her voice low; the husky tones feathered across his senses.

"No." He turned; leaning against the tallboy, he shoved his hands in his pockets and faced her, and ruthlessly refocused his mind on his mission. "He's avoiding me, hardly surprising, but it's not only that. He's distracted—I think he's looking for Drake's man among his Anglo-Irish friends."

Antonia pulled a face. "I had wondered if Drake's peculiar message might backfire." She was stunned to hear how calm and collected she sounded; inside, she felt as if she was teetering at the edge of some dangerously high precipice, her nerves taut as a bowstring one twist away from snapping.

Her lungs felt locked; she was so tense, she thought she might be quivering.

She kept her eyes locked on Sebastian's shadowy figure. The curtains on the window between them had been left open, and faint moonlight streamed in—strong enough to see shapes, but not to make out expressions. But he stood outside the shaft of light, and she sat outside it as well. That left them searching with and relying on their other senses as much as, if not more than, their eyes.

In the instant he'd walked in and his gaze had fallen on her, she'd felt a jerk of awareness—a visceral tug unlike anything she'd ever experienced. Some part of her mind was still reeling from that; the rest of it understood all too well that, entirely unwittingly, she'd placed herself in a predator's lair.

On his bed.

She'd always known, instinctively had known, what manner of man he was. Although she'd never seen him like this, with his shields—the sophisticated and highly polished surface he displayed to their world—down, she'd always sensed the reality of him, the ineluctable masculine threat he posed—powerful, virile, and compelling.

She hadn't intended to provoke him, but the single heavy armchair in the room had its back to the door, and she hadn't felt comfortable sitting there.

As she watched, Sebastian pushed away from the tallboy. Slowly, with a gait that could only be described as a stalking prowl, he closed the distance between them.

His voice seemed impossibly low as he murmured, "I'll catch him tomorrow."

She nearly asked "Who?" then realized he meant Ennis.

He passed through, then beyond the fall of moonlight and became a large, dark figure steadily, step by step, looming nearer.

She'd forgotten how to breathe. A tiny, very small and craven, part of her wanted to flee; the rest waited, breath bated, needing, quite desperately, to see what he would do.

He halted a bare foot away, and she discovered her mouth had gone dry.

She looked up at the pale oval of his face and knew beyond question that something fundamental between them had changed, literally in the blink of an eye, and they would never go back to the way they'd been...

A shiver—one of sheer, reckless anticipation—slithered down her spine. The atmosphere felt so charged, she was surprised she saw no sparks.

Then he raised one hand—slowly—to her face, and his long fingers touched, then traced the curve of her cheek.

He lowered his hand. When he spoke, his voice was so deep, so gravelly, she could only just make out the words.

"Get out of here, Antonia. Now."

There was no real force behind the command, as if only a part of him meant it.

Yet the unspoken warning was clear.

The sense of standing on a precipice expanded and grew…and she chose the path of wisdom. Of immediate safety.

Despite her quaking limbs, she managed to—carefully—rise. It was an effort to wrench her gaze from his, but once she had, a curious defiance bloomed. Moving slowly, deliberately, she smoothed her skirt, then she raised her head, looked directly into his shadowed eyes, less than a foot away, and despite being entirely unable to draw breath, coolly said, "Do let me know when you succeed in speaking with Ennis."

He'd asked for her help with his mission several times, had availed himself of her social skills; she wasn't about to allow him to keep her in the dark over what was going on. As he would, if she let him.

Boldly, she stepped past him. Her nerves leapt as she sensed him tense and swivel as if to seize her, but he didn't. Exhaling silently, head high, she walked toward the door. "Goodnight."

She opened the door and stepped outside. Without looking back into the unlit room, she started to draw the door closed behind her—and heard from within a dark murmur, "Goodnight."

She shut the door, released the doorknob, then paused, for one instant, savoring the thrill of having played—just for a moment—with fire. Of having faced such a challenge—unknown and dangerous, at least to her—and survived the encounter.

Then she realized a silly, far-too-smug-for-her-own-good smile had curved her lips. She forced them straight, shook her head at her delusions—dealing further with Sebastian was not going to be so easy—and walked slowly up the dim corridor.

To reach the door to her room, she had to pass the archway to the gallery; as she did, from the corner of her eye, she glimpsed a dim figure lurking in the shadows on the other side of the archway. From the hairstyle, she instantly recognized Cecilia.

Antonia gave no sign of having seen their hostess hovering in the dark. She reached her door, opened it, then paused and frowned. There'd been something about the way Cecilia had been standing, dithering…

*That* was it. She'd intended to visit Sebastian, but had seen Antonia come out of his room and had drawn back, uncertain.

Antonia glanced along the corridor. She didn't think Sebastian was expecting Cecilia; if he had been, he would have got rid of her much more quickly and with much less…tension. Still, she waited and watched.

After a minute or more had ticked past, her straining senses picked up the soft swish of silk skirts, but Cecilia didn't step into the corridor.

Antonia debated, then quit her door and crept silently back to the archway. Peering into the gallery, she saw Cecilia retreating, then Cecilia opened a door, went through, and shut the door behind her.

Antonia drew back. Proprietorial satisfaction bloomed again. "Good," she murmured.

Then she smiled and headed for her bed.

Things had changed—or perhaps evolved—between her and Sebastian. She reacted as if he was hers, and he did the same over her. Well and good. As for the tension—the visceral connection—that had erupted between them in the dark of his room…she wasn't entirely sure *exactly* what that presaged, but she was ready and distinctly eager to find out.

# CHAPTER 4

$S$ebastian bided his time through the morning—through an extended breakfast in the breakfast room, then, as the day was once again fine, he followed the other guests outside. The younger ladies set off for the folly from which they planned to sketch the views; after exchanging a coolly challenging glance with him, Antonia joined their ranks.

Connell Boyne and his friends went out onto the rear lawn to smoke cheroots. After strolling the rear terrace and evaluating their options, the older men retreated to the library; Hadley Featherstonehaugh and Sebastian trailed behind.

Sebastian and Hadley settled in comfortable chairs at one end of the library; Ennis, Parrish, and McGibbin appeared to be discussing business of sorts at the other end. The table between Sebastian's and Hadley's chairs held a stack of gentlemen's sporting journals; they spent a quiet half hour flicking pages and trading the occasional remark.

Then Filbury looked in. "Connell suggested a croquet tournament. Who's in?"

As it transpired, all the men were gripped by competitive zeal. The entire male half of the company duly gathered on the croquet lawn where Connell and Worthington had already set out the hoops. Mallets were passed around and various structures for a tournament were discussed before a series of games was decided, and they settled to play in rotating groups of three.

Knowing that playing croquet in groups was as much about arguing line and tactics, and that such a game never progressed quickly but rather with long pauses for evaluation and dissection, Sebastian saw the perfect opportunity for speaking privately with Ennis looming.

Although he had to wait for more than an hour, eventually, he and Ennis were playing against each other, with Hadley as the third of their group. Hadley had proved a past master at taking forever to line up his shots. That left Sebastian and Ennis standing to one side of the green, watching.

Sebastian waited until they were at one end of the oval-shaped course. After taking his shot, he walked to the edge of the clipped expanse to allow Hadley to essay his. Sebastian halted alongside Ennis—who shifted as if to move away, but then, as if realizing how that would appear, settled again.

"Indeed," Sebastian murmured, his gaze on Hadley. "I am most assuredly the last man you would want to see."

He turned his head and met Ennis's widening eyes.

"You?" Ennis looked stunned.

Sebastian nodded and looked away. "Winchelsea is a good friend." He paused, then went on, "I feel I should apologize for his inappropriate sense of humor. It was his idea to label me thus, but I realize, in the circumstances, the words might have led you to suppose his stand-in was someone else."

"Just so." Ennis sounded aggrieved.

Sebastian glanced sharply at him. "You haven't spoken of this to anyone else by mistake?"

"No—no." Ennis put a hand to his neckcloth as if it was suddenly too tight. "Look here—I can't talk to you here. What I have to tell Winchelsea is too…complicated to be conveyed in a few words."

His gaze once more on Hadley's antics, Sebastian slowly nodded. "Very well. When and where?"

"Tonight. In my study." Ennis paused, then added, "I'll meet you there at ten o'clock."

"Yes." Sebastian raised his voice. "Look at that—straight through both hoops!" Walking to Hadley, Sebastian clapped him on the shoulder, then glanced at Ennis. "Your turn."

They continued their game. Sebastian estimated his exchange with Ennis had taken no more than two minutes. If, as Ennis's nervousness suggested, someone of the company was connected with the plot Ennis intended to expose, even if that person had been watching them, there was no reason they would have imagined he and Ennis had discussed anything more enthralling than Hadley's game.

The tournament eventually concluded, with Worthington declared the outright winner, with Hadley in second place.

The younger ladies returned from the folly, and Cecilia, Mrs. Parrish, and Mrs. McGibbin returned from their exploration of the rose garden just as Blanchard appeared on the rear terrace to strike the gong summoning the party to luncheon.

Antonia appeared by Sebastian's side and boldly wound her arm with his.

He wasn't entirely certain he approved of the bolder, wilder side of her—certainly not when she allowed it out in public.

"So have you managed to corner Ennis?" Her words floated to him on a whisper.

"Yes." The others had started across the lawn to the terrace. He and she fell in at the rear of the company. He dipped his head and murmured, "He elected to meet at ten o'clock tonight in his study. He's definitely nervous of someone here."

"Hmm...if he is, that suggests that someone must have some sort of connection with whatever group Ennis intends to inform against—doesn't it?"

"So one would infer." He paused, then said, "While we're whiling away the day waiting for this meeting, we should see what more we can learn about the other Anglo-Irish here."

She nodded. "You'll be largely restricted to the men. I'll see what I can extract from the women."

They joined the other guests in the dining room. As the seating at breakfast and luncheon was informal, and they were the last to reach the table, they perforce had to take the two remaining seats—the pair in the middle of the table on either side. That left Sebastian to entertain Miss Bilhurst and Miss Boyne, while Antonia was left to the dubious delights of Worthington—still crowing about his croquet win—on one side and Wilson on the other.

As it happened, that suited Sebastian and Antonia; they diligently applied themselves to their joint undertaking, and the meal passed off more quickly and satisfactorily than either had expected.

When the company rose, Antonia left Sebastian to his own devices and concentrated on cultivating Mrs. McGibbin, who was as Irish as her husband, unlike Mrs. Parrish, who was English through and through.

But she quickly discovered that Mrs. McGibbin belonged to that class of wives who paid no attention whatsoever to the details of their husband's business. Beyond what she'd already imparted about McGibbin's interest in the local fishing fleet, she knew no more; she did not even know if her husband belonged to any particular club.

Antonia shifted her sights to Melinda Boyne and was pleased to discover that the younger woman had something of a tendre for Filbury. Consequently, Melinda was a font of information on Filbury's background, friends, and associates, and, even more importantly, his views—and those of his close friends—on such matters as Irish independence.

On the latter subject, Antonia had to reach deep and project an artlessness bordering on the inane; as the daughter of a very English earl, she had to phrase her questions exceedingly carefully and, as Melinda was by no means witless, pretend to a lack of comprehension that was profound, yet at the same time believable.

The careful interrogation took time and skill and lasted until teatime. During the half hour spent over the cups in the drawing room and the amble about the rose garden with her friends that followed, Antonia learned little else. Instead, she sifted through the numerous hints and facts Melinda had let fall.

By the time the gong to dress for dinner sounded, she was ready to retire and refresh herself, body and mind, before participating in dinner and the musical evening Cecilia had arranged.

She climbed the stairs with Claire and Georgia. Claire headed into the west wing, while Antonia and Georgia walked into the east wing to their rooms.

"See you downstairs." Georgia waved and went into her room.

Antonia opened her door, walked inside, and saw Sebastian seated on the window seat.

He didn't rise. Odd. Normally, inculcated manners would have brought him to his feet. Only in private and only with a lady with whom he considered himself very close—such as a lover—would his instincts allow him to remain seated... Had he remained seated on purpose to send her some message? Or had he not even noticed that he hadn't risen?

One brow arching, she shut the door. A quick glance around informed her that Beccy wasn't in the room.

"Your maid was here. I sent her off and told her to wait for you to ring."

*High-handed of you.* Antonia didn't bother saying the words; she just threw him a haughty, disapproving look and walked to the dressing table. With a swish of her skirts, she subsided onto the stool. "So what have you learned?"

She reached for the pins that held the bun at the back of her head in place. As she pulled the first free, she met Sebastian's eyes in the mirror.

Yes, she was teasing him—challenging him—by letting down her hair like this, but...too bad. Her wild side felt like it, and if he could arrogantly presume to send her maid away...

She felt certain that, as in so many endeavors, he assumed that he would be in complete and absolute control of any relationship between them—that it would proceed and develop as he dictated.

That certainty only prodded her into seeing how far she could push him—how far she could provoke him before he realized his assumption wasn't correct.

A frisson of danger—of anticipation—fizzed through her veins.

She pulled out the next pin.

Sebastian felt he should—somehow—stop her unraveling her hair; the action created a far-too-intimate atmosphere, yet he couldn't summon the necessary will to override his more primitive side. That part of him, the sensual, sexual being, wanted to see that crowning glory rippling over her shoulders. She'd been wearing her hair up for over a decade; he couldn't recall exactly what it had looked like when, as a girl, she'd worn it down.

And it would be different now—lusher, thicker, more vibrant.

Surreptitiously, he cleared his throat and ignored his ever-sharpening appetite. "From all I gathered from Worthington and Filbury—both of whom gossip far too readily, useful though that trait is in this instance—I suspect Ennis has, at the very least tacitly and possibly through donations, been a supporter of the Young Irelander cause. However, despite possessing a large and well-established estate over there, he hasn't been back much in the past decade, and he certainly wasn't directly involved, any more than Parrish, McGibbin, or the younger men were, in the recent rebellion. Added to that, Cecilia is English to the bone, and according to Wilson—another likely Young Irelander-sympathizer—her influence is definitely anti-Irish."

"So although Ennis might retain a sympathy for the Irish, it's sympathy-at-a-distance, and, overall, he's settled into and is accepted by English society—and by all the evidence, he values that position." Antonia continued easing pins from her tightly coiled hair and laying them on the dressing table. "I gathered from Mrs. Parrish and Mrs. McGibbin that the Ennises have lived here or at their town house in London consistently since their marriage."

He nodded. "I can see plenty of justification for Ennis, if he'd heard of something beyond mere protests—for instance, of some plot that bordered on treason—feeling compelled to contact Drake. As for whom among the guests he fears…I can't see why it would be Parrish or McGibbin. Although both live in Ireland and, therefore, presumably have closer ties to those there, I get the sense they're exactly as they appear—gentlemen devoted to the managing of their estates and businesses and having no special interest in any political intrigue."

"I got the same impression from Miss Bilhurst—although she's English, I gather she's been close to her aunt and uncle for most of her life and has visited them frequently—and also from Melinda Boyne, who has known the Parrishes and McGibbins for years. Later, I overheard Cecilia talking to Mrs. Parrish and Mrs. McGibbin about their homes and children—again, there was no whiff of anything that might remotely suggest any political interest at all, not on the ladies' or even on their husbands' parts." Antonia let her coiled hair fall. The mass unfurled in a waterfall of wavy black tresses that spilled over her back, almost to her waist.

Sebastian clenched both hands on the edge of the window seat, gripping against the impulse to rise and stroll to stand behind her—to where he could reach out and run his fingers through the silken fall of her hair; if fingers could slaver, at that moment, his did—hungry for the feel of black silk sliding across his palms and over and around his fingers. Antonia sighed as if in physical relief, then raked her fingers under and back through her hair, lifting the long tresses, then letting them slither free. He tried to block the sight from his mind and forced himself to speak, although to his ears at least, his tone was flat, devoid of enthusiasm. "Assuming that Ennis is, indeed, fearful of someone present at the house party and not someone outside the company, then it seems we're looking at the younger men."

Antonia picked up her hairbrush. "Through my discussions with Worthington and Filbury at the luncheon table, and what Melinda Boyne—who's sweet on Filbury—let fall later, I gather both Worthington and Filbury are sympathetic to the cause, but neither go beyond good wishes. I seriously doubt either of them would be actively involved in any plot, but they might be informants to those who are."

She set the brush to her hair and started plying it—running down each long strand from her scalp to the wavy ends. "From what Cecilia let fall, she doesn't approve of any of the four. She tolerates Connell because he's Ennis's brother, and it's a family tradition that this house party is held to coincide with his annual visit to report to Ennis about the Irish harvest. Because Cecilia wanted to invite us—me, Melissa, and Claire, as well as Georgia and Hadley—she needed to make up the numbers, so to keep peace with Ennis, she invited Filbury, Wilson, and Worthington." She paused, busily brushing, then went on, "That said, Cecilia's attitude to the four younger men is dismissive rather than condemnatory—more because she doesn't consider them up to snuff socially than because she imagines they're up to no good."

The sight of her steadily, rhythmically running the brush through her hair was literally mesmerizing.

After several seconds, Sebastian blinked, then dragged his eyes from the sight. He focused on the floor. After a moment, he frowned. "Ennis is anxious, even fearful, of someone, but it's possible the reason for that has nothing to do with his message for Drake."

"Another coincidence?"

He looked up and, in the mirror, met her eyes, took in her cynically disbelieving expression. He felt his jaw set. "Quite." He hesitated, then took the bit between his teeth and did what he'd come there to do. "Tonight, after dinner, don't go anywhere near Ennis—especially don't go near his study."

In the glass, she held his gaze, then she arched a coolly imperious brow.

"I promise I'll come and tell you what he says afterward." He'd told her of the meeting and would tell her of its outcome for one simple reason; it was senseless to keep such information a complete secret, to have no one but himself knowing, not when she was there, knew Drake, and understood the mission, and he knew he could trust her.

She studied him—searched his face—for several seconds, then she nodded. "Very well. Just as long as you tell me later."

That had gone better than he'd hoped. He hadn't been sure how she would react to what she might well have interpreted as an attempt to rein her in.

The warning *was* an attempt to keep her away from any potential action; while talking to Ennis should, theoretically, be safe enough, Sebastian's thumbs were pricking. He didn't like not knowing the source of Ennis's underlying fear.

But he'd accomplished what he'd come there to do—he'd learned what she'd found out about the other guests and had ensured she would keep her distance that evening.

His gaze had drifted and was once more transfixed on her brush, traveling languidly through the thick fall of her hair. He inwardly shook himself free of the distraction and rose. "I'll see you in the drawing room."

She met his gaze, then pointed to the bellpull. "You can ring for Beccy before you leave."

He hid a grin at her tone; she hadn't liked him dismissing her maid. So he dutifully tugged the bellpull, then opened the door and slipped out, closing the door quietly behind him.

Antonia paused in her brushing and stared at the closed door for several seconds. Ennis was frightened of someone or something. Frightened people were unpredictable.

Then again, she'd never known Sebastian not to be able to take care of himself.

Turning back to the mirror, she set down her brush and reached up to remove her earrings.

\* \* \*

At two minutes to ten o'clock that evening, Sebastian pushed away from the balustrade at the east end of the terrace that ran along the front of the house and ambled back toward the front door.

Half an hour earlier, after they'd finished with the port and brandy, Ennis had been the first to rise from the dining table. He'd excused himself on the grounds of having some urgent estate matter to deal with and had gone off, presumably to his study.

After a day spent in each other's company, the guests had grown more relaxed with each other; the other men had drifted from the table in twos and threes. Sebastian had retreated to the front terrace—deserted at that time—to avoid being roped into another billiards game or some conversation; he didn't want to have to make his excuses at ten o'clock, thereby calling attention to a meeting.

He opened the heavy front door, stepped inside, and let the door quietly close behind him. His shoes made little sound as he walked slowly down the long front hall. He halted just short of the archway giving onto the corridor leading to Ennis's study; earlier, he'd asked a footman where it was. From the sound of feminine voices and the tinkling of a piano, it seemed the ladies had remained in the music room whither they'd retreated on rising from the table.

The green-baize-covered door at the rear of the hall swung open, and Blanchard appeared, pushing the tea trolley. He saw Sebastian and inclined his head, then turned the trolley toward the music room.

Sebastian stirred and walked forward. He turned into the corridor leading toward the study just as, with a series of whirrs and muted clangs, the clocks in the house geared up for the hour, then bonged and chimed in unison.

As the tenth bong resonated through the house, he reached the intersection where the corridor he was in met another to the left; the intersecting corridor led to Ennis's study and ultimately to the billiards room. The door to the study lay three paces along the corridor. Somewhat to Sebastian's surprise, the door stood slightly ajar.

He halted outside the door and rapped on the panel. He heard nothing from inside—no sound at all bar the clink of billiard balls coming from the end of the corridor. Increasingly wary, he pushed the study door further open.

Ennis's desk, a large, polished mahogany affair, stood at one side of the room, set square and facing across the width, with the chair behind pushed back against a wall of shelves. Sebastian stepped over the threshold and looked around the door, but there was no one sitting in the armchairs angled before the hearth.

A fire crackled cheerily in the grate.

On the opposite side of the room, the lamp on Ennis's desk was lit, shedding a steady glow over several letters and papers left strewn across the blotter—as if Ennis had been there, but had just stepped out.

Then a gust of cooler air drew Sebastian's gaze to the long window directly opposite the door. The curtains were pushed aside, and the sash was raised…curious, given it was cold and misty outside.

Sebastian hesitated, yet it was ten o'clock. He reached back, returned the door to its almost-closed position, then strolled toward the desk and put out a hand to draw back one of the pair of chairs angled before it.

The chair behind the desk was pushed hard—jammed—against the shelves. Almost as if…

Swallowing an oath, Sebastian strode around the desk—and looked down at Lord Ennis.

Ennis was lying on his back, one arm outflung, his other hand pressed to a wound on his left side from which blood was steadily pouring.

Sebastian leapt to the bellpull and yanked hard three times, then he lifted the heavy chair, set it aside, and crouched in its place beside Ennis. Even from his first rushed glance, Sebastian knew Ennis was done for; his lordship's eyes were closed, but, this close, Sebastian could just hear the man's shallow breathing. "Ennis? Who did this?"

Surely the most important question.

At the sound of his voice, Ennis rallied. He opened his eyes, then fractionally shook his head. He shifted his outflung arm, raised that hand, and gripped Sebastian's wrist.

Ennis tensed, plainly fighting for breath.

Sebastian leaned nearer.

Ennis's mouth worked. His lips moved. "Gunpowder." The word was a thready gasp. Ennis gripped Sebastian's wrist as if to draw strength from him and forced out, "Here."

The effort was too much. Ennis's eyes lost focus, then his lids fell, and all tension left his body. At the last, his fingers relaxed, and his hand fell limply from Sebastian's wrist to the floor.

Sebastian closed his eyes. He hung his head for a moment, then, slowly, he rose.

A sudden rush of footsteps sounded in the corridor. Blanchard pushed the door wide and raced in.

He saw Sebastian and pulled up short. "My lord?"

Blanchard glanced around, clearly expecting to see his master.

His face like stone, Sebastian gestured to the figure at his feet. "I was to meet with Lord Ennis at ten o'clock. I arrived to find the door ajar and your master…" Sebastian looked at the body on the floor.

Blanchard came around the desk. The butler's eyes grew huge. "Oh, my good Lord."

"Indeed. I found his lordship lying there dead—murdered." Sebastian glanced at Blanchard, who was now chalk white. "Who is the local magistrate?"

Without looking away from the body, Blanchard answered, "Sir Humphrey Rattle, my lord."

Sebastian drew in a not-quite-steady breath. "I suggest you leave a footman on guard in this room, put another at the door to keep everyone away, and send for Sir Humphrey immediately."

Blanchard drew in a deep breath and straightened. He nodded. "Indeed, my lord." Then Blanchard looked suspiciously at Sebastian. "And you, my lord?"

"I," said Sebastian, most unwillingly, "will break the news to the others." He thought, then added, "Please summon everyone to the drawing room. I'm sure Sir Humphrey will prefer us all to be together in one place when he arrives."

# CHAPTER 5

$S$hock was never a pleasant experience. Sebastian had seen dead men—

even murdered men—before. He'd killed three himself in the furtherance of one or other of Drake's missions, but they'd been villains and not men he knew.

Finding Ennis dying, stabbed in his own study, had been an experience of a different caliber.

Despite having drunk a cup of tea followed by a large brandy, he still felt chilled and was grateful for Antonia's soft warmth close beside him as they sat on one of the smaller sofas in the drawing room.

The members of the house party had dutifully congregated, summoned by Blanchard and the footmen with the message that there was some serious news Sebastian had to impart to them. Once they'd all assembled, he'd told them of Ennis's death; for Cecilia's sake, he'd been as gentle and as vague as possible.

Cecilia now sat huddled between Mrs. Parrish and Mrs. McGibbin, weeping quietly; Sebastian judged her to be shocked and truly grieving. He could see no reason for Cecilia to have murdered her husband; despite her affairs—and Ennis's—they'd been sincerely attached in the way of couples who rub along well enough together, and who had made a life and had children together. Although desire might have waned, affection had remained.

The other guests sat in small groups around the room; most still looked stunned. He'd told them the magistrate had been sent for and that it would

be best for them to await Sir Humphrey's arrival, rather than retire.
Blanchard had advised that Sir Humphrey lived less than fifteen minutes
away and would most likely ride to the Hall.

Over the soft sound of Cecilia's weeping, the guests exchanged
comments in hushed tones.

Sebastian scanned the faces, wondering which of them, if any, was the
murderer. Despite the apparent message of the open window, he was
disinclined to believe that the murderer came from outside the house—
not with the way Ennis had been behaving.

Someone presently under Ennis's roof had murdered his lordship.

Why wasn't quite so clear.

Sebastian glanced at Antonia. Other than an initial "Oh, no!" she'd said
nothing, just sat beside him and offered wordless support. He studied her
face; her complexion was paler than usual, but her eyes were clear as they
moved from face to face around the company.

He reached out and took her hand.

Immediately, she glanced at him, but didn't draw her fingers from his.

He lifted her hand across so that he could cradle it between both of his.
Just the simple fact of feeling her fingers under his soothed some part of
him and cleared some of the fog from his mind. Looking at the other
guests again, under his breath, he murmured, "I need you to do something
for me."

"What?" she murmured back. Instantly, without the slightest hesitation.

He would have grinned if the matter wasn't so serious. "Should
anything occur to delay me—like the magistrate insisting on taking me
off somewhere for questioning—I need you to return to London and tell
Drake, or if he's not back, then his masters in Whitehall, what Ennis
said."

There was a second's silence, then she breathed, "What he said?"

Until then, he hadn't mentioned Ennis's last words, not to anyone.
"When I found him," he continued, his words a bare whisper, "he was
still alive. I asked who had stabbed him, but instead of answering that, he
used the last of his strength to say two words. Gunpowder. Here."

She, too, appeared to be looking idly across the room. She stiffened,
then drew a slow, shallow breath and murmured, "Good Lord."

"Indeed. He clearly believed those two words were more important
than naming his murderer."

Antonia shifted her hand in his hold and gripped his fingers as he was
gripping hers. Her mind darted this way, then that, evaluating, imagining.
Despite the scarifying implication of Ennis's last words, she didn't like
the notion of leaving Sebastian to his fate, but he was a marquess and
perfectly capable of acting as one of the higher nobility and pulling rank
when he chose to do so. She felt confident he wouldn't be taken up, but

she could understand that, to him, having her agreement that, in such an eventuality, she would take Ennis's words back to Drake was important... She forced herself to nod. "All right. If anything happens to detain you, I'll take the message to London."

And then, if he had, indeed, been detained, she would come straight back, dragging Drake, or St. Ives, or even her own father with her to ensure Sebastian was immediately released.

Unaware of her full intention, he squeezed her fingers in wordless thanks.

Instinctively, she returned the comforting pressure, then they heard voices outside. He released her hand, and she drew it back. Along with the other guests, they looked expectantly toward the drawing room door.

But the sound of heavy footsteps marched past, and the door did not open.

"The magistrate will have gone to examine the body," Sebastian stated, his gaze resting on Cecilia, who gulped and tried valiantly to contain her sobs.

Five minutes later, they again heard footsteps approaching. This time, the door opened to admit a robust gentleman of above middle years, yet still hale and hearty. His face looked the sort that would normally be graced with a genial expression, but tonight, Sir Humphrey Rattle looked grave. After one swift survey of the room, with a brisk gesture, Sir Humphrey directed a constable to wait unobtrusively beside the door, then he walked forward and bowed before Cecilia, who, with an effort, managed to give him her hand.

"Dreadful business, my dear." Sir Humphrey patted Cecilia's hand, then released it. "You stay where you are—I'm sure your guests and I can introduce ourselves."

Sir Humphrey proceeded to circle the room. He didn't shake hands but attentively noted every name, asking the obvious questions that allowed him to link this one with that. As he moved on, the gentlemen, who had risen at his approach, remained standing.

Eventually, Sir Humphrey reached Sebastian, who, like the others, rose to face him. "Earith," Sebastian said, "I'm here as escort to Lady Antonia Rawlings." He waited while Antonia gave Sir Humphrey her hand, and the magistrate bowed over it.

As Sir Humphrey straightened, Sebastian said, "It was I who found the body."

Sir Humphrey eyed him shrewdly. "You did, heh?" After a second of studying him, Sir Humphrey turned to face the room. "I'm afraid, ladies and gentlemen, that due to the serious nature of this crime, I am obliged to report the matter to Scotland Yard. I've already sent off a courier to notify the Yard, and I expect we'll see an inspector here by tomorrow morning. Until then, you will all need to remain at Pressingstoke Hall. As I gather the house party has only just commenced, that shouldn't create any difficulties for any of you."

Sir Humphrey paused as if waiting for a protest that didn't come. He cast a sidelong glance at Sebastian, then said, "Now, ladies and gentlemen, if you would oblige me by waiting here for the next few minutes, I'll have a quick chat with Lord Earith and then decide what's best to be done."

"It was Cynster—Earith—who found Ennis." Worthington looked unnaturally pale. "None of the rest of us even went near—the butler and the footmen kept us away. Can't see what good keeping us cooped up here will do."

"Nevertheless," Sir Humphrey said, and now there was steel in his tone, "for the moment, I require you to remain in this room. My chat with Lord Earith will not take long."

With that, Sir Humphrey directed an inquiring look Sebastian's way and, with a tip of his head, indicated the door.

Sebastian fell in beside the magistrate. As they neared the door, Sir Humphrey, his head lowered and his hands clasped behind his back, murmured, "You're St. Ives's son, aren't you?"

"Yes. The Marquess of Earith is a courtesy title."

"I see." Sir Humphrey opened the drawing room door and waved Sebastian ahead of him. After closing the door behind them, Sir Humphrey said, "I'll get Blanchard to find us a room, and you can tell me—"

"Actually"—Sebastian halted in the middle of the hall and, looking back, met Sir Humphrey's eyes—"might I suggest we speak outside?"

"Outside?" Sir Humphrey frowned.

Sebastian gestured to the front door. "There is a reason for my request. If you would humor me?"

Sir Humphrey debated for all of one second; he couldn't gainsay a man of Sebastian's lofty rank, not without having a very good reason. He nodded curtly. "Very well."

Sebastian led the way to the door; a footman sprang to open it. Walking onto the front porch, Sebastian noted a constable standing in the shadows along the front terrace. Looking ahead, he pointed to the circle of open lawn beyond the sweep of the drive. "There should do." He started down the steps, making it clear he expected Sir Humphrey to follow.

Sebastian crossed the gravel drive and walked on until he was several yards beyond its edge. Then he halted and waited for Sir Humphrey to join him.

The magistrate stopped and faced him, regarding him through

narrowed eyes. "What's the reason for this, heh?"

Sebastian met his gaze. "I want to be one hundred percent certain that what I say to you will not be overheard."

Sir Humphrey blinked.

Before the magistrate could pose another question, Sebastian asked, "Have you heard of Winchelsea? Of the role he plays?"

Sir Humphrey's expression grew wary. "You mean Wolverstone's heir? Another marquess like you?"

Sebastian nodded. "Just so. But the important point is whether or not you know what Winchelsea does."

Sir Humphrey studied Sebastian for a moment, then grudgingly admitted, "I've heard he works for the Home Secretary in some secretive sort of capacity."

"Indeed." Sebastian judged he had to take the chance and tell Sir Humphrey of the mission. "What I am about to tell you must be held in the strictest confidence. I'm attending this house party ostensibly squiring Lady Antonia, who is a family friend, both of my family and also of Winchelsea's. In reality, I'm here in Drake's—Winchelsea's—stead. He sent me here to act as his surrogate and receive a message from Lord Ennis."

"A message?"

"Ennis wrote that he had information of vital significance to lay before Winchelsea, but that he would not commit that information to writing. Instead, he wanted to meet Winchelsea face-to-face and suggested he attend this house party for that purpose. Unfortunately, Winchelsea had a pressing engagement elsewhere—in Ireland, as it happens. Consequently, he was very interested in hearing what Ennis had to say, but couldn't be in two places at the same time. I've occasionally assisted Winchelsea before, so he asked me to stand in for him and come to the house party—and we arranged for me to attend as Lady Antonia's escort. My brief was to contact Ennis and receive whatever information his lordship wished to divulge."

"I see." Sir Humphrey frowned; he stared at the trees bordering the lawn. "So what happened? Did you get the information?"

"Yes and no. I only managed to speak privately with Ennis this morning, when I alerted him to the fact that I was Winchelsea's surrogate. We couldn't talk further then—we were in the middle of a game of croquet. Ennis suggested we should meet tonight at ten o'clock in his study, the implication being that he would give me the information for Winchelsea then. I arrived outside the study door just after the clocks struck ten, and found the door ajar. I went in and, subsequently, found Ennis stabbed and dying—you saw where the body was."

"Dying?" Under his bushy brows, Sir Humphrey's eyes flew wide.

"Blanchard said Ennis was already dead when you found him."

"He wasn't, but I let everyone assume he was."

"So did he say anything?"

"After summoning the staff, before they arrived, I asked Ennis who had stabbed him. He shook his head and, instead of answering, used his last breaths to say two words. Gunpowder. Here." Sebastian heard the grimness in his tone. "Then he died."

"Gunpowder? *Here?*" Sir Humphrey all but goggled.

"Indeed. And no, I have no idea what that actually means."

The night's cold silence engulfed them. From deep in the wood to the side of the house came the hoot of an owl.

Sir Humphrey shifted, then he cleared his throat and gruffly said, "No insult intended, my lord, but do you have any proof of this business?"

Sebastian stirred. He reached into the inside pocket of his coat. "I have the letter from Ennis to Winchelsea—you'll be able to verify it's Ennis's handwriting—and a copy of Winchelsea's reply." He offered the folded sheets to the magistrate.

Sir Humphrey took the letters, walked back to stand beside one of the lanterns lighting the edge of the drive, and silently read both.

Sebastian followed. Facing the house, he halted beside the magistrate and waited.

Then Sir Humphrey frowned and shot him a look from under his shaggy brows. "Why call you 'the last man Ennis would want to see?'"

Sebastian sighed. "That was Drake's misplaced sense of humor. Six years ago, Lady Ennis and I were, for a short time, lovers. Ennis was aware of that. Hence, Drake surmised I was not a man Ennis would want to see."

"Ah." Sir Humphrey glanced again at the signatures on the letters, then refolded them and handed them back. "I rather think those are proof enough. I know Ennis's signature. This sounds like a serious business, and clearly you wouldn't have killed Ennis when he was the source of the information you and your friend Winchelsea wanted."

"Just so." Sebastian tucked the letters back into his pocket. "It's possible that Ennis was killed to prevent him passing on the information. Alternatively, he might have been killed for some other reason entirely. At this point, there's no way to tell."

"You'll have to show those letters to the inspector when he arrives." Sir Humphrey grimaced. "Reading between the lines, I take it the Irish are involved?"

Sebastian admitted, "We're assuming we're dealing with some offshoot of the Young Irelander movement. I suspect Ennis was a sympathizer, but most in the movement would see the use of gunpowder as a step too far."

"Indeed." Sir Humphrey tugged one ear lobe and frowned at the lawn. After several moments, he said, "So how do you think we should proceed?"

"Until the murderer is caught, I would caution against allowing anyone—English or Anglo-Irish—to leave. As you mentioned, all the guests had expected to be here until Thursday, so there's no reason they can't remain until then, at least."

"Oh, we'll definitely keep everyone here. The inspector should arrive in the morning, and we can decide what's next then." Sir Humphrey turned toward the house. "I'd best get back to the others. I have a few questions, then I'll tell everyone they can find their beds. I'll leave constables on guard to make sure no one bolts."

Sebastian fell into step beside Sir Humphrey; as they crossed the forecourt, he said, "One thing—if you would, please instruct your constables to allow myself and Lady Antonia to ride out tomorrow. There's a gentleman who lives nearby who might be able to shed some light on whatever plot Ennis had got wind of—especially given Ennis's 'here.' If there's some local connection, this gentleman might know more of it. As Winchelsea is almost certainly still in Ireland, there's no sense in me rushing to get Ennis's two words back to London. It would be more profitable for me to see what I can find out at this end—and to wait to see if you and the inspector can identify the murderer."

Sir Humphrey nodded. They reached the porch, and he halted and beckoned the constable who'd been standing unobtrusively against the house's front wall. "Sergeant Crickwell." Sir Humphrey waved at Sebastian. "This is the Marquess of Earith. He and a lady—Lady Antonia Rawlings—have permission to ride out as they wish. Everyone else, however, staff as well as her ladyship and the guests, are to remain at the house. They can walk the lawns, but for the moment, no farther."

"Yes, sir. I'll pass the word." Sergeant Crickwell nodded and stepped back into the shadows.

Blanchard had heard their voices; he opened the front door before they reached it. Sebastian walked beside Sir Humphrey into the house. Blanchard closed the door and followed; he anticipated their direction and moved to stand by the drawing room door.

Frowning, Sir Humphrey halted and turned to Sebastian. "A man, don't you think?" he murmured.

Sebastian considered, then said, "Most likely, but not necessarily. Whoever stabbed Ennis, he had to have known them to allow them to get that close." He saw the scene in his mind, imagined how it would have played out. "As I recall, there was one clean strike—angled upward to hit the heart. I didn't see any signs of a scuffle, did you?"

"No." Sir Humphrey grunted. "And I suppose you're right. With a sufficiently sharp weapon, a woman could have delivered that blow."

"I believe," Sebastian said, "that from the time they quit the dining table, all the ladies were together in the music room. If so, they can vouch for each other."

"Excellent. We'd best get that out of the way first."

Blanchard was hovering, his gaze flicking from Sebastian to Sir Humphrey, presumably seeking some hint of Sir Humphrey's stance on Sebastian's possible guilt.

Sir Humphrey noticed. He humphed and gave Blanchard the same instructions he'd given Crickwell. "No one at all to depart, mind, and that includes all the staff, although his lordship here and Lady Antonia are free to come and go."

"We will, however, be remaining as part of the house party," Sebastian clarified.

Blanchard inclined his head. To Sir Humphrey, he said, "The murder has shaken the staff, sir, as one might expect. If there's any reassurance I might convey…?"

Sir Humphrey sighed. "At this moment, Blanchard, there's nothing I can say that would reassure anyone." He nodded toward the drawing room. "I'm going to ask a few more questions, then allow everyone to retire for the night. I'll leave constables on watch inside and outside the house—that should calm any imminent hysteria. I expect to be back tomorrow morning with the inspector Scotland Yard will send down. You might ask among the staff if anyone saw or heard anything that might be relevant—for instance, whether anyone unexpected was seen leaving the house around ten o'clock."

Blanchard bowed. "Very good, sir. I will inquire." He moved to open the drawing room door.

Sir Humphrey led the way in. Sebastian followed. As the door closed behind him, he surveyed the company spread around the room. Everyone had looked up, but most gazes flitted over him and fixed on Sir Humphrey as the magistrate walked forward.

Only Antonia continued looking at Sebastian, incipient concern in her eyes. He met her gaze, infinitesimally shook his head, and strolled to reclaim his position on the sofa beside her.

Sir Humphrey, meanwhile, took up a stance at the end of the rug directly opposite the fireplace and faced the assembled company. "Now, if you will bear with me, I have a few simple questions, and then you may retire. I understand that, on rising from the dinner table, the ladies gathered in the music room, which from memory is toward the rear corner of the ground floor, beyond the breakfast room. At what time did you rise from the dinner table?"

The ladies exchanged glances, then Cecilia mumbled something around the handkerchief pressed to her lips, and Mrs. Parrish, beside her, spoke up. "It was about twenty minutes past nine o'clock."

A murmur of agreement came from various female throats, and some of the men nodded as well.

"Excellent. So the ladies gathered in the music room. Did you all go there directly?"

"I believe so." Mrs. Parrish looked at the other ladies for confirmation.

Antonia's clear voice cut across the resulting chatter. "Miss Wainwright and I were the last of the ladies to reach the music room. As I recollect, all the other ladies walked ahead of us, and all of us went directly into the music room."

Melissa Wainwright nodded. "That's correct. We brought up the rear, and all the others were ahead of us. No one went anywhere else."

"And you all remained in the music room until the murder was discovered?"

"Yes" and "Definitely" came from all sides.

Then Miss Bilhurst said, "I was at the piano for most of the time—until we heard the alarm. I was playing, and from the stool, I could see all the ladies and the door. No one was rude enough to leave—I noticed. Everyone was still there when we heard…" She waved vaguely.

"Thank you." Satisfied, Sir Humphrey cast his gaze over the gentlemen. "So the ladies left at twenty minutes past nine. I assume the gentlemen remained to pass the decanters?"

Most of the men nodded.

Sebastian stated, "As I recall, all the gentlemen remained in the dining room, at the table, for only a relatively short time. About ten minutes after the ladies left, Ennis excused himself on the grounds of having some pressing matter of business to deal with."

Sir Humphrey glanced around, and a number of men murmured agreement. "So," Sir Humphrey concluded, "the critical question for all the gentlemen will be where each of you were between half past nine and ten o'clock, when Lord Earith found Ennis dead."

There was silence for a moment, then Mrs. McGibbin exclaimed, "Great heavens, sir! You can't possibly think that any of those here stabbed his lordship." She sounded faintly incredulous and genuinely shocked.

"I gather the study window was open," Hadley Featherstonehaugh said. "Surely Ennis came upon some vagrant rifling his desk, and the miscreant stabbed him and escaped."

Sir Humphrey inclined his head. "We are pursuing that notion."

"Good Lord!" Mrs. Parrish had paled. "A murdering vagrant on the loose. Why, any of us might be murdered in our beds!"

Antonia uttered a muted but plainly derisive sound.

With his hands, Sir Humphrey gestured for calm. "There's no cause for panic—I will be leaving constables on watch inside the house and around about. You needn't fear any villain will get in. However, I must insist that, until the inspector arrives and gives you leave, you must all remain at the house."

The announcement elicited various mumbled comments and several grumbling ones, but in the face of Cecilia's grief, her guests refrained from making any more strident complaint.

"So can we go to our rooms, then?" Melinda Boyne asked somewhat plaintively.

"Yes, indeed." Sir Humphrey gave a short bow. "Thank you for your forbearance. I will return in the morning with the inspector, and we'll evaluate where we are then."

The company didn't wait for further encouragement. Most rose and made for the door in twos and threes.

Sir Humphrey walked to where Cecilia sat, exchanged a few quiet words, then, with a last general nod, headed for the door.

Antonia looked at Sebastian. When he met her eyes, she murmured, "We can't talk here. Let's go up."

Together, they rose and fell in behind Mrs. Parrish and Mrs. McGibbin, who between them were supporting Cecilia upstairs.

Considering Cecilia—considering the depth of shock he'd glimpsed in her eyes—Sebastian wondered if she'd known anything of Ennis's fears. He did not for a moment imagine she was in any way complicit in her husband's murder; quite aside from her eminently sincere grief, he couldn't imagine that becoming a widow would ever have been a part of the future Cecilia had planned. If he'd been asked, he would have said she'd enjoyed her life as it had been; she and Ennis had understood each other, and regardless of their dalliances, had got along well.

He and Antonia left Mrs. McGibbin and Mrs. Parrish helping a wilting Cecilia into her room.

The instant they'd passed under the archway and into the east wing, Antonia's fingers curled into his sleeve, and she tugged, then towed him up the corridor to her room.

She opened the door. He glanced quickly down the corridor—confirming it was deserted—then followed her inside and shut the door behind him.

Antonia lit the lamp that stood on a side table by the armchair near the fireplace. She adjusted the wick until the lamp shed a golden circle of light over the area before the hearth. Then she straightened and looked at Sebastian; he'd followed her and had halted before the hearth, and now stood gazing into the fire. "What on earth did Ennis mean?" she asked. "Gunpowder *here*. Here, where?"

Lit principally by the firelight, Sebastian's features appeared chiseled and harsh. His lips thinned. "Precisely. Here meaning England. Here meaning south-east England, including London. Here meaning Kent or this stretch of coast. Or here meaning this estate or even just the house."

She folded her arms and gripped her elbows. She felt chilled, as if the proximity of violent death had cast an icy pall over her. "He could have meant any of those as far as I can see." She started to pace back and forth, a yard before the hearth and parallel to it—driven by restlessness more than anything else.

"Hmm." Sebastian straightened his shoulders, then glanced at her and saw her pacing. He hesitated for a second, then turned and fell to pacing, too. His longer strides carried him around her on a roughly oval track.

She knew he paced when deep in thought. Fixing her gaze on the floor, she paced in more restrained fashion. "Presumably, 'gunpowder here' is the crux of the message Ennis intended to give Drake. If they—whoever they might be—have some gunpowder here—wherever 'here' is—what are they planning to do with it?"

"Blow something up." Sebastian paced on. "But what?"

"But that's a clue, isn't it?" Antonia swung around and paced back. "Who would think to gather gunpowder and blow something up?"

"Given Ennis's connections to the Young Irelanders, I can't see the 'who' being any other group."

"I thought the Young Irelanders—those left after the rebellion was put down—were more peaceable, these days."

"Those remaining in the public eye are, but no doubt there are more militant elements still skulking in the shadows."

"So if it is the Young Irelanders, what would they be likely to want to blow up?"

His gaze on the floor, he shook his head. "Most likely something in London, but it might be elsewhere—for instance, Windsor Castle."

The edge of her skirts flicked into his field of vision. Abruptly, he halted—just in time.

With a suppressed squeak, she pulled up—less than an inch away. With a sliver of air—heated and heating—separating her breasts from his chest.

She swayed with the suddenness of her halting, even as her head jerked up, and her eyes met his.

Wide gray eyes, roiling with surging heat, with passion, with desire—with hunger. In that instant, he saw it all—and was seized with a powerful, nearly overwhelming urge to reach out and take—to raise his hands, close them about her waist, and jerk her the last inch to him.

And what then?

His mind reeled. He felt himself teetering at a metaphorical fork in his path. This way—or that?

But the decision was irreversible.

Antonia stared into pale green eyes—warlock's eyes with the power to mesmerize. She couldn't breathe. She couldn't think. But she could feel temptation—rich, alluring, compelling—slide across her skin.

It whispered to her senses, stroked them beguilingly.

Enticed her...

Her lips felt fuller; the lower throbbed.

As if he knew, his gaze fell to fasten on her mouth.

For a second, they stood frozen.

Then he hauled in a breath and stepped back. Without meeting her eyes, he turned to the door. "We should sleep on our questions."

*The ones about you and me, or the ones about gunpowder?* As he crossed to the door, she was tempted to ask. Once she was free of his immediate orbit, her wits functioned with their customary facility.

"No doubt we'll see things in a clearer light come morning." He paused at the door, his hand on the knob, and through the shadows looked back at her. Then he nodded somewhat curtly and went out.

She watched the door quietly close behind him, then heard his footsteps, muted by the runner, continue down the corridor to his room.

She discovered she could breathe again, although her lungs still felt constricted. Standing, staring at the space where he'd last been, she considered what her senses told her was the portent of that last dark look of his.

He'd been as tempted as she, but he'd set the personal aside and stepped back from taking the next obvious step in what seemed to be evolving between them in favor of dealing with the mission—the mission that was increasingly looking as if it involved a threat to the realm. Gunpowder suggested a fairly major event and a significant target.

She supposed she had to accept his decision as the sensible way forward.

She rang for Beccy and spent the next twenty minutes immersed in the commonplace, in the routine of preparing for bed.

But once Beccy had left, and she lay under the covers, shrouded in darkness, she finally allowed her mind to refocus on the evening's events...

Sebastian had been right, but for her, clarity had already arrived.

And courtesy of that, concern was slowly welling inside her.

If Ennis had been killed in order to prevent him from speaking to Sebastian, then presumably the killer had guessed that Sebastian was Drake's surrogate. But the killer had fled before Ennis had died.

What if the killer started to worry that, despite being at death's door, before he'd died, Ennis had managed to pass his message on to

Sebastian—not just two words but the whole message?

Wouldn't the killer seek to kill Sebastian?

Sebastian, who was being accommodated by Sir Humphrey and already being treated differently than the other guests.

There was more than enough in the situation to make any killer nervous.

Admittedly, Sebastian had let everyone else believe Ennis was already dead when he'd reached him, but being Drake's surrogate, he would have done that regardless. Such a pretense wouldn't protect him from a nervous killer.

Should anything occur to delay me...

Her eyes narrowed. Sebastian had suggested that the magistrate might detain him, but how likely was that? As he'd already demonstrated, he'd had no difficulty winning Sir Humphrey to his cause.

No—he'd foreseen the possibility that the killer might come for him, and that was why he'd extracted that promise from her.

Fierce determination rose within her—a compulsion powered by potent and forceful emotions. The feeling was so startlingly strong, it took her several moments to identify it. Protectiveness, but of a strain she'd never before experienced.

Now she'd finally come to her senses and fully appreciated what Sebastian was to her—and it appeared he'd finally focused on her, too— she was not going to allow any killer to get in the way of what she already considered their joint future.

Of course, that future was still undecided and might not come to be, but if so, it would be at their determination; she was not of a mind to allow any killer to interfere, much less dictate.

She lay staring up at the ceiling as possibilities and options revolved in her mind.

As it happened, the best way forward was relatively easy to define.

She would stick like glue to Sebastian's side through whatever investigative forays he made; that, she felt certain, as her lids fell and she slid toward slumber, was the only viable way of ensuring that the killer in their midst had no chance to derail the future she was now determined to explore.

# CHAPTER 6

*T*he following morning, feeling decidedly grim, Sebastian walked along the gallery and started down the stairs. He'd spent far too many hours over the past night thinking—of Antonia and that fraught moment in her room.

If he had the time again, he was almost certain he would react differently—that he would give in to the urgent compulsion that had gripped him, if only to see where it led.

Anything would be better—less aggravating—than all the hours he'd spent tossing in his bed.

Yet despite the lust that hovered like a combustible cloud between them—a cloud he knew very well would grow only more dense, more intense, the longer they refrained from igniting it and letting it burn—despite the fact the scales had now fallen from his eyes regarding her, and if he was any judge, had fallen from her eyes regarding him as well, now was not the time to pursue such a connection. Not with a murderer under the same roof, and God alone knew what danger hovering.

Gunpowder. Here.

Ennis's words haunted him, constantly replaying in his mind.

Duty and Drake's mission came first. Antonia and whatever might come of their new level of interaction could safely wait until later.

That said, he'd already realized that he wouldn't be able to concentrate on the mission, on figuring out which 'here' Ennis had meant, if he—the less civilized male inside him—wasn't assured of Antonia's safety.

With a murderer in the company, the only way to ensure she was safe was to keep her with him.

Given her typical feminine curiosity and her predilection for involving herself in whatever was going on, he felt confident keeping her by his side wouldn't require any great effort.

Thus resolved, he stepped onto the tiles of the front hall, turned left, and entered the breakfast room.

Somewhat to his surprise, he discovered he was the last of the company to approach the sideboard. Knowing that due to the distance from London, the inspector—and therefore Sir Humphrey—wasn't likely to arrive at the house until after nine o'clock, he'd slept late. He'd thought others would have, too, but one glance at the faces around the table suggested few had found any true rest; most looked strained, but were endeavoring to rise above it.

He was less surprised to find Cecilia at the table, nibbling a slice of toast and sipping tea. She'd never been a social hypocrite, and although she'd cared for Ennis, her feelings for him hadn't run deep enough to excuse any histrionics. She had endeavored to find a black gown; the color made her blond paleness appear even more wan.

After filling his plate from the silver serving dishes arranged along the sideboard, he carried the plate to the empty chair between Antonia and Filbury. Antonia welcomed him with a small smile, Filbury with a nod.

As Sebastian sat, Antonia returned her attention to what he realized was a watchful examination of the others at the table.

On his other side, Filbury leaned nearer and murmured, "Dashed awkward, if you ask me. I hope this inspector knows his place and allows us to leave. Seems pointless to keep us all here when it's plain as a pikestaff that some blighter climbed into the study, thinking to steal things, Ennis surprised him, and the blighter did for him. Wouldn't surprise me if there were gypsies camped nearby."

Sebastian used a mouthful of food as an excuse to make no reply.

Most were eating in silence, with only a few soft-voiced conversations among the ladies springing up and then quietly fading. As he ate, he studied the faces—as Antonia was doing. Cecilia was clearly saddened and sorrowful but not distraught. Virtually everyone else looked unsettled and uncomfortable; none were sure how they should behave, and most showed signs of lingering shock and not a little uncertainty.

A few of the men, like Filbury, were hovering on the brink of belligerence, but Sebastian judged that was nothing more than their way of dealing with a situation they didn't understand and couldn't control.

He'd just pushed his empty plate away when sounds from the hall suggested Sir Humphrey had arrived.

The company exchanged glances, very much of the "What do we do?"

variety, but before any answer was formulated, Sir Humphrey walked through the open doorway.

A tall, thin, middle-aged man garbed in a neat but undistinguished suit accompanied the magistrate; the man, presumably the inspector, had a long, thin face and a long, thin nose, and his brown eyes were sharp and watchful. Both men halted just inside the room and waited for those about the table to turn and face them.

Sir Humphrey greeted them all with a crisp nod and a brisk, "Good morning." He waved to the man beside him. "This is Inspector Crawford of Scotland Yard. He will, henceforth, be in charge of the investigation."

Crawford stepped forward. "Lady Ennis." He half bowed to Cecilia, then, with a more general nod, let his gaze travel around the table. "Ladies and gentlemen. I understand you will wish to know how the investigation into Lord Ennis's murder stands, and I will endeavor to answer that question as soon as may be." The inspector had a dry, precise way of speaking that was curiously calming. "But first, I need to examine the study in which his lordship was killed. Subsequently, I will interview each of you, one by one, in the estate office. Purely routine—we need to determine where each of you were over the critical period, which I understand to be between nine thirty and ten o'clock last evening. Until you are called to the estate office, I would ask you to remain in this room, the music room, or the drawing room. Once you've been interviewed, you will be free to move about the house and grounds, but at this stage, it's imperative that you all remain here, at this house."

Several mouths opened, no doubt to protest, but before a word was uttered, Crawford smoothly rolled on, "Rest assured we will release you as soon as possible." He nodded to the company—a nod that was nicely gauged to be civil and appropriate, yet in no way servile. "Thank you for your forbearance. We will attempt to minimize the disruption to your day."

With that, the inspector turned to Sir Humphrey, and together, the pair walked out.

"Well!" Mrs. McGibbin said. After a moment, she added, "At least he seems a sensible-enough person."

By which, Antonia wryly thought, returning her gaze to her teacup, you mean the man was wise enough to appear conciliatory.

She'd been the second of the party to arrive in the breakfast room. Only Worthington had been before her. She'd sat toward one end of the table and had paid particular attention to the faces of all the men as they'd joined the gathering. She felt that a man who'd murdered his host the evening before should carry some sign of guilt in his countenance.

Sadly for her theory, while all the men appeared somber and even rather grim, none had looked remotely guilt-ridden. Several looked worried, even anxious, but more in the way of being concerned that they might be looked at askance by the other members of the company; all of the men seemed to have realized that suspicion might, at some point, focus on them, and they were all watching each other closely, searching, as she was, for some hint of who was the guilty party.

No one stood out. There was nothing to distinguish one from the other.

Now that the inspector had made his appearance, several members of the group eased back their chairs, preparing to rise.

Before anyone did, Cecilia cleared her throat and raised her head. In a voice made husky and scratchy by weeping, she said, "I fear I must apologize—such a dreadful business to engulf us all."

Instantly, there was a chorus of disavowals and assurances that no one could possibly blame her, not at all.

Cecilia smiled weakly. "Thank you, my friends, not just for your understanding but also your support." She smiled at Mrs. Parrish and Mrs. McGibbin in particular.

Seated beside Cecilia, Mrs. Parrish patted Cecilia's hand. "There's no need to worry your head over us, my dear. I'm sure we'll all cope."

Several hear-hears supported that assertion.

"I'm sure that's so," Cecilia allowed, "but as the inspector has decreed that we are all to remain here for the time being, I wish to assure you that, while our planned excursions beyond the estate cannot now proceed, the amenities of the house and grounds will continue to be available for your use as previously, and while I'm sure you will understand if I retreat somewhat from your company, I would encourage you to make use of the avenues the house affords to divert your minds from this distressing situation."

Everyone, Antonia included, approved of their hostess's speech; in Antonia's opinion, it hit just the right note.

Cecilia rose and excused herself; she dissuaded the other ladies from accompanying her, stating she intended to rest quietly in her room.

Once she had left, pausing only to speak briefly with Blanchard in the doorway, the others of the company, apparently feeling rather better over disporting themselves while their host lay dead, started making plans for the day. On the ladies' part, the plans were restrained, but as Antonia listened, she realized that, as the shock wore off, the younger ladies— Melissa, Claire, Georgia, and Melinda Boyne and Amelie Bilhurst—were rather titillated by the drama; none of them had known Ennis well, and his murder was, she supposed, more excitement than they'd previously encountered in their conventional lives.

Most of the ladies had made some attempt to find dark colors to wear. Being black haired, Antonia rarely wore darker hues, but she had brought a navy-blue walking dress with her and had donned that this morning.

Casting her gaze over the men of the company, she noted that, unlike the ladies, they seemed much more hesitant over committing themselves to any particular diversion in any other man's company. All appeared to be keeping their distance—mentally, at least—from each other, even Mr. Parrish and Mr. McGibbin, who, if she'd understood correctly, were old friends.

Before she could decide what the gentlemen's behavior meant, Blanchard materialized between her chair and Sebastian's.

"My lord, Inspector Crawford and Sir Humphrey have requested your and Lady Antonia's presence. If you and her ladyship will follow me, I will show you to the estate office."

An immediate and distinctly avid silence fell.

"Yes, of course." Sebastian pushed back his chair and got to his feet. He waved the footman back and drew out Antonia's chair.

She rose and smoothed down her skirts. She met Sebastian's gaze; he smiled faintly and offered his arm, and she placed her hand on his sleeve.

Utterly ignoring all the fascinated watchers, Sebastian turned her toward the door. "Lead on, Blanchard."

Leaving a pregnant silence reigning in the breakfast room, they followed Blanchard across the hall to the first door in the corridor leading to Ennis's study.

Blanchard opened the door and announced them.

Sebastian steered Antonia before him into the office. It was a decent-sized room, with a large desk placed before the far wall on which a detailed map of the estate was displayed. Pigeonholes and cabinets lined one side wall, with bookshelves covering the other. The shelves were packed with ledgers, all neatly arrayed spine-out. The room drew light from high windows in the wall it shared with the front hall, itself well supplied with natural light courtesy of the cupola in its ceiling.

The inspector and Sir Humphrey rose from chairs behind the large desk. The inspector nodded politely. "Good morning, my lord. My lady." He waved to two comfortable chairs angled before the polished expanse. "If you would be seated?" He looked past them at the constable standing at his ease inside the door. "Wait outside, please, constable, and make sure no one disturbs us."

"Yes, sir."

Sebastian guided Antonia to the chair on the right, then sat in the other chair, directly in front of the inspector. Antonia settled her skirts, then clasped her hands in her lap and fixed her gray gaze on the inspector, but said nothing.

Sebastian took pity on the man. "I take it Sir Humphrey has explained the background to my presence here."

"Indeed, my lord." Crawford studied Sebastian for several seconds, then leaned forward, placing his forearms on the desk and clasping his hands. He fixed a level look on Sebastian's face. "I'll be frank, my lord. On the one hand, I'm not at all thrilled to discover that this murder might be connected with some political intrigue in which Whitehall's agents are involved. On the other hand, I have to admit to a...certain curiosity. Not every murder has wider implications."

"I should think that was just as well, at least from your perspective. However, that is the hand Fate has dealt us in this instance." Sebastian hesitated, then said, "It might help to mention that both myself and Lady Antonia are acquainted with your Chief Inspector Stokes, and even more with Mr. Barnaby Adair. We therefore appreciate the...restrictions and requirements, and indeed, the limitations of your position."

Crawford pursed his lips, then his features relaxed somewhat, and he nodded. "I believe we understand each other, my lord. My lady. So if you would tell me all you know of Lord Ennis, up to the point of finding him dead?"

Antonia listened as Sebastian concisely explained what had brought him to Pressingstoke Hall, then described their arrival and the various events that had occurred since. He told of arranging to meet with Ennis at ten o'clock and outlined his movements after the ladies had left the dining table to the moment of finding Ennis dying.

When informed that Ennis hadn't yet been dead, and hearing Ennis's last words, Crawford widened his eyes. "Gunpowder? And what did he mean by *here*?"

"Precisely our questions. With Ennis dead, we'll need to find the answers." Sebastian glanced at Antonia, who had remained uncharacteristically silent throughout. "I suggest that while you and Sir Humphrey search for Ennis's murderer, Lady Antonia and I should use the time to pursue the—as you labeled them—wider implications."

Crawford slowly nodded. "Sir Humphrey mentioned some letters you hold. If I could see them? Purely a formality."

Sebastian gave him the letters; he kept them on him at all times.

After perusing the second, Crawford glanced sharply at him. "Why are you the last man Lord Ennis would want to see?"

Sebastian inwardly sighed and explained. He could almost see the obvious suspicion rise in Crawford's mind, but then the inspector glanced at Antonia, then looked at Sir Humphrey, both of whom appeared bored and transparently saw nothing of concern in a long-ago liaison. Sebastian sensed Crawford's bubble of suspicion deflating.

With that issue dealt with, the inspector humphed, glanced at the letters again, then refolded both and handed them back. "I agree that the best way forward is for us to work in parallel. It's entirely possible, even likely, that someone here—almost certainly one of the guests—learned that Ennis was about to reveal something of vital importance regarding their efforts to you—to Winchelsea—and so killed Ennis before he could."

Sebastian nodded. "If I'd found him a minute later, the killer would have succeeded, and we wouldn't have learned anything."

Crawford regarded him with a level gaze. "You might want to bear in mind that the killer might grow nervous over whether or not Ennis managed to say anything to you."

"I took care to let everyone suppose that Ennis was already dead when I found him. At this point, only Sir Humphrey, you, and Lady Antonia"— Sebastian glanced briefly her way—"know that he managed to utter even those two words. Two words that raise more questions than they answer."

The inspector nodded decisively. "I'll leave you to pursue them. Meanwhile, Sir Humphrey and I will hunt our murderer."

"I feel I should point out that, once you have him, Winchelsea and his masters will have a very real interest in interrogating him. They'll want to learn all they can, not just about the details of whatever plot's afoot but about the organization behind it."

Crawford pulled a face. "We'll deal with Whitehall's interest once we have him. Meanwhile"—he looked at Antonia—"if you would, my lady, could you describe where the ladies were during the half hour before the murder was discovered?"

Antonia repeated the information she'd given Sir Humphrey, adding that, in her opinion, Miss Bilhurst was the definitive source on the ladies' movements. "She was at the piano the entire time and had a clear view of the room and the door. Although she was playing most of the time, she's accomplished enough to have been observing her audience more or less constantly."

Crawford thanked her, then asked Sebastian to detail what he knew of when the other male guests left the dining room.

Sebastian obliged.

When he fell silent, Crawford looked over the notes he'd jotted down. "So Ennis left the dining room first, followed a short time later by McGibbin, Worthington, Filbury, Wilson, and Boyne. Exactly where they went, you can't say, but some, at least, said they were headed for the billiards room. A bit after that, you left and walked onto the front terrace, leaving Parrish and Featherstonehaugh still seated at the table, talking." The inspector looked up and met Sebastian's eyes. "Is that correct?"

Sebastian nodded. "And when I came in from the terrace a few minutes before the hour and walked to the study, I didn't see any of the others on the way."

Crawford humphed. "I believe," he said, glancing at Antonia, "that we can discount the ladies, at least for the role of murderer." He looked at

Sebastian, then returned his gaze to Antonia. "I have one more question for both of you. When the alarm was raised, did you see anyone—anyone at all—whose reaction seemed odd or out of place? Did anyone behave in a way you wouldn't have expected?"

Antonia exchanged a glance with Sebastian, then looked at the inspector and shook her head. "No. I saw no one behaving in any way oddly."

Sebastian grimaced. "I didn't actually see any of the guests—just Blanchard and two footmen, all of whom were shocked and aghast, as one might expect. I didn't see anyone else until later, and by then everyone simply appeared shocked."

Crawford slowly nodded as he scribbled another note in his book.

Then he looked up, his gaze once more sharp and incisive. "I understand from Sir Humphrey that you wish to ride somewhere."

"There's an old gentleman who, during autumn, usually rusticates nearby. He knows a great deal about politics and plots, and I'm hoping he might have some insight to offer into how best to respond to Ennis's warning. I also need to get a message to Whitehall regarding Ennis's death and his last words, preferably faster and with greater security than via the Royal Mail."

"And this gentleman can arrange that?" Crawford looked skeptical.

Sebastian smiled. "If he's in residence." He uncrossed his legs and rose. "I propose to ride out with Lady Antonia and find out. His house is quite close. We should be back for luncheon."

The inspector glanced at Sir Humphrey.

Sir Humphrey nodded. "Any help in this matter is to be welcomed." The magistrate got to his feet as Antonia rose.

Crawford hurriedly stood and half bowed to her. "Lady Antonia." Then he looked at Sebastian. "If you learn anything that sheds light on who the murderer might be—"

"We will bring it to your attention without delay." With a faintly ruthless smile curving his lips, Sebastian inclined his head to Crawford. "I hope you will reciprocate should you discover anything pertinent to our interpretation of Ennis's last words."

"Of course."

Antonia saw Sebastian hold the inspector's gaze for a second, then he stepped back and waved her to the door.

She waited until they were sufficiently distant from the constable on duty outside the office before slanting a glance at Sebastian's face. "Where are we going? And who are we visiting?"

He met her eyes. They'd reached the front hall. He halted before the stairs.

She halted beside him and noted the way his gaze swept their surroundings before returning to her face.

"Go and change," he said. "I'll meet you at the stable."

She threw him a haughtily censorious look—those words had sounded far too much like an autocratic command—but knowing his imperviousness on that front, without further ado, she went up the stairs.

* * *

By the time Antonia had changed into her dark-gray velvet riding habit, pulled on her boots, settled her riding cap at the correct angle on her piled hair, swiped up her gloves and crop, and started down the stairs, her mind had had time to sort through the morning's exchanges, and once again, concern floated at the forefront of her brain.

Concern for Sebastian, that the fact he was being accorded special freedoms beyond that granted to other guests would mark him as in some way associated with the authorities—and he had been the one to find Ennis.

Surely the murderer would be moved to wonder if Ennis, when found, had, in fact, been dead or still dying. Still able to speak.

She asked directions from a footman, then strode briskly out along the path to the stable.

Sebastian was standing in the stable yard, the reins of a large gray hunter in his hand. A lighter-weight, leggy chestnut mare bearing a side-saddle was tied to the railing nearby. Sebastian was chatting to the stable master, a grizzled older man with a knowledgeable eye. He smiled when he saw Antonia and dipped his head.

Sebastian turned. His pale green gaze raked her. "Good." He handed the gray's reins to the stable master.

Antonia went to the side of the chestnut, intending to free the reins and walk the horse to the mounting block, but before she even touched the reins, Sebastian caught her about her waist, turned her, then lifted her to the saddle.

She lost her breath; for a moment, she lost her wits and all ability to think.

But the instant he released her, her wits returned in a rush.

When he handed her the mare's reins, she narrowed her eyes on his faintly smug expression—yes, he'd definitely done that on purpose, just to see what would happen. And he'd seen and now knew. As she watched him stride to the gray, take the reins, then fluidly mount, she silently vowed revenge.

He compounded his sins by arrogantly collecting her with a mere glance, then urging the gray into a trot.

Counseling herself against acting precipitously, head high, she brought the chestnut alongside the gray and bided her time.

Once they were out of sight of the stable, trotting briskly across the fields and angling toward the coast north of the estate, recalling her earlier worry, she called to him, "Don't you think us being allowed to ride out is going to mark you as working for the authorities?"

He met her eyes. After a moment, he looked forward. "I'm my father's son. You're your father's daughter. We outrank all the others here by a country mile. No one's going to wonder over a police inspector allowing us to wander as we please—they'll just see it as proof that rank still wields power."

"Ah." She hadn't thought of it in those terms, but now he mentioned it...

"Come on." He urged the gray into an easy gallop. "We need to find out if he's there."

*He, who? And there, where?* But there was no point trying to converse at this speed. She thumped her heel against the chestnut's side and pushed the horse faster.

Presumably, she would have her answers soon enough.

The first answer—where they were going—came sooner than she'd expected. They'd veered to the coast and followed the bridle path along the top of the cliffs, but had gone only a few miles when she saw the uniquely curved walls of Walmer Castle ahead. Shaped like a four-leaved clover, the official residence of the Lord Warden of the Cinque Ports was impossible to mistake.

And that, of course, answered the question of whom they were hoping to speak with.

As Sebastian led the way up the graveled drive, she shook her head. "Wellington?"

Sebastian glanced back at her. "He comes down here every autumn. He may be nearly eighty years old, but he's still sharp as a tack, and he's still Commander-in-Chief of the army and keeps his ear close to every political ground there is. If anyone can give us a rapid but accurate assessment of the potential of a gunpowder threat, it's him."

They left their horses at the stable. The stable lad confirmed that the Lord Warden was, indeed, in residence. Side by side, Sebastian and Antonia strode along a hedge-lined walk to the drawbridge leading over the dry moat to an iron-studded double door made of ancient timbers inches thick.

Sebastian tugged the bell chain. A minute later, one door was hauled open by a neat individual, who left them standing in the panelled entrance hall while he took Sebastian's card to his master.

Wellington's secretary soon appeared with the news that His Grace would be delighted to grant them an audience.

Antonia hid a grin and followed the secretary, a dapper little man, along a corridor and up a curving stair to a large room in one of the towers. She'd met the Iron Duke several times, although not recently, but his acerbic wit and sharp tongue were legendary, and she remembered them very well.

The long room into which they were shown was instantly identifiable as Wellington's own. A narrow camp bed rested against the wall farther down the room, and various mementos of his numerous victories were mounted on the walls or lay scattered here and there on side tables and chests. The great man himself was seated in a Bath chair, a shawl draped over his knees. He still sat rigidly upright, and there was nothing whatever impaired about the mind behind his large, slightly protuberant eyes. As they entered, he set aside the clutch of papers he'd been perusing and, with a smile, waved them to the chaise at his left.

With an answering smile, Antonia curtsied, then rose and went forward.

"My dear Antonia." Wellington held out his hand, fingers waving for her to give him her hand. "This is an unexpected pleasure." Taking her fingers, he gallantly raised them to his lips, then gently squeezed them and released her. "I hope you will forgive an old man for not rising—the manners are willing, but the flesh, I fear, has grown frail."

"Of course, Your Grace. I'm delighted you were able to receive us." She glanced at Sebastian. "I had no idea we would be calling on you, or I would have brought a gift."

"Huh." Wellington's still-incisive gaze shifted to Sebastian. "Playing his cards close to his chest, is he? I wonder why?" Wellington's lips quirked as he held out a hand to Sebastian. "Well, young pup? What can I do for you in your father's name?"

Sebastian smiled and shook the duke's hand. "Not in my father's name this time. As it happens, he doesn't yet know about this. I'm here—staying at Pressingstoke Hall—at Winchelsea's behest."

"Aha! Another of our more promising youngsters." Folding his hands in his lap, Wellington waited until Sebastian settled on the chaise beside Antonia, then commanded, "Start at the beginning, go through to the end, and don't leave anything out."

Sebastian complied. Wellington might be already at an age that, in others, would be regarded as their dotage, but there were few in England with a clearer grasp of all matters political and military, and Sebastian had enormous respect for the duke's unique combination of experience and acuity.

As if demonstrating that he hadn't lost any of his famed mental sharpness, Wellington posed several pertinent questions, pushing Sebastian to elaborate on his suspicions alongside his facts.

He concluded his recitation of events with his and Antonia's recent meeting with Inspector Crawford and Sir Humphrey. "The most urgent issue on my plate as of this moment is to get a letter to Whitehall detailing Ennis's warning, such as it is."

Wellington nodded. "Yes—that must go and with all speed. Winchelsea is unlikely to be back from Ireland, but regardless, the Home Secretary needs to know of this, early days though it is. One never knows with matters such as this what snippet of information will connect with another and give warning of something major. Have you written this missive yet?"

"Yes." From his pocket, Sebastian drew the letter he'd prepared during the restless watches of the night.

"Good man." Wellington pointed to the bellpull. "Ring for Moreton."

His secretary answered the summons, and after scrawling his name across one corner of the envelope, Wellington consigned the letter into Moreton's care with explicit instructions it be sent off by courier immediately.

When the door closed behind Moreton, Wellington returned his attention to Sebastian. "Now as to this plot." Wellington paused, then he sat back, once more folding his hands in his lap. "What are your thoughts on it?"

Understanding that his grasp of the situation was about to be tested, Sebastian marshaled his wits. "The two words Ennis uttered…the way he said them was distinct. The first word was gunpowder, and that, itself, was the point. It stood alone. To me, it seemed that Ennis saw the fact that gunpowder was involved was the most critical point he needed to convey."

Wellington nodded. "Indeed. Impending death, I have often observed, sharpens the mind wonderfully. I believe you're correct in thinking that the involvement of gunpowder is of paramount significance."

"So what does that tell us?" Sebastian answered his own question. "That whatever is planned, it's deadly serious and likely to end in deaths. If gunpowder is involved in a secretive way, there really is no likelihood that the proposed use will be either innocent or minor."

"Precisely." His gaze locked on Sebastian's face, Wellington continued, "Ennis said gunpowder because he knew he hadn't time to say much more, and that single word establishes not just the substance but also the seriousness of the threat he sought to expose."

Sebastian nodded. "So to the second word, which, as I said, was separate. Here. Although distinct, I believe it was secondary to the first— that Ennis meant that the gunpowder was here, not that he intended to tell me something else about 'here' but ran out of time."

"But where is here?" Antonia asked. "There are so many possible interpretations."

Wellington inclined his head. "I take your point. However, given this is gunpowder we're talking about, I believe your best option is to assume Ennis meant the specific—namely that he meant Pressingstoke Hall itself—and then, if there is no sign of it there, or of it ever having been there, extend your search outward to the immediate area." He paused, then went on, "Given Ennis was dying and knew it, we have to assume that his 'here' means somewhere close. Anywhere farther than the immediate neighborhood, and I think he would have tried for another word."

After a moment, Sebastian said, "That brings us to the next question arising from Ennis's warning—who is behind this?"

"Certainly, the evidence points to the Young Irelanders, or at least their more militant fringe. However..." Wellington paused as if consulting his capacious memory. Eventually, his expression faintly puzzled, he continued, "I have to say it's not something I would have expected. The government came down hard on those involved in organizing the rebellion, and that was only two years ago. It takes time to regroup after a defeat like that. I wouldn't have anticipated any violent attack—much less one involving gunpowder—from that quarter so soon."

Wellington grimaced. "However, with Winchelsea hearing rumors of a Young Irelander plot, and Ennis being Anglo-Irish and possibly a sympathizer, as well as having other Anglo-Irish in the house, it's difficult not to make the obvious connection." Wellington stared at the floor in front of his chair, then raised his head and frowned at Sebastian. "I don't like wagering the nation's security on what might, in the end, be mere coincidence. We have precious few facts to draw on in terms of who might be behind this—for all we know, it could be the Chartists, although, in their case, even more than the Young Irelanders, we're dealing with a group who have been reduced to a vestige of their former strength."

"And if it isn't either of those two groups?" Antonia asked.

Wellington snorted. "Then it could be anyone. Anyone with some wild idea of upending the government. Or, indeed, the Crown." Several moments passed in silence as the great man cogitated, but then he looked at Sebastian and shook his head. "My advice, young Cynster, is to put aside the question of who is behind this action and, instead, focus on what Ennis rightly identified as the item of critical importance—the gunpowder."

Sebastian held Wellington's gaze for an instant, then nodded. "Yes. That needs to be first in our order of battle."

Wellington grinned. "Your father always knew to keep his priorities in mind..." Wellington's expression grew distant, then he refocused on Sebastian. "Ring for Moreton again. There's something I should give you before you go."

Moreton duly appeared, and Wellington demanded his writing desk. With it balanced on his knees, he swiftly wrote, then signed. After blotting the document, he handed it to Sebastian. "If you run into officious difficulties, just wave that in their faces—it should get you through."

Sebastian read the document and smiled. "Thank you." He folded it carefully and tucked it away with the other letters he was carrying. Then he rose and looked at Wellington. "And thank you for your counsel, Your Grace."

Wellington wagged an admonitory finger at him—at them as Antonia rose and joined Sebastian. "Don't get sidetracked—locate that gunpowder. Once you do, how much of the stuff has been assembled will give you a clue as to the target. Once you have the target, you'll be several steps closer to identifying who the devil is behind this plot. Eliminate the danger first, identify the target, then go after the perpetrators."

\* \* \*

They'd spent longer than they'd bargained for with Wellington; consequently, they galloped most of the way back. It had been years since Antonia had enjoyed such an exhilarating run, with the fresh breeze off the sea rushing past her cheeks. After one brief, assessing glance, much to her appreciative approval, Sebastian concentrated on nothing more than keeping his gray in the lead.

He was only a yard ahead of her when they thundered onto the rear drive. Reluctantly, they drew rein, easing the horses to a trot, then a walk as they turned into the cobbled stable yard. The stable master saw them and sent grooms running to take their reins.

With his usual fluid grace, Sebastian dismounted.

Antonia slid her feet free of the stirrups. But before she could slide down, Sebastian reached her mount's side and, with his customary high-handed arrogance, reached up, closed his hands about her waist, and lifted her down.

She'd been expecting him to do so and had planned her revenge.

She tipped forward as he lifted her; the shift in her weight had him taking a half step back, then he instinctively locked his legs and steadied…but by then she'd placed herself in the same space, so close that he had to ease her down his body, more or less breast to chest.

She'd thought she'd been prepared for the jolt to her senses.

She'd been wrong.

It was searing, like a sensual flame passing down the front of her, leaving an urgent longing—to seek more of the contact, more of the heat, more of him—in its wake.

Her heart raced; her lips throbbed. She felt warm all over and faintly giddy with wanting.

But the effect on him—the tension that gripped him—was even more telling.

More thrilling and enlightening.

She kept her eyes locked on his as she battled the urge to reach up and drag his lips down to hers—and let the thought shine in her eyes.

His muscles locked; his features set like stone.

He was waging a battle of his own.

If they'd been anywhere more private, she might have added her weight against his good intentions, but...

Instead, she found enough strength, enough determination, to shift one hand and pat his chest while she smiled into his sea-green eyes.

His grip about her waist tightened; his jaw looked like it might crack.

When he finally lowered her the last inch, and her boots touched the cobbles, she made no effort to step back.

Her message was simple: Two could play at this game.

And she was only too willing to engage.

Sebastian recognized a gauntlet when he saw one at his feet, but this was one challenge he'd elected to defer.

The sane part of his mind reminded him of all the good—nay, excellent—reasons why. The rest of his brain was urging him to pick up her gauntlet and counter—to riposte.

This was the sort of game in which that other side of him delighted; the temptation to engage was well-nigh overwhelming.

But he had his own agenda and had no intention of allowing her to divert him from it.

The need for control, to remain in control, especially in this game, and even more especially with her, came to his rescue.

With adamantine will, he set her down and stepped back—away.

He ignored his howling demons, but the best retort he could muster as he all but peeled his fingers from her waist was "We don't want to be late for luncheon."

Her eyes widened, then she looked down and obliged by turning toward the house.

At least she didn't laugh.

He swallowed his hunger and strode sedately—distinctly stiffly— beside her.

After several paces, she glanced up at him.

He didn't meet her gaze but felt the quality of it—pure female curiosity.

"I wanted you to kiss me, you know."

Damned impertinent and overbold female. "I know."

His tone should have been enough to end that discussion, yet he was rather surprised when she didn't reply.

They arrived at the side door. She paused, waiting as he reached out to open it.

Before he did, her gaze once more on his face, she murmured, "So what now?"

He faced her and narrowed his eyes on hers. Deliberately ambiguous or…was she referring to both endeavors on which they were, apparently, now mutually engaged?

He gripped the door handle and, reminding himself of the propensity of females in his and her family to act on their own initiative, repressively replied, "Now we join the others for lunch, then check in with the inspector, and then we concentrate on locating the gunpowder."

# CHAPTER 7

*A*ntonia hurried upstairs to change out of her riding habit into a walking gown suitable for the afternoon. Sebastian waited impatiently in the front hall, then together they walked into the dining room.

As they joined the others already seated about the luncheon table, Antonia wasn't sure what she felt. Decidedly smug on the one hand—not victorious, but against Sebastian, she'd held her own, which, against him, was as good as winning. Yet she also felt distinctly puzzled.

Why hadn't he kissed her?

She'd wanted him to—and had told him so, an invitation impossible to mistake—and he had definitely wanted to, or she'd eat her best bonnet. She'd given him the perfect opportunity—not in the stable yard but outside the side door. There'd been no one near, a fact she was sure he'd known. He could have kissed her then.

Why hadn't he?

As she pretended interest in the various viands on her plate, she assessed, evaluated, and wondered.

Control was important to men like him—being in control and not ceding it, not even sharing it.

Would he seek to control their interaction?

Silly question. Of course he would.

She permitted herself a small smile; he would learn soon enough that she was his equal in all ways.

She was about to relegate the interlude to the back of her mind when a rather less comforting thought impinged.

Yes, he liked control. So how far would he go to retain it?

Might he, iron willed as he was, decide she posed too much of a threat to his vaunted and much-prized control and draw back from engaging with her? What if he thought to ignore the attraction welling between them?

She didn't like that prospect at all.

"Lucky you being allowed out for a ride." Melissa leaned forward, peering around Filbury, who was seated between Melissa and Antonia. "How far did you go?" Speculation glowed in Melissa's eyes.

Noting it, Antonia quashed the impulse to glance at Sebastian and dismissively replied, "Just around the grounds and surrounding fields, but with the constables watching, and having to keep close to the house, we may as well have remained indoors."

Filbury humphed. "Dashed inconvenient having those blighters lurking. One never knows where they might be."

"So what did the rest of you do with your morning?" Sebastian asked.

A series of rather desultory replies suggested that most of the guests had mooched about the house.

"After you two," Mr. Parrish said, "Sir Humphrey and the inspector spoke to each of us alone." He glanced at his wife and Mrs. McGibbin, seated side by side along the board. "Even the ladies."

"Can't see the point in it," Mr. McGibbin stated. "If they have questions, why not just gather us together and ask? No need for all this rigmarole. It's not as if any of us did for Ennis."

There were murmurs of agreement from all around, but Sebastian noticed several of the younger men glancing assessingly at each other, and at Parrish and McGibbin, as if they were no longer quite so certain.

Sebastian wondered what questions Crawford and Sir Humphrey had asked. Clearly, something had opened the men's minds to the likelihood that, despite their hopes, the murderer walked among them.

Filbury turned to Antonia. "I wonder, Lady Antonia, if you would care to join us—Wilson, Miss Boyne, and myself—for a round of tennis?"

From across the table, Worthington suggested, "Or perhaps a turn about the croquet course? Very ready to make up a team, what? It could be fun."

Mrs. Parrish and Mrs. McGibbin bent disapproving looks on the younger folk, clearly deeming any notion of "fun" in a household in which someone had recently died to be in poor taste, but those involved didn't seem to notice.

Sebastian, meanwhile, tightened his grip on his knife and clamped down on what he knew was an entirely uncalled for—and very unwise—reaction. In situations such as this, Antonia could take care of herself; she certainly wouldn't thank him for stepping in and dismissing both importuning gentlemen for her.

He kept his gaze fixed on his plate, but from the corner of his eye, he saw her smile—a practiced social gesture, cool and distancing.

"Thank you for the invitations, gentlemen, but I fear neither activity calls to me at this moment. Perhaps another day."

Filbury and Worthington were disappointed, but accepted their dismissals with good grace.

Farther up the table, Georgia Featherstonehaugh and Miss Savage had been chatting with Miss Bilhurst. Claire Savage turned to Melissa and Antonia. "We thought we'd go back to the folly and continue our sketches and paintings. You haven't finished yours yet, have you?"

"No." Antonia paused as if considering joining the group.

Sebastian reached for his wine glass. If she went sketching with the other younger ladies, surely she would be safe enough. Yet what if one or more of the men wandered up? One was a murderer, although why a murderer would focus on Antonia…who knew?

He would rather have the reassurance of having her with him.

Melissa agreed to join the excursion to the folly.

Sebastian was contemplating wasting his afternoon watching the ladies paint when, to his relief, Antonia said, "I'm not such an enthusiastic artist as all of you, and after the exertion of the morning, I believe I'll spend a quiet afternoon about the house—perhaps in the library."

The last words were said with a swift, sidelong glance at Sebastian— one he felt, but didn't meet, being too busy noting the exchange of glances between Filbury and Wilson. Were they planning on following the ladies to the folly, or Antonia to the library?

Mr. McGibbin humphed. "Seems a pity to waste a clear day—we're not likely to get many more. What about taking out some guns?" He paused, casting a glance up the table, but Cecilia, if anything looking even more drawn, was absorbed in a discussion with Mrs. Parrish and Mrs. McGibbin. McGibbin lowered his voice a trifle. "Ennis mentioned there was some decent grouse and woodcock to be had in the far reaches of the Home Wood."

The suggestion found favor with most of the men. Hadley Featherstonehaugh declined, saying he would play escort to his wife and her friends at the folly.

When asked if he would join the shooting party, Sebastian simply declined. "But you might want to let Sir Humphrey know of your plans."

The men exchanged glances, then Mr. Parrish pushed to his feet. "I'll go. I'll meet you in the gun room."

Chairs scraped as, in groups, most of the company rose. The younger ladies gathered and bustled out, trailed by Hadley, with the other men straggling behind. At the end of the table, Mrs. McGibbin, Cecilia, and Mrs. Parrish still had their heads together.

Sebastian, who had risen with the others, pulled back Antonia's chair. He murmured, "We'd better check in with Sir Humphrey and the inspector before deciding what to do."

She rose with alacrity, and they walked out of the dining room.

In the front hall, she slowed. "Mr. Parrish will be with them..." On the words, they heard footsteps approaching from the corridor leading to the estate office. "Ah. Here he is."

Parrish, looking slightly peevish, walked into the front hall. He saw them. "Dashed ridiculous, having to ask permission just to go out."

"I take it no objections were raised?" Sebastian asked.

"No. They just said they wanted us back by evening—as if we're children. Pah!" Parrish turned toward the corridor leading past the stairs. "At least they didn't try to stop us." He raised a hand in farewell. "I'll see you at dinner."

Sebastian and Antonia murmured goodbyes. They waited until they heard the gun room door open and the rumble of male voices cut off as the door closed again, then they exchanged a glance and walked on through the archway into the corridor beyond.

The constable on guard outside the estate office saw them and straightened.

"We'd like to speak with Sir Humphrey and Inspector Crawford," Sebastian said.

"Aye, my lord. I'll just ask."

The constable did, and seconds later, Antonia preceded Sebastian into the estate office.

Sir Humphrey and the inspector rose.

Antonia claimed the same chair she'd occupied that morning and sat. The men settled; before any of them could speak, she asked, "Have you learned anything of the murderer, Inspector? Sir Humphrey?"

Sir Humphrey humphed. "I was called away and just arrived back myself." He glanced at the inspector. "Well, Crawford, do we have any prime suspects?"

"As to that, I've yet to reach any conclusion." Crawford appeared resigned. "We've now interviewed all the guests and established their movements during the critical period—in the half hour leading up to the murder and the minutes immediately after it." The inspector clasped his hands on the desk and fixed his gaze on his fingers. "While I'm happy to eliminate all of the ladies—each and every one was in the music room with all the others—the gentlemen..." He grimaced. "I'm increasingly certain one of the male guests is our murderer, but at the moment, all appear accounted for."

Concisely, he listed each of the gentlemen and where they said they
had been, plus who else had seen them, or what other observation
corroborated their whereabouts during that time. "Each of them is
vouched for by at least one of the other guests in such a way that makes it
difficult to see how they might have stabbed his lordship. And although
some form of conspiracy might be possible, given those involved in each
alibi, it seems unlikely."

Sir Humphrey shifted in his chair. "There must be some hole in
someone's tale—some gap in the evidence we haven't yet stumbled
over."

Sebastian nodded. "Some anomaly—something that someone's said,
and perhaps even believes, that isn't actually perfectly correct."

"Well," Sir Humphrey said, "we can rule out any vagrants or gypsies. I
checked with the bailiffs—there aren't any in the district at the moment,
and as the bailiffs pointed out, we don't usually get vagrants out this way,
so close to the coast, this late in the year." After a second, he added,
"That doesn't mean it couldn't have been some unusual vagrant, but it
does make the prospect much less likely."

Crawford snorted. "Despite the fond hopes of those attending this
house party, I think we can discount any vagrant or gypsy. Aside from all
else, I had Lady Ennis check, and the butler and parlormaid, too, and
none of them could say that anything was missing from the study."

Sebastian put in, "From the moment I set eyes on that open window, I
felt it was staged—a diversion executed under pressure. A red herring to
lead us astray, but not one that had been planned or carefully thought
out."

"That's how I see it, too," Crawford said. "And that only makes me
more certain that the murderer is one of the gentlemen guests, and
furthermore, that the murder wasn't planned. As I see it, one of the men
grasped the chance of Ennis going to his study alone. No reason our gent
needed to know Ennis was preparing to speak with you—he might just
have seen the opportunity to have a few words with his lordship. But then
Ennis told this gent something, or revealed something, and the gent
panicked and killed Ennis to shut him up."

"What did the murderer use to stab Ennis?" Antonia asked. "Could that
shed some light?"

Crawford pulled a face. "His lordship was stabbed with a letter knife
that he apparently kept on his desk in a tray above his blotter, in full view
of anyone about the desk. The murderer had tossed it in a corner of the
room."

Frowning, Sir Humphrey tugged at his ear lobe. After a moment, he
glanced at Sebastian. "We've assumed the subject that presumably was
discussed between Ennis and the murderer that resulted in Ennis being

stabbed had something to do with Ennis's last words, but that's not necessarily so."

Sebastian inclined his head. "Logically, there's no reason it has to be, but..." He grimaced. "Ennis with such a secret, in such company, is murdered—it's hard to look past this putative Irish plot as the motive behind it. Not unless Ennis knew other secrets that affected one or more of these men."

Sir Humphrey grunted. "Possible, certainly, but how likely?" He looked at Crawford. "I agree—unless we find evidence to the contrary, the most likely motive for Ennis's murder is something to do with this gunpowder plot."

Crawford reached out and lifted a paper onto the blotter. "I'll be interviewing all the staff this afternoon, and in particular, checking the male guests' alibis. With luck, someone will have seen something that doesn't fit with the picture we've had painted for us thus far."

Antonia murmured, "Sadly, you might not get much joy. At that time of evening, any staff in the front of the house would have been clearing the dining room, while the majority of the staff would have been in the servants' hall or kitchens. It's not a time staff are generally about, wandering the corridors—not unless someone has rung for something."

The inspector stared at her, then humphed. "We'll see." He looked at Sebastian. "So how did you two get on with your old gentleman?"

"He was in and spoke with us." Sebastian reached into his coat pocket for the letter from Wellington. "He has a better understanding than most of the likely implications of Ennis's last words." He handed Wellington's letter to Crawford. "He clarified what my focus needs to be in this matter and gave me his support"—he nodded at the letter—"as you can see."

The inspector unfolded the sheet. The instant he saw the letterhead, his eyes flew wide. He scanned the letter.

Peering across, Sir Humphrey glanced over the document, which amounted to a thinly veiled blanket order to whoever was presented with the letter to render all assistance to Lord Sebastian Cynster, Marquess of Earith, in whatever manner he required. Sir Humphrey humphed. "I wondered if that was whom you had in mind. Clearly, His Grace views the matter seriously."

Sebastian nodded. "He recommended that I"—he glanced at Antonia and smoothly amended—"we leave pursuing the murderer to you and the inspector and concentrate our efforts on locating the gunpowder. As he pointed out, learning how much of the stuff is involved will help define the target, and the target, in turn, will help identify who exactly is behind this."

"But obviously," Antonia put in, "seizing the gunpowder and nullifying the danger should be our first priority."

Crawford humphed and handed the letter to Sir Humphrey, who glanced swiftly over it, then handed it back to Sebastian.

"It seems," Crawford said, "that we each have our tasks laid squarely before us. You two search for the gunpowder, and Sir Humphrey and I will pursue this murderer."

"Agreed." Sebastian tucked Wellington's letter back into his pocket. "Apropos of that, we need plans and local maps—plans of the house and associated structures, the layout of the grounds, and a map of the estate." He glanced at the framed map on the wall behind the desk, then looked around. "Did Ennis keep any maps and plans in here, do you know?"

Sir Humphrey glanced at the shelves and cabinets. "I don't know, but let's see."

The four of them rose and quickly searched through the various shelves, cupboards, and drawers.

"Here it is." From a drawer beneath a set of bookshelves, Antonia drew out a map of the estate, a smaller version of what was displayed on the wall. "But this just shows the estate's fields—it doesn't show the house in any detail."

Sebastian took the unwieldy map from her and held it up so they could examine it. The other men gathered around and studied it, too.

"It doesn't show details of the grounds, either," Sebastian said. He looked at the shelves they hadn't yet searched. "Let's see if we can find anything else."

Ten minutes later, they'd scoured the office, but had unearthed no further maps, plans, or diagrams.

"Perhaps it's not surprising that's the only map here," Sir Humphrey said. "Although Ennis occasionally used this room, it was more the domain of his farm manager, who wouldn't have any need for plans of the house or grounds."

"True." As he rolled up the map, Sebastian looked at the inspector. "Can we search the study? I see you still have a man at the door."

"More a precaution in case there's anything there we've missed." The inspector waved to the door. "Come and I'll have a word with the constable. I don't mind you two going in and searching, but I don't want him thinking that it's therefore all right to let anyone else in. But while you're looking for your plans, you could do me a favor and search again for anything that might point to the murderer."

Two minutes later, Sebastian followed Antonia into the study and closed the door on the interested constable. Antonia halted in the middle of the room. Her gaze had gone to the desk, and there it remained.

Sebastian glanced at the desk, then at her. "Why don't you take that half of the room"—he waved at the area around the fireplace, opposite the desk—"and I'll search this half." The half containing the desk behind which Ennis had died. The window and door were in the middle of their respective walls, so dividing the room into two was easy.

Antonia drew in a breath, hauled her gaze from the desk, and nodded. "All right." She looked around. Apart from the window, the door, and the space taken up by the fireplace, all the walls were covered in densely packed shelves. They contained not just books and ledgers but also stacks of loose papers weighed down with, apparently, whatever had come to Ennis's hand. She considered how best to tackle her assigned half, then started with the shelves beside the window.

Ten minutes later, she reached the fireplace. She was about to move past it when a thought struck. She studied the large portrait of Cecilia Ennis as a young lady that hung above the mantelpiece, then reached out, raised one corner of the heavy frame, and peered behind it. A safe was recessed into the wall.

She let the frame hang straight again and turned to Sebastian, who was pulling out and replacing books on one of the high shelves behind the desk. "Has the inspector looked in the safe?"

Sebastian glanced at her, then raised his gaze to the portrait. "He didn't say. I'll ask." He went to the door, opened it, and left.

Antonia progressed to searching the shelves on the other side of the fireplace.

Several minutes later, Sebastian returned. He closed the door. "There's nothing in there but Cecilia's better jewelry and two hundred pounds in cash."

"Exactly what one might expect and nothing more." Antonia continued to search through the ledgers, but more to be thorough than in any real hope of finding any plans.

Sebastian returned to the shelves behind the desk.

Eventually, she asked, "How long do you think there's been a house on this spot?"

She felt Sebastian's sharp green gaze, but didn't bother meeting it.

"Why do you ask?"

"Because at Chillingworth—and I'm sure at Somersham, too—because the house is so old, the plans are kept—"

"In the library."

"Precisely. The plans of the house are bound in one large volume, and the landscaping plans are kept in a separate folio, because they keep being updated."

"So we're looking in the wrong place."

"Perhaps." She glanced at him, a wryly questioning look in her eyes. "But we wanted to search here anyway, didn't we?"

Fleetingly, he grinned. "Indeed." He turned to a shelf by the door. "And I'm almost finished on this side, and I haven't found anything."

She replaced the last stack of loose papers on their shelf, then stepped back and visually checked. "I've finished here." She turned to survey her side of the room one last time. Her gaze swung over the grate, and she froze.

Then she went forward and, crouching, carefully teased a paper—the left half of an envelope—free of the ashes that had almost obscured it.

She rose with the remnant in her hand. Frowning, she angled it so the light from the window fell on the words scrawled across the envelope's face.

"What is it?" Sebastian came to see.

"It's part of an envelope. The writing on it says 'Three hundred pounds for'—and the rest has burned away."

He halted by her side, close, and leaned closer still to examine the black scrawl.

She fought to keep her hand—and her breathing—steady.

"Damn!" he murmured.

"Indeed." She glanced sideways at his face. Firmly quashing her unhelpful reaction, she managed, "The fire was burning when you came in to see Ennis, wasn't it?"

"Yes. Just crackling away, nothing out of the ordinary." He straightened, and she could breathe a touch easier. He added, "I didn't notice that in the grate, but then I didn't really look."

"And the staff haven't been allowed in this room since, so whatever's in this grate—"

"Had to have been there when I found Ennis dead."

Tilting her head, she studied the envelope. "Did he put it in the flames, or did someone else—like the murderer?"

"Hard—if not impossible—to say. But as to that, Ennis was with us—his guests—throughout yesterday. In the afternoon, he came in with the rest of the men with only time enough to change for dinner, and I saw him come upstairs. So he didn't come in here during the day, not for more than a minute at most. So the fire in here, which would have been laid earlier in the day, almost certainly wouldn't have been lit until dinnertime."

As accustomed to the ways of large houses as he, she nodded. "Blanchard would have ordered it lit while dinner was being served."

"Exactly. So that envelope couldn't have been fed to the flames until after dinner—which means by either Ennis or his murderer."

"By which, I take it, we can infer that the name of the person for whom the three hundred pounds was intended was, in fact, the murderer."

Sebastian stared at the envelope for a second more, then met Antonia's gray eyes. "We should take this to Crawford and Sir Humphrey immediately. Three hundred pounds is a large amount for any man to carry in notes."

Her lips firmed. "Thinking himself safe, the murderer might still have the money on him or have hidden it in his bags."

They found Sir Humphrey and the inspector just finishing their interview of one of the footmen. On seeing their faces, Crawford wound up the interview, got to his feet, and sent the footman on his way.

The instant the door closed, Sir Humphrey, who had also risen, said, "You've found something?"

Sebastian waved Antonia forward. He let her explain how she'd found the envelope and its significance—and what he and she thought the inspector's next step ought to be.

Crawford was eager, but he turned to Sir Humphrey. "A search will cause a ruckus."

Sir Humphrey glanced inquiringly at Sebastian. "Only if they know."

Sebastian's smile was intent. "They've all gone shooting. You can search their rooms now."

"And if you don't find anything," Antonia said, all the hauteur at her command on show, "make them turn out their pockets when they come in—in the gun room, before any of them have a chance to go upstairs."

Again, Crawford glanced at Sir Humphrey. "They'll squeal."

"Not"—Antonia slanted a glance at Sebastian—"if you tell them it's to eliminate them as suspects, and that Earith has already complied."

Sebastian promptly started emptying his pockets onto the desk's blotter, starting with the three very important letters he was carrying. "And you have my permission to search my room—and indeed, you should also search the rooms of all the visiting staff, maids as well as valets."

"Yes, and you have my permission to search my room, too." Antonia held her arms out to either side. "As is obvious, I have no pockets in this gown that could hold three hundred pounds."

The bodice of her walking dress was a very snug fit.

Instinctively, Crawford had run his gaze down her figure; abruptly, he realized what he'd done and looked down at the desk as a wash of color crept into his cheeks. He gruffly cleared his throat. "As you say, my lady." Then he glanced at Sir Humphrey. "Shall we?"

"Why not?" Sir Humphrey looked almost belligerent. "This is a murder investigation, after all, and Lady Antonia and Earith have just cleared the way for us."

"That's it." Sebastian patted his pockets, demonstrating that they were empty.

Antonia glanced at the items piled on the blotter and fought to hide a grin. The expensive pocket watch, engraved silver billfold, heavy silver card case, coin purse, fine embroidered handkerchief, notecase, and silver capped pencil were to be expected, along with the silver hip flask and the three letters, but the two pieces of string, several crumpled notes, a short section of candle plus a box of Congreve matches, a button, a lady's ornamental buckle, and a pebble—river-washed to smoothness—were more appropriate to a boy's pockets.

She knew he had a habit of slipping random things into his pockets; she'd always assumed he later discarded them. She felt his gaze touch her face as he reached for the pile—as his hand closed over that river-washed pebble, hiding it from her sight.

Abruptly, memory seized her and jerked her back into their long-ago past.

That pebble came from the Lambourn, the river that flowed past her family home. He'd picked it from her hair when, on one hot summer's day, along with his siblings and several of his cousins, all of whom had been visiting, he and she had gone down to the banks of the river, and during a game, she'd fallen in.

The river had been deep where she'd entered it, but as the season was mid-summer, the currents had been flowing lazily, and like all the group, she could swim. She hadn't been in any danger, yet Sebastian had immediately dived in, swum to her, seized her, and hauled her to shore.

They'd come to the bank farther along the river, screened from the others by an outcrop.

She'd waded out alongside him. But once they'd reached solid ground, he'd narrowed his green eyes at her and lambasted her for her carelessness. During his tirade, he'd reached out and plucked that pebble from her hair.

Her memories were so vivid, she felt a phantom tug.

Drenched and infuriated by his high-handedness, she'd narrowed her eyes back and, in no uncertain terms, had told him what she thought of his behavior—of his entirely unnecessary rescue.

Beyond furious with each other, they hadn't exchanged so much as a word for the rest of his stay.

But he'd kept that pebble.

It *had* to be the same pebble.

She blinked, then glanced at his face, but he was stuffing all his belongings back into his pockets and didn't look at her.

Crawford waved Sir Humphrey to the door. "We should start our search immediately—speaking to the rest of the staff can wait."

Sir Humphrey glanced at Antonia and Sebastian. "Did you find what you were looking for?"

"No," Sebastian said. "But we think we'll find the house plans and diagrams of the grounds in the library." He picked up the rolled map of the estate they'd found earlier. "We'll hunt them out, then start our search."

They filed out of the estate office. Crawford, followed by Sir Humphrey, strode off up the corridor and into the front hall, taking his constables with him.

To Sebastian's surprise, Antonia turned in the opposite direction. For an instant, he thought she was heading back to the study for some reason. Instead, she opened a door—a secondary door more or less concealed in the wall the corridor shared with the library—and led the way into the large room.

He followed and closed the door, which clicked shut, fitting neatly into the wall in a way that rendered it not readily discernible. He walked deeper into the room, then halted and surveyed the shelves lining the walls. Interrupted only by gaps for the doors, windows, and the large fireplace, the open shelves were packed with leather-bound tomes of every description.

"Luckily," Antonia murmured, "we're looking for folio-sized books, and there aren't so many of them."

He set the map of the estate on a small circular table. "I see some." He walked to the wall shared with the corridor and crouched to scan the tall volumes filling the bottom shelf. Antonia trailed after him and halted beside him. He forced his mind to remain on track, to take in what his eyes were seeing in terms of the words etched on the spines and not drift... "Ah—this might be it." *Thank God.*

He hauled out a large, heavy volume covered in maroon leather with "Pressingstoke Hall" inscribed on the spine. He hefted it into his arms, rose, and carried it to the central library table.

Antonia followed eagerly, her attention plainly diverted by the find.

They opened the book and saw a copy of an early plan of the house when it had been a medieval hall. Like many large houses, Pressingstoke Hall had gone through various iterations, with new versions built onto or over earlier structures.

"This book looks like it was compiled early this century. We need the latest plan." Antonia turned the pages until they were looking at an exquisite rendering of what was obviously the current Pressingstoke Hall.

Antonia studied the plan. "There are too many rooms to remember, especially on the lower level and in the attics. We'll need to make a copy." She looked around. "There's a writing desk."

She crossed to the desk, sat in the chair behind it, and searched in the shallow drawers, eventually unearthing several sheets of paper and a handful of pencils.

He carried the large book over and placed it open on the desk. "You're unquestionably better at drawing than I am."

"True. But before I start on this, let's see if we can find the plans of the grounds."

They hunted through the folio-sized volumes and finally found a box stuffed with loose sheets. He carried the box to the library table, and she quickly sorted through the pages.

"This is the one—done in 1827." She studied it for a moment, then handed it to him. "You can manage a reasonable copy of that, I'm sure."

So while she settled at the desk to make a copy of the plan of the house, he sat at the library table and did his best—his distinctly poor best—to draw what was at least a passable representation of the grounds, noting the location of the various buildings and structures that dotted the cultivated area around the house.

Antonia diligently copied line after line, an activity that required attention, but not a great deal of active thought. Her mind, unsurprisingly, reverted to contemplation of what was fast becoming her dominant obsession.

Sebastian.

He who apparently carried around a pebble he had drawn from her sodden hair some fifteen years ago.

*If* it was the same pebble.

It had to be the same pebble; why else had he glanced at her and moved to hide it?

So why had he kept it? Why did he carry it in his pocket to this day?

She knew all about his protectiveness; it was something that had always been there—that had simply come to be the way he related to her, unchanging and absolute.

She'd grown so accustomed to it—that overbearing protectiveness— that she'd long ago stopped being surprised by it, or by anything he did while in its throes.

What she hadn't previously realized was that he was as aware of his reaction to her as she now was, as aware of the longevity of those feelings, as demonstrated by that pebble.

It meant something to him. Something definite. Something important. Something very real.

That longevity, that constancy—the fact that his protectiveness toward her had never ever faltered, and it certainly hadn't waned—wasn't something she should have been so cavalier in taking for granted.

Given what she now knew, all that she'd seen and felt, put that obsessive protectiveness together with all that had flared between them since they'd left their normal world behind, and what did that add up to?

It was tempting—oh, so tempting—to leap to conclusions, but she wasn't about to do that. This was too important. Far too important.

Yet whatever the reality was, she needed to know and was determined to find out.

But if she left further exploration of that topic until after they returned to town…she would never learn what she needed to know. She understood him well enough to be one hundred percent certain of that. No matter whatever happened in the future, if she wanted a clear and unequivocal declaration of what drove him, she would have to push for one now—while they were there, away from their families and the world they usually inhabited.

The simple truth was, once they returned to London, any further interaction between them would be at his discretion, not hers. She could refuse to engage with him, but she couldn't make him engage with her. She wouldn't have any opportunity to initiate anything he wasn't prepared to allow.

That prospect thrilled her not at all.

If she was reading the signs correctly, them being thrust into this situation—one neither of them, of their own accord, would have instigated—had stripped away the veils and screens they both normally kept in place, especially with regard to the other.

Whether intentionally or unintentionally, wittingly or unwittingly, until now, neither of them had faced, much less focused on, what was, in truth, between them.

But courtesy of the hours they'd spent there, in each other's company, they now recognized what that potentially was.

Both of them knew that much.

But he liked control—more, he insisted on control, on control remaining in his hands.

Ergo, he would put off dealing with what lay between them, at the very least until they returned to town.

And possibly even after that.

She had no idea how he saw the lady he would wed, but it was perfectly possible he had some entrenched notion of eventually marrying some meek and mild miss he could easily control.

That was not just possible but likely.

She hadn't ever thought about being the Marchioness of Earith. Knowing him as she had, it had simply not occurred to her—much as a prize she wasn't at all sure she would want to win. Marrying Sebastian hadn't ever featured on her list of things to do because…

Carefully drawing in the final lines on her copy of the plan of the basement, she realized that she'd always known that marrying him would be a challenge—one she hadn't been sure she could win.

She still didn't know if she could win.

If she could win the one thing that, according to all those ladies who knew, was the only viable guarantee when marrying a nobleman.

She knew how he felt about her protectiveness-wise.

She had no idea about his heart.

Holding up her copy, which she knew to be exact, she pretended to compare it to the original while her heart thudded, slow and certain, and her mind raced.

Would she attempt it—would she open Pandora's box and find out what their truth really was?

Or would she cling to safety and let the moment—the next few days—pass without risking it?

She stared unseeing at her copy for several silent seconds, then she compressed her lips, picked up the four sheets she'd prepared—one for each level of the house—rose, and shut the heavy volume with a thump.

She looked at Sebastian, seated at the nearer end of the long library table. As he looked up, she met his eyes. "I'm ready."

He pushed back his chair, picked up the single sheet on which he'd sketched the grounds, tucked it into his pocket, and rose. "Let me put these away."

He lifted the box, came and fetched the volume of house plans, and carried both to the shelves.

She followed.

After he'd slid both box and tome back into their places, he straightened, picked up the rolled map of the estate, then caught her gaze and arched an arrogant brow. "Logically, we should start with the house and work outward. Let's begin in the basement."

She met his eyes and smiled intently. "That sounds as good a place as any."

# CHAPTER 8

*A*rmed with Antonia's copy of the house plans, they consulted
Blanchard and, under his aegis, ventured through the green-baize-covered
door and down a set of stairs into the servants' hall, beyond which lay the
kitchen and a warren of other rooms.

"We'd like to start at the lowest level of the house." Sebastian looked
at Blanchard. "I assume the cellars are in use?"

"Indeed, my lord. If you will come this way?"

They followed Blanchard into the kitchen, where preparations for the
evening meal were in full swing. The cook and her helpers saw them and
froze, then downed tools and bobbed curtsies.

Antonia calmly smiled. "Don't mind us. Do carry on."

Blanchard led them down the long room, past the curious staff, and
into a smaller storeroom. "The cellars are quite extensive, but we use only
the nearer sections." Blanchard halted and waved to a heavy door set into
the wall at the end of the storeroom. "You will need these." Blanchard
turned to where lanterns sat on a bench and proceeded to light two. "Are
you looking for anything in particular?"

Behind the butler's back, Sebastian exchanged a look with Antonia.
"This is one of those instances in which we'll know what we're looking
for when we see it."

Blanchard nodded, then turned and handed one of the lighted lanterns
to Antonia. "If you would, my lord—the door's not locked."

Sebastian lifted the latch and swung the heavy door wide, noting as he did that not only was the door not locked, it didn't even have a lock. Nor was there any sign of a bolt. Reaching for the other lantern, he frowned. "This door is never locked?"

"No, my lord. As long as I've been here, there have been no locks or bolts on it, and, indeed, we've never seen the need."

Sebastian raised his brows. "What about Ennis's wines and spirits?"

"Ah—they are stored in a room in the cellars, and that door is locked. The wine room is to the left at the bottom of the stairs."

"Just so we're thorough, might we have the key to that door?" Antonia asked.

"Of course, my lady." Blanchard hauled out a key ring and started searching through his many keys.

Two minutes later, armed with the key to what Blanchard had assured them was the only locked door in the cellars, Sebastian led the way down a long flight of worn stone steps.

"Judging by the dip in the middle," Antonia murmured, "these date from medieval times."

Sebastian grunted. The atmosphere in the cellar was cool, but not damp; the air smelled musty, but not oppressively so. Beyond the area lit by their lanterns, the darkness was absolute.

He stepped off the last stair and halted. He raised his lantern and played the beam around, illuminating a collection of stores arranged on wooden shelves, along with a group of wooden crates holding apples and root vegetables. Swinging the beam to the left, he saw the locked door. "Let's try the wine room first."

"Yes—*oh!*"

He spun in time to catch Antonia—or rather, to bodily break her fall. She'd lost her footing and pitched forward. She slammed into him, breast to chest; instinctively, his free arm clamped about her, and he clutched her close.

His senses rioted; valiantly, he beat them down. Her eyes, wide and shadowed in the diffused light, locked with his. For several heartbeats, they froze—both intensely aware, the air around them inexorably heating…

He forced in a tight breath. With it came some semblance of control. Moving slowly, he bent his knees and set her on her feet, then he released her and forced himself to take a step back.

"Thank you." She sounded breathless. She smiled apologetically at him. "These half-boots are new, and the soles are still slippery."

He swallowed a grunt. The front of him felt aflame, not just with heat but also with longing.

He stepped around her to the door to the wine room, slipped the heavy key into the lock, turned it, then pushed the door wide. He shone his lantern into the space, then led the way in.

Wine racks were arranged in four rows stretching down the long, narrow room, forming two aisles, each with bottles stacked on either side.

"Look." Antonia gripped his sleeve. She'd directed her lantern toward the room's far end. "Barrels!" Twenty or more barrels were stacked end-out against the rear wall.

They both started forward, but chose different aisles—her to the left, while he went right.

"And there are more barrels here." She halted, playing her lantern against the wall of the aisle in which she stood. "Gunpowder comes in barrels, doesn't it?"

"Yes. Check every barrel. Tell me if you find anything that's not marked cognac, armagnac, whisky, or some other spirit you recognize. And tap every barrel—the sound will be different if it's filled with powder rather than liquid."

They spent the next minutes checking the barrels stacked at various places around the room.

Eventually, she joined him in examining the bulk of the barrels, those stacked along the rear wall to a height higher than his head. She placed her lantern at the end of a rack, as he had; the overlapping beams illuminated the wall quite well.

They peered at labels and tapped and listened.

At last, she stepped back; he was crouching by her feet, sounding out the lowest row of barrels. Her hands on her hips, she looked down at him. "I haven't found anything but spirits."

"The same. And that's the last of them." He braced one hand against a barrel and started to rise.

The wall of barrels creaked and shifted.

Half smothering a squeal, Antonia grabbed his shoulders and hauled, attempting to drag him away from the barrels. She caught him off balance and sent him and her stumbling and careening into the side wall.

He fetched up with his back against the cold stone, and she landed hard—body to body—against him.

And again, he fell victim to his slavering senses and reacted as those senses decreed; before he registered what he was doing, his arms had risen and locked her against him.

The impulse to crush her closer yet, to appease the welling, insistent ache, flared hotly.

"Oof!" She blew out a breath, fanning the fine tendrils of black silk that framed her pale face. Then she focused her wide eyes on his. "Sorry. I thought you were about to get buried."

His gaze had locked with hers; feeling as if he was all but drowning in the silver of her eyes, he fought to compress his lips against a searing need to find out what hers tasted like. After a fraught second, he managed to reply, "No. The barrel I leaned against shifted a trifle—that's all. The stack's stable."

Even to his ears, his voice sounded rough, deeper and more gravelly.

The battle to set her away from him was significantly more difficult to win than before.

He succeeded. Just.

He eased past her and turned to look up the room. He set his hands on his hips, drew in a tight breath, and pretended to survey the area as if searching for anywhere they'd overlooked, while inside, he wrestled his demons back into their cage.

He was supposed to be protecting her—even from himself. At least for now.

She, too, had fallen to studying the room's contents again. "We haven't found anything here, but regardless, might they have disguised the gunpowder? Perhaps put it into old brandy casks, for instance."

He drew in another breath, forced his wits to function, then shook his head. "I don't think so. That would increase the risk that someone—thinking it was brandy or whatever else—might steal it, or open it, find gunpowder, and raise the alarm." He reached for his lantern. "And whoever brought the gunpowder here had no reason to imagine anyone would start actively searching for it. Better to just hide the gunpowder barrels somewhere—either somewhere sufficiently secret or among other barrels."

"By the latter theory, this is the most likely place the gunpowder would have been hidden, but it's not here." She retrieved her lantern, and side by side, they started up the room toward the door.

He glanced back. "There's no sign of any barrels being recently brought in or removed, either."

"Well, the door is locked, and it's a heavy old lock, so they—whoever they are—would have to have had access to the key."

"If Ennis was directly involved, then they would have had no problem getting the key." He held the door, then followed her through. "If by 'here' Ennis meant inside the house, then this was the most likely place to hide any barrels." He hauled the door closed and relocked it.

After pocketing the key, he raised his lantern and played the beam into the surrounding darkness. "It's possible they didn't bother trying to hide the barrels among others, but simply hid them around some corner down here. We'll have to search the entire area—even if you don't see barrels, look for any sign that they might have been here. Any sign of recent activity."

They spread out and quartered the cellars, which, once they moved away from the storage areas immediately around the bottom of the steps, proved to be largely empty. The floor was paved with stone flags throughout, and their footsteps echoed hollowly.

The beams from their lanterns marked their progress, but between them, silence reigned. Until they met once more at the bottom of the cellar stairs.

Sebastian looked into Antonia's eyes, steel gray in the lantern light. "Where else in a house are barrels found?"

She pulled a face. "No doubt there'll be one or two in the storerooms around the kitchen, but unless we're looking for just one barrel, I can't think where more could be hidden above this level."

He considered, then said, "I can't imagine an amount smaller than several medium-sized barrels being threat enough for Ennis to have felt compelled to report it."

"In that case"—Antonia raised her skirts and started up the stairs—"let's check the kitchen storerooms just in case, then take a closer look at the house plan and see if there are any other places in which several medium-sized barrels might be concealed."

With a grunt of agreement, Sebastian followed her up the stairs.

Antonia took the lead in examining the barrels in the various storerooms, but found nothing beyond two barrels of herrings, one of vinegar, and a large vat of cider. She was glad of the minutes of being in charge; the exercise demanded she keep her mind focused on their search, allowing her senses time to recover from the jolts she'd given them.

In deciding to batter through Sebastian's armor-plated control, she hadn't considered how such an endeavor would affect her. In truth, the thrill of those moments—the anticipation of when, exactly, he would break, and what would happen next—was distinctly addictive.

Deciding she needed a little more recovery time—and she needed to be careful he didn't realize her actions were deliberate, so a longer period of perfectly innocent behavior on her part wouldn't go astray—as they emerged through the green-baize-covered door into the front hall, and found it empty, she glanced at him. "There's a morning room that no one seems to use." She pointed to the closed door at the front of the hall, opposite the drawing room. "Why don't we go there and study the house plans for anywhere else we should search?"

"Good idea."

He walked at her shoulder down the front hall, reached past her and opened the door, then followed her inside and shut the door.

Although no one was using the room, the curtains had been opened and a small fire was burning. A well-padded sofa faced the fireplace with a low table before it. Antonia sat on the damask and spread the four sheets of her copy of the house plan on the table.

The cushion next to her depressed as Sebastian sat beside her. "I really can't see anyone carting several medium-sized barrels upstairs." He leaned forward to study the plan, then reached out and drew the sheet representing the ground floor closer. "Is there anywhere on this level that would make any sense as a place to store gunpowder?"

"The gun room?"

"Not for a whole barrel, let alone two or more."

They pored over the relevant sheet. Antonia tapped her sketch of Cecilia's recent addition; she'd found the plans for it stuck into the back of the tome of house plans. "What about Cecilia's new conservatory?"

"Too humid." He paused, then said, "But there might be a storage area underneath it—one accessible from outside."

They asked Blanchard, only to be informed that the conservatory was built on a solid base that contained the latest type of heating pipes connected to the kitchen stoves. They retreated to the morning room and, standing before the low table, resurveyed the plan of the house.

Sebastian humphed. "Let's agree that no one would have hidden barrels of gunpowder anywhere upstairs. Quite aside from the difficulties inherent in ferrying heavy barrels up and down either the main stairs or the servants' stairs undetected, and subsequently, the very real risk of the barrels being discovered while here, it's hard to see why, with the many alternatives apparently available"—he pointed to the outbuildings Antonia had marked on her plan—"our villains would have chosen to hide the gunpowder inside the house, let alone upstairs."

"Agreed. So let's start on the outbuildings." All were at the rear of the house. Antonia gathered up her four sheets and refolded them. "Let's try the stable first."

They did and found nothing at ground level, but Antonia insisted on climbing the ladder to the extensive loft and searching there.

Sebastian gritted his teeth and followed her up the ladder. He gave up trying to keep his gaze from her trim ankles, lovingly encased in her leather half-boots; with her skirts held up, said tantalizing ankles were more or less directly in front of his eyes.

He consoled himself with the thought that that was better—less arousing, ergo less painful—than allowing his gaze to drift higher.

Predictably, no villain had hauled barrels up to the loft, although as there was a hay door and a winch, he had to admit it wasn't such an inaccessible hiding place as he'd thought.

The trip back down the ladder was less of a trial, given he descended first and kept his gaze away from her.

Briskly, she led the way onward—through the barn and the milking shed, both deserted at that time of day, and into an apple store. In all the buildings, he checked for concealed cellars or locked rooms, but discovered nothing to excite their interest.

"And why would there be any such place," he said as they emerged from the apple store, the last of the outbuildings, "when there's so much unused space in the cellars beneath the house?"

"Hmm." Antonia glanced at him. "So to our next question. Is there anywhere in the gardens and grounds that might have been used to store gunpowder?"

He halted, reached into his pocket, and pulled out his sketch of the grounds. He unfolded it and held it so she could see. "Aside from the folly—and we'll have to check that to see if there's any room below it—there's a grotto, and a dovecote, and a ruined chapel just inside the wood."

She leaned closer, peering at his sketch; the swell of her breast briefly brushed his arm, but she shifted back immediately.

Much to his inner self's disappointment.

She glanced at the sky, then pointed at the buildings he'd depicted on the sketch. "We can start at the dovecote, then go on to the grotto. By then, the light will have started to wane and the other ladies will have left the folly, so we can check there, then continue on our circuit to the ruins."

He nodded and started refolding the sketch. "If there's water in the grotto, we won't need to search inside—it'll be too damp for gunpowder. And going via your route, by the time we reach the ruins, the shooting party should have returned to the house, too." He tucked the sketch into his pocket, then waved her on. "Come on. We'll need to hurry, or we'll run out of light."

The dovecote was still in use, but the shadowy lower level proved to be half full of feathers and droppings and devoid of barrels. The grotto did, indeed, contain a pool fed by a small stream; they wasted no time there, but walked straight on to the folly, a typical replica of a small Grecian temple. They reached it in time to see the ladies almost back at the house. A quick examination of the folly's tiled floor and the outside of the plinth on which it stood convinced Sebastian that there was no hidden room beneath the colonnaded structure.

They strode toward the wood and the ruins of the old chapel. The soft light of afternoon was well and truly fading by the time Antonia, reinterpreting Sebastian's somewhat crude and inexact sketch, found the opening of the path into the wood.

The path wasn't long and ended in the clearing in which the ruins of the chapel stood, forgotten and forlorn. They halted just inside the clearing to take stock. Judging by the wear on the walls still standing, the rounding and smoothing of the top course of stones, the roof had fallen in perhaps a hundred years ago. Lichens had encroached, forming scab-like patches here and there on the pale yellow stone. The surrounding trees had already blanketed the ground in a thick carpet of red, brown, and faded golden leaves.

There was a silence there, beneath the louring trees, that was not quite menacing, yet faintly unsettling. Atmospheric, certainly, Antonia thought. As, side by side, she and Sebastian walked forward to what appeared to be the chapel's front façade, she murmured, "I should mention this place to the other ladies. In stronger light, it would make a good subject for a painting or a sketch."

"Hmm." Sebastian halted just before the arch that was all that remained of the chapel's entrance. He put out a hand, placed his palm against the side of the arch, and pushed, then drew back his hand and dusted his palm and fingers. "What remains seems stable enough." With that, he walked beneath the arch into the chapel.

Antonia followed, but immediately halted, her way blocked by rubble. Sebastian had halted, too.

The chapel had been a simple one. A single room with a stone altar raised on a shallow stone dais that ran across the other end of the room. Formed from a large rectangular block, the altar was still there, but any lectern or pulpit would most likely have been wooden and was long gone.

What they could see of the central aisle was paved in a herringbone pattern, with more-simply paved areas to either side that must once have played host to pews. But the pews, too, were gone, and stone blocks from various places on the walls had tumbled down and now littered the chapel's floor, creating an obstacle course between the front door and the altar.

Sebastian stepped onto and over the first large block.

Antonia raised her skirts and shifted her feet, trying to work out how to follow; the block was sizeable, and her legs weren't as long as Sebastian's.

He turned, saw her difficulty, and offered his hand.

Hiding a grin, she placed her fingers in his and felt a sharp jolt of sensation—and more, of recognition of a sort—as his hand closed about hers. She tensed to step up onto the block—

A furtive rustling reached her ears, and she froze.

Eyes widening, she glanced at Sebastian. His hold on her hand had tightened as he'd readied to pull her onto the block; he'd heard the noise, too, and his grip hadn't eased.

He held up his other hand, gesturing her to silence.

They both glanced around, straining their ears.

The noise came again. This time, they both placed it—outside and close to the chapel's rear wall.

Was someone following them—perhaps spying on them?

She turned back to the front archway as Sebastian stepped silently back over the block and joined her. With him still holding her hand, she leaned into him and whispered, "Could it be rats?" She hated all rodents.

He bent his head and breathed in her ear, "Rats look for food—there's no food here."

So it might be a person.

They crept back under the archway. She stuck close to Sebastian's side—and he seemed in no hurry to release her hand—as he led the way, stealthily stalking around the outside of the chapel's ancient walls.

For a large man, he moved silently, but she knew he hunted in Scotland with his cousins and was considered an expert deerstalker. She was a fair hand at stealthy creeping herself. They made very little sound as they steadily progressed along the side wall.

Sebastian slowed even more as they neared the rear corner. Even with his senses open wide, he couldn't detect any hint of another person, yet there was something there—hunkered at the rear of the chapel.

Carefully, he released Antonia's hand.

Tensed to react, to defend against any attack, he stepped past the corner and looked.

A vixen stood over the entrance to a den and bared her teeth at him.

In stepping forward, he'd left a gap between him and the wall. Antonia filled it, leaning forward to look—startling the fox.

Sebastian swore. Without taking his eyes from the now-snarling and darting fox, he put out a hand and pushed Antonia back.

Entirely unintentionally, his hand pressed fully over one firm breast.

The jolt that racked him almost made his eyes cross and nearly made him forget the fox.

Still, his action had the desired effect—Antonia uttered a strangled squeak and leapt back.

His eyes still locked on the fox, he waved his now-burning palm, signaling Antonia to retreat, and for once, she obeyed without argument, although he heard her mutter something.

Smoothly, he stepped back. He continued to watch the fox as, step by step, he steadily retreated; the farther he went, the more the vixen stood down.

He wished he could say the same of his own anatomy. But the sensation of firm, distinctly feminine flesh pressing into his palm...more than anything else, the recognition that it had been *Antonia's* flesh had been galvanizing. His now-empty palm itched. A large part of his awareness had followed Antonia, utterly diverted.

When he'd retreated halfway along the chapel's side, he turned and strode the rest of the way to the front of the ruins.

Antonia was standing outside the chapel's entrance. Arms crossed, she'd been staring toward the path that had brought them there.

The instant he appeared, she turned her gaze on him, meeting his eyes with a steely, stormy warning, as if daring him to comment on their recent contact.

He clamped down ruthlessly on the ridiculously dangerous impulse to ignore that warning.

When, with an assiduously impassive expression in place, he held her gaze steadily, halted beside her, and said nothing at all, she lowered her arms and waved into the chapel. "If we're checking cellars and hidden storerooms, then in a chapel of this age, there's likely to be a crypt."

He glanced through the archway. "A ruined chapel most likely with a crypt in an area rife with smuggling. Yes, we need to check."

"In a chapel of this size, the entrance to any crypt is likely to be somewhere around the altar."

He walked back under the archway, climbed over the first block, then turned and offered her his hand—exactly as if the entire incident with the fox hadn't occurred.

She cast him one swift, assessing glance, then she took his hand and allowed him to steady her over and around the blocks. As they progressed up the aisle, the sensation of her delicate fingers in his grip was another little prick to his libido, but by dint of telling that side of himself that the right time would come soon enough, he managed to keep a reasonable focus on what they were supposed to be doing.

Antonia struggled to cope with the new and even more potently distracting plane of awareness of Sebastian onto which the unexpected contact at the rear of the chapel had catapulted her senses. Thank the heavens she'd had a moment to gather her wits before he'd rejoined her. As she'd fled back around the chapel, her breasts had positively ached.

But he'd elected to play the gentleman and had kept his mouth shut and his thoughts shielded behind that impassive mask of his, and she'd managed to bludgeon her witless senses into submission—only to have them flaring again. Not, this time, at the sensation of his hand gripping her fingers—it seemed she was finally growing accustomed to that—but at the unwitting demonstration of the innate power in his body, of its steely strength as he effortlessly supported her weight here, there, as she clambered over the stones in his wake.

She had never, ever, been as aware of a man's body as she now was of his.

Purely on the grounds of self-preservation, she was going to have to bring their ever-intensifying interactions to a head, but sadly, not now, and definitely not there.

By the time they'd gained the clearer space about the altar, the light was almost gone.

"We'll need to search quickly." She slipped her fingers free of Sebastian's and started walking slowly around the altar, peering closely at the floor as she went; this area was largely free of rubble.

He paced in the opposite direction, his gaze trained on the worn flagstones.

Several times, she kicked aside leaves and twigs to examine one of the flags. She'd reached the rear left corner of the altar when a darker piece of what looked like iron among the detritus closer to the side wall caught her eye.

She crossed to it, with her boot swept the litter aside—to reveal a heavy iron ring set in the floor. "Sebastian! This must be it—the entrance."

He strode over, looked at the ring, then at the litter she'd swept to the side. "If it was covered by that, I doubt this slab has been lifted recently."

"Never mind that. There might be another way in." She all but jigged with impatience. "The light's almost gone. We need to go down and check, regardless."

Sebastian grimaced, but obediently reached for the ring, braced himself, then hauled—he was rather shocked when, albeit with a deep groan and the expected scraping noises, the slab pulled up relatively smoothly. As it swung and settled in place, he leaned around it and studied the mechanism. "Very neat. It's perfectly balanced and pivots."

"Yes, well—excellent." Antonia waved him to precede her.

The trapdoor had revealed a steep set of stone steps leading into darkness. Now as eager as she, he went down the first steps, bent, and peered inside, but the shaft of weak light provided little illumination. Antonia prodded his back. "Wait a minute," he said. He searched in his pockets and found the candle stub and his matchbox. He crouched, set the candle on the step, and quickly lit the wick.

There was virtually no breeze; the candle flame flared, then settled. Slipping the matchbox back into his pocket, he picked up the candle, straightened, then holding the candle before him, he went down the rest of the steps.

Antonia peered down, then quickly followed.

As she joined him on the dusty floor, he held the candle high—almost brushing the low ceiling—and turned slowly, taking in all he could see. It was a typical small crypt with stone tombs lining the walls, with burial niches above them. "There's nowhere I can see where any tunnel might come in—the niches are in every wall, and the tombs block anything lower."

"Look!" Antonia gripped his arm. "There are barrels in that corner." She pointed, then released him and hurried forward—only to recoil and bat her hands in the air before her face. "Ugh! Cobwebs!"

He hid a grin and followed her, holding up the candle. The faint light fell on four barrels, dark with age and covered in dust and cobwebs, stacked two by two in front of the tombs in the far corner.

Somewhat gingerly peeling aside cobwebs, Antonia bent over the barrels. She brushed down the end of one. "I can't see any writing."

"It might have faded with age." He studied the barrels, then held out the candle. "Here—hold this."

She took the candle.

He bent, gripped the upper edge at each end of one barrel, and lifted it. He swung the barrel slightly and felt the weight of liquid shifting inside. They both heard the faint sloshing. He set the barrel down. "Brandy at a guess. It might well be over a hundred years old."

She glanced around. "I suppose this crypt must have been used by smugglers once upon a time."

"On this coast, that's a certainty. A gang must have delivered this, most likely for whoever was living at Pressingstoke Hall at the time, and then whoever was to retrieve it either forgot or perhaps died."

She held the candle high and looked back along the crypt toward the steps.

He followed her gaze; from this spot, they could just make out the far wall of the crypt. "Regardless, there's no gunpowder here, and given the cobwebs and the dust, no one's been down here recently."

She sighed. She reached for her skirts and was about to start back for the steps when a faint skittering scurrying noise reached his ears.

Then she screeched, and the candle went flying—plunging them into darkness. Before he could blink, she turned and flung herself into his arms.

Full body-to-body contact in the dark.

For a moment, his inner self gloried and gloated, imagining the time had finally come.

After all, she was clutching him frantically, and his arms had locked around her.

But he could sense her heart beating wildly, could hear her suddenly quickened breaths. "It's all right," he soothed. "It's nothing."

"It's not *nothing*!" she wailed. "Some horrible beast ran over my foot!" He felt her lift her face—even through the darkness, felt her accusing glare. "I thought you said there wouldn't be any rats if there wasn't any food."

He could hardly point out that there had been food, but by now the rats would be long gone. "Trust me, there aren't any rats down here."

"What was it, then?"

She had him there. Tentatively, he offered, "It might have been a mouse."

"A mouse?"

Apparently mice were worse than rats. "Or maybe a vole. Or a mole.

Or even a bat."

"Bats?"

He pressed his lips tight against a laugh. He'd forgotten about her aversion to rodents, but he was definitely enjoying the result. She was still pressed against him, still holding onto him, a warm bundle of distinctly feminine curves with her arms looped around his neck.

For several long moments, he simply stood there with her held fast against him, telling himself he was merely waiting for his eyes to adjust well enough to guide her toward the lighter oblong that was the opening above the steps.

Even as temptation welled, he remembered his sane and undoubtedly wise resolution. This—and all that flowed from it—would be best left until later.

He bent his head and murmured, "I'm going to let you go, then I'll take your hand and lead you back to the steps and up. All right?"

"Are there any more bats—or whatever that was?"

"I think you probably scared them away."

After a second, he felt her nod, then her arms eased from about his neck.

She stepped back.

He felt the loss keenly, but he'd expected that. He ran one palm down her arm to her hand and laced his fingers with hers. "Come on."

Without further incident, he led her back along the crypt, up the steps, and helped her through the trapdoor and back into the chapel.

She stood and watched as he lowered the trapdoor back into place. "We should tell Blanchard about that brandy."

He nodded and reached for her hand. She surrendered it without a word. Her fingers clutched his as he helped her over the shattered blocks and up the aisle.

By the time they reached the arched entrance, night was closing in. "What time is it?" she asked.

Still holding her hand, with his other hand, he fished out his watch and checked. "It's after half past five." Tucking the watch back, he started for the path. "We'd better get back to the house."

She fell in beside him, striding freely. With her long legs, she could cover distance nearly as fast as he.

She made no move to extract her fingers from his clasp.

But they couldn't be seen by other guests openly holding hands.

The trees thinned. As they neared the end of the short path, he started to ease his grip.

Abruptly, she tripped.

Instantly, he tightened his hold and held her up until she caught her balance.

She glanced back along the path and sighed. "Just a tree root. I must be tired."

After that, of course, although he released her hand, as they stepped into the open, he offered her his arm. She smiled at him gratefully and wound her arm in his.

Side by side, they walked back to the house without further accident and entered via the rear terrace and the French doors of the music room. Once inside, they went into the front hall. Hearing voices from the drawing room, they exchanged a glance, then quietly made their way upstairs. They reached the corridor outside their rooms just as the dressing gong sounded.

She drew her arm from his. "I'll see you in the drawing room."

He nodded, watched until she'd gone into her room and shut the door, then continued to his room.

Wilkins was waiting with a bath prepared, along with information as to how the staff and the visiting servants had reacted to being interviewed by Inspector Crawford. Sebastian stripped and bathed while Wilkins filled him in.

"And now there's quite the excitement, what with everyone trying to predict who the murderer might be. As the inspector's made it plain he doesn't suspect any of the staff, they all feel free to speculate."

Sebastian rose, water cascading down his body. Wilkins handed him a towel.

Sebastian mopped his face and chest. "Have you heard anything the inspector might not have?"

"I don't think so." Wilkins was vigorously brushing Sebastian's coat, frowning over clinging cobwebs and dust. "But the inspector had me in for a quick word this morning, and he said as he'd call me back tomorrow to compare notes, as it were."

"Good. We need all the information we can get, and the inspector most of all." Sebastian finished drying himself and strolled across to the bed. He pulled on fresh drawers, then reached for the clean shirt left on the coverlet.

Given he and Antonia had covered the house and grounds and seen no hint of any gunpowder, not even any indication of where barrels might recently have been stored, he was increasingly convinced that no matter where they searched, the only way they would find the gunpowder was to find Ennis's killer. The murderer was the key to the plot.

He was standing before the mirror, tying his cravat, when, his thoughts of the plot and the murderer temporarily suspended as he concentrated on getting the linen folds just so, a sudden revelation on an entirely different subject bloomed in his brain.

Antonia had tripped on the stairs going down to the cellar—and landed in his arms.

Then in the wine room, on what was, in fact, a very weak pretext, she'd flung herself at him.

In the crypt, she'd reacted to a noise and flung herself into his arms. He had only her word that some beast had run over her foot—her booted foot.

Then, just as he'd been about to let go of her hand and create distance between them, she'd tripped on a root on the woodland path. Supposedly.

And this was Antonia, who before today, he would have described as innately surefooted, light on her feet, and never, ever clumsy.

He stared at his reflection. "Huh."

A moment of self-examination was enough to inform him that the particular brand of tension that owed its existence to sexual frustration had escalated significantly over the day, until now it thrummed just beneath his skin.

Waiting. Just waiting.

He couldn't be certain, but he had to wonder.

Had Antonia's uncharacteristic clumsiness throughout the day been entirely genuine? Or had she, with full intent, elected to play with fire?

# CHAPTER 9

*S*ebastian entered the drawing room and paused on the threshold to sweep the company with an outwardly languid gaze. He located Antonia standing with her female friends before the long windows. Worthington, Wilson, and Filbury had joined the younger ladies' circle. Unhurriedly, Sebastian crossed the room, pausing to exchange greetings with Parrish and McGibbin before fetching up by Antonia's side.

She'd seen him approaching and shifted to make space for him beside her—much to Wilson's poorly concealed annoyance.

Sebastian smiled genially at the ladies and exchanged nods with the men, then asked Wilson whether he'd had any luck with his gun that afternoon, effectively distracting the man from his sulk.

He didn't do anything so gauche as to claim Antonia's hand, but under cover of the conversation, he ran his fingertips down the inside of her forearm, bared beneath the elbow-length sleeve of her gray silk gown.

She didn't start, but he sensed the jolt she fought to suppress; she stiffened, and from the corner of his eye, he saw her eyes widen fractionally.

His easy smile deepened just a touch. This was a game at which he excelled.

He focused on Melissa Wainwright, currently holding center stage in the group.

"It's such a strange situation—I confess I'm not at all sure how we should behave." With one hand, Melissa waved at their clothes. "We've all managed some degree of mourning, but we didn't know Lord Ennis, we're not connected to the family, and overdoing things seems hypocritical and rather disrespectful."

Filbury nodded. "Ennis was our host, but we really didn't know him. It's Connell we know, so it's mourning at one remove, so to speak."

Georgia and Hadley Featherstonehaugh walked up and joined the circle. On being informed by Claire Savage of the topic under discussion, Georgia said, "Hadley and I were just talking about the very same issue with Mrs. Parrish and Cecilia. Consider—if one is at a house party at which the host dies, we all know what we would do."

"We'd pay our respects and leave the next morning," Hadley put in.

"Exactly," Georgia said. "But Ennis didn't just die, he was murdered, and although we all feel as if we should leave, I gather Sir Humphrey and the inspector are adamant we must remain until the murderer is caught, or at least until the day the house party was supposed to end."

"Cecilia, Mrs. McGibbin, and Mrs. Parrish have been discussing what's best to be done," Hadley revealed. "I gather Cecilia is thinking of making an announcement at dinner."

"Good," Claire said. "It's the uncertainty of not knowing if one is doing the right thing that's so discombobulating."

The conversation swung to what sort of group outings, if any, might be acceptable, both socially and to the inspector.

Sebastian bent his head toward Antonia's and murmured, "Stroll with me. We need to discuss strategy."

She glanced at him, curious but wary. He made sure no hint of any predatory smile showed as he ignored her wariness and offered his arm. She hesitated for a second, then with a tiny inclination of her head, she set her hand on his sleeve. Glancing at the others, she murmured an excuse, and together, they stepped away from the circle.

Slowly strolling across the room, he said, "Before we get to strategy, apropos of the Featherstonehaughs' recent remarks, earlier, you told me Cecilia had wanted to invite you and your friends to this event. I assumed that some friendship with Cecilia was involved, but that doesn't appear to be the case."

"No." Antonia paused, then went on, "As I understand it, Cecilia and Ennis were expecting the Parrishes and the McGibbins and had arranged for their visit to coincide with Connell's stay and Cecilia's annual house party. From what I've now gathered, I suspect Cecilia wanted to…underscore her and Ennis's position in English society for their visitors. Cecilia and Georgia are connected, albeit distantly, and it's well known the four of us—me, Claire, Melissa, and Georgia—are old friends and often pay visits together. And as our group consists of the daughter of an earl, the daughters of two viscounts, and the granddaughter of a duke now married to the grandson of an earl, we're seen as highly desirable guests. Precisely the sort of guests Cecilia wished to flaunt."

He'd steered her to a spot sufficiently distant from the other guests to be able to converse without being overheard. As he drew Antonia to a halt and shifted to face her, she lightly shrugged. "So Cecilia invited us, and Georgia's mother urged Georgia to help Cecilia out, and as the rest of us had nothing else on, we all accepted and here we are." She raised her eyes to his and cynically arched a brow. "So what about our strategy?"

He met her gaze. "There's nothing more we can do to advance our search for the gunpowder tonight. I suggest that instead, we should concentrate on seeing if we can narrow the candidates for the role of murderer."

She agreed with a dip of her lashes and a graceful inclination of her head. Calmly, she surveyed the gentlemen scattered about the room. "The generally accepted avenue to learning more about a gentleman than he intends to reveal is to encourage him to talk about himself, about his life."

He felt his brows rise. "It is?"

She nodded. "Flattery will get you even further with men than it will with women. Given the right encouragement, men will prattle away quite happily."

"I feel as if I'm seeing the ladies of the ton from an entirely new angle."

Her lips curved cynically. "With whom would you suggest we start?"

He glanced around. "Parrish and McGibbin. I don't see either as the murderer, but I'm unclear as to what their relationships with Ennis were based on—how closely were their business dealings intertwined?"

She nodded. "Very well. Let's see what we can learn."

Intrigued, and interested in observing her approach in action, as he led her to where the two older gentlemen were standing before the fireplace, he refrained from distracting her.

Antonia was relieved that Sebastian's focus on identifying the murderer had trumped his rakish inclinations. She'd never been the target of his roving eye—never been his prey—for which she gave thanks. At least that was what she told herself.

She knew his reputation and could imagine that, if he put his mind to it, he would be utterly diabolical in driving a lady to distraction. She was quite sure he knew all the ways. That earlier, thoroughly unnerving caress of his had proved that.

What she wasn't sure about was what that sudden, unprecedented action of his presaged. Did it signal intent on his part, or had it been more instinctive?

Or had he done it in revenge for all the jolts she'd given him over the long afternoon?

She wasn't sure what answer or answers she hoped were correct, which was another level of distraction altogether.

Regardless, she'd spent the last decade in the far more demanding circles of the haut ton. With easy assurance, she chatted with Mr. McGibbin and Mr. Parrish, both of whom she judged to be in their early forties, and by dint of subtle flattery and understated encouragement, soon had them both vying to tell her—and Sebastian, who stood quietly absorbing all by her side—everything about their recent successes in their various endeavors. Along the way, both imparted a large amount of information about their lives. Nevertheless, it took more than twenty minutes before she managed to winkle from them the basis of their friendship with Ennis.

"We formed a landowners' association, you see. Way back…" McGibbin looked at Parrish. "Well, must be nearly twenty years ago, now."

Parrish nodded. "Although McGibbin here and I now live elsewhere in Ireland, we still retain our holdings north of Limerick. Our origins, so to speak."

"It's those holdings and the landowners' association that made Ennis and us friends and kept us in touch over the years." McGibbin pulled a face. "Shared interests." He glanced at Parrish. "I suppose Boyne over there will continue to run the Ennis estate—he has for the last eight or so years—but we should tell Cecilia that we'll be happy to help out with teaching Ennis's boys the ropes."

"Early days, yet," Parrish replied. "But when the boys reach an appropriate age, it'd be a blessing to be able to do that for Ennis. He was a good friend."

Antonia exchanged a glance with Sebastian. McGibbin and Parrish were wearing black cravats and black armbands, and seemed to have sunk into their memories of Ennis.

Before Sebastian could respond, the dinner gong sounded, and Blanchard appeared in the doorway to summon them to the table.

Cecilia, tonight dressed in unrelieved black crepe, rose from the sofa. Pale and drawn, she pressed her hands together and said, "If you would, I suggest we keep the seating informal." She gestured vaguely. "There seems little reason to impose unnecessary strictures on ourselves. Not in these circumstances."

Sebastian, who, had they been adhering to formality, would have led Cecilia in, half bowed to her. "Whatever you wish, Cecilia. I'm sure all of us here are happy to do whatever we can to make this stressful time as easy as possible, for you especially."

Smiling a touch wanly, Cecilia inclined her head. "Thank you, my lord."

The company rose and, in twos and threes, made their way into the dining room.

Antonia rested her hand on Sebastian's sleeve. As they joined Melissa and Wilson, and Claire and Filbury, Sebastian closed his free hand over hers—abruptly jerking her attention from everything and everyone else.

She managed to keep her expression relaxed and unconcerned, but that touch! It was overbearingly, domineeringly, ridiculously possessive—and set her nerves jangling.

Worse was to come. Releasing her to guide her to a chair, his hand settled at the small of her back, burning through three layers of silk. Scrambling to tamp down her reaction, feeling as if her until-then-easy smile was pasted on her lips, she managed to subside onto the chair he held for her with reasonable grace.

Finally free of his touch, while he claimed the seat beside her, she seized the moment to draw in a deep, calming breath. She didn't immediately meet his eyes but instead engaged Hadley, opposite, with a smile.

Then Cecilia, about to take her seat at the foot of the table, waved her brother-in-law, who had escorted her in, to the empty carver at the head of the table. "Connell—if you wish...?"

Already pale and thoroughly overset in the wake of his brother's unexpected death, Connell paled even further. He shook his head. "No. I can't." He glanced at Cecilia. "It wouldn't be right. That's..." Connell blinked, then drew in a tight breath and went on, "James's place."

Cecilia smiled weakly. "Of course. As you wish."

Sebastian placed two fingertips on the back of Antonia's wrist.

Although the touch sent sensation streaking through her, she tipped her head his way and murmured, "James is Ennis's older son and heir."

Sebastian nodded, and the disturbing touch vanished.

Contrarily, she immediately wanted it back.

Connell claimed the empty place between Georgia and Miss Bilhurst, both of whom murmured their support for his decision—an approval shared by all. The ladies endeavored to entertain Connell, and after drawing in another breath, he made an effort to respond.

Seeing nothing in Connell's attitudes or behavior to raise anyone's suspicions, Antonia shifted her attention to Filbury, intending to further her—and Sebastian's—acquaintance with him and his background.

Somewhat to her surprise, while Sebastian did nothing to undermine her efforts directly, indirectly...every time an opportunity to discompose her, to capture her senses and derail her wits, presented itself, he was quick to seize it.

At first, she battled to keep her mental feet, but as his surreptitious actions continued, she discovered she could, indeed, successfully split her attention. She could continue to converse rationally with Filbury, and with Hadley and Melinda Boyne opposite, while simultaneously engaging with Sebastian and his game of sensual distraction.

She no longer harbored the slightest doubt that he was retaliating for her behavior of the afternoon. But having realized that his new direction played directly into—indeed, aligned perfectly with—her own plans, she was only too delighted to not just respond but encourage him.

In terms of touching, of artfully caressing without appearing to do so, he had the advantage; he could touch her by "accident" much more easily than she could innocently touch him. But this was a game she couldn't lose.

She found herself smiling rather more delightedly than the conversation called for while inwardly thrilling to the way her nerves leapt and her senses sizzled at his covert caresses.

When he handed her a serving spoon for the trifle, she reciprocated by sliding her fingers over the back of his hand, and sensed him still—freezing in that way she now recognized as him jerking his own reins taut.

A minute later, under cover of shifting and reaching past her to hand a heavy cream bowl to Filbury, Sebastian skated his palm up her side, from her hip to the outer curve of her breast.

She nearly choked on the trifle.

Understanding that tit for tat was an unwritten rule in this game, she bided her time.

When Blanchard and the footmen started clearing the dessert plates, Cecilia tapped her glass with a spoon; the tinkling sound drew everyone's attention to the foot of the table.

Cecilia directed a weak but commiserating smile around the company. "It seems we are trapped in one of those situations that our customary social prescriptions—the accepted patterns of behavior we normally adhere to—fail to cover. If Ennis had simply passed on, then you would have offered your condolences and departed this morning, leaving me and Connell to arrange the funeral. However, as Ennis was murdered, you are not free to leave, and today, I have learned that my husband's body will not be released for burial for at least several more days."

Cecilia clasped her hands tightly and glanced at Mrs. Parrish, who nodded encouragingly. After glancing at Mrs. McGibbin, on her other side, and receiving a similar nod, Cecilia looked down the table. "We—several of us"—she waved vaguely—"have discussed how best to go on. What will be acceptable and also most comfortable for us all. We are, in effect, in a social limbo. We are cut off from all other society. I doubt there are any of our number who feel we must eschew all form of entertainment in the name of being respectful to the dead—to Ennis. I can assure you he would not see us sitting around being mournful as being in any way desirable." Cecilia paused and, down the table, met Connell Boyne's eyes. She smiled faintly. "As Connell will testify, and the Parrishes and McGibbins as well, Ennis was, at his core, an Irishman, and the Irish have a tradition of celebrating a person's life with a wake—with music, singing, and dancing."

Cecilia glanced to right and left, meeting many gazes. "While a good half of us are English, I would ask you all to join with the Irish among us to celebrate Ennis's life tonight. Not wildly, but with joy in our memories. As there is no one but us to view what might, in other circles, be taken as inappropriate levity, there is no barrier to us making of the evening what we choose."

"Hear! Hear!" came from several male throats up and down the board.

"Excellent." Cecilia managed a more convincing smile. "I've asked for the piano to be moved into the drawing room. Melinda and Miss Bilhurst have both agreed to play for the company. Might I suggest we adjourn there?"

With newfound alacrity, the company rose; Cecilia's suggestion had breathed fresh life into the house party.

And Antonia seized the moment. In that instant before Sebastian pushed back his chair, she reached across beneath the table, laid her hand on his thigh, just above his knee, and squeezed lightly—not that her fingers made the slightest impression in taut muscles that, at her touch, had turned to iron—then easing her grip, she trailed her fingers upward in a blatant caress before drawing her hand away.

She'd kept her head turned away from him and her gaze fixed down the table.

For what felt like long moments, stillness seemed to have engulfed him, then from the corner of her eye, she saw him push to his feet.

He leaned over her—closer than necessary. "Allow me." The dark whisper shivered over her senses.

Then he drew her chair out.

Clinging to wholly spurious serenity, she stood, then turned to follow the others as they filed out of the room.

Sebastian appeared beside her and offered his arm.

Drawing breath into lungs constricted and still tightening, she placed her hand on his sleeve and looked up, a smile on her lips.

Her eyes met his—and she caught her breath.

She'd never before seen his pale green eyes burn, not with that particular flame.

His face appeared graven, all hard edges and sharp angles, but those eyes...they were molten.

Feminine satisfaction of a quality she'd never felt before bubbled up inside her; she fought to keep it from infusing her smile, but in that, she knew she failed.

The slight narrowing of those gorgeously revealing eyes, the increasing intentness she sensed emanating from him, confirmed that.

Glancing forward and finding the other guests now ahead of them, she waved. "Shall we?"

He glanced at the departing backs and seemed to suddenly recall where they were. With a sound like a growling grunt, he steered her toward the door.

What am I doing?

After guiding her out of the dining room, Sebastian lowered his arm. Clasping his hands behind his back, thus ensuring he kept them to himself and wasn't goaded into any further unwise reaction, he stalked beside Antonia at the rear of the crowd making for the drawing room. While he knew why he'd indulged his inner self by paying her back for her afternoon's endeavors, he also recalled that he hadn't intended to send them hurtling down this particular path—not yet.

Yes, he'd intended to play on her senses, to prick and spark them, but he hadn't allowed for her reaction, or rather the effect her reactions would have on him, spurring him on to more explicit touches—which had only encouraged her to even more daring, more blatantly sexual responses…

He felt as if they were on a runaway carriage, rocketing along with no reins.

Temporarily thrilling, yes, but ultimately destructive.

This—their interaction—had got out of hand.

Entirely unintentionally.

But control lay in his hands, no matter what she might imagine.

As they entered the drawing room, he swore to himself that no matter what the vixen did, he was not going to follow her lead. He was going to retreat to his previous line and hold firm against any actions that would escalate that telltale mutual awareness to any greater heights.

No more touching; no more suggestive remarks. No more playing at all.

With that resolution ringing in his mind, he glanced around. Melinda Boyne had already settled at the piano. She started playing a pleasant Irish tune. Filbury came to stand beside the instrument. Melinda smiled up at him, then he started to sing.

After the first verse, Wilson joined him, their voices blending in a soothing harmony.

Sebastian approved. Nothing remotely encouraging—to his inner self or Antonia.

He touched her arm briefly—just enough to get her attention—and when she glanced at him, with his head he directed her gaze to a nearby sofa on which Georgia Featherstonehaugh and Claire Savage had already taken up residence. There was space enough for Antonia, but not for him, which he deemed wise.

She hesitated, but then fell in with the suggestion and crossed to sink onto the sofa beside Claire.

The next half hour passed in unexceptionable fashion, with various ladies playing and singing, and several gentlemen adding their voices to the harmonies. As befitted daughters of the nobility, Antonia and her three friends were all accomplished pianists and also possessed well-trained voices; they combined to sing a ballad in four-part harmony, entrancing the entire company.

After the applause had died, as Antonia made her way back to the sofa against the back of which Sebastian had propped, he noticed a small conference being conducted on the other side of the room. Cecilia was at the heart of it, with Connell Boyne, Melinda Boyne, and the two older ladies all discussing some subject.

Then there were smiles all around, and the group dispersed. Connell and Melinda went to the piano; Connell summoned Filbury and Worthington to help him move the instrument into the corner of the room.

Halting before the sofa, Antonia followed Sebastian's gaze. Beside her, Claire looked, too.

"What's going on?" Antonia murmured at the same time Claire asked, "Why are they moving the piano?"

Then Connell directed Wilson to move the low table that stood on the Aubusson rug before the other sofa, then called Hadley to help him as he rolled up the carpet.

"Dancing?" Georgia murmured as she joined Antonia and Claire.

As if in reply, Cecilia rose from the other sofa and clapped her hands. "No Irish wake would be complete without dancing, as I'm sure you're all aware. However, as too few of us are familiar with the usual jigs and reels, we thought to make do with waltzes. Rather more sedate, which should suit us better. Indeed—" Cecilia broke off as if to master an upswell of emotion. When she continued, her smile wobbled and her voice shook slightly. "Ennis loved to waltz. I'm sure he would approve."

With that, she sat down rather abruptly. But her words had made certain no one would argue the propriety of waltzing—and as they'd already agreed, there was no one to play censor.

Once again seated before the piano, Melinda Boyne sounded out the introductory chords of a traditional waltz.

Sebastian glanced at Antonia. She was still looking toward the piano.

Hadley, smiling, was already on his way to claim his wife.

Filbury was crossing the room, his eye on Claire.

In the time it took to blink, Sebastian foresaw the problem—having to watch Antonia whirl about the room in some other gentleman's arms—evaluated the danger—of him being goaded to the point of breaking his firm resolution and striding across the floor to claim her in front of the entire company—and decided on his best, and indeed only, way forward.

He straightened and stepped around the sofa. Antonia glanced at him, and he held out his hand. Commandingly, because, in truth, it really wasn't a request. "My dance, I believe."

Her brows rose, haughtily quizzing him. "Your name is not on my dance card."

"You don't have a dance card." *Thank Christ.* He reached out, trapped her hand, and closed his fingers around hers—and tried not to register the feel of her slender digits within his grasp or the instinctive response that leapt within him. "You're not going to argue, are you?"

Her eyes laughed up at him; her lips weren't straight. "Would it do any good?"

"No."

"Well, then." With her free hand, she gestured to the dance floor where other couples were already revolving, then she stepped toward him, and he smoothly drew her nearer, and she placed her hand on his shoulder.

In perfect synchrony, they stepped into the dance.

He reminded himself that he should keep her at a distance, with the regulation however-many inches between their bodies.

Not so easy when she swayed so enticingly, when the fluid flow of her slender form drew him on and urged him to hold her tighter. Closer. In the end, he told himself it was simply easier to draw her more firmly within his arm so that their long legs interleaved as they whirled through the turns.

Being who they were, they were accomplished dancers. They'd waltzed since their early teens; the activity required very little of their minds. They could carry on a complex conversation if they so chose, but conversation, he judged, looking down at her face, a perfect pale oval with those strikingly dark brows and long lashes, and that lush, ripe, oh-so-tempting mouth, would be entirely superfluous.

Her expression was serene, composed; her lids were at half mast, screening her eyes from his gaze.

Leaving him free to study her face as he wished. If she was aware of his scrutiny, she didn't let it show.

He should ask if she'd heard anything that might point to their elusive murderer, but couldn't summon sufficient interest to do so, not while she was in his arms.

Melinda Boyne segued smoothly from one waltz to the next. The dancing couples were, in the main, not changing partners.

After several measures, Amelie Bilhurst spelled Melinda at the piano.

The dancers stood smiling, relaxed, some chatting, waiting for the music to resume; when it did, they stepped out once more.

Outwardly, it appeared to be a soothing interlude, yet beneath his skin—beneath Antonia's—Sebastian could sense the fires building. Could feel the insistent compulsion to act—to do something about the flaring attraction that, even now, seemed to flex its claws, preparing to sink them deep—rise. And rise.

Being this close, even without any suggestive, seductive caresses, without any further incitement at all, was playing on them both.

Escalating the hunger their earlier touches had irrevocably awoken.

Like a hunting cat, desire—a very different desire to anything previously between them—prowled through them, and he was sufficiently attuned to her, and sufficiently experienced, to know that those increasingly powerful impulses were only going to get harder to restrain, and they weren't affecting only him.

And therein lay a very real danger.

She was no meek and mild miss. She was no stranger to instigating action, to leading and not simply waiting to follow.

Maintaining control, as he very well knew, often lay in ensuring others didn't seize it.

But was the danger she posed so real—so immediate? Or would he still be able to leave dealing with her until after they returned to town, as he'd intended and had assumed he could and would do?

They were circling fluidly, revolving down the room. His attention had drawn in to lock on her, on them.

He couldn't tell where her attention was, but she didn't seem aware of the others around them any more than he was.

*Hmm.* He mentally paused, then lowered his shields and opened his senses to all the impacts he'd been holding at bay. And the lure of her, the physical reality of the sensuous woman she had grown to be, flooded his mind; the whirlpool of temptation swirled to the circling of their feet— and nearly pulled him under.

He slammed shut his mental doors at the very last moment. Then slowly drew breath and steadied his giddy head.

*Good Lord!* Their burgeoning attraction had grown even more powerful—infinitely more compelling than he'd realized.

As the current measure drew to a whirling close, he accepted that talking to her directly about what lay between them had become imperative—he couldn't afford to delay and risk her seizing their reins.

Given the reality of what he'd just glimpsed, if she tried to seize control, she might well succeed, and he had no idea what would happen then.

He steered their circling feet toward the open doors. When the music ended, he halted and released her, but changed his grip on the hand he'd held and tipped his head toward the front hall. "We need to talk."

She opened her eyes wide, but then made the decision—a deliberate concession he was intended to see—and inclined her head. "Very well." She wriggled her fingers, and when he released them, she wound her arm in his.

He started for the doorway, and without a single glance behind, she walked with him out of the room.

Just before they passed beyond the doorway, he looked back, but everyone else had turned toward the piano, where Worthington was being prevailed upon to play; no one had seen them leave.

"Where to?" She slanted a glance at him. "I assume we need privacy?"

He nodded and mentally scanned the house plan they'd worked from during the day. "The conservatory. Everyone else seems intent on waltzing or listening to the music—we should be safely private there."

But not *too* private. Unlike the morning room, someone else might walk into the conservatory at any time; he judged that was one risk she wouldn't as yet be likely to take.

The conservatory lay at the end of the corridor that led right from the rear of the front hall. They passed the music room, and he opened the door with its glass panes, and Antonia preceded him into the humid warmth.

Shutting the door, he surveyed the room.

Greenery abounded on all sides, mostly ferns with the occasional palm lending height. The plants grew in pots of all shapes and sizes placed on a floor of glazed tiles. The central section of the roof was composed of glass panes, and the end wall and half of the outer wall were completely glazed, no doubt affording vistas of the moonlit grounds, of the manicured lawns rolling away to the lake, with the dark shapes of the trees in the Home Wood looming to one side.

The plants were densely packed and had been arranged to create a weaving path that led across and then down the length of the room. Sebastian hadn't been in the conservatory before, hadn't explored its amenities.

Antonia walked to where the path turned. Glancing back at him, she waved down the room. "There's a clearing of sorts at the end." Without waiting for any agreement, she started strolling.

He followed. Halfway down the long room, the path straightened, and over Antonia's head, he saw a circular area ringed by low shrubs before the wall of windows at the end of the room. Two white-painted wrought-iron chairs and a small matching table were set against the green backdrop. The spot seemed designed as a place to share secrets.

Antonia led the way into the circle of ferns, some large-leaved, others with lacy fronds that bobbed in the faint currents created as she and Sebastian passed. Moonlight struck through the panes above, bathing the area in a silvery glow. To their left, a narrower path led through the ferns to a door giving onto the rear terrace, presently deserted.

There was no one else around; they were entirely alone.

Expectation welled; anticipation gripped her. Surely they weren't there to talk about the murderer.

She halted and swung to face Sebastian.

He'd been scanning their surroundings and hadn't been watching her; he abruptly pulled up with a scant few inches between them.

She fixed her gaze on his eyes. "What—"

The click of the door latch froze them both.

"I've never known much about Ennis's Irish holdings."

Cecilia; she'd apparently halted just inside the door—out of sight of the area where Antonia and Sebastian stood. The glass surrounding them seemed to reflect Cecilia's words, rendering them with bell-like clarity.

"We wondered if you'd heard of any changes to the management—the people running things there?"

Filbury.

Sebastian frowned. They heard the click of the door as it shut.

"There's still a bit of unrest over there, you see."

That was Wilson.

Her eyes locked with Sebastian's, Antonia's mind raced. What did the men know? What did Cecilia know? What were the men trying to learn—and why?

"As far as I know, there have been no changes, at least not to the senior staff," Cecilia said. "But why not ask Connell?"

"He's rather overset by Ennis's death, don't you know—and we thought you might know." Filbury continued, "We're just a touch concerned."

"We're Connell's friends," Wilson put in, "and we wouldn't want to see the estate get caught up in anything…well, untoward."

"Untoward?" Cecilia said.

By their voices, the trio had been moving slowly away from the door. Any minute, they would reach the central path.

There was nowhere Antonia and Sebastian could hide and continue to listen. If they moved onto the path to the terrace door, they would remain shielded for only a short time, and if they opened the door and tried to slip out, the cold air from outside would give them away.

She evaluated their options at frantic speed, knowing Sebastian would be doing the same. They'd already heard too much; they needed some excuse—better, some screen that would suggest that they hadn't heard a word…

They both knew their world. There was only one way.

She hauled in a breath and stepped forward, boldly closing the distance between them, reached up, framed the long planes of his face between her hands, stretched up on her toes, and pressed her lips to his.

In the instant her lips met the cool firmness of his, she realized that, while this kiss was a subterfuge to excuse their presence and reassure Cecilia and the two men that it was unlikely they'd heard anything, she—the passionate woman inside her she so rarely let free—had been waiting for this moment for much of her life.

It was that passionate woman who swept to the fore and took charge—who pressed her lips firmly to his and, with absolutely not a shred of reservation, boldly incited.

Sebastian reacted instantly—instinctively. First, to the unvoiced understanding that they needed to excuse and defuse their presence, to leave the others assured that they'd been far too distracted to have heard anything, much less taken anything in.

But even as his arms swept around Antonia and he drew her flush against him and swung them so her back was to the path and, from beneath his lashes, he could observe the steadily approaching trio, even as he angled his head, covered her lips with his, and seized control of the kiss, he sensed another imperative—another demand—one he equally instinctively moved to meet...

She and the kiss dragged him under.

Into a whirling cauldron of hunger, of greedy, ravenous need fueled by surging desire—hers as well as his.

The exchange was supposed to be just a kiss, a pretense, a façade.

It was anything but.

Passion erupted; too long denied, it geysered between them, drowning them in a raging tide of wanting.

Hunger drove them. She parted her lips on a gasp, and he dove into the honeyed warmth of her mouth, plundering, claiming, needing to do so with an intensity that overwhelmed him. That seized him, shook him, and enslaved him.

She pressed nearer; one hand slid from his cheek, and her fingers speared through his hair, then splayed and gripped.

He tasted her joy, her effervescent delight, her enthusiasm and unbridled desire.

She'd set herself free and ensnared him.

She threw caution to the winds and effortlessly drew him with her.

They strove to get closer, to taste more, to devour. Their mouths merged, lips melded, tongues tangling, stroking and inciting and blatantly claiming.

He—and she—lost all touch with the world.

The entire company could have been standing, gawping, on the path, and he wouldn't have known and wouldn't have cared.

In that instant, the only thing that mattered was her—the fiery, feisty woman she truly was, the woman he'd always instinctively known lived beneath her cool, composed exterior. The only imperative remaining in his mind was to appease her demands, to lure her and capture her, just as she had already captured him.

It was tit for tat, a natural search for balance between them, and this time, she was leading the dance, forging the way, and for once, he didn't mind.

Her lips were ambrosia, her mouth a dark paradise. The pressure of her body against his completed the lure—one that, for him, was utterly irresistible.

Not that he had any wish to resist...

Yet protectiveness remained, alert and watchful; some distant part of his brain informed him that the trio had come farther along the path and seen them.

But the intruders had halted, no doubt transfixed by the sight of him and the woman held tightly in his arms standing in the clearing and bathed by moonlight.

A soft male chuckle reached him. "Half his luck." Then Cecilia murmured something, and the sound of footsteps creeping away faded.

Good.

The need for their charade had passed. They could end the kiss. But the man he was when she—the woman she truly was—was in his arms had no intention of doing anything so senseless.

This—her as she was, in his arms, with her lips under his, her hands in his hair, and her mouth and her pliant body surrendered—was exactly what his inner self craved.

Now he had her where he needed her, he was in no hurry to let her go.

No more than he did she evince any desire to break from the engagement.

Instead, she pressed more firmly into his embrace.

Antonia had given up all hope of rational thought. All notion of following any plan. Feelings, impulses, and compulsions battered at her and drove her; recognizing and appeasing them made her wits spin. But of one thing she was ineradicably certain—she wanted more.

More of everything.

In that instant, she needed more of the sensation of Sebastian's muscled body riding against her heated curves. Deliberately—blatantly provocatively—she pressed her breasts to his chest and shifted, needing to ease the ache that had spread over her skin and sunk into her flesh.

Into her very bones.

An urgent ache, one some primitive side of her recognized, an ache she yearned to ease.

With her hands clutching his head, the soft feathery caress of his silky locks on the backs of her hands another temptation, she held him to the kiss, held herself open to it, and gloried in the exchange—in the fiery flow of desire between them. Hot, stirring, and flagrantly needful, a steadily rising tide of wanting that was not just hers but theirs, that compulsive passion swirled and welled and linked them.

He responded to her tempting, her bold provocation, and closed one hard hand over her breast.

Her heart leapt, then hammered—not in shock but in giddy delight.

He caressed, stroked, then palpated the suddenly swollen mound, then his clever fingers found her nipple beneath the silk of her bodice and circled teasingly. Then he closed his fingers and gently squeezed.

Her senses spiked, her nerves seized, and she lost what little breath she had.

Eagerness swamped her. More—more...

"Antonia?"

They broke from the kiss. Eyes wide, for an instant, they stared at each other. Claire's call had acted like a pail of cold water dumped over them both.

Abruptly, Sebastian's arms fell from her, and he looked up the path. Her heart tripping, she swung around to see, but her friend hadn't come far enough into the room—yet.

"Antonia—are you there?" Melissa, this time.

Struggling to catch her breath, Antonia glanced at Sebastian. Features setting, he stepped back. He straightened his coat, then raked a hand through the hair she realized she'd thoroughly mussed.

She glanced down at her gown and hurriedly tugged the somewhat rumpled bodice into place, then looked up. Only a few seconds had elapsed.

His expression close to its usual arrogantly impassive mask, he met her eyes and nodded.

She hauled in a still far-too-tight breath. "Yes—I'm—we're here."

Even drawing on her years of social experience, she discovered it took every ounce of her will to keep her voice steady and her tone coolly composed, to plaster on an expression of serene assurance and get herself moving in a reasonably smooth glide up the path.

Sebastian followed close behind—strolling easily, as if they'd merely been admiring the views.

Her pulse seemed to throb just beneath her skin. She felt flushed all over and hoped it wouldn't show in the poor light.

Melissa and Claire appeared on the path. "There you are," Claire said.

"Cecilia said she thought you were in here."

Ignoring the large presence at her shoulder, Antonia airily waved down the path. "The view is quite pretty in the moonlight."

Her friends were too well bred to stare suspiciously at Sebastian. Instead, they smiled as if they believed her story.

Melissa gestured toward the door. "We're all going up."

In a group, the four of them made for the front hall, where they found the rest of the company gathering at the foot of the stairs.

Over the heads, Sebastian glimpsed Worthington and Connell returning from the direction of the billiards room. A quick scan of the company showed everyone else was there.

Cecilia made a gesture toward the stairs, and the ladies started up, the older ladies and Cecilia in the lead. Melinda Boyne and Amelie Bilhurst followed, then Antonia and her friends. Sebastian started up beside Hadley, who was trailing his wife.

Sebastian threw Hadley a questioning look.

Hadley rolled his eyes. He lowered his voice and said, "The older ladies, and Miss Boyne and Miss Bilhurst, have talked themselves into a tizzy over some itinerant having broken into the house and killed Ennis. Ergo, said itinerant might come back—God knows why—and we'll all be better off safely in our rooms upstairs."

When Sebastian just looked at him, Hadley sighed. "Yes, I know. It makes no sense, but the rest of us decided we could do with an early—or at least earlier—night."

Sebastian glanced at the long-case clock on the landing—just as it whirred and started to toll ten o'clock.

At the head of their small procession, Cecilia gained the top of the stairs and stepped into the gallery. She paused by the balustrade and glanced down at the rest of the company. "I'm hoping tomorrow will see us released. I'm sure we'll all feel relieved to be able to escape this place."

The comment—and her tone—struck Sebastian as odd. Still slowly climbing, he focused on her. "Will you be returning to London?"

She shrugged and didn't meet his eyes. "It's the atmosphere here." She gestured vaguely. "The sense of being under the same roof beneath which violent murder took place so recently—especially as the victim was my husband…"

"Indeed!" Mrs. Parrish put a motherly arm around Cecilia. "Hardly surprising that you would want away from this place, my dear."

"Even arranging poor Ennis's funeral," Mrs. McGibbin stated, "can just as easily be done from elsewhere." She patted Cecilia's shoulder in passing. "Just get a good night's sleep, dear. Everything will seem more settled in the morning."

Sebastian watched Cecilia as she allowed Mrs. Parrish to guide her into her room. There was a certain brittleness about Cecilia's demeanor that made him wonder...

Directing his gaze at the floor, he blindly followed Antonia, Georgia, and Hadley to the east wing.

He'd been Cecilia's lover once upon a time; he knew her well enough to be certain she was nervous or acting a part. Or both. Experience—and what he'd overheard of that conversation in the conservatory—suggested it might well be both.

He was fairly certain that neither Sir Humphrey nor the inspector would have pressed Cecilia—the grieving widow, and her grief was real enough—over whether she knew anything. Or suspected anything, which was rather more likely.

Both Sir Humphrey and the inspector would have assumed that Cecilia knew nothing about her husband's dealings. That was most likely true, but in this case, when those dealings involved plots and betrayal...

They reached the corridor leading to their rooms. The others called goodnight, and he raised a hand in acknowledgment.

He felt the very pointed look Antonia directed his way, but didn't meet it. With a distant nod in her direction, he went into his room and firmly shut the door. He wasn't ready to even think about what had erupted between them in the conservatory—what genie they'd released. He definitely wasn't ready to take their interaction any further that night; on that score, he needed to think long and hard about how best to proceed.

As he shrugged out of his coat, his mind swung back to Cecilia.

She wasn't stupid. Despite their various affairs, she and Ennis had still lived as a couple; he might have mentioned something over the breakfast cups that Cecilia remembered and that Ennis's murder might have recast as having some deeper significance.

Or she might have sensed something between Ennis and someone else—some man at the house party.

He didn't bother to ring for Wilkins but draped his coat over a chair. He stripped, tossed aside the silk pajama jacket, but donned the trousers, then slid between the sheets, turned down the lamp, slumped back, and stared at the ceiling.

Courtesy of that incendiary kiss, he wasn't going to find sleep any time soon. He was still half aroused, and desire thrummed through his veins, tensing his muscles and leaving his skin taut.

Making a mental note to suggest to the inspector that questioning Cecilia more forcefully might bear fruit, he closed his eyes, willed his mind away from Antonia—from anything to do with her—and valiantly tried to think of something else.

# CHAPTER 10

*A*n hour later, he was still wide awake.

Lying on his back, his arms crossed behind his head, he stared moodily at the shadowed ceiling.

Hunger still prowled beneath his skin, yet he was determined to ignore it. To deny it. Taking any further step with respect to Antonia no longer featured in his plans for this house party. Not even simply to discuss what he'd intended to discuss with her before they'd been sidetracked; given what had occurred in the conservatory, he could imagine all too well how any such discussion—which would necessarily have to be conducted in private—would end.

She'd wanted more. She'd had no intention of calling a halt, not until they'd been forced to.

Recalling her responses—her blatant encouragements—he seriously doubted he could rely on her to toe any conventional line.

And given how far their runaway passions had swept them, he couldn't be one hundred percent certain *he* would be able to rein them—him and her in the grip of said passions—back.

He could foresee the problem looming—one with which he'd never before had to contend.

While he wasn't about to make the classic mistake of imagining he could predict what she was thinking, he didn't believe he was indulging in any overweeningly arrogant self-confidence. If he made it clear he wanted her, she would invite him to her bed.

With alacrity.

And then…heaven alone knew how matters would evolve.

The threat of being unable to exert control—of not being in the driving seat—bothered him. Troubled him. A lot.

If he was brutally honest, it made him nervous.

Control—as in being in control of himself and any situation in which he found himself—was something he strove always to maintain. He'd been trained to wield power more or less since birth, and in almost all situations, control was power.

He shifted in the bed, still restless—still nowhere near relaxed enough to fall asleep.

Outside his door, the house had quieted, settling, as large houses did, into brooding stillness. His eyes had grown accustomed to the dimness; the moon had shifted and now shone sufficiently strongly through the uncurtained window to the side of the bed for him to see across the room quite clearly.

The gentle creak of a floorboard outside his door drew his gaze to the panel.

He blinked, focused, and confirmed that the door handle was slowly turning.

He tensed to rise, then remained as he was. The shaft of moonlight fell across the bed; his face was in shadow. Anyone coming through the door wouldn't immediately see he was awake.

The latch clicked back; the door was slowly—very slowly—pushed inward.

Eyes glued to the spot, he waited, breath bated, to see who would appear.

Cecilia?

The murderer?

* * *

Antonia drew in a tense, tight breath and slipped through the doorway into Sebastian's room.

One swift, wide-eyed glance at the bed showed the molded line of his long legs, unmoving beneath the covers. The upper half of the bed lay in shadow, but surely by now, he would be asleep.

It had taken nearly an hour to conclude her internal debate. For her true self to win out—for her to accept that no matter the arguments against it, her best interests lay in pursuing their attraction to its logical conclusion there, at Pressingstoke Hall, where he and she stood on level ground.

If she was ready and willing to forge ahead, so should he be.

After that kiss, she had absolutely no doubt of what their future relationship would be, and if there was one fact that interlude in the conservatory had made abundantly clear, it was that he knew that, too.

Regardless, she could readily imagine he would seek to put things off until they returned to London—and the ability to manage their interactions tipped his way.

It would be unwise to allow that to happen—to allow them to return to their normal lives without establishing at least a basic framework for their future relationship. If she didn't make a push to get that much settled now, while they were there, she might well find herself married without having gained the assurances she needed to make marriage with a man— a nobleman—like him work. And then getting that necessary framework in place would become a protracted battle.

Such a scenario found no favor with her. If he had any sense, it wouldn't find favor with him, either, but then, he was a man. A nobleman. One who thought he could manage damn near anyone.

So it had to be there, and her moment was now.

It was time for her to put her stamp on the relationship she was determined they would have.

And regardless of whatever plans he might have made to the contrary, as witnessed by the fact he hadn't come to her room, she knew perfectly well that if she issued a challenge, he wouldn't—simply didn't have it in him to—refuse to engage.

Turning back to the door, she carefully eased it shut. No sense waking the tiger too early.

She stood staring at the panel—this was her moment of no return.

She drew in a breath, swung around, and determinedly walked to the bed.

She halted beside it, blinking as she saw he was definitely not asleep.

Blinking as her eyes drank in the sight of his bare chest, displayed in its muscled glory given he was lying with his hands behind his head, and the sheet lay across his waist.

It had been a decade and more since she'd last seen his chest bare, and the image she retained from then was very, very different to what lay before her now.

What lay before her now made her senses sing.

Made her mouth water.

Several more seconds elapsed before she finally dragged her gaze up to his face.

And despite the dim light, met a look that was one step away from a glare.

"What the devil are you doing here?"

His voice was low, his tone aggressive, his diction clipped and forceful.

Had she harbored any doubt that he held a definite view as to how their relationship should evolve—specifically, under his direction—those words would have eradicated it.

She took her time studying him, then opened her eyes wide. "With all your years of experience, after that kiss in the conservatory, I would have thought you would know."

Her inner wildness had well and truly taken over; even to her ears, her voice sounded sultry, converting the simple words into a blatant provocation.

She saw tendons in his arms shift as his hands fisted in response, but his lips had set in a hard line, and, stubborn to the last, he didn't move. "I decided," she continued, her tone a conversational purr, "that it was time we dealt with this—with what's grown between you and me."

"Undoubtedly." Sebastian seized on her words like a drowning man. "But is this the best venue for a rational discussion?" With her standing by his bed, gilded by moonlight, her hair cascading over her shoulders, her curves wrapped in a pearl-pink silk robe—with, he fervently prayed, a nightgown beneath—she was a sight designed expressly to addle his wits. Rational discussion was already far beyond him.

It was all he could do to keep himself locked in position in the bed. His inner self was scrabbling to break free of his reins and seize her. And...

Thrusting such thoroughly unhelpful thoughts aside, he fought to keep his eyes glued to her face and ignore the impulses pummeling him.

Her fine brows arched. Although her expression conveyed taunting amusement of a distinctly feminine flavor, he sensed something else in her shadowed eyes, in the steadiness of her gaze—a quality of steely determination, again with a definitely feminine feel that, he realized, he associated with her. Like a hallmark.

A hallmark that declared her backbone was of the same tempered steel as her mother's. As his mother's, his sister's. And all their ilk.

He was a nobleman, but she was his equal.

That last scale fell from his eyes as she quietly replied, "Who said anything about discussion—rational or otherwise?"

And he knew from her tone this was one battle he wasn't going to win.

He made one last desperate bid for the reins. "Antonia—"

Smoothly, with a determination that was all the more impactful because of her gracefulness, she drew the sash at her waist undone, and the sides of her silken robe gaped.

He broke off with a damned-near-audible gasp as he saw his prayer for a nightgown had been rejected.

Beneath the robe lay long, delicately curved limbs, perfectly rounded shoulders, breasts that promised to fill his hands, and hips that formed a perfect cradle that was—at least as his primitive mind saw it—shaped specifically for him, all sheathed in skin one shade away from alabaster white; the moonlight struck, caressed, and turned that skin exquisitely pearlescent.

He felt as if he'd swallowed his tongue. He certainly couldn't find it.

His mouth had dried—he couldn't remember the last time he'd been struck speechless at the sight of a woman's body.

He had a sneaking suspicion he never had been—not until now.

She took his silence as acquiescence—as surrender, which it was. She shrugged off the robe, letting it slide with a sibilant susurration down her delectably long limbs to pool about her slender feet.

Completing his capture. Starting the torture.

He had, he realized, no defense against her. None whatsoever.

Had he ever had?

He'd always thought, being dark haired himself, that blondes were the right foil for him. Virtually all his lovers had been blondes; the few who hadn't had been redheads. He'd never taken a brunette as a lover, but as he—his senses—drank her in, he had to wonder if some part of him had always known, always recognized that she, black haired, was his one true lover—his perfect mate—and consequently he'd shied from taking any like her, any his senses might see as a substitute for her, to his bed.

He was already so ferociously aroused, if he thought about it, he would be in pain.

Unable to summon either strength or will to stop her, he watched as she knelt on the bed and—with that grace that was so much a part of her—in a crawling prowl, came up the bed toward him.

He assumed her aim would be to lie by his side, but then she shifted, slid a leg over his hips, and sat on the sheet across his waist.

He closed his eyes and only just bit back a groan. Behind his head, he held his wrists in a death grip to stop himself from reaching for her. The warm, alluring pressure of her weight over his waist and upper belly, the firm press of her inner thighs against his sides, was temptation incarnate.

She had him trapped—physically trapped. He couldn't move. And there was nothing he could do.

"Hmm," she purred—and it was definitely the purr of a cat surveying her own bowl of cream. "Where to begin?"

The question sounded distinctly rhetorical—which calmed him not at all. Her hands hadn't yet touched him.

He cracked open his lids; his gaze fell on her breasts. The luscious mounds, pearlescent in the silvery radiance of the moon, their peaks tipped with rosy pink aureolas and nipples, made his mouth water.

She'd straightened, and her hands rested on the sleek muscles of her widespread thighs.

He hauled in a tight breath and forced his gaze up to her face—to her

perfectly sculpted chin, to the fullness of her lips...eventually, to her
eyes; he trapped her gaze as she raised her eyes to meet his. "You're a
virgin." He couldn't remember the last time he'd had a virgin beneath
him—sometime in his schooldays?

She blinked her eyes wide. "I know." Her lips slowly curved in another
of those amused female smiles—the sort women used when they knew
they had the man in question exactly where they wanted him. Helpless.
"I'm fairly certain you're up to dealing with that little matter for me."

Then the damned woman swayed, sensuously shifting the globes of her
derriere so they brushed the head of his straining erection.

He couldn't stifle his groan. Again, he closed his eyes, clutched his
wrists. His jaw felt as if it would crack.

Why am I resisting?

He'd known the reasons before she'd walked into the room, but they
escaped him now. Was there any sense in prolonging his resistance to
something that was clearly—whether there or in London—going to be?

"Antonia..." His voice was almost gone—so deep, so rough, it was
more growl than diction. He dragged in another breath—and realized he
didn't have any idea what he wanted to say.

Then he felt her weight shift.

Is she pulling back?

A wholly contradictory panic assailed him.

He opened his eyes.

As she put her hands on the bed on either side of his shoulders and
leaned close.

Much closer. From a distance of mere inches, her gray eyes met his.
Fearlessly, she held his gaze.

And catlike, dipped, so her breasts—delectably warm, deliciously
weighted silken mounds—caressed his chest as she closed the last inch
and breathed over his lips, "Sebastian..."

Then she covered his lips with hers, and he was lost.

Utterly and completely vanquished.

Not by her but by the primitive force she unleashed in him.

That she was there—patently recognizing that she was his, by her own
wordless declaration accepting that truth—and offering herself so
blatantly to him... There was no way he couldn't seize.

His hands whipped from behind his head, clamped about her hips, and
he rolled, bringing her down to the bed beside him.

Then he rolled further, and she was beneath him.

The movement had trapped the sheet between them; he considered that
a bonus given she was, as he'd reminded her, a virgin. This engagement
would have to be slow, even though every impulse he possessed
hungered. Wanted. Now. This second.

Ruthlessly, he seized control of the kiss—and kissed her ravenously, rapaciously, with a plundering voraciousness he couldn't tame.

Didn't want to. Saw no need to. This—him and her like this, rolling naked in a bed—had been written in their stars.

As if confirming that, she matched him to a large degree; only his years of experience distinguished their efforts—in their intent, in the strength and sheer power of their desire, they were otherwise well matched.

And there was, he discovered, as her hands found his chest and stroked, caressed, and then blatantly possessed, nothing wrong with her imagination. Or her inventiveness.

She caught his lower lip between her teeth and tugged, then nipped, sending a surge of sheer lust to his groin.

Not that that part of his anatomy needed further urging; he ached to join with her, but…first things first.

Antonia had always wondered how she would feel in this position—naked with a man's weight pinning her to a bed. As it was…she couldn't stop smiling. Even as she answered his searing kisses with fiery kisses of her own, even as her fingertips sank into the broad sweep of muscles banding his chest, and she battled to hold onto her whirling wits, her lips were curved, and inside, she was grinning.

With effervescent joy and not a little satisfaction. She'd wanted this; she'd played her hand and risked an embarrassing scene—had gambled on his desire for her being strong enough to break free of his restraint and answer her call—and he'd proved her right, and she'd won.

But oh, my Lord, *this* was better than she'd expected—even better than her wildest fantasies. The scalding heat, the earthy promise, the spiking sensations were all heralds of a deepening intimacy. Above all else, the elemental power—the raw possessiveness—that flexed beneath his skin, that invested his every muscle, that, although still under his command, strained to snap its leash, called to her inner wildness as nothing else ever had.

Well matched? No—they were more.

Perfect complements.

Even as the concept flashed through her mind, distracted to the limit by so many novel sensations—the erratic, abrasive brush of the wiry dark hair adorning his chest over the fine skin of her already sensitive breasts, the ruthlessly commanding pressure of his lips, the all-too-evocative probing of his tongue, the flexing of his fingers as they gripped her hips and held her down—she suddenly understood her own instincts.

Understood why she'd been so set on pressing on with this engagement here and now.

Because the marriage she wanted with him was one of perfect complements. Not precisely equals, but balancing halves.

They were different, had different strengths, and although their weaknesses were few, they differed in those, too.

With his hands drifting upward from her hips, cruising over her sides, she couldn't corral her wits sufficiently to ponder her new insight. Yet as those distracting hands closed possessively over her breasts, one goal shone, compulsively demanding, in her mind.

She needed to establish the necessary framework in which that perfect complementarity could flourish—here, now, in this bed.

In this arena, one in which he was regarded as an expert, and she had no training. No experience.

But if she didn't succeed here, didn't set their course correctly tonight...

Even as his fingers played, and she felt her spine bow, tensing in response to the most exquisite pleasure, even as her wits deserted her, she committed herself to her goal.

But wresting control from him in this sphere was easier thought than done. Every time she tried to focus on him, he distracted her—with a touch, a caress, each laden with such blatant demand, such domineering possessiveness that her mind seized, caught on the cusp of wanting to protest and wanting to savor.

Time and again, savoring won; he steadily swept her into deeper sensual seas, and rather than cavil, she urged him on.

Sebastian hadn't expected anything else; she had instigated this, had climbed naked into his bed and insisted they take this road—here, now—and his inner self had never been of a mind to argue. But even as he indulged his fascination with her breasts, with the superfine skin with a texture that was a cross between peach-silk and satin, even as he finally bowed to his inner demons' ranting, wrenched his lips from hers, bent his head, and tasted one delectable curve, he was conscious of an elusive novelty, of something being different.

He'd been along this road so many times, it was impossible not to notice the deeper thud in his veins, the evidence of something beyond mere desire. With any other woman, such an encounter would have been about nothing beyond pleasure, an appeasement of a mutual desire that, although it might flare hotly, was destined to burn for only a short time.

With Antonia...that quest for pleasure—hers even more than his—remained, but beneath that pulsed another drive, one he recognized as having elements of possessiveness.

Of a need to claim. To brand her as his and no other's.

With a woman, a lady—a noblewoman—like her, thinking in terms of ownership was as futile as it was archaic.

That said...

As he bent his head and took one rosy, tightly puckered nipple into his mouth, licked, laved, then suckled—and she clutched his head and moaned—he was acutely aware of an impulse to mark her, but reined himself back.

He reminded himself she was new to this, and this time, her pleasure would be his first reward.

He set out to claim it—to distract himself from that surging, underlying emotion by reducing her to gasping surrender.

Beneath his expert ministrations, she writhed and clutched. He achieved the gasps, but instead of surrender, those gasps came with increasingly insistent, increasingly explicit demands.

She seemed intent on pushing him, on testing his control. With her hands, with her lips and tongue, with the untutored undulations of her body beneath his, she persisted in driving him on.

Driving him just a little insane.

He didn't realize just how truly enthralling the web of desire she'd cast over him was, not until her greedy, grasping hands slid evocatively down his back, long fingers reaching for the waistband of his silk trousers, but lying as they were, she couldn't quite reach—something he'd made sure of—yet in instinctive response to that unvoiced demand, he rolled to his side and whipped off the offending garment, even as she eagerly thrust aside the sheet, the last barrier screening their hips and legs.

Only then did he remember that they were supposed to be going slowly.

Too late. Even as the thought bloomed in his brain, she hooked a hand around his nape and hauled him into a searing kiss—as she twisted and brought her body and long legs flush against his.

The sudden contact, burning skin to burning skin, sent fire leaping down every vein.

Then their legs were tangling along with their twining tongues, and with blatant provocation and flagrant invitation, she arched against him.

Something in him broke, shattered, then her other hand slid between their hips, and she cradled his erection in her hot palm, then closed her fingers—in incendiary possessiveness and unadulterated demand—about him.

And her conquest was complete.

Not a single thought—not a single glimmer of self-protectiveness, of any need for caution or restraint—remained to deflect the driving need to be inside her. To join with her and ride with her into ecstasy.

He couldn't breathe other than in shallow drafts, and he didn't think she was any better.

Need consumed them, hot and demanding, and they fumbled and shifted and rolled and writhed.

Fire burned wherever they touched; their bodies flamed with near-incandescent passion.

With their lips locked, he raced his hands over her one last time, then he gripped her upper arms, rolled her onto her back, and came up on his elbows over her.

His hips pressed hers to the bed; he had to use his weight to corral her. But her hand hadn't released his erection, and with every caress, she stole his breath, his wits, his very will.

Roughly, he caught first one hand, then the other, then drew back from the kiss long enough to haul her hands over her head and, with one hand, anchor them in the pillows.

Her black hair a silken mass cast over the white pillows, she lifted beneath him, twisting to see.

With his free hand, he caught her chin, drew it down, bent his head, and took her mouth—this time, without the slightest finesse.

Not that she seemed to care; every ounce of demand, of command and scorching hunger he poured into the kiss, into her, she returned in full measure.

Further heating them both.

He'd never in his life felt so consumed, so driven.

But they both needed this, it seemed.

Plundering her mouth, holding her to the kiss, he released her chin and skated his hand over her breast—paused to knead and claim again, first one mound, then the other—then he sent his palm gliding over her desire-dewed skin, tracing a path downward to where a patch of black curls hid the delicate folds of her sex.

He wasn't surprised when she gasped at his first touch, or that she shifted and squirmed as he wedged her thighs open, parted her folds, and learned her secrets.

Antonia's mind felt overwhelmed. So many sensations—so many startlingly new. So much to absorb. But this, this intimate exploration, was something she'd heard of, but had never fully comprehended; she'd never grasped how intensely pleasurable it would be.

His lips remained on hers, languidly supping, and while all but instinctively, she returned the slow caresses, her focus had shifted, registering and recording each glide of his fingers, each stroke, each intimate probing.

Then he circled the nub of flesh at the apex of her thighs, and her nerves sparked, and heightened tension shivered through her.

That tension sank deep, seeming to pool in molten waves in a cavern low in her body.

She'd barely adjusted to the latest sensations, to the sparking pleasure as he touched her just there, when he kissed her more deeply, temporarily deflecting her attention, and with his thumb riding against that nub of sensitive flesh, he slid one long, heavy finger deep into her sheath.

Her nerves leapt. Her senses constricted, locking on the intrusion. She lost all awareness of the world beyond the bed—beyond them, him and her, in the heated darkness.

That he knew what he was doing, she had not a single doubt. In climbing into his bed, she'd already made the decision that she would trust him with her body; she already trusted him with nearly everything else. So she drew breath through the kiss and let him show her—let him open her eyes to the extraordinary pleasures of lovemaking, of such intimate sharing.

And that heated tension—born of need, of hunger and yearning— changed, coalescing into a spiral that constantly shrank, cinching tighter into an ever hotter knot of need that the rhythmic glide of his finger in her sheath only heightened. Tightened.

Then he shifted the hand between her thighs, pressed more firmly with his thumb as he reached deep into her body—and the spiral imploded.

Fractured and shattered.

Her spine bowed, and she cried out—the sound muffled between their lips.

Pleasure—sharp, exquisite, excruciatingly intense—flashed down every nerve, followed almost instantly by a sensation of suffusing heat and a feeling of blessed ease—of release.

She sighed into his mouth, and her spine eased back to the bed. Pleasure and that sudden loss of tension seemed to reach to her toes.

Yet inside, in that heated cavern, she still felt strangely empty.

He drew back from the kiss. She sensed him studying her face.

Her lids were too heavy to lift, but she let her lips curve. "Very nice," she murmured. "For the first course."

He huffed out a laugh that sounded ridiculously breathless.

"So...what's next?"

He dropped his forehead to hers. "You're going to be the death of me."

"*Le petit mort?* I certainly hope so."

He groaned. She realized he was...quivering, his muscles quaking as if they were under enormous strain...

"We don't have to. Not yet. We could wait until later—"

"No. *Now*, Sebastian." Of that, she was quite sure.

She opened her eyes as he shifted, easing to her side. His grip on her wrists loosened, and she slid her hands free and lowered her arms.

He looked into her eyes.

She wondered if he knew his were molten—the usually cool green was anything but. His irises glowed as if banked fires burned inside him.

Despite that, he met her gaze levelly and said, "You're slender, and I'm not. The first time is going to hurt, no matter what. Are you truly sure?"

She didn't bother answering—not with words.

She reached for his erection—and found it as hard as iron. He hissed in a breath and closed his eyes. She ran her fingers up the impressive length, then swiped her thumb wonderingly across the baby-fine skin stretched across the broad head. A pearl of liquid rubbed onto her thumb—and he wrapped his fingers in a brutally tight grip around her wrist.

She didn't release him, but shifted instead, raising one leg and wrapping it about his hip, opening herself to him as she guided his erection to the cleft between her thighs.

He exhaled in a rush, then released her wrist, gripped her hip and her raised thigh, and anchored her as he obliged and eased, slowly, into her channel.

Just a little. Just past her entrance, not enough to breach her.

She caught her breath and let her lids fall as the sensation rolled through her.

His eyes still closed, Sebastian rocked shallowly, savoring the gentle clench of her inner muscles as the scalding slickness of paradise's vestibule coated the head of his erection.

The position wouldn't do to breach her, but it had been her choice, her doing, and he saw no reason not to honor that and allow her to grow more accustomed to the sensation of him entering her body.

But the moment couldn't last long; he couldn't hold back the raging tide of desperate need that crashed and churned inside him.

When he could withstand it no longer—when his body felt aflame—he rolled her fully onto her back, planted his hands palms down on the sheet on either side of her shoulders, braced his arms, and raised his chest.

The movement pushed him deeper into her scalding sheath.

He withdrew as far as her entrance. She didn't tense, expecting him to rock in just a little way.

He locked his gaze on her face, shadowed now as the moonlight had faded—and with one sharp, powerful thrust, seated himself fully in her softness.

She arched and cried out, the sound well-nigh breathless. He saw the spasm of pain that crossed her face—the sight scored him like a blade, and he held still. Desperately fought not to move, battled to hold against the instinct to plunder.

He clung to the sight of her face, watched, waited, and sooner than he'd expected, he saw the tension born of pain fade...

Then she opened her eyes.

The gray orbs, brilliant and bright, stared into his eyes.

Then she smiled.

Not tremulously, but intently.

Then she reached up, dragged his head down to hers, brushed a kiss across his lips, and ordered, "Ride."

She shifted beneath him in blatant invitation.

He'd never before laughed at such a moment in his life, but a bark escaped him even as he did exactly as she wanted.

And at first slowly, but increasingly forcefully, he drove them back into the fire and the flames.

If he'd had any notion she might be a passive lover, she promptly shattered it. Her body rose to his. She quickly caught his rhythm, and then she was riding with him, faster, more urgently, more powerfully, on through their landscape of passion.

Antonia had never dreamt such closeness could be. Had never comprehended what physical intimacy truly entailed. The slide of naked limbs and intimate caresses had been one thing, but the moment when he'd thrust deep and filled her, the sensation of him there, at her core, had branded itself forever on her mind. So alien, so him, so very male. He'd held her trapped, impaled, but he'd hung suspended over her and watched her as if, in that moment, she'd been his entire world.

Now, her heart swelled, and her spirits rejoiced, and they thundered on through a haze of heat and hunger, and passion seared, need soared, and desire thrummed—until ecstasy hove on their horizon.

Her senses had abandoned the world and shrunk to him and her and their joining.

In that moment, nothing else existed but this. Nothing could be so important as this.

This seizing, this claiming, this possession.

His of her, and hers of him.

They were united in that, too. In their commitment, their intention, their unswerving direction.

The tension mounted, stronger, more potent, more intense than before. Now that he'd joined with her, there was an urgency, a building desperation that flayed them and drove them both on, ever on. She clung and sobbed as that unrelenting tension ratcheted thrust by thrust—then abruptly, the world fell away, and she flew.

Her senses imploded in a blaze of white heat and mind-numbing pleasure. Scintillating shards of golden glory flew down her veins and cindered her hold on reality.

For one instant, he held her there, on the cusp of paradise, then on a deep groan, he went rigid in her arms, and she felt the hot spurt of his seed deep within.

Then all tension left him.

As if his arms could no longer hold him, he tumbled down onto her; instinctively, she wrapped her arms around him as far as she could reach and held him.

Pleasure, bone-deep, flooded her, along with a sense of togetherness she hadn't expected. His weight held her trapped, but she didn't mind.

She held him close, shut her eyes, and let the oblivion that hovered just out of her senses' reach rush in and buoy them both on its tide.

\* \* \*

Antonia awoke to find herself lying on her side with Sebastian spooned around her. She vaguely recalled, in the heated depths of the night, that he'd woken, lifted from her, then tugged her sleepy self around so he could cuddle up behind her...

She grinned at the memory.

And the more she recalled, the more success, sweet and very pleasurable, flowed through her veins.

Then she realized she could see—that although the sun was not yet up, pre-dawn light was washing through the window.

She didn't know the rules of conducting a liaison, but she was fairly certain being discovered with Sebastian in his bed by some footman or maid was likely to cause a scandal.

Sebastian's arm lay heavy over her waist. Moving slowly, she eased out from under it, reluctantly shifting away from the heat of his body until she could swing her feet to the floor. She pushed up to sit on the side of the bed.

And felt fingers lock like steel about her wrist.

She glanced over her shoulder and met surprisingly intense pale green eyes.

"You do realize," he rumbled, "that this means we're getting married?"

*Of course.* The words leapt to her tongue; she arched her brows haughtily, but at the last minute, held those particular words back.

Instead, she smiled and let her confidence and assurance fully invest the gesture. Twisting her wrist from his grasp, she patted his naked—still quite fabulous and exceedingly distracting—chest. "Let's leave that discussion for another day."

That, of course, was a red rag to a bull. He immediately pushed up; leaning on one muscled forearm, he narrowed his eyes on her face. "What discussion? Your boldness in..." He paused.

Rising, she looked at him inquiringly. In seducing him? Would he say it?

His eyes narrowed even further, and his face set. "In coming to my room last night means we've leapt over all discussions. There's no longer anything left to discuss."

That was what he thought, arrogant nobleman that he was. But telling him that she wanted him to admit what he felt for her—more than anything else so that she would know he knew—wouldn't get her what she wanted. But given what was at stake, she was willing to be patient. Heaven knew, she'd waited years—more than a decade—to get to this point. What were a few more months if that was what it took to gain everything she'd ever sought in a marriage?

She bent, scooped up her robe, and shook it out. "You're just put out that I took the initiative and filched those particular reins from your grasp." She shrugged on the robe. "As I see it, as matters stand, there's no reason we need to rush into anything—we can safely leave all details until later."

Tying the sash, she flashed him a calm smile, then headed for the door.

Sebastian shook his head. His wits were still not functioning. She was teasing him—wasn't she?

But what the hell did she mean by leaving details until later? Details like a wedding?

He glared at her silk-clad back. Then he realized and called, "Wait."

She swung around and arched a brow.

He kicked off the covers and got out of the bed. "I'll escort you back to your room." He reached for his clothes.

And was grateful that she waited without further comment. Distantly, he could hear the sounds of staff rattling coal scuttles downstairs, but none would have yet ventured upstairs to the bedchambers. Given the only others along their corridor were the newly married Featherstonehaughs, Antonia returning to her room unseen should be straightforward, but still…

Tucking in his shirt, he waved her back and cracked open the door. After confirming the corridor was deserted, he escorted her to her door, waited until she opened it and went in—and with a swift scan over her head, he confirmed there was no one else there.

Who he'd imagined might be waiting, he had no idea—and didn't want to think too much about the impulse that had prompted him to check.

With a curt nod, he left her; he halted along the corridor and waited until he heard her door shut, then returned to his room.

He stood in the room's center and stared at the bed while memories of the night poured through his head.

He grunted, then walked to where he'd left his coat, fished in his pocket, drew out his watch, and opened it.

It was just after five o'clock.

He closed the watch, slipped it back into the pocket, and set about stripping again.

Naked, he tumbled onto the bed. The scent of her—of the herbs in her soap and the elemental perfume of well-loved woman—wreathed through his brain.

He tugged up the covers, closed his eyes, and imagined she was still there, beside him.

After their activities of the night—because of those activities—he needed more sleep if he was to have any hope of coping with her and her machinations, let alone locating the damned gunpowder.

\* \* \*

Safe inside her room, Antonia snuggled down in her bed. She might as well get another hour or two's sleep while creating the impression she'd spent the night there.

Smiling exceedingly smugly, feeling thoroughly pleased with herself and her world, she closed her eyes.

# CHAPTER 11

*A* horrendous scream rent the morning.

Sebastian sat bolt upright. A second, strangled scream reached him; he flung back the covers, leapt from the bed, and hauled on his trousers.

Shrugging on his shirt, he strode to the door, flung it open, and stalked into the corridor. The scream had faded to sobbing whimpers coming from not that far away—on that floor, in the gallery.

He strode rapidly in that direction, hearing voices in the Featherstonehaughs' room as he passed. He turned under the archway and paused.

A maid stood backed against the gallery balustrade, her hands to her face, staring in abject horror through the open door to one of the main bedchambers. She was the source of the whimpers and, presumably, the scream.

A chill touched Sebastian's nape.

He strode forward. Ignoring the maid, who, seeing him approaching, pointed into the room and gibbered, he walked to the open doorway. He halted on the threshold and looked into the room.

As he'd feared, it was Cecilia's bedroom.

From where he stood, he could see only the end of the large bed.

And her feet—one bare, the other with a feathered high-heeled slipper dangling. The other slipper lay on the rug at the foot of the bed.

The hem of a filmy peignoir lay rucked about Cecilia's calves.

Away from the bed, closer to the door, a heavy pewter jug lay rolling on one side, the water it had contained pooling on the floorboards.

The sounds of rushing footsteps, of exclamations and questions, fell on Sebastian's ears, but he blocked out the distraction. He drew in a too-shallow breath, held it, and stepped into the room.

Two paces, and he halted, his gaze riveted by the crumpled doll-like body tossed on the bed.

Cecilia was dead. Her eyes were wide open, staring up at the ceiling; her fair hair was still up in the elaborate French knot she'd favored the previous evening. She was clad in a silk nightgown and the peignoir, both in shades of pink; neither garment hid the bruises circling her throat like some gruesome necklace.

Sebastian exhaled in a quiet rush. Despite her faults, Cecilia had been a lively woman with whom he'd once shared a bed. She hadn't been evil, but evil had come looking for her.

Behind him, the maid was now sobbing freely. He felt cold—chilled—and hollow.

Brusque voices drew nearer; some of the other men entered the room. Like him, they halted just inside the door.

A detached part of his brain noted that the bed was still made; Cecilia's body had been flung on the undisturbed coverlet. There was no sign of a struggle on the counterpane; she'd been dead before she'd been tossed there.

He scanned the room. There was no sign of a struggle anywhere—no rucked rug, nothing disturbed or out of place.

Amid the press of males all uttering horrified exclamations, Sebastian sensed a softer presence slip through the door and draw nearer.

Instinctively, he shifted to block her view, but Antonia gripped his upper arm and held him still. She glanced at the body on the bed, then she looked up at him—briefly studied his face.

Then her fingers slipped into his.

He closed his hand around hers and gripped. Tightly, as if she was his anchor to the world.

Hadley Featherstonehaugh, who had halted, transfixed and aghast, at Sebastian's side, was the first to voice the obvious question. "What should we do?"

Drawn back to reality by the feel of Antonia's fingers in his, Sebastian hauled in a deeper, freer breath and stated, "We send for the doctor. And we send word to Sir Humphrey's house and summon Inspector Crawford."

* * *

Sebastian stood before the fireplace in the estate office and stared at the flames leaping in the grate. "I didn't kill her." His tone was flat, emotionless; he honestly wasn't sure what he felt.

Crawford humphed. "At least, this time, you weren't the one who found the body."

"Could the maid tell you anything?" Antonia asked.

Sebastian glanced at her. She was sitting in one of the chairs before the desk behind which the inspector and Sir Humphrey sat.

The two men had arrived several hours ago. They'd consulted with the doctor, who had been waiting to make his report before continuing with his day. Then magistrate and policeman had been waylaid by several of the guests, with whom they'd briefly spoken. Subsequently, they'd examined the scene and talked with a number of the staff. When, eventually, Crawford and Sir Humphrey had come into the drawing room, where all the guests had gathered after a hurried breakfast, they had made a general statement that they intended to interview everyone again, then they'd asked to speak with Sebastian. He'd pushed away from the mantelpiece against which he'd been leaning and joined the two men, and Antonia had risen and walked with them into the front hall.

When he'd turned to her, intending to insist she remain with the others, she'd been waiting to catch his eye. With a very definite challenge in hers.

Instead of imposing his will, he'd cravenly surrendered; he hadn't been up to fighting himself as well as her. Neither Sir Humphrey nor the inspector—both of whom had taken in that brief but wordless exchange— had ventured to try to dissuade or deny her.

In reply to her question, Sir Humphrey snorted. "Silly female keeps dissolving into hysterics, but in between, we got out of her that she'd opened the door to take in her mistress's washing water, saw Lady Ennis as we found her, dropped the jug, screamed, and backed out of the room." Sir Humphrey raised his gaze to Sebastian. "She said you were the first to arrive."

Sebastian nodded. "Her first scream woke me. Unsurprisingly, I rushed to see what had happened."

"Who was the next to arrive?" Crawford asked.

Sebastian frowned. "I'm not sure—I was transfixed by the body—but it might have been Featherstonehaugh." He drew breath and exhaled. "I heard his voice as I passed their room on the way to the gallery, and Cecilia's room is closer to the east wing, where our rooms—mine, the Featherstonehaughs', and Lady Antonia's—are."

"When I arrived"—Antonia's voice was calm and composed—"most of the men were already there. Mr. Parrish and Mr. McGibbin were just going into the room, and Mr. Boyne followed me in. The women were still arriving, but most stayed in the gallery."

The inspector grunted. He read through the notes before him, then glanced sidelong at Sir Humphrey.

Antonia watched the magistrate and the inspector exchange a long glance—some wordless communication—then Sir Humphrey grimaced faintly. He shifted, then clasped his hands on the desk and looked at Sebastian—who was, once again, staring at the flames.

Sir Humphrey cleared his throat, then said, "It's been suggested—not an accusation, mind, but merely a mention—that, on the face of things, you, Lord Earith, might be seen as the most likely suspect for both murders."

Antonia watched as a curious—quite menacing—stillness stole over Sebastian's tall frame. Then, slowly, he turned his head and looked at Sir Humphrey.

For long enough for Sir Humphrey's normally ruddy complexion to pale.

Then Sebastian blinked, slowly, his long lashes momentarily screening his piercingly pale green eyes, and in a tone of voice that reminded any who heard it just who and what he was, he quietly asked, "On what grounds?"

The inspector darted a glance Antonia's way. "The motive appears somewhat hazy."

"Indeed?" Sebastian's diction—clipped, hard, and rigidly even—was the equivalent of a screamed warning to any who knew him. He straightened and took two prowling steps to stand behind the vacant chair facing the desk—the better to fix both Sir Humphrey and the inspector with his intimidating gaze.

Antonia knew perfectly well what motive had been mooted, and knew he knew it, too. But he would put Sir Humphrey and the inspector through a metal-spiked wringer before allowing his long-ago liaison with Cecilia to be mentioned in such a context—and they didn't have time for such distractions. She fixed her gaze on the inspector and, her own voice even but considerably lighter in tone, asked, "Did the doctor give you an estimate of when—what time—Lady Ennis was killed?"

From the corner of her eye, she saw Sebastian's eyes widen fractionally, then he turned his intimidating look on her.

She ignored it and kept her gaze on the inspector.

Faintly puzzled but willing—anything to ease the oppressive tension in the room—Crawford hurriedly consulted his notes. "It seems clear that her ladyship was killed in the hours after she retired. She summoned her maid at about half past ten o'clock, and the maid left her mistress sitting at her dressing table at eleven o'clock—the clocks were striking the hour as the maid left. The doctor has declared that her ladyship was murdered sometime in the following three hours."

"So between eleven o'clock and two o'clock in the morning." Antonia arched her brows. "In that case—"

"Antonia..." Sebastian's warning growl, gritted out through clenched teeth, held overtones of disbelief.

Unperturbed, she continued, "Earith couldn't possibly have murdered her ladyship. Throughout those hours, he was with me—or rather, I was with him, in his room, and I would definitely have noticed if he'd left."

Silence greeted her pronouncement—as if all three men couldn't quite believe she'd said what she had. Crawford stared at her. Sir Humphrey blinked several times and looked increasingly uncomfortable and unable to decide where to look—at her or Sebastian or the desk.

As for Sebastian, she could feel his gaze locked on the side of her face. She was about to glance his way when he gripped the back of the chair in front of him, straightened to his full height, and faced the other two men. "Lady Antonia and I are unofficially betrothed."

She managed to stop her reaction from showing—her eyebrows from flying upward.

When Antonia glanced at him, Sebastian met her gaze levelly. He felt curiously calm—as if stating the truth aloud had been somehow freeing. Settling.

It had certainly given his inner self an unanticipated degree of satisfaction.

He held her gray gaze, daring her to attempt any contradiction; she briefly searched his face, his eyes, then her fine brows faintly arched, and she turned back to the inspector and Sir Humphrey and let the statement lie unchallenged.

*Thank God.* Given the cauldron of emotions the current situation had stirred inside him, he wasn't sure how he might react if she attempted to argue.

He refocused his attention on the inspector and Sir Humphrey. "To have two murders committed in the same household in the space of little more than twenty-four hours...it's hard to avoid the conclusion that the murders are connected. It's possible whoever murdered Ennis feared he had shared something with his wife, enough for her to prove a potential threat. And so her ladyship was silenced, too."

Crawford was happy to move on. "I agree—that is, indeed, the most likely scenario."

"As to that," Antonia said, "when the company was going up the stairs last night, Cecilia seemed...anxious, even nervous, over something. We all heard her." Antonia glanced up at Sebastian.

He met her gaze and nodded. To the inspector and Sir Humphrey, he said, "She spoke of escaping this place. She claimed it was the atmosphere, but..." He shrugged. "I felt she was bothered over something, but also playing some sort of role."

Antonia added, "I thought she seemed frightened, but it was an amorphous fear—as if she suspected one of the company of murdering Ennis, but didn't know who—which one—it was."

Sir Humphrey tugged at his ear lobe. "That she was frightened suggests she had reason to imagine the murderer might come after her."

"True." Sebastian let go of the chair, rounded it, and sat. "It's possible she didn't know who the killer was but had guessed what motive lay behind Ennis's murder, and knew, therefore, that the murderer might suspect she knew enough of the plot to also pose a threat to him. Regardless, she didn't suspect the man who murdered her. There was no sign of any struggle. She was taken entirely unawares." He paused, then arched his brows. "Much as with Ennis. Neither he nor Cecilia felt threatened by the murderer until he struck."

"Very well." Crawford looked down at his jottings. "The murderer is a man—no woman could have strangled her ladyship, not with their bare hands, as was done. So who among the male guests remain on our list of suspects?" The inspector looked at Sebastian, then at Antonia. "Could any of the other men have been…involved with her ladyship?"

Antonia glanced at Sebastian. "I saw nothing that made me think so."

Sebastian looked at Sir Humphrey. "It's possible, but I wasn't specifically watching for signs of it."

"You might try asking the older ladies—Mrs. Parrish and Mrs. McGibbin," Antonia said. "If Lady Ennis had had a lover among the guests, they are more likely to have noticed. However, those ladies' husbands would have to go on your list of possibles—with the Ennises, the Parrishes, and the McGibbins, husbands and wives have separate rooms." She paused, then added, "The only men you can strike from your list are Earith and Mr. Featherstonehaugh. Hadley and Georgia are newlyweds, and Georgia would certainly know if Hadley crept out, quite aside from him not being that way inclined."

Sir Humphrey cleared his throat. "Just so." He glanced at the list the inspector had compiled. "That leaves us with rather a lot of possibles for the positions of murderer and her ladyship's lover."

"And," Sebastian added dryly, "the murderer and her lover could be one and the same."

Antonia blinked. "Actually, there's something we've forgotten to mention." She glanced at Sebastian. "In the conservatory yesterday evening, we overheard Filbury and Wilson speaking with Cecilia—we were out of sight, and they assumed they were speaking in private. This was a little before we all retired."

Crawford looked keen; he leaned forward. "What was said?"

Antonia frowned, clearly trying to recall.

Sebastian couldn't help her; his recollection of those moments had been largely overwritten by more vivid memories of the taste of her lips, the feel of her in his arms.

"They—the two men—were asking about the Irish estate." Antonia glanced at him; he met her gaze and fractionally shook his head. Apparently realizing he couldn't remember, she looked at Crawford and went on, "They couched their queries in terms of being friends of the family and friends of Connell. In essence, they wanted to know if there was anything going on there—on the estate—to cause concern. Cecilia didn't seem to know of anything amiss."

"So..." Sir Humphrey narrowed his eyes. "Filbury and Wilson could simply have been asking as concerned friends, as they claimed, or they might have been sounding out her ladyship to see what she knew of...whatever this is that's going on, which seems somehow connected with Ireland."

"Exactly." Antonia nodded.

After a moment, Crawford sighed and closed his notebook. "If only Lady Ennis had told us what she'd suspected, she might still be alive."

Sebastian stared at the inspector for a moment, then grimaced. "In defense of her ladyship, there might not have been time. I think her suspicions evolved through the day—the longer she thought about her husband's murder."

Crawford grunted, but acknowledged the point with a nod. "We're going to be busy all day here, interviewing everyone again—all of the guests and then all of the staff, one by one. If luck comes our way, we might find one of the staff—either those of the household or those visiting—who glimpsed one of the male guests slipping through the corridors. That said, the way these cases tend to go, I won't be holding my breath. No one ever seems to witness the murderers moving back and forth."

Sir Humphrey looked questioningly at Sebastian. "Any luck with your search for this gunpowder?"

"No." He glanced at the magistrate. "But we did find four very old casks, most likely of brandy, hidden in the crypt of the old ruined chapel."

"Did you, by Jove!" Sir Humphrey looked enthused. "Any good?"

Sebastian suppressed a wry grin. "I've yet to tell Blanchard. No doubt he'll send a couple of footmen to retrieve the casks. However, the find made me wonder if there might be other hidden places—or perhaps a secret tunnel connecting the house to caves or even to the shore. Pressingstoke Hall isn't that far from the sea, and this has been a smuggler's coast for centuries." He fixed Sir Humphrey with an inquiring look. "I've heard that was often the way with old houses in this area in times past, but I checked this morning, and there was no hidden place or tunnel marked on the house plans, even on the older iterations."

"Ah." Sir Humphrey tapped the side of his nose. "But there wouldn't be anything marked on the plans—wouldn't be a secret then, what? But indeed, you're right. While what's around us"—with one hand, he waved at the walls surrounding them—"is relatively new, it's built on a much older base, one dating from an age when having a secret tunnel into a cave system at least, if not directly to the shore, was the norm."

The inspector looked intrigued. "Wouldn't the finding of casks in this crypt suggest there wasn't such a tunnel?"

"Not necessarily," Sir Humphrey said. "Two different routes for two different levels of involvement. If the master of the house was dealing directly with the smugglers, the secret tunnel and the caves it accessed would be used. But if the master wasn't involved, then the casks left in the crypt are the smugglers' payment for him looking the other way. That's how the system worked in these parts."

Sebastian pulled a face and uncrossed his legs. "Regardless, we've found no hint or trace of anything resembling barrels of gunpowder inside the house or in the grounds. We'll need to expand our search to the rest of the estate."

He rose, and Antonia smoothly came to her feet.

Crawford and Sir Humphrey rose as well.

Sebastian nodded to them both. "If you need us, we'll be riding over the fields, quartering the estate from the western edge to the coast."

Crawford glanced at Sir Humphrey. "We'd better get on interviewing the rest. One of the men has to be our murderer—we just have to find clues enough to point to him."

"We'll leave you to it." Sebastian took Antonia's elbow.

"Gentlemen." With a nod to Sir Humphrey and the inspector, she let him escort her to the door.

\* \* \*

Antonia changed into her riding habit, then joined Sebastian at the side door; he'd already been wearing buckskin breeches and riding boots, topped with a soft linen shirt and a hacking jacket. A plain cravat completed the outfit; he might have been the model for what the fashionable marquess was wearing this year for riding about the countryside.

"So where are we heading first?" She stepped through the door he held for her, then, tugging on her gloves, walked briskly down the path toward the stable.

He fell in at her side, striding with long-legged ease; it occurred to her that the shock of Cecilia's murder had leapfrogged them—her and Sebastian—over the awkwardness she'd assumed would attend their first meeting after being intimate.

They'd been plunged into dealing with the ramifications of the murder and, of course, instantly—without the slightest hesitation on either of their parts—had banded together to face the situation.

"Before we get to that"—his voice was a deep murmur, but his tone was definite enough to be one step away from invincible—"I should make clear that, as far as I'm concerned, all that I told Sir Humphrey and Crawford about us—you and me—is the simple, unvarnished, and inviolable truth."

She considered that—considered how she wished to respond—then briskly nodded. "Duly noted."

From the corner of her eye, she saw his expression fleetingly register complete bafflement, then his features hardened, and he shot a glance brimming with suspicion her way. She pretended not to notice; only her excellent training allowed her to keep her grin from her face.

They reached the stable yard, and he asked for their mounts of yesterday to be saddled. Had it been only yesterday? It seemed longer; so much had happened in such a short time.

She'd appropriated the map of the estate they'd found and had made a rough copy on a smaller sheet; she drew it from her pocket and unfolded it. Studying it, she tried to estimate the area they had to cover. "Where to first?"

He came to look over her shoulder. After a moment, he grunted. "North or south. We can't effectively do both in what's left of today."

It was already late morning.

She turned as he fished a coin from his breeches pocket.

He tossed the coin, caught it, slapped it onto his wrist, and covered it with his palm. "Heads, we search north. Tails, we look to the south."

He lifted his hand.

She leaned nearer to peer at the coin. "Tails." She straightened and looked southward.

"I meant search the southern half of the estate." He turned as, with hooves clopping, the horses were brought out. "We'll go west to the road, then zigzag over the southern half of the estate and return via the coastal path, stopping at all possible hiding places we come upon."

She steeled herself to weather the sensual jolt as he grasped her waist and hoisted her to her saddle—as if she weighed very little, which she knew was not the case. She was pleased to discover that, although the thrill to her senses was still there, the discombobulation had faded; her wits remained hers to command.

The instant he'd swung up to his saddle, she shook the chestnut's reins and led the way out of the yard—but then had to wait for him to set their course, which he did by taking the lead on the large, raw-boned gray. She urged her mare up to keep pace, riding to the side and half a length behind—sufficiently to the rear to respond to any change in direction he made. Although she suspected her map-reading skills were superior to his, he had a landowner's sense of north, south, east, and west; he led them unerringly west, toward the road linking Deal with Dover that formed the estate's western boundary.

But as they rode, they zigged and zagged, stopping at barns and sheds to search.

At the third such stop, when they emerged from a shed having found no sign of any barrels, she halted and glanced up at the sky—at the sun moving steadily west behind the scudding clouds. "I wonder what the others will think of us being allowed to ride out freely even after Cecilia's murder." She glanced at Sebastian as he halted beside her. "You don't think it'll mark us as working with the authorities—especially to the murderer?"

His gaze scanning the fields before them, he considered, then shook his head. "Even now, I think their first assumption will be that I—and you, too—are pulling rank, purely to get out of the house. After all, if we insisted on riding, what could Sir Humphrey or Crawford do to stop us? The others know we haven't left, and as for the murderer, although he has no doubt guessed that I was the one Ennis intended to speak with, as apparently Ennis was dead before I found him, there's no sense in the murderer risking showing his hand by attempting to silence me." He met her gaze. "As I learned nothing from Ennis, I can't be a threat. Unlike poor Cecilia, who Ennis might have confided in."

She humphed and tried to stifle a persistent sense of unease—not on her account but on his.

He gestured to their horses, and she walked beside him to where they'd tethered their mounts to the branches of a stunted tree.

"Still," she persevered, "I can't help feeling that the company at large might start to question your purpose in being here. Our excuse—that you're here as my father-decreed escort—while acceptable, is hardly unshakably convincing."

He lifted her to her saddle. As he swung up to his, he slanted an amused glance her way. "After the events of yesterday evening and this morning, I believe my presence here will have been adequately explained to all. Far from imagining I'm here pursuing some intrigue, I'd wager the question exercising Mrs. Parrish's and Mrs. McGibbin's minds will be whether your father knows I'm here with you at all."

She humphed and turned the chestnut's head once more to the west. "Our relationship—our connection—is not that obvious, and I'm sure

Wilson and Filbury are gentlemen enough to be discreet."

His expression stated he thought she was indulging in fantasy, but he said nothing more, just nudged the gray into the lead again.

But when next they stopped—at a hayshed—and he lifted her down, he said, "You need to remember that all those remaining at Pressingstoke Hall know me only by repute. Not even Cecilia knew I know Drake beyond a nodding acquaintance. You know otherwise. You also know Drake. But for most of the haut ton, let alone wider society, there's no reason for anyone to suspect that the Marquess of Earith might occasionally undertake missions for Winchelsea and his Home Office masters."

She considered that as they circled the hayshed, then checked inside. And some of her nebulous anxiety faded.

After concluding that there was nothing concealed among the bales of hay, they walked back to the horses.

She halted by the mare's side and faced him. "How occasionally do you work for Drake?"

He lifted her to her saddle, then shrugged as he turned and gathered the gray's reins. "A few times a year." He mounted, then widened his eyes at her. "But of course, the sons of dukes can't ever be even *vaguely* associated with anything like work."

She grinned at his tone. Then he wheeled the gray, and she followed him on.

They reached the Deal-Dover road at the village of Ringwould and stopped at the inn, the Five Bells, for lunch. While seated at a table in the corner of the tap and consuming portions of an excellent rabbit pie, they debated the wisdom of asking the locals about any recent smuggler-like activity and decided against it.

Sebastian grimaced and concluded, "It's too difficult to clarify exactly what we're asking about."

To Antonia's mind, it was simply too risky; people asking about smugglers on this coast...she'd heard too many tales. "Besides, we aren't really concerned with the mechanism by which the gunpowder got here but rather with the stuff itself."

His eyes on his plate, Sebastian nodded. "True." He swallowed. "And even if they know something, they won't tell us—neither of us are locals."

After finishing their meal, they mounted up again and, this time, swept south, riding a few hundred yards inside the boundary and diverting to search any building they spotted.

They halted at two cottages, and Sebastian used his title as license to search the associated sheds and barns—to no avail.

After searching two more haysheds, they reached the estate's southern boundary and swung east toward the coast. They came upon three abandoned huts and an isolated ruin of a cottage, but none of the structures held barrels of anything.

Eventually, with the sun sliding down the western sky and the clouds massing more thickly overhead, they reached the coast just north of the next village. The tide was out, and the increasingly brisk wind set narrow white crests rearing on the gray-green waves. A bridle path meandered along the edge of the cliffs; they turned their horses' heads to the north and cantered along the path, scanning both the sands below and the nearby fields.

Again, they turned aside to search cottages, barns, and sheds; again, they found nothing. The sands at the base of the cliffs along which they rode remained smooth and unmarred.

Drawing rein at a point he judged to be level with Pressingstoke Hall, Sebastian studied the pale sands. "It looks like the tide comes up high enough to wash away any signs of activity on the beach." He looked northward along the cliffs. "If tomorrow we find nothing on the northern half of the estate, we'll try riding along the beach. There'll be caves in the cliffs, but whether we'll come upon the right one, much less that there'll be anything there to find…who knows?"

Beside him on her chestnut, Antonia shrugged. "If we find nothing tomorrow, it'll be worth a try."

While they continued northward, keeping to the bridle path, Sebastian pondered the likelihood of caves and how best to address that. They spotted two more haysheds and turned aside to search them, but there was nothing to be found amid the tightly packed bales.

The day was closing in. He halted the gray above a steep dip where the bridle path dropped to cross a tiny lane that led all the way down to the sands. On the other side of the lane, there was a scattering of cottages built on a narrow rocky shelf that jutted out from the base of the cliff.

Folding his hands on the pommel, he revisited their strategy. "Gunpowder. Here." He could still hear Ennis's strained voice gasping the words. "What precisely did Ennis mean? Was the gunpowder already here—or was it going to be brought here sometime in the future?" He glanced at Antonia; she had halted the chestnut alongside the gray. "Is gunpowder here now? Or is it on its way here, or was it here last week or earlier, but even when Ennis died, had it already been moved on? Or did Ennis mean something else entirely by the word 'here'?"

She met his eyes, then shook her head and looked out at the pristine, wave-washed sands. "There's no way we can tell and no benefit in speculating. All we can do is what we're doing—searching everywhere we can think of to at least confirm that the gunpowder is, as far as we can tell, not in Ennis's house or on his estate. At least, not at this time."

He thought through her words, then grimly nodded. "You're right. And if we find no trace here in the next few days, we'll take what we know back to London and hope Drake's returned so he can decide where next to search—or what next to do."

The chestnut shifted. Acting instinctively, she settled the horse, then said, "Would it be better to leave and go back to London immediately?" She met his gaze. "Even if Drake's not back, you or your father—or Drake's—could find out who to contact in the Home Office."

He considered that, then slowly shook his head. "Crawford and Sir Humphrey will hold those at the house party at Pressingstoke Hall as long as they can in the hope of identifying the murderer. Crawford is thorough—there's a good chance he'll flush the beggar out. If he does, then assuming we don't find the gunpowder ourselves, learning the identity of the murderer and all he knows of the plot will be our best route to locating the stuff."

Elucidating his thoughts aloud confirmed their logic. He glanced at her, saw her agreement in the set of her features, smiled faintly, and turned the gray's head for the house. "It's starting to get dark. We'd better get back."

She nodded and wheeled the chestnut. "And tomorrow we'll search the northern half of the estate—assuming we don't ride in and discover that Sir Humphrey and the inspector have the murderer by the collar."

# CHAPTER 12

*T*hey clattered into the stable yard with the shadows deepening and discovered Inspector Crawford seated on the mounting block.

He rose and stretched, then waited while Sebastian dismounted, lifted Antonia down, and the stable lads gathered their reins. As the boys led the horses away, Sebastian and Antonia turned to the inspector.

Crawford tipped his head toward the house. "My lord, my lady—if you would walk with me a little way, I'd like to pick your brains."

Antonia shot Sebastian a questioning look, but when he just took her hand and wound her arm in his, she fell in beside him.

With Crawford pacing on Sebastian's other side, they strolled to a point halfway back to the house where the rising slope and a stand of trees combined to screen them from the windows.

Crawford halted and faced them. "I take it your search wasn't successful."

"No." Sebastian's reply was colored by his frustration. "But we've yet to search the northern half of the estate. We'll do that tomorrow. If we find nothing...we might well have to rely on the murderer for further information."

Crawford's brows rose. "Do you think he'll talk?"

"Eventually."

Crawford eyed Sebastian's face for a second, then plainly decided to let that subject go.

"Did you find the money?" Antonia asked. "The three hundred

pounds."

"No." Crawford glanced at Sebastian. "The search went well enough—we searched all the gents' rooms and those of the visiting staff, and none of them the wiser, but came up empty-handed." Crawford looked at Antonia. "So we used your suggestion to get the gents to turn out their pockets, but no one was carrying any roll of banknotes."

Sebastian grimaced. "It was worth a try." He paused, then in a more pensive tone added, "So where has the money gone?"

His expression tending grim, Crawford nodded. "I've been wondering how much gunpowder is worth."

"But if the money's been handed over"—Antonia met Sebastian's eyes—"doesn't that mean the gunpowder is here—somewhere near?"

Sebastian's expression hardened, and he nodded. "Or at least it was. And that line of thinking confirms that the murderer—who must have taken the money from Ennis—is also the person involved in this plot. The person dealing with the gunpowder." He focused on the inspector. "Are you any closer to identifying the murderer?"

Crawford sighed. "That was why I was waiting for you two. I wanted to discuss with you both"—the inspector included Antonia with his gaze—"the matter of alibis. All the guests have alibis of sorts for Ennis's murder, but only a few guests have alibis for her ladyship's murder. Yet the simple truth is that, other than the pair of you and the Featherstonehaughs, none of the other guests *can* have any reasonable alibi for the second murder—they were all in their beds in their separate rooms, all supposedly alone. So we're back to focusing on who had the chance—the opportunity—to murder Lord Ennis. Sir Humphrey suggested I run the gentlemen's alibis past the pair of you in the hope you'll see something neither of us have."

Sebastian nodded and settled to listen.

Crawford tugged his notebook from his pocket. "If we assume that the murders were committed by the same person—and, please God, that's true—then the one thing we can take from her ladyship's murder is that the murderer is a man. So we're concentrating on the alibis of the men—and that the ladies all had solid alibis for Lord Ennis's murder only underscores that our approach is correct. The murderer must be one of the male guests." Crawford glanced at Sebastian.

Again, Sebastian nodded. "That conclusion seems inescapable. I can't see Cecilia, dressed as she was, opening her door and admitting a male servant. Whoever strangled her was a gentleman she knew—ergo, one of the male guests."

"Indeed." Crawford flicked open his notebook. He leafed through several pages, then tapped his finger on an entry. "Here we are—the alibis of the male guests for the time of Lord Ennis's murder. To remind you, my lord, other than yourself and Lord Ennis, there are seven male guests to account for, and the period in question is quite short—from roughly half past nine to ten o'clock. For argument's sake, let's say that Ennis left the dining room at nine thirty and, as he'd intimated, went straight to his study. We have no reports from anyone of seeing him anywhere else. So Ennis was in his study by, say, nine thirty-two. Next, McGibbin, Worthington, Filbury, and Wilson left the dining room for the billiards room. According to McGibbin, that was at nine forty.

"McGibbin and Worthington went straight to the billiards room—passing the study on the way. According to the pair of them, the study door was closed. They stayed in the billiards room, chatting and waiting for the other two. According to McGibbin and Worthington, neither of them left the billiards room until the ruckus when you found Ennis dead."

The inspector paused to turn over a page. "Filbury and Wilson, however, did not go directly to the billiards room. They parted from McGibbin and Worthington in the front hall—and this is where things get interesting.

"According to Filbury and Wilson, they paused to chat near the gun room. They saw Boyne—who we'll come to in a moment—go into the library, but they don't think he saw them, and Boyne said he didn't. Filbury and Wilson then went out through the door onto the rear terrace and so down onto the lawn. There, they smoked cheroots, but they didn't remain together. Wilson says he went off to wander through the rose garden—apparently the design of such places is of interest to him—while Filbury says he ambled slowly around the lawns to the western side of the house. As you're no doubt aware, my lord, there's a small porch and an external door to the billiards room—Filbury, and later Wilson, entered the billiards room through that door, joining Worthington and McGibbin. Of necessity, both Filbury and Wilson passed Ennis's study window, but apparently neither noticed whether it was open or not. Neither of them heard anything, either." Crawford humphed. "Worthington, McGibbin, Filbury, and Wilson then started their game of billiards, and it was some time later—between five and ten minutes, they all say—that you raised the alarm."

Crawford glanced up. "So that's those four." He turned another page and went on, "The next gentleman to leave the dining room, virtually on the earlier four's heels, was Boyne. He says he went into the library, to the far end, sat in an armchair, and settled to read a book. Filbury and Wilson saw him enter the room, more or less at the time he says he did. Later, Parrish and Featherstonehaugh came into the library and saw him in the armchair at the far end, reading. They joined him and spoke with him for several minutes before the alarm was raised. According to Boyne, he remained in the chair in the library the whole time."

Sebastian shifted his weight. His eyes narrowed, his gaze distant, he said, "I left the dining room a minute or so after Boyne. I didn't see him, but if he'd gone into the library, I wouldn't have. I did glimpse Filbury and Wilson strolling down the passage alongside the gun room—they looked to be heading for the door to the rear terrace, which fits with what they said." He paused, then frowned. "When Filbury and Wilson went out onto the rear terrace, they should have been able to see Boyne walking down the library—if they happened to glance that way and the curtains hadn't been drawn." Sebastian met Crawford's eyes. "You might ask Filbury and Wilson if they noticed Boyne in the library."

Crawford nodded and made a note in the back of his notebook.

"I paused in the front hall and checked the time," Sebastian went on. "It was just coming up to nine forty-five. I didn't want to get caught in any conversation with the other guests—I didn't want to have to excuse myself at ten o'clock and indirectly call attention to my meeting with Ennis. So I went out of the front door and onto the front terrace—the stretch that runs beside the drawing room. There was no one in the drawing room—the ladies were in the music room—so I knew no one would spot me and come to chat. I waited on the terrace. It was quiet outside...and, now I think of it, I heard the billiards room door open and shut twice—that must have been Filbury and Wilson returning, one after the other. That was only a few minutes before I returned inside. I waited until nine fifty-eight, then went in via the front door. I walked down the front hall, into the side corridor, and so to the study."

He paused, letting the memories roll through his mind. "While I was in the front hall, I remember hearing the ladies in the music room, and then Blanchard walked out through the servants' door, pushing the tea trolley. He saw me and nodded, then went on to the music room. I turned into the corridor leading to the study. The clocks started to whirr...but underneath that, I remember hearing the murmur of men's voices as I walked along the corridor—that must have been Boyne, Featherstonehaugh, and Parrish in the library. Then the clocks chimed the hour. I reached the study door—which was ajar—as the last chime was fading. I heard the clink of billiard balls—the door to the billiards room is at the end of that corridor, and the door was open, but from where I stood outside the study door, I couldn't see anyone in the billiards room."

Crawford had been scribbling madly. He paused and looked at what he'd written. "That's a good bit more detail than you mentioned before, but it all fits with where everyone else says they were." He flicked back to his earlier notes. "The only others to account for are Parrish and Featherstonehaugh, who had remained in the dining room. Parrish says they finally got up from the table at about five minutes to ten and ambled into the library. They saw Boyne sitting in an armchair at the far end of the room and walked down and started chatting. They were still chatting when all hell broke loose—and that fits with what you said."

Antonia looked from the inspector to Sebastian, then back again. "So where does that leave us?" The inspector was starting to look a trifle worn down.

Crawford scratched his temple with the end of his pencil, then sighed. "If we discard any notion of conspiracy and agree this is all just one man, one murderer with no help from anyone else, then there are three men who might have done it—three who were out of sight of any others for long enough during the critical time. But even for those three, it would have been tight. Very tight." Crawford glanced at Sebastian. "I had another chat with the doctor. Sound man—ex-army. I asked how long he thought Ennis might have hung on after he was stabbed and fell. The doctor's estimate was five minutes—seven at the very outside."

Sebastian narrowed his eyes. "That leaves us with Filbury, Wilson, and Boyne as potential candidates for the role of murderer."

Crawford nodded. "Either Filbury or Wilson could have doubled back, returned through that rear terrace door near the gun room, then gone to the study. There was a decent window of time for either of them to have done that, when none of you others were in the front hall. Then they stabbed Ennis, left through the study window, and joined the others in the billiards room—and that's the one scenario that gives a purpose to that open window." He shuffled through his notes. "Boyne...he had time to come out of the library and go to the study, but it's harder to see how he could have returned to the library in time. Even going out through the window and in again through that rear terrace door, he would have had to avoid crossing paths with Wilson and Filbury as they headed to the billiards room, or being seen by Featherstonehaugh and Parrish as they left the dining room." Crawford shook his head. "It's difficult to see how he might have managed it, time-wise."

Sebastian grimaced. "All three are Anglo-Irish, and all three spend a good part of their time in Ireland. There's also that snippet of conversation we overheard in the conservatory—Filbury and Wilson asking about conditions on Ennis's Irish estate."

"Sir Humphrey and I tried to ask them about that." Crawford's expression hardened. "Let's just say, both were evasive. They certainly didn't want to reveal, much less discuss, whatever the matter giving rise to that conversation was."

Antonia studied Sebastian's frowning expression and the inspector's puzzled face. She cleared her throat. "I hesitate to mention it, but there's one other possible candidate for the role of murderer—someone from outside who came to the house in secret. Ennis was expecting him"—she looked at Sebastian—"perhaps as a part of his revelations to you. Ennis opened the window and let this man in. Having learned that Ennis was preparing to speak to the authorities, the man killed Ennis, then escaped via the window."

Crawford shot her a glum, distinctly unhappy look.

"No." Still frowning, Sebastian shook his head. "It can't have been that."

Crawford perked up. "Why not?"

"Because while that neatly accounts for Ennis's murder, a mysterious man from outside the house party can't account for Cecilia's murder." Sebastian grimaced and met Crawford's gaze. "Not unless you're willing to entertain the possibility of two different murderers."

Crawford groaned. "Heaven help us—no." He closed his notebook and tucked it back inside his coat. "One murderer is bad enough. No need to imagine a second."

Sebastian grunted. "I agree."

Antonia had been picturing where all the men had been, like a play on a stage with characters moving here and there. "Of our three men who might be guilty, Connell Boyne was out of sight of anyone else for the longest period of time."

Crawford nodded. "True. But he's also the one it's hardest to see being able to stab Ennis in the study late enough to fit the doctor's timetable, then get back to where he was seen several minutes before Lord Earith here raised the alarm." The inspector grimaced. "He's Ennis's brother, too—not that that makes him any less likely as the murderer, sad to say."

"As to that," Antonia said, "another possibility we haven't properly canvassed is whether the motive for these murders is something quite other." She looked at Sebastian. "Something not in any way linked to Ennis's message for Winchelsea."

Both Sebastian and the inspector stared at her impassively.

Then Crawford heaved another sigh. "And that's entirely possible, too."

Sebastian snorted. "If it comes to that, Blanchard could have done the deed. He—or any of the staff—had as much opportunity as any of the guests."

Crawford nodded. "I'll be interviewing the staff again tomorrow. We'll see where that gets us."

"We can discount the obvious other motive," Sebastian said. "Ennis had at least one son, so his heir isn't his brother, Connell, so the inheritance can't be a motive in these murders."

"There are two sons," Antonia put in. "Cecilia mentioned they were at boarding school."

"Poor tykes. They haven't been told yet," Crawford said. "Sir Humphrey is getting Ennis's solicitor down tomorrow, and we're hoping he can take on the estate for the moment. Until we free Connell Boyne of suspicion in his brother's murder, no matter the motive, it isn't appropriate for him to take up the reins."

Crawford looked at Sebastian, then at Antonia. "Sir Humphrey and I would appreciate it if you both could keep your eyes on our three prime suspects. It's possible that our villain will let something slip when he's in what he deems less threatening company."

Antonia added her agreement to Sebastian's, then Crawford nodded politely, and they parted—the inspector heading back down to the stable while, arm in arm, she and Sebastian continued to the house.

\* \* \*

Sebastian and Antonia entered the house with just enough time to bathe and dress for dinner.

They met in the corridor outside their rooms and descended to the drawing room side by side. Once inside the room, they halted. Both surveyed the subdued company, then they met each other's eyes and, in wordless accord, separated.

Antonia strolled to join the ladies gathered on the sofas before the fireplace. A roaring blaze sent heat into the room, but seemed unable to lift the chill from the company's collective spirits. Mrs. McGibbin and Mrs. Parrish looked much older tonight; they sat with their heads together, conversing in murmurs. Amelie Bilhurst, quiet but holding her own, sat beside Melinda Boyne and was patently attempting to keep Melinda's spirits up, a task at which she wasn't succeeding all that well; Melinda looked...spooked.

Antonia wondered if Melinda—a Boyne, after all—knew anything about the murders. Or anything that might shed some light on who the murderer might be.

But Claire, Melissa, and Georgia, all with somber expressions on their faces, were waiting to draw Antonia down to sit on the arm of the sofa the three shared.

"Where did you get to today?" Georgia asked.

Antonia hid a grimace. "I went with Sebastian to check on nearby farms for Sir Humphrey and the inspector, asking if they'd noticed any strangers about. Sebastian didn't want to leave me here alone—well, without him." A twist on the truth, perhaps, but essentially true.

"Well, it's been deadly here," Melissa whispered. "They—Sir Humphrey and that inspector—questioned us all, one by one."

"Not that any of us have been able to tell them anything," Georgia said.

"Have you heard any word on when we might be allowed to leave?" Claire asked.

"With two murders to solve, I don't think Sir Humphrey and the inspector are yet ready to allow anyone to depart." Antonia glanced across the room and saw that Sebastian was surrounded by the men—no doubt being questioned much as she was.

Other than glum rumblings of discontent, nothing of note was said in her hearing before Blanchard appeared and announced that dinner was served.

Sebastian came to give her his arm, a signal for others to adhere to the social habit and pair up, which they did. As a company of couples, they trooped into the dining room and claimed seats as they would.

No one made any move to sit in the carvers at either end of the table.

Blanchard surveyed the company, then proceeded to serve the meal with butlerish imperturbability, as if not having a master or mistress present was an irregularity he was determined to ignore.

The meal was consumed largely in silence—a sober, even somber, and exceedingly weighty silence—broken only by occasional murmurs as people commented desultorily on this or that.

At the end of the meal, Mrs. Parrish and Mrs. McGibbin exchanged a glance, then both rose—bringing the rest of the company to their feet. With nods, the ladies departed for the drawing room, clearly assuming the gentlemen would want their port.

But after exchanging glances themselves, the gentlemen—led by the married men, who seemed to feel a need to remain within sight of their wives—fell in and trailed in the ladies' wake into the drawing room.

Sebastian was only too happy to stroll with Hadley to where the younger ladies had gathered at one side of the room. He gained Antonia's side as Georgia Featherstonehaugh, looking longingly out of the window at the front drive, murmured, "I wonder how long we'll be stuck here?"

Hadley caught her hand and squeezed it. "I'm sure they won't keep us much longer, not once they've gathered all the information they need."

Georgia summoned a weak smile and trained it on her husband.

Sebastian exchanged a look with Antonia, but neither of them said anything. Informing the company that they might well be held there for days yet—or until the murderer was caught—wouldn't raise anyone's spirits.

Claire Savage shook herself, then raised her head and somewhat bravely said, "I heard there's a new play in production at the Theatre Royal. Has anyone heard more?"

After an instant of something akin to shock, Melissa Wainwright leapt in to share what she'd heard.

Gradually, minute by minute, although the atmosphere remained strained, it became clear that the general consensus was to carry on as best they could and ignore—as best they could—the pall the murders had cast. Difficult given the company was lacking both host and hostess, but they gamely soldiered on.

But when Blanchard wheeled in the tea trolley, he was greeted with an undercurrent of relief. Mrs. Parrish and Mrs. McGibbin shared the honors, and all the gentlemen leapt to assist by ferrying the cups around.

As soon as the tea had been consumed, the company—still moving as if with one mind—rose, and everyone stated their intention to retire. En masse, they moved out of the drawing room and started up the stairs.

Following at Antonia's heels, Sebastian detected a certain watchful wariness, arising, no doubt, from latent yet unspecific and undirected suspicion that seemed to have afflicted everyone.

"Anyone for billiards?"

Along with all the other men, Sebastian glanced down to see Connell Boyne hovering at the foot of the stairs.

Boyne scanned the faces in a half-hearted way; his tone hadn't suggested any real enthusiasm. More as if he thought he ought to offer the invitation.

Murmurs in the negative came from all the other men. Sebastian briefly shook his head and continued climbing in Antonia's wake.

On gaining the gallery, he looked down into the hall and saw Connell, left alone on the tiles, vacillating—clearly debating whether to come upstairs or head for the billiards room. In the end, Connell thrust his hands into his trouser pockets and slouched slowly off—toward the library or the corridor to the billiards room, Sebastian couldn't tell which.

He turned and followed Antonia and the Featherstonehaughs into the east wing.

* * *

Sebastian dawdled in the corridor outside his room until Hadley and Georgia had gone into theirs, and the door had shut behind them. The instant it did, he turned and walked silently back along the corridor, scratched at Antonia's door, then opened it and walked in.

She was seated at the dressing table, her arms raised as she pulled a pin from her hair. She leveled a look he couldn't quite read at him.

He ignored it and quietly shut the door. "Have you rung for your maid?"

"No—not yet."

"Good. Don't." He crossed to where a straight-backed chair stood against the wall, lifted it, turned it, and set it down behind and a little to one side of the dressing stool, so when he straddled it and sat, resting his forearms on the raised back, he could see Antonia's face in the dressing table mirror.

She arched a haughty brow at him. "You presume."

He snorted softly. "Did you really imagine I would allow my de facto affianced marchioness to sleep alone and unprotected under the same roof as a murderer?"

She looked at him, then lightly shrugged. "Put like that...I suppose not."

He had the distinct impression that, despite her neutral expression, she was laughing at him. She was amused, at the very least.

She returned her attention to freeing her long hair. "Did you hear anything useful?"

"Nothing at all. You?"

"Likewise. But while no one has actually said the words, and despite the ladies' earlier talk of gypsies or an itinerant being responsible for killing Ennis, it's clear the realization that there's almost certainly a murderer among us has started to sink in and take hold."

"Ah. That was what was behind the men sticking by their wives' sides, and the company as a whole acting like a herd."

"I daresay such behavior is natural in the circumstances." She withdrew a last pin, and the mass of her hair tumbled free. A rippling wave of black silk, it reached down her back, almost to her hips.

His palms itched; his gaze had already fixed on the black-as-deepest-night waterfall.

She reached for her brush. He watched as she raised it and set the bristles to that silken mane and, slowly, drew the brush down.

Hypnotized by the unbidden, innocent sensuality of the repetitive, rhythmic movement as she continued to brush the long tresses, his gaze remained transfixed, his senses flaring, even as he wondered. Pondered.

Control.

How effortlessly she tried his. How she challenged it—even unintentionally, as now.

On a flash of insight, he realized why—why she and only she had always possessed the power to deflect and distract him.

Because he couldn't control how he felt about her, how he reacted and responded to her, over her, about her.

When he was with her, not only in a bedchamber but wherever they happened to be, there was no such thing as control—as his customary absolute and inviolable mastery over himself and all he did.

When he was with her, control faded and lost its hold; when he was with her, he was driven by instinct, by reactions and feelings.

Feelings engendered by an emotion too powerful to deny...

He blinked back to the present, to the faint *shush* as she plied her brush.

And frowned.

In the mirror, her gaze flicked to his face, then fastened on his eyes. To excuse the frown, he said the first words that slid into his mind—into the space vacated as that too-powerful emotion eased its hold on his wits. "Where the devil is Ennis's gunpowder?" His frustration had bubbled up and infused the words. He crossed his forearms on the upper edge of the chair's back and leaned his chin on them. "More—what's the damned stuff for? Who organized for it to be here—wherever here is? And is it still here—wherever here is—or has it already been spirited away?"

She switched her gaze forward. Staring into the mirror as if focusing on some distant point beyond her own reflection, she continued to steadily wield her brush. "It was only two nights ago that Ennis used his last words to tell you the gunpowder was here. There's been no evidence of any relevant activity around the house and grounds, so taking the simplest interpretation of his words, presumably the gunpowder is still here—wherever here is."

He grunted. Grumbled, "If they—whoever they are—learned Ennis was about to betray their plot and were in a position to kill him before he could, then surely they would also have moved the gunpowder at the same time—on that night."

"Only if they could. If they could arrange to move it—and could risk moving it—immediately." She paused in her brushing, head tilted as she thought, then she resumed the slow, evocative stroking. "And only if the gunpowder was already here. Ennis might have meant the gunpowder was *on its way* here. If it had already been moved on, he would have told you—or at least tried to tell you—where it was going."

He turned all the aspects—all the disconnected elements of the situation—over in his mind. "I keep coming back to the apparently inescapable truth that, in light of Ennis's last words, the question of whether Ennis and Cecilia were killed because of this plot or for some other reason is entirely beside the point."

"It's impossible to make sense of the motive for their murders—even to be sure that they're connected—without knowing who the murderer is."

"True, but why they were murdered doesn't change the fact that we came here with a specific goal in mind—to receive Ennis's message for Drake. We have that message, such as it is. Gunpowder. Here. That's all we have, and given the effort Ennis made to give me those words, it's most likely those words are, in fact, the gist of what he wanted to communicate. So we've done what we came here to do." In the mirror, he met her gaze. "We could leave tomorrow—Sir Humphrey and Crawford won't try to stop us. We could return to London and put everything we've learned into Drake's hands." He grimaced. "Assuming he's back, but even if he isn't, we could place our information into the hands of his masters in Whitehall."

Antonia set down her brush, swiveled to face him, and rapidly searched his face. After a moment, she said, "We could…but we're not going to, are we?"

His gaze shifted from hers. All she got was a faint grimace in reply.

She went on as if she hadn't noticed, feeling her way through his thoughts, "You've already sent word to Whitehall. Wellington's imprimatur would have ensured the message got delivered with all speed to the right people." She studied Sebastian's expression, what little of his feelings she could read from it. Frustration, disgruntlement, disappointment, yes—but not defeat. Never that. She made an educated guess. "Correct me if I'm wrong, but there aren't that many of you, are there? Gentlemen like you who occasionally work for Drake—who step in when, for whatever reason, he can't do something."

His gaze returned to her face. Several seconds elapsed, then he shrugged. "As far as I know, Drake relies on only a handful of…sons of the nobility."

"Exactly." Knowing Drake, she hadn't imagined anything else; high-handed selectiveness was entirely in keeping with the Marquess of Winchelsea's character. "And Drake left for Ireland when?"

He had to think back. "On the sixteenth or seventeenth."

"So five or six days ago. And I also assume that he isn't swanning about Ireland as the Marquess of Winchelsea."

"I seriously doubt it."

"So even if he'd been able to travel rapidly on this side of the Irish Sea, even if he's been able to complete his business over there in just a few days—which I take it is unlikely—then he wouldn't return to London until tomorrow, or the next day, or more likely some days after that."

He held her gaze levelly. "There's nothing in your assessment with which I disagree. However—"

"Bear with me." She tried to see what lay behind his pale green eyes. What was driving this—a wish to take her back to London, leave her there, and then return? That, she could believe. "Your letter to Whitehall would have been received this morning. As I understand matters, it's highly unlikely they can or will send anyone else down to look for this gunpowder. Yet gunpowder is a word that conjures up destruction. And just attempting to convey that word to Drake was enough to get Ennis killed. As Wellington said, having received Ennis's message, our goal now must be to locate the gunpowder."

She paused, continuing to hold Sebastian's gaze. "Ennis died to get those two words to you—to Drake. To people who would care enough to do something about it—to stop whatever destruction is planned. You can't turn aside." Finally, she caught the flash of something she recognized in the back of his eyes—offended pride, which he immediately buried. Sure, at last, on what ground she stood, she let her lips curve, just slightly. "And you're not going to convince me that you ever would. And I'm not about to sit meekly and let you wrap me in cotton batting and tuck me away somewhere safe while you continue to search for the damned gunpowder."

He sat up and uncrossed his arms.

Before he could growl a word, she rose and caught one of his hands. "I'm now a part of this, too—you involved me, and so did Drake. You can hardly complain over the outcome. Now"—she tugged on his hand; she didn't want him dwelling on that for too long—"stop being such a grump. We still have the northern half of the estate to search tomorrow. And yes, I will be searching it with you."

He looked disgusted, but at her insistent tugging, got to his feet. "It was worth a try."

She threw him a look—disapproving but resigned—as she drew him around, then, backing toward the bed, she allowed thoughts of a completely different nature to infuse her gaze. "We can't do anything more until tomorrow."

The atmosphere between them changed in just a heartbeat to one of leaping senses and tightening nerves. She smiled, confidence and self-assurance rising. "Come to bed." Her voice had grown sultry. "I guarantee you'll see matters in a more positive light come morning."

His gaze remained locked with hers. His brows slowly rose.

And he allowed her to tow him toward the bed.

Mentally, Sebastian threw up his hands—surrendering, even if he wasn't entirely sure to what.

To compulsion, yes. To hunger, definitely.

To need?

As she halted by the bed, grabbed the sides of his coat in both fists and hauled him to her as she stretched up, and he bent his head, it certainly felt like that.

Their lips met—and that swelling need ignited. No tentative dipping of toes into desire's sea—not for them. The tide raged, and they plunged in, and it swept them, swirled them, then dragged them under.

And they went. Gladly jettisoning all vestige of restraint and all pretense of rational decision, with blatant abandon, they let passion have them.

Their lips meshed and melded, their mouths devoured, greedy and needy, then she parted her lips, and he thrust his tongue past and claimed every lush inch of her mouth. He possessed and branded in flagrant mimicry of what was to come, then her tongue boldly tangled with his, and they fell into a duel of wills and wants, and he lost his last anchor to the world.

She pushed, she challenged, and he instinctively met her, on this plane as on all others.

Ardor burned brightly within them both, a near-incandescent flame. It heated, it lured—it drew and drove them on.

Into ever-escalating hungers, into turbulent seas of passions unleashed.

Desire burned, a fire in their blood, and hunger and need thudded in their veins.

And compulsion reigned.

Her small hands were everywhere, tugging at his clothes.

He finished unbuttoning her gown, then acquiesced to her insistence and shrugged off his coat and waistcoat, both of which she'd already undone.

An errant thought whisked through his mind; one day, they might manage to take this slowly, to draw the moments out, but that day was not today. Driven by something that was close to desperation, an increasingly urgent need to feel the other close—*that* close—they shed clothes like leaves swept away by the gale of their need.

Until they came together, skin to skin, senses to achingly yearning senses, bodies flush and limbs embracing in the space beside her bed.

Hands—hers and his—reached, stroked, and caressed. On a panting breath, he broke from the kiss and sent his lips cruising—over the delicate curve of her jaw, down the long column of her throat, following the sculpted line of her shoulder wide, before swooping down to pay homage to one breast. He filled his hand with her other breast, kneaded the already swollen mound as he suckled, and she cried out, her fingers digging into his scalp as she arched in his arms.

As her naked hips pressed tight, then provocatively ground against his bare thighs.

They stilled, all breathing suspended. Their eyes met for a fleeting instant, then they tumbled onto the coverlet, landing in a tangle of long limbs and searching, grasping, greedy hands. He seized the moment of unscripted wrestling to catch his breath, physically and mentally, and reached for what, in that sphere, passed for patience. For some lever—anything—that would slow them down; control might be beyond him, but surely experience would afford him some ability to at least guide…

She wasn't of a mind to allow it. She caught his head between her hands and yanked him back into a searing kiss—one that cindered all restraint. Then she undulated beneath him, her body sinuously tempting in a move as old as time.

He reacted—it was impossible not to, to keep his body from answering her call.

From covering her, settling heavily into the cradle of her hips, into the embrace of her slender, welcoming thighs—and then, with one thrust, he was inside her.

Pleasure, laced by something far more profound, more acute, infinitely more heady, lanced through him.

The jolt was a sensual shock potent enough, glorious enough, to make him draw back from the kiss simply to better savor it.

From beneath his lashes, he looked into her face. Shadowed though it was, he saw her eyes gleam from beneath her weighted lids. For an instant, their gazes locked, held.

And an ineluctable sense of togetherness welled—clicked, locked, and bound them.

An invisible strand, one of pure physical sharing. A connection nonetheless, one they'd both intuitively reached for.

In that split-second exchange, he and she both acknowledged that reality.

Then her lashes lowered, and her lips curved.

He bent his head, covered those alluring lips with his, and together, they plunged into their fire.

They rode and burned, gripped and clung.

Antonia thrilled to the beat, to the heavy, repetitive rhythm of their joining. Her skin was aflame, while he was pure heat. The sensation of his body moving on hers, against hers, into hers, sent her senses spinning, spiraling through a universe of ever-expanding awareness—of touch, of fire, of molten heat. Of the thud of their hearts, the compulsive surge and retreat, and the steady rise of that glorious, scintillating tension.

Almost there.

She gasped, clung, sobbed, and urged him on.

The climax rushed up, an eruption of sensation that wiped all else before it and exploded across her senses in a starburst of glittering, unadulterated pleasure.

Leaving behind a clean slate. And an emptiness that, a second later, he joined her and filled.

As if they were two halves of one entity.

An entity formed through long association, perhaps, yet forged in this fire.

Welded in this furnace of passion and desire.

Her senses slowly returned to earth. She realized he'd collapsed upon her, heavy muscles and bones slumped, wrung out, in abject surrender, and felt her lips spontaneously curve.

If anyone had told her mere days ago that she would welcome his weight lying so heavily on her, trapping her and pressing her into the bed, she wouldn't have believed them. But now...

Lazily, languidly, she lifted her arms, reached as far around him as she could, and held him to her.

There was a sharing in this moment, an intimate closeness that nothing else and no other situation could even aspire to; she held that closeness to her as she held him.

She closed her eyes and let her mind drift into the beckoning, blissful oblivion.

* * *

Eventually, Sebastian returned to the land of the living. He had no idea how much time had elapsed. Which was…unusual, to say the least.

Slowly, he raised his head, taking care not to jar Antonia awake. He looked down into her sleeping face, drank in her expression—Madonna-like in its moon-washed serenity—and mentally shook his head.

He'd had women beyond counting, yet he couldn't recall ever being this… Wrung out? Hollowed out? Whatever it was. So deeply sunk in the moment, so deeply enthralled, so profoundly connected and exercised—exorcized?—that it took such a long time for him to reconnect with the world.

Moving slowly and carefully, he disengaged from her clinging embrace, then slumped beside her in the bed. He reached down, freed the covers, and tugged them over their cooling bodies. He felt ridiculously gratified when she turned on her side and, apparently still asleep, snuggled against him. He settled one arm around her, holding her close, then, feeling oddly mind-clear and nowhere near sleep, he raised his other arm, put his hand behind his head, and stared up at the ceiling.

Unsurprisingly, his thoughts circled the conundrum curled, a warm and soft armful, by his side.

She'd always been there, a part of his world, as far back as his memories ran. She'd always been different in some unspecified way—occupying a slightly different category than anyone else. She'd been one of the few, possibly the only person inside his inner palisade—able to connect with him on a different, more personal, more direct, and no-subjects-barred plane. That connection had been outside his control—not something he'd allowed so much as something that had simply been—a link she had, from her earliest years, instinctively exploited and used.

Yet when he'd started looking for a wife, he hadn't thought of her.

If he was honest, he *specifically* hadn't thought of her.

Because he hadn't wanted to risk what she could—would—do to his ability to control…himself. Her. Them.

But now they'd flung caution aside, and there they were, with their feet inexorably following a path into matrimony.

How was he—were they—to manage?

Instinct, more primitive than educated, suggested he would be wise to set all thoughts of control aside. Witness his signal lack of success that evening.

Even had he succeeded, she would have realized all too soon and wouldn't have readily forgiven him—and would, no doubt, have taken steps to counter his manipulation, steps of which he wouldn't have approved and wouldn't have liked...

Trying to exert control, even by his favored method of subtle manipulation, might well lead to worse problems than any he sought to solve.

Now they'd embarked on this path, he needed to accept that reality.

He would never control her, and she would never control him.

So where did that leave them?

As essentially equal partners, with different abilities and different strengths yet on a par with each other, as powerful as each other in this domain they were creating and shaping between them.

The landscape of their future, of the life they would share.

He stared unseeing at the ceiling. He had to admit there was temptation of a sort in that challenge.

For it would be a challenge—of that, he had no doubt.

He dipped his chin and glanced down at her. At the curve of her face he could see.

Resolution, determination, strength—much of what he recognized in her he knew also lived in him.

He'd lowered his arm. Caught in his web of contemplation—of her, of them—he ran a gentle finger down her nose. Like the rest of her, it was long, but in perfect proportion with the rest of her face.

He shifted his attention to one lithely muscled arm and traced its length with his palm.

He loved—

His mind froze.

After a moment, he tentatively considered, for once truly looked, then he shied away from the thought.

But he didn't bury it—just left it, unaccepted but not dismissed.

He'd heard all the tales of Cynsters marrying only for love. Always for love. That any attempt to do otherwise—like his great-uncle Arthur's first marriage—was doomed.

But...the stories of the grandes dames were just stories, weren't they? What currency did they have in the modern world? In the world he and Antonia inhabited.

Another set of questions to which he didn't have answers.

He didn't need more frustrations.

Satiation still lay heavy in his veins. He closed his eyes, opened his awareness to the mind-numbing sensation, embraced the bone-deep glow, and surrendered to whatever dreams awaited him.

# CHAPTER 13

$S$ebastian left Antonia's room and returned to his as late as he dared, gaining his bed just before a footman crept in to lay and light the fire.

Once the footman had gone, Sebastian lay beneath the covers he'd artistically disarranged and weighed up competing compulsions. Should he make another—most likely futile—bid to somehow convince Antonia to remain in safety with the other ladies? Or should he acknowledge his newly recognized reality and accept that she would be riding out with him?

In the end, he realized that with a murderer among the guests, even with Sir Humphrey, Inspector Crawford, and the constables around the house, his inner self did not deem the company sufficiently safe for her, not without him by her side.

He wasn't sure how to regard that conclusion—was it realization or rationalization? Regardless, with his way forward clarified, he rose, washed, and dressed, and was loitering in the archway leading to the gallery when Antonia emerged from her room.

She saw him and arched a faintly haughty brow, but made no other comment. That she'd donned her riding habit was a sufficient declaration of her expectations of the day.

They walked side by side through the gallery and down the stairs.

As they stepped onto the tiles of the front hall, she murmured, "It appears to be a good morning—given the lack of screams, it seems no one died in the night."

He humphed.

A footman was passing, ferrying an empty dish back to the kitchen. Sebastian halted him and asked for a message to be relayed to the stables, to have the horses he and Antonia had ridden the previous day saddled and waiting in half an hour.

The footman bowed and retreated.

Antonia had halted and waited, listening. As Sebastian turned back to her, she bestowed an approving smile on him, then turned and walked on.

Schooling his features to impassivity, he followed her into the breakfast room. They greeted the other guests already present—all the younger crew except for the Featherstonehaughs—then helped themselves from the sideboard.

After piling several sausages onto a mound of kedgeree, Sebastian eyed the excellent spread laid out along the board. "With both master and mistress dead, who is running the household? Do you know?"

"I believe Blanchard and Mrs. Blanchard have stepped up to the mark, and Mrs. Parrish has offered to assist if needed." A plate containing one slice of toast, a small mound of scrambled eggs, and one slice of ham in her hand, Antonia turned from the sideboard, surveyed the table, then elected to sit beside Claire and Melissa at one end.

Her friends eyed her riding habit with ill-concealed envy.

"Half your luck," Claire grumbled as Antonia set down her plate and paused to allow Sebastian—who had, of course, followed at her heels—to draw out the chair beside Claire's for her. Claire went on, "I take it you plan to ride out again today?"

Antonia sank onto the chair. "Yes." She glanced at Sebastian as he circled the end of the table and helpfully claimed the place opposite her; she briefly met his eyes—he hadn't heard the excuse for their absence she'd given her friends the previous day. "So far, we've covered only half the area Sir Humphrey and the inspector asked us to check for strangers. With luck, we'll finish today."

"Well," Melissa said, "I sincerely hope Sir Humphrey and the inspector bring their investigations to a speedy conclusion so we can leave tomorrow, as planned. I had to get out of bed at cock's crow to move the chair I'd wedged against my door so the tweeny could come in."

"Cecilia had planned a ball for tonight"—Claire put down the slice of toast she'd been nibbling and reached for her teacup—"but I understand Sir Humphrey has sent word to all the neighbors, informing them of the murders and asking them to stay away."

"Just as well," Antonia said. "This is the country. News of the murders is sure to have spread by now, and as we all know, nothing short of an instruction from a magistrate is likely to keep the curious at bay."

"That's the last thing we need," Melissa stated. "Having to receive the local gossips all agog for the scandalous highlights."

"Actually," Sebastian murmured, his gaze on his plate, "the last thing any of us need is the press."

Melissa and Claire stared at him. "What an horrendous idea." Claire sounded aghast. After a second, she asked, "When do you think they'll arrive?"

Sebastian looked at Melissa and Claire. "When did Sir Humphrey send word to the neighbors?"

"Yesterday," Melissa said. "Mrs. Parrish mentioned the ball to him, and he said he would call at the appropriate houses and ensure the word was spread throughout the neighborhood."

Sebastian's expression turned cynical. "Twenty-four hours for the news to reach Fleet Street, then twelve or so hours before the hounds reach here. If we are released tomorrow, even if the constables succeed in keeping the newsmen off the property, you can expect to run a gauntlet at the gate."

A short silence fell while Antonia exchanged horrified glances with her friends as they digested that unwelcome prediction.

Melissa slumped. "This was our first excursion out from under our mothers' wings. We'll never be allowed out alone again."

Claire pulled a disgusted face.

Sebastian grinned. "Wear veils and have your coachman whip up the horses twenty yards before the gate. The good gentlemen of the press will be too busy scrambling for their lives to notice who you are, much less demand answers to unwelcome questions."

Melissa and Claire considered that image; both perked up.

Sebastian pushed aside his empty plate and caught Antonia's eye. "We should get going."

"Yes. All right." She drained her teacup, pushed back her chair, and rose. She glanced at Melissa and Claire, who were once again regarding her with resigned envy. "Pray God nothing else bothersome happens today."

"Amen," Melissa said.

"And that Sir Humphrey and the inspector either find the murderer or else decide he's flown and allow us to go home." Claire flashed a weak grin at Antonia. "Have fun."

Antonia hesitated, then replied, "Take care." She looked at Melissa as well. "Both of you. And tell Georgia, too."

"Oh, all the ladies plan to stick together," Melissa said. "It's boring, but we all feel safer that way."

Sebastian, who had risen as Antonia had and circled the table to pull back her chair, nodded in approval. "An excellent idea." He glanced at Antonia, hesitated for a second, then waved to the door giving onto the rear terrace. "Let's walk around rather than go through the house."

With a last smile for her friends and a nod to the others about the table, Antonia led the way. Sebastian reached around her and opened the door, then followed her out and closed the glassed pane behind them.

The day was overcast, but although darker clouds were massing to the north, there was no scent of rain, and the breeze, blowing fitfully from the west, was mild.

They went down the steps from the terrace to the lawn, then strode side by side around the short central wing which, at ground level, housed the kitchen and associated facilities. A brick wall enclosed the kitchen garden, but archways in both side walls allowed them to walk through to emerge on the lawn below the rear terrace running beside the library. They cut across toward the stable, eventually joining the path from the side door.

Antonia noticed Sebastian studying the house as they walked. "What are you looking for?"

"Any sign of unexpected basements. Of anywhere we haven't yet searched." He faced forward as they left the house behind. "I swear we've searched all possible places inside the house."

She nodded.

And continued to wonder at his apparent ready acceptance of her company. After his attempt to remove her from the house party—and all danger—last night, she'd expected him to try again, or at least to try to dissuade her from accompanying him. She would have sworn that in the moment when they'd taken their leave of Melissa and Claire, and he'd hesitated, he'd debated suggesting she remain with her friends in safety…but he hadn't.

Instead, he seemed not just resigned but acquiescent over her presence.

That was a great deal more than she'd hoped for.

Almost as if, with respect to her, he was changing his spots…only she didn't believe that for an instant.

She and her sister had heard countless tales from their mother of their father's smothering protectiveness and had endured enough incidents of that on their own accounts to have formed a very clear idea of the only possible way to deal with a similar man—with a nobleman who, when in the grip of instinct, would behave as if he owned them. As if they were somehow his—his to dictate to, at least when there was any danger involved.

She wasn't foolish enough to discard or denigrate the protectiveness such men—men like Sebastian—personified. Protectiveness was welcome; any sane lady would agree. But possessive protectiveness was something else again and needed to be guarded against.

Needed to be trained out of those so afflicted.

She bit back a smile; Sebastian wouldn't see that conclusion as amusing, much less approve of such a tack.

Too bad. That was the price if he wanted her hand in marriage.

They reached the stable yard to find their mounts waiting. When Sebastian lifted her to her saddle, she discovered she now enjoyed the thrill, the spiking of her senses.

He mounted up—she enjoyed watching that, too—then they wheeled the horses and clattered out of the yard.

Only to almost immediately rein in as the inspector, flanked by a bevy of constables, came trotting up.

Crawford halted his good-looking bay, doubtless borrowed from Sir Humphrey's stable, waved his men on to the stable yard, then politely lifted his hat to them. "Good morning, my lord. My lady."

"Inspector." Sebastian steadied the gray, who had taken exception to the other horses; at the same time, he glanced about, confirming none of the stablemen and no one else was close enough to overhear. "We're about to ride out and search the northern half of the estate for any sign of the gunpowder."

Crawford nodded. "I don't suppose you've anything enlightening to tell me as to who the murderer might be?"

"Sadly, no," Sebastian said.

Antonia took pity on the inspector. "Last night, everyone was very subdued. We all retired early. This morning, the main subject of conversation about the breakfast table was whether you will allow us to depart tomorrow, as was originally planned."

Crawford sighed. "That's a decision Sir Humphrey and I will have to make later today, and frankly, I'm not looking forward to it. With all evidence pointing to the murderer being one of the guests, the new rules that apply to investigations such as this say we keep you all here, contained, until something breaks. That said, I can see that's not going to be so easy in this case and might not even be possible."

Sebastian hesitated, then nodded and tightened the gray's reins. "If anything occurs to us, or if we find anything to point to the murderer, we'll let you know as quickly as we can."

"In that case"—Crawford half bowed to Antonia—"I'll wish you good riding and good luck."

They parted. With Antonia beside him, Sebastian set course for the fields lying to the northwest of the grounds surrounding the house.

When they reached the area they hadn't yet explored, once again, they zigged and zagged, working their way toward the western boundary, stopping at all structures no matter how small to search for hidden barrels.

The first place they stopped at was a farmhouse that stood isolated on its own plot. The farmyard with its associated buildings was a short distance away, around the flank of a low hill. Sebastian dismounted and came to lift Antonia down. Together, they walked up the gravel path. The door opened before they reached it; the tenant farmer's wife blinked at them, then colored and bobbed a curtsy. "Sir. Ma'am. What can I do for you?"

Sebastian glanced at Antonia.

She smiled at the woman. "We're searching for some barrels that those at the house"—she waved toward Pressingstoke Hall—"believe might have been hidden somewhere about the estate. Have you or your husband seen anyone moving barrels about recently?"

Clearly mystified, the woman shook her head. "No, ma'am. Can't say as we have. Not much we have that's brought in by the barrel-load, so we'd've noticed, I'm sure."

Sebastian shifted. "Do you know of any old cellar or cave where barrels might have been hidden?"

The woman studied him for a second, then said, "I was born on the estate, so I know most places, but other than the caves in the cliffs, I've never heard tell of any hidden place—not in the fields."

Sebastian regarded the woman for an instant, then nodded. "Thank you."

He took Antonia's arm and walked with her down the short path. As soon as they were out of earshot of the woman, he bent his head and whispered, "I want to search the cellar—in a place that size, there's bound to be one. Can you get her out of the house?"

The cottages they'd stopped at the previous day had been too small to boast cellars. Antonia halted, studying his face, then she nodded and turned.

The farmer's wife was still standing in the open doorway.

Antonia walked back, smiling easily. "I wonder if I could trouble you for a glass of water?"

The woman straightened. "Of course, ma'am." She stepped back. "Come in."

Leaving the front door wide, Antonia followed the woman down a corridor that led to a large kitchen at the rear of the house. The woman went to the dresser, picked up a pewter mug, and reached for a jug. Antonia stayed her with a raised hand. "If possible, I would prefer water straight from the pump."

The woman nodded. "Of course." She set down the jug and made for the back door. "The pump's just out here."

Antonia followed the woman out of the door; as she had hoped, the pump stood in the middle of the rear yard. She offered to hold the mug while the woman plied the pump handle. Once the mug was full, Antonia sipped, then asked the woman about her family.

They were still standing by the pump, swapping observations on male children, when Sebastian came striding around the side of the farmhouse. He halted and frowned at her. "We need to be getting on."

She smiled sweetly at him, then turned her smile on the woman and handed back the mug. "Thank you."

The woman took the mug and bobbed a curtsy. "Ma'am."

Antonia joined Sebastian, and they walked around the farmhouse and back to the horses. Only once they were mounted and had wheeled the horses did she ask, "Anything?"

He grunted. "A root cellar, but no barrels." He set the gray trotting. "Come on."

They halted in the nearby farmyard, which proved to be deserted. "I suppose all the men are out in the fields at this hour," Antonia said.

"At least we don't have to make excuses." Sebastian led the way into the barn.

Their search of the barn and hayshed didn't take long.

In silence, they remounted and rode on.

Antonia set the chestnut to pace the gray. "Is gunpowder transported in anything other than barrels?"

Sebastian frowned. "It can be. But only smaller amounts would be in boxes or paper packages, and not generally for transporting any distance. I can't imagine Ennis wasting his last breath to warn us about any small amount. Also, the powder needs to be kept dry, and oak barrels are best for that."

She sighed. "So barrels it is."

Another farmhouse, somewhat larger than the last, sat in a dip ahead. Again, they halted and questioned the farmer's wife, who confirmed that, at that time of day, all the men were out in the fields. Again, the woman knew nothing of any barrels being moved about the estate. She went with them to look into the barn and hayshed. Antonia distracted her by professing an interest in her extensive vegetable garden while Sebastian circled the house and searched its cellar, but all for the same result.

"Nothing," he somewhat tersely informed Antonia before she'd even asked. He urged the gray on, and she followed.

To that point, she'd had no reason to complain about his behavior. However, the next structure they came upon was a lone hayshed. On reaching it, Sebastian quickly dismounted, waved her to remain ahorse, handed her the gray's reins, and stalked off to swiftly search.

She told herself he was simply growing impatient, and it really didn't take two to search a hayshed that was open on three sides.

But their next stop was at a derelict barn, and once again, he was off his horse and waiting to hand her the gray's reins the instant she halted the mare. "This won't take long" was all he said before stalking into the barn.

Leaving her to wait outside.

She humphed. She glanced around, looking for a tree or bush to which to tie both sets of reins...only to realize there wasn't anything suitable nearby.

Maybe that was why he'd left her holding the reins. She returned her gaze to the barn door, sagging on its hinges, and narrowed her eyes... Perhaps. But she had to wonder.

The barn proved uninteresting. His expression hard and unrevealing, Sebastian returned, reclaimed the gray's reins, mounted up, and they continued quartering the fields, moving steadily westward.

They saw no other structures requiring searching before they reached the Deal-Dover road, once again not far from Ringwould, although this time to the north of the village.

Sebastian drew rein and looked toward the cluster of village roofs. "Let's go back to the Five Bells and have an early luncheon. There's unlikely to be anywhere else on our route where we might get food."

"An excellent idea," she returned and led the way. She'd discovered her appetite had grown; even the extra scrambled eggs she'd eaten that morning hadn't entirely assuaged her hunger.

At the Five Bells, the day's main dish proved to be mutton stew, hearty and filling and almost as tasty as the previous day's pie. They spoke little while they ate; for her part, she was absorbed with thoughts of where barrels of gunpowder might be hidden, and what next they might do if their search today proved as futile as yesterday's.

Suitably fortified to face the afternoon, they quit the inn, remounted, and rode northward, steadily traversing the fields of the estate bordering the road.

That tack revealed no structures of any kind and landed them at the northwestern corner of the estate, where a large coppice filled the triangle between the fields, the road, and the northern boundary fence. The coppice hadn't been harvested for some time and was overdue for attention; the trees grew thick and dense.

Antonia drew rein facing the coppice. Sebastian rode closer, ranging between her and the trees. He appeared to be peering into the massed thickets.

She noticed a path leading into the coppice. "There's a path there." When he glanced at her, she pointed. "Should we get down and search?"

Sebastian rode to the opening of the path. Standing in his stirrups, he looked down it, then he shook his head, resat, and turned the gray toward her. "It's just a clearing. Nothing there. If whoever's behind this has a grain of sense, then assuming they want to use the gunpowder to blow something up, they won't risk leaving it in the open, even under a tarpaulin. In this season, damp will get in, and that will be the end of their plans."

"We could hope," she replied and turned the chestnut's head to the east.

They rode on, again taking a zigzag route across the fields as they covered the last section of the estate they hadn't yet searched—the fields inside the northern boundary from the road to the shore.

The next feature they came upon was another large coppice, a roughly circular one surrounded by fields. Sebastian had been riding on Antonia's left, but when they slowed before the coppice, he urged the gray forward and across, coming between her and the trees. This coppice had been recently harvested; perched on their horses, they could easily see through the thin young shoots. But with Sebastian between her and the coppice, Antonia had to lean sideways and crane her neck to see around him.

"Nothing there." He nudged the gray on.

Her view finally clear, she cast a swift glance over the coppice, confirmed there was no structure of any kind hidden in its depths, then raised her reins and pressed the chestnut into motion again.

Still keeping station between her and the trees, Sebastian led the way on.

From beneath her lashes, she cast him a narrow-eyed sidelong glare. Did he even realize what he was doing? Where was the danger here? What did he imagine—that someone was hiding in the coppice waiting to take a shot at her?

She humphed and shifted her gaze forward. Were noblemen in the grip of this particular affliction really so illogical? So driven by instinct that common sense fell by the wayside?

She had a sneaking suspicion her mother would assure her that they were. That she—Antonia—should expect such behavior.

She felt like snorting.

She bit back an acerbic comment when they came to another coppice, this one on the other side of their route, and he behaved in the same shielding way, wheeling the gray around her to do so.

But when a large barn, not derelict and apparently very much in use, loomed ahead, she scanned the area, spotted a small tree to one side, and planned her approach. At the last moment, she pushed the chestnut into the lead, headed straight for that useful tree, pulled up, slid from her saddle to the ground—an admittedly precarious undertaking given the chestnut stood a good sixteen hands tall—regained her balance, and swiftly tied the chestnut's reins to the tree.

She turned to find Sebastian scowling down at her.

But "Wait" was all he said.

She hid her grin and decided not to take umbrage at his tone. He would learn.

She duly waited while he dismounted and tethered the gray. She even allowed him to lead the way into the barn.

Searching that barn took some time—there were piles of hay to poke beneath and stalls, presently empty, to explore. But, once again, they found nothing.

In disaffected silence, they returned to the horses and mounted up again. As Sebastian turned the gray eastward once more, she glanced at him. His face, with its angular features and chiseled planes, would never be described as soft, but his expression was even more granite-like, more impenetrable than usual.

There was a hint of bleakness in his gaze as he scanned the area ahead of them.

She could understand. This might be something of an adventure, but it wasn't a game. Gunpowder destroyed, not just buildings but people, too. There was duty of a sort weighing on Sebastian's broad shoulders, and, now she thought of it, she felt she shared that burden.

They needed to find the gunpowder.

Not finding it would feel like failure.

And failure wasn't something he was conditioned to accept, any more than she was.

They came upon two abandoned huts; one showed evidence of being used as a shed. Although she sensed it went against his grain—that he had to rein in his impulses to do it—he refrained from trying to stop her following him into the huts.

They shifted tools and checked the floors and, again, found nothing.

When they mounted and rode on, they could smell the sea.

Minutes later, they reached the bridle path that followed the edge of the cliffs. Judging by the position of the sun, barely discernible through the thick clouds, it was midafternoon. The breeze had picked up, and it was chillier this close to the sea.

They halted and looked around. Sebastian pointed to a fence a little way to the north. "That's the boundary line. This is the northeastern corner of the estate."

Looking farther to the north, Antonia glimpsed the distinctive walls of Walmer Castle a mile or so away.

Sebastian followed her gaze, then looked away. The sight of the castle was a stark reminder of his failure to locate the gunpowder. He turned the gray's head to the south and nudged the heavy beast into a walk.

Antonia brought the chestnut alongside.

After a moment, he gave voice to his frustration. "I cannot believe Ennis used his last breath to tell me something that didn't matter. So the threat posed by the gunpowder is real. More, it's significant. And by here…he *must* have meant, at the very least, this estate. The missing three hundred pounds confirms that. And while it's now nearly three days since he was murdered, and the barrels might well have been moved, we haven't found a single place in which they might even conceivably have been kept."

He glanced at Antonia.

Her gaze fixed ahead, she lightly shrugged. "So we keep searching. Ennis said the gunpowder was here, so it will be, or will have been, here, somewhere."

He snorted disgruntledly. "*Where* remains our abiding question."

She tapped her heel to the chestnut's side and moved into a trot. "You scan the land, and I'll search the sands."

It was the same division of labor they'd used the previous day. He spotted an isolated cottage, and they diverted inland to search. Although a couple clearly lived there, the building stood empty. They searched, but found nothing.

Feeling increasingly helpless, he led the way back to the cliff path, and they continued southward.

After several minutes, she asked, "If they want to blow up something in England, why bother bringing gunpowder from somewhere else?" She looked at him and, when he met her gaze, arched a brow. "Don't we have enough gunpowder in England?"

"We have plenty, and a lot of it is in and around London. But the Office of Ordnance keeps a strict tally of how much there is and where it's stored. For someone wanting gunpowder to use illegally, stealing it would instantly raise an alarm."

"All right." She nodded. "So they have to bring it into the country, and that means by sea, and given we're searching for hiding places along this coast, that means they've brought it this far by ship." She glanced at him. "So why not take it directly to London? By water, it's not that much farther."

"No, it's not, but any ship coming into the Thames has to deal with Customs and Excise, so again, that route would risk failure or, at the very least, raising an early alarm."

The horses clopped on. He swayed with the movement, mentally filling in the picture her words had sketched in his mind. "Assuming the gunpowder was here, and the target chosen for destruction is somewhere in London, then…I assume they plan to move the barrels to London by road. As far as I know, if they just loaded the barrels onto a wagon, there would be no checks or hurdles for them to overcome. They could cover the load and cart it into London without anyone knowing what they were transporting."

"That must be their plan."

She sounded as bleakly grim as he felt.

They continued along the bridle path, the cliffs and shore stretching southward before them.

Just ahead on the seaward side, the cottages they'd seen the previous day—clustered on a semicircle of rocky land that ran out from the base of the cliffs—crouched above the waves. The cottages faced the cliffs, separated from them by a narrow path. He considered searching the cottages, but discarded the notion.

When Antonia glanced questioningly at him, he shook his head. "They're too close to the water to safely store gunpowder even for a short time, and given their lack of elevation, any cellars or underground passages leading to the cliffs would fill with water."

She grimaced and looked ahead, and they rode on.

Soon after, they neared the place where they'd broken off their search the previous afternoon. Sebastian halted the gray above the dip concealing the tiny lane giving access to the shore; this time, they were on the northern side of the lane. Away to the southwest, they could see the chimneys of Pressingstoke Hall rising above the canopy of the Home Wood.

They'd searched the entire estate and found nothing—no barrels, no sign of them, nothing at all.

He drew in a deep breath, folded his hands on the pommel, and thought. Rethought.

Antonia halted the mare alongside the gray; he felt her gaze on his face, but didn't meet it.

After a moment, he mused, "It all hangs on what Ennis meant by 'here.' If I was inside Somersham Place and said something was 'here,' I would mean…something either in the house or close by—attached to the house." He finally met Antonia's gaze. "When we searched the house, we were looking for places where barrels might have been stored. But what if the place the barrels are or were stored is attached to the house via one of those secret tunnels Sir Humphrey confirmed are common in large houses hereabouts?"

Her gray gaze grew distant. After a moment, she said, "We looked for entrances to secret passageways in the cellars. We didn't search above ground—and we didn't look for hidden entrances to tunnels in the parts of the house in everyday use." She glanced at him, her expression growing animated. "But entrances such as those could be anywhere, even on the upper floors."

Grimly, he nodded. "That's where we search next." He gathered his reins. "And we need to do it now, because we—and Crawford and Sir Humphrey—are running out of time."

He tapped his booted heels to the gray's sides, and the horse surged.

A second later, he heard from behind him, "Sebastian! *Wait!*"

His instincts informed him Antonia hadn't followed, hadn't moved. He muttered an oath, slowed the gray, then wheeled.

He saw Antonia in her dark gray habit silhouetted against the paler gray of sea and sky. But she was transformed; her eyes were wide, her face alight, and she was pointing insistently into the dip, toward where the tiny lane ran down to the sands.

He couldn't see what was exciting her interest from where he was. He rode back, scanning the sands as they came into view. "What?"

"There!" She pointed again. "See that churned-up sand?" Her eyes glowed as they met his. "That patch of sand was perfectly flat when we were here yesterday afternoon. I looked."

He studied the area again. A section of sand at the end of the lane had, indeed, been trampled by many feet. The tide had come in and washed smooth the sands farther down the beach, but had only lipped the seaward edge of the churned-up section.

Antonia all but jigged in her saddle. "It's as if, since yesterday, men have walked back and forth along the base of the cliffs on the other side of the dip—the trail disappears around the cliff there, heading farther along the beach. Perhaps they were carrying barrels to a wagon that waited in the lane!"

Her excitement was infectious. He could see the scene she was painting. The lane itself was surfaced in flints embedded in clay; there would be no wheel marks or boot prints to be found there. But the sands… The trail did seem to lead farther south; they couldn't see how much farther from their present vantage point.

He glanced in the other direction, at the cottages on the shore. Sensing his rising excitement, the gray shifted restlessly. "For anyone in those cottages…at night, the sound of the wind and the waves would drown out any other sounds."

"Come on!" Antonia's patience had run out. "Let's see where the trail leads." She shook the chestnut's reins and rode down into the dip, then urged the mare up the other side.

He caught up with her as she trotted along the coastal path, keeping as close to the edge as she could and peering down. The cliffs along that section weren't precipitous. They sloped sharply downward, and scrubby trees and bushes studded the slopes.

"There!" Looking down through a gap between the trees and shrubs, Antonia pointed again. "See? They're still trudging along."

She drew rein and glanced at him. "Should we stop and go down and follow along the sands?"

He looked back at the Hall's chimneys. He had an idea. "No. Let's continue up here for as long as we can see the trail in the sand."

She was perfectly happy to comply. Her eyes were sharp; so were his. They caught sufficient glimpses of the sands bordering the foot of the cliffs to know almost immediately when the trail ended.

They pulled up and wheeled. Without exchanging a word, they walked the horses back to the last point at which they could see churned sand below.

Sebastian halted the gray and looked inland. "As I thought." He smiled intently, then met Antonia's questioning gaze. "We're almost directly east of Pressingstoke Hall."

"You think there's a cave here that's connected to the house?"

He nodded and dismounted. "The cliffs here are limestone—it's fairly soft. Easy to tunnel through. They probably started from the house and tunneled until they joined a natural cave system closer to the shore."

He tied off the gray's reins, then went to lift her down. He had already evaluated the dangers with respect to her; leaving her here, alone on the cliffs, while he investigated below, out of sight or hearing, wasn't in anyone's best interests.

She rapidly tied the chestnut alongside the gray, then peered down the cliff. "It's not impossibly steep. We should be able to manage it."

That was his assessment, too. "Let me go first." As he moved past her, he felt her sharp glance and added, "If I'm behind you and lose my footing, I'll take you down with me. If you're behind me and fall, I'll catch you."

The only response he got to that inarguable logic was a humph.

The scramble down the cliff wasn't as bad as Antonia had feared; they'd both scrambled over enough rough hillsides and craggy slopes during their childhoods to still remember the tricks. But the last section of the descent was down the sheer face of a single block of stone. Sebastian dropped down easily, landing in a crouch. She dithered at the edge.

He turned, saw, and grinned. He positioned himself, raised his arms, and beckoned. "Jump. I'll catch you."

She narrowed her eyes on his face; he was enjoying this far too much. But... She dragged in a quick breath, held it, and jumped.

He seized her about the waist in midair and swung her around and down, finally setting her gently on her feet.

She brushed down her skirts—tamped down her leaping senses; the strength he'd just displayed was ridiculously impressive—then she squinted up at him and, with dignity, said, "Thank you."

He laughed.

Then they turned to look at the trampled trail in which they now stood, and all impulse to levity faded.

She tensed to follow the trail forward—southward—but he put out a hand, grasped her arm, and gently pushed.

"Move toward the water a little way."

She complied, stepping out of the churned track to where the tide had left the sand smooth.

He followed. He walked on a few feet, then hunkered down and studied the imprints in the sand.

She waited with what patience she could muster.

Eventually, he straightened. Before she could ask, he pointed to the footprints visible in the sand. "Men came from the end of the lane and trudged that way." He pointed south, along the cliffs, then looked down at the trail again. "And then they came back, retracing their steps, but this time, they were each carrying something very heavy. You can see that the boot prints heading toward the lane overlie those coming from the lane, and the prints going back are deeper."

"Yes. I can see that." With her eyes, she tracked the trail of footprints onward. Ten yards farther south from where she and Sebastian stood, the trail ended, and the footprints veered into a dark cleft in the cliff.

"There'll be a cave in there," Sebastian said.

"That's where they hid the gunpowder," she breathed. "We've finally found it."

She glanced at Sebastian in time to see him grimace.

"We've found where it *was*." He caught her eye. "Judging by these footprints, they moved the barrels out last night."

"Still…" She looked at the gap in the cliff face; it was only a yard or so wide with nothing but blackness beyond. "There might be some signs— some clues—inside." She looked at Sebastian and found him striding past her. She picked up her skirts and hurried in his wake. "We are going to go in and look, aren't we?"

Sebastian halted and felt her run into him. He swung around and caught her elbows and steadied her. "*I* will go in and look." He drew his hands from her and forced himself to rein in the overriding impulse to issue an order. "You need to remain out here." Translation: *He* needed her to remain safely on the beach. There was no one near, and who knew what dangers might lurk in the darkness inside?

He'd thought he'd muted his tone to at least reasonably acceptable, but the look on her face—stunned, eyes wide and widening, jaw dropping, mouth agape, disbelief in every line—suggested he'd fallen far short.

For several seconds, she simply stared at him, then, slowly, she started to shake her head. "Oh, no, no, no."

He felt his jaw set, his features instinctively hardening.

Her mouth snapped shut. Her lips compressed to a thin line, and something fiery leapt in her eyes before they narrowed to sharp gray flints. "*No.*" She punctuated the emphatic declaration by jabbing her index finger into his chest. Hard. "I am not—I repeat, *not*—going to be left out here, supposedly in safety, while you go in there to face God knows what."

Her diction was precise, forceful, with a hint of queenly power; she almost sounded like his mother.

"Besides, you great arrogant oaf"—she stepped close enough for him to see the fire in her eyes and drilled her jabbing finger into his sternum— "if you truly want me to be safe, from whatever *I* might do as well as all else, then you'll get it through your thick skull that the safest place for me to be *at any time* is right by your side."

Her chin set; her gaze bored into his.

For an instant, they teetered, will against will.

Time froze.

Waves softly shushed on the sand, and high overhead, a seagull wheeled and screeched.

He had time enough to study her face, to sense the temper, the strength, the unbending will behind her demand.

He could crush it; he was the stronger.

But should he?

To have that—that feminine power—on his side, aligned with him through the rest of his life…

What was he willing to pay as the price?

He'd held her gaze throughout, just as she still held his. Neither of them would look away. Back away.

Both of them recognized the significance of the moment; given their characters, their temperaments, it was one they would have had to face at some point, at some time.

Climbing down was not something he did—could do—easily. It took significant effort to draw in a slow breath. He felt his chest rise beneath her finger. Then he fought to unlock his jaw and get his tongue around the words he'd elected to say.

"All right."

She blinked, just once. Very slowly, she drew her finger back. "All right?" Uttered as if she wasn't sure she believed her ears.

"Yes. All right." He bit off the words; his jaw was still clenched. He reached out and seized her still-raised hand. "You can come with me." He stepped back, swung to face the cleft, and started marching through the sand.

He felt her jerk into motion, then she hurried to keep up with him.

He reached the cleft. It was intensely dark inside.

As they passed through the opening and cool blackness fell over them, he adjusted his hold on her hand. "Stay close. And for pity's sake, don't dart ahead."

His tone made the words an outright order; too bad—he'd bent as far as he was going to.

# CHAPTER 14

*A*ntonia blinked and blinked, trying to get her eyes to adjust. The opening in the cliff faced east, and it was afternoon; very little illumination reached into the passageway they seemed to have stepped into. The area in which they stood was wider than the entrance, but her senses informed her the walls and roof were not that far away; it wasn't as if they stood in a cave.

Sebastian had taken only three paces, then stopped, bringing her to a halt beside and a little behind him.

Now he stepped forward again, slowly.

She remembered and asked, "Do you have your candle and matchbox?"

"The matchbox, yes, but you dropped the candle in the crypt, and I forgot to pick up another."

"Oh." She peered into the blackness. "Can you see at all?"

"Not well. But then neither could they, so… Ah. Here we are." He let go of her hand.

She immediately clutched his coat. "Here we are what?"

She sensed him reaching upward with both hands.

"There's a ledge up here—with candles." He lowered his arms, then reached around and caught her hand.

She felt him press a candle into her palm and grasped it. "Just as long as there are no mice, rats, or bats," she muttered.

He chuckled. She sensed him searching in his pockets, then he struck a match, and it flared. He caught her hand, held it steady, and lit the candle. Once the wick caught, he released her hand and reached into his pocket. "This time, I'll carry one as well. Just in case of bats."

He'd murmured the last sentence under his breath. She pretended she hadn't heard it. Holding her candle high, she turned, examining the area in which they stood. "It's like a small antechamber."

"Indeed." He reached over and lit his candle from hers. Once it was alight, he faced away from the entrance, then reached back and took her free hand. "And there is a tunnel leading toward the house."

He walked forward, and she followed close behind.

They'd gone only a few yards when he said, "Steps." Holding his candle aloft, he started up them. Crudely hacked into the stone, the steps weren't steep; they were like stair steps and easy enough to climb.

She tugged her hand from his; he halted and looked back.

"My skirt." The candle in one hand, with the other, she raised her heavy skirt and climbed in his wake.

He faced forward and continued.

Her gaze on the steps, she counted twelve, then they reached a level stretch. She released her skirt, and he reached back and took her hand again, and they walked on. As far as she could tell, they were traveling in a roughly straight line, perpendicular to the beach—which meant directly west, more or less directly toward Pressingstoke Hall.

After a moment, she asked, "Wouldn't gunpowder stored in a cave in the cliff get damp?"

"Normally, yes, which is why I wasn't in any great hurry to search for smugglers' caves, which are usually by the shore. But we're already some way from the water, and limestone is drying. The air here is already bone dry."

"So perfect for storing gunpowder."

"Indeed."

An unsettling thought occurred. "What if the candles burn down?"

He didn't immediately reply. But after several more steps, he said, "I assume that, as there weren't any lamps, only candles, then wherever the area for storing things along here is, getting to it and getting back can be done within a candle's life. There were stubs left on that ledge, but I chose two unused candles."

The existence of candle stubs was, she decided, sufficiently reassuring.

Then they passed through a roughly hewn archway and stepped into a large space—so large, the candles' light didn't reach any walls. She looked up and couldn't see any roof, either.

"This has to be the place." Sebastian studied the cavern's sandy floor. "It's clear those men have been here. The floor all the way along has had boot prints the same as those on the beach." He looked ahead. The boot prints led on. "Let's see where they go."

Stepping to the side of the well-tramped trail, he drew Antonia behind him, and they moved steadily forward.

He sensed a stir in the air and stared ahead. There was a darker patch in the dimness before them—perhaps the opening of a tunnel leading onward.

"Look!" Antonia tugged his hand and halted.

He glanced at her and saw her pointing at the floor ahead and to their right with the hand holding her candle. He followed the direction, then grinned. *"At last."*

He let go of her hand and walked to the marks she'd spotted, then crouched and examined the circular impressions left in the sandy floor.

Antonia came to stand at his shoulder. She raised her candle, illuminating the line of circles. "Ten. Ten barrels stood here."

He released a breath, then straightened. "Until last night."

She glanced sharply at him, as if hearing more in his tone than he'd intended. "How much gunpowder is there in ten barrels?"

He glanced again at the impressions by his feet. Heard the grim note in his voice as he replied, "Barrels this size would each hold a hundredweight." He'd expected fewer barrels, maybe three or four. Not ten.

"A hundred and twelve pounds *each*?" When he nodded, she paused, then said, "But...that's over *one thousand pounds* of gunpowder!"

His face felt like stone as he nodded. "Indeed. Enough to blow up something very large." And the barrels were already on their way to London.

Urgency gripped him. He reached out and caught her hand. "We need to get news of this to Whitehall immediately—"

"Oh, no, you don't."

The voice came out of the darkness ahead.

Sebastian swung to face the threat, and light—a strong, brilliant beam of it—hit him in the face.

Some man—just a vague shadow in the opening of what, in the faint light reflected from the distant cavern walls, was revealed as a tunnel leading onward—ruthlessly directed a powerful lantern beam into Sebastian's and Antonia's eyes.

Sebastian raised the hand holding his candle and tried to shield his face, but he couldn't escape that disorienting, blinding light.

He and Antonia were standing together; a mistake.

He released her hand and stepped away from her. "Drop the candle," he murmured and tossed his away.

She did the same.

He took another, larger step away from her, forcing the man to swing the lantern beam more widely to keep them both in sight.

"Stop!" the man ordered.

Antonia gave up trying to see the man clearly and looked at Sebastian—saw him disregard the man's order and keep edging away from her.

Then the lantern beam locked on Sebastian, and the sound of a pistol being cocked echoed through the cavern.

She knew that sound. Knew what she was seeing—and immediately realized Sebastian had it wrong.

He was ensuring the man shot him and not her.

But if the man wounded Sebastian, who would protect her? The man wouldn't allow her to live. And if he killed Sebastian…

Her heart seized.

Sebastian's gaze swung from the man to her.

*"No!"* She flung herself toward him.

Sebastian felt his heart stop. He saw Antonia spring toward him, distantly heard her scream.

He was already moving, launching himself at her—forced by instincts too powerful to resist to change direction and protect her.

The pistol roared, the sound magnified by the rock around them.

The ball sliced through the air where, a split second before, he'd been, and ricocheted into the darkness.

He collided with Antonia, clutched her to him, and let his momentum, dampened but not negated by hers, carry them on and down. He rolled, shifting to cushion her head as they landed. Then he pushed her from him and turned onto his side between her and their assailant, and frantically reached for his right coat pocket.

The lantern beam swung wildly as the man tried to locate them. Then it steadied above their heads and started to lower.

Searching desperately, Sebastian slumped onto his back.

A second before the light reached his face, his fingers closed around the butt of his pistol. He hauled it from his pocket, sighted, and fired.

The man cried out. The lantern wobbled crazily, but the bastard didn't fall, just cursed.

In the reflected glow from the now-erratically swinging lantern beam, Sebastian saw the man heave something their way; he reached up and batted the projectile—the man's spent pistol—aside. It clattered to the rock floor.

Glancing back at the man, Sebastian started to push to his feet—only to realize the bastard was fleeing.

The lantern light winked out.

Leaving him blinking into complete and utter darkness. "Damn!"

He dropped back to sit on the floor.

"*My God*—are you hurt?" Suddenly, Antonia was clambering over him—in the dark patting him, working her way to his face. "Sebastian? Say something! Did he shoot you? *Where*, for heaven's sake?"

He caught her hands, one in each of his, and yanked her to him. He released her hands, found her face, held it immobile, and crushed his lips to hers.

The emotions crashing through him were too many, too great, to make any sense of. All he knew was that if she hadn't acted—hadn't flung herself at him—he would, almost certainly, be dead. And she might have been facing a worse fate.

It seemed all wrong—completely and inescapably wrong. She shouldn't even have been there. If he'd had his way—if she hadn't pushed, or if he'd pigheadedly insisted on letting his protective self hold sway as he'd been so very close to doing—she would have been waiting in safety on the shore for him.

And he would never have returned to her.

He would never again have felt the indescribable thrill of her hands desperately clutching at him, of her fingers winding in his hair, never again have experienced the transcendent glory of her lips soft and pliant under his, kissing him back with a fervor and a passion to match his.

A maelstrom of feelings wracked him—wracked them. He kissed her ferociously, and she responded in kind, as if letting him go was something she couldn't yet manage.

Relief, and the knowledge that they were still there—alive, hale, whole, and together—eventually seeped into their brains.

A storm of reaction still roiled inside them, but they couldn't let it rage—not now. Not here.

Not yet.

He filled his lungs and drew back.

They broke from the kiss; his hands cradling her face, her hands framing his jaw, each holding the other captive, with their breathing still ragged, each leaned their forehead against the other's in wordless communion.

In wordless support.

Several seconds passed, then they both drew deep breaths and moved apart.

Refocused.

He glanced toward where he judged the mouth of the onward tunnel lay. "Did you see who it was?"

"No. You?"

"Just that it was one of the younger men."

In the dark, he felt her push to her feet. "And from his accent, it was one of the Irishmen—so Filbury, Wilson, or Connell Boyne."

He nodded, then realized she couldn't see. Moving slowly so he wouldn't bump into her, he drew his legs in and stood. "We need to get back to the house and see which one is wounded."

"Are you sure you hit him?"

"Yes. But he knows I know, so he'll be running as fast as he can. We need to hurry."

"I can't see anything," she said. "We both dropped our candles."

He felt in his pockets and was relieved to discover his matchbox still there. "I have matches, but we'll need to find at least one of the candles." Carefully, he opened the matchbox and extracted one of Congreve's matches. "Ready?"

"Yes."

He struck the match. As soon as it flared, he held it at head height, and they both searched the floor.

"There!" She pounced. Just as the match burned down, and he swore and dropped it, she triumphantly rose, holding one of the half-burned candles.

He drew out another match, lit it, then he lit the candle, and they finally had light enough to see each other.

For an instant, they stared—and it felt as if a rush of urgent things both needed to say passed between them in a second.

Then they both drew in a breath, and she looked toward the tunnel leading onward. "Do we follow him? That will be the fastest way, won't it? On to the house?"

He considered. "No, we can't go that way." An explanation of the dictate leapt readily to his tongue. "If I were him, I would wait along the tunnel somewhere and hope we come along. It's still very much in his best interests to make sure we don't reappear—at least not alive."

She drew in a quick breath and, in a brisker tone, said, "Very well. It's back to the beach. At least we know it's not that far."

And they knew the terrain; they accomplished the return journey to the beach in a matter of minutes. They stumbled into the deeper sand on the shore. Sebastian blew out the candle, stubbed it on his boot sole, stuffed the remnant into his pocket, then caught Antonia's hand and helped her run back through the sands to the spot where they'd come down the cliff.

Because of that last large stone, they had to find an alternative route up.

He studied the climb, then glanced at her. "Can you manage it?"

She threw him a look he remembered from long ago, reached up, caught a branch, and swung herself onto the slope.

This time, he let her go first. He followed close behind, lending a steadying hand whenever she needed one.

It was a scramble, but she uttered not one word of complaint, just grabbed branches and bushes and hauled herself up.

Finally, they gained the top of the slope.

They both paused to catch their breaths.

Then their eyes met, and they raced for the horses.

* * *

They thundered across the fields. Sebastian didn't need to glance over his shoulder to check on Antonia. He knew she was an accomplished rider; he trusted in her abilities to keep up.

She was only two lengths behind him when, eschewing the path to the stable yard, he veered across the side lawn. He rode directly to the side door; it was their fastest route into the house.

He hauled the gray to a halt, flung himself from the saddle, and was waiting to lift Antonia from hers the instant she drew up.

She did, and he seized her about the waist, swung her down, released her, took her hand, and together, they ran for the door.

He thrust it open. "Pray he lingered, hoping to catch us in the tunnel."

They strode straight down the corridor toward the estate office, but as they neared the office door, they saw Crawford and Sir Humphrey in the front hall. The men's backs were to the corridor, and they were being railed at by Parrish and McGibbin.

"Damned man came barreling out through the servant's door." His face ruddy, McGibbin pointed down the front hall. "No consideration as to who might be out here."

"He slammed into my wife and sent her spinning." Parrish was well-nigh apoplectic. "But did he stop? Did he even pause?"

"Inspector! Sir Humphrey!" Sebastian strode out of the corridor.

Keeping pace at his side, her hand still clamped in his, Antonia noticed Mrs. Parrish sprawled limply in a chair against the wall by the side of the stairs. The older woman had one hand pressed to her ample bosom; her eyes were closed, and she was breathing stertorously.

Parrish and McGibbin broke off at Sebastian's hail. Crawford and Sir Humphrey spun around.

"Earith!" Crawford recovered first. His sharp eyes raked them both. "You have news?"

"Yes," Sebastian said, "but there's no time to explain." He switched his gaze to Parrish and McGibbin. "Who was it who came charging out just now?"

McGibbin blinked. "Boyne. Connell Boyne. He came racing out and sent poor Mrs. Parrish flying."

"He didn't so much as glance her way." Parrish returned to his complaint. "He just raced on"—Parrish waved up the front hall—

"straight out through the front door. Disgraceful behavior!"

Along with Sebastian, Antonia had followed Parrish's gesture; looking toward the front door, she saw that it stood wide.

She met Sebastian's gaze briefly—Connell Boyne was their murderer, and he'd fled—then Sebastian looked at the inspector and Sir Humphrey and urgently said, "Lady Antonia and I found those signs we were searching for in a cavern off the beach to the east. But some man—one of the three younger Irishmen—found us there and shot at us. He missed. I didn't—I'm sure I winged him. He escaped up a tunnel that we think leads back to the house. We couldn't follow and had to race back across the fields."

Sebastian looked at Parrish and McGibbin. "Was Connell Boyne injured when he came through here?"

McGibbin and Parrish blinked, then they exchanged a long look. "Yes. He was."

They all looked at Mrs. Parrish. Antonia had noticed that, as Sebastian had spoken, Mrs. Parrish had opened her eyes and slowly sat up. She'd been listening closely.

Now, her lips set grimly, she nodded to Sebastian, the inspector, and Sir Humphrey. "Connell was clutching his left arm, just above the elbow. I noticed when he ran into me." She paused as if remembering. "I believe I saw blood."

She looked down at the floor, scanning a certain area. "He ran into me about there." She waved vaguely at the space before the side corridor. "Then he ran that way..." She followed the line, then triumphantly pointed. "There! That's a spot of blood, isn't it?"

Antonia slipped her fingers from Sebastian's hold and walked over to look.

She was joined by the inspector, who crouched and examined the spot, then he rose and nodded to Sebastian and Sir Humphrey. "It's blood." His gaze locked with sudden intensity on Sebastian's face. "Is Connell Boyne our murderer?"

His expression grim, Sebastian hesitated, then grimaced. "I can't say—there might have been someone else working with him. But Connell Boyne is connected with the secret Ennis was killed to protect, so..." His voice hardened. "Regardless, Boyne's fled, and we need to catch him."

"Right, then." Sir Humphrey looked up the hall to the front door. "He might have gone that way, but no doubt he circled around to the stable."

"He was heading for the side door," Mrs. Parrish said, "but he ran full-tilt into me, and then we were all milling there, so he changed direction and rushed for the front door."

Sebastian swore beneath his breath. "We left our horses at the side door. We didn't go to the stable yard."

His gaze met Antonia's, then as one, they turned and rushed back down the corridor to the side door.

As she passed them, Antonia saw the inspector and Sir Humphrey exchange a look, then both men fell in at her heels.

From farther back, she heard Mrs. Parrish saying, "I'll tell the others. Go! *Go!*"

Sebastian hauled open the side door. He and she rushed down the steps onto the lawn. Their mounts had been grazing. They caught the reins and turned them, then, with the inspector and Sir Humphrey now leading the way, strode on toward the stable yard.

Sir Humphrey marched in under the stable arch. The stable master was standing in the open stable door. Sir Humphrey hailed him and demanded, "Did Connell Boyne come this way?"

"Aye—you've just missed him." Frowning, the stable master walked out to join them. "Came racing down in a right state and yelled for his horse. He was nursing one arm, but he wouldn't let me see. Just insisted he have his horse, and the instant it was brought out, he hauled himself up and took off."

"Which way?" Sebastian asked. "Did anyone see?"

"I didn't." The stable master turned and looked back toward the stable.

The youngest stable lad had gathered with his fellows in the entrance; it was he who volunteered, "Went northwest, he did." The lad pointed. "Up toward the road."

"We need horses." The inspector stood at Sir Humphrey's shoulder. "Right now."

Increasingly grim-faced, the stable master nodded and signaled his lads, and they leapt toward the stalls.

Crawford turned to Sebastian and Antonia. "You two need to wait for us. You can't go after him alone—he might well have rearmed himself by now, or met up with others."

Sebastian frowned. "He must be heading toward Canterbury and the London road."

Sir Humphrey humphed. "That's a decent ride across country, and he's wounded—he won't be able to ride that hard. We'll catch up with him before he gets far."

Sebastian glanced at Antonia, then nodded. "Very well. We'll wait and ride with you."

They heard footsteps on the path and the sounds of male voices exclaiming. The four of them turned and beheld the rest of the male guests; as a group, led by Parrish and McGibbin, they came striding into the stable yard.

Parrish and McGibbin halted before Sir Humphrey and the inspector, with the other four men ranging at their backs. "We understand," Parrish said, "that Boyne—Connell Boyne—is somehow behind what's been going on here over the past week. If you're riding out after him, we want to come, too."

"It's only fair," Wilson put in. "He murdered his brother and sister-in-law and caused suspicion to fall on all of us."

The inspector stared at the group, then glanced at Sir Humphrey. "More eyes and hands, more witnesses. It can't hurt."

Sir Humphrey pursed his lips, but then nodded.

"Excellent." Hadley Featherstonehaugh stepped around the inspector and Sir Humphrey and led the other men to the stable.

Two stable lads led out saddled horses for Sir Humphrey and the inspector, then rushed back to help saddle the rest.

Antonia brought the mare around, then glanced at Sebastian.

He handed the gray's reins to the inspector, then grasped Antonia about the waist and hoisted her up.

She slid her feet into the stirrups and settled her skirt.

Sebastian retrieved his reins from Crawford. He met Crawford's eyes, then glanced at Sir Humphrey. "We need Connell Boyne alive."

"Because of that business with the gunpowder?" the inspector asked.

Sebastian nodded. "You've both seen my authority."

"Oh, you'll get no argument from me." Crawford looked at Sir Humphrey. "I'd prefer him alive, too. I like all my loose ends neatly tied off, even when they aren't, strictly speaking, mine."

"Apropos of loose ends"—Sebastian looked to where the other men were emerging from the stable one by one, each leading a saddled horse—"we agree that most of the male guests could have killed Lady Ennis, but I've always wondered about which man she, dressed as she was, would have allowed into her room at that time of night without her being very much on her guard. If she had no other lover among the guests, then aside from myself, the only other man of the company I could imagine her inviting in without a qualm would be her brother-in-law. As far as she knew, she had nothing to fear from Connell. To my mind, he should be at the top of your list of suspects for her murder, but we'll never have any proof short of a confession." He focused on Crawford. "Unless you learned anything from the staff?"

Crawford shook his head. "Not a thing. None of them were in that part of the house at that time."

Sebastian nodded. "That was to be expected. However, there's something that's been nagging at me about Connell's alibi for Ennis's murder. You told Lady Antonia and me that it was difficult to see how Connell could have stabbed Ennis late enough to meet the doctor's timetable, then got to the end of the library in time to be seen sitting there by Parrish and Featherstonehaugh without also being seen going into the library by them." Sebastian paused as Worthington, Filbury, and Wilson, now mounted and looking intent and grim, walked their horses up and reined in to wait for the others.

Featherstonehaugh had already walked his horse out; he brought his gelding to join the other three and swung up to the saddle.

Sebastian looked at Hadley. "Featherstonehaugh, on the evening that Ennis was murdered, when you and Parrish came upon Boyne reading in the library, how long was it between the time you set eyes on Boyne in the chair at the end of the library and the clocks striking ten?"

Hadley met Sebastian's gaze, then he frowned, and his expression grew distant. "More than one minute. Two? Probably." He refocused on Sebastian. "We came into the library and saw Boyne at the end. Parrish and I exchanged glances, then we ambled down the room—it's a long room—and then started chatting with Boyne. So all in all, I would say between two and three minutes passed before the clocks struck. I doubt it was longer."

Sebastian looked at the inspector. "When you considered Connell's alibi, did you take into account the second door into the library—the one in the corridor wall directly opposite the billiards room door?"

Crawford's expression drained. "What?"

Sebastian went on, "It's not a concealed door, but it fits so well into the paneling it would be easy to miss seeing it. Connell would have known about that door. It's at the end of the library where he was found sitting, and it's only a few paces from the study door. He didn't need to go around into the front hall to enter the library through the main door. If Connell left the study at the same time as Featherstonehaugh and Parrish left the dining room, they wouldn't have seen him, and he would have been in that chair when they entered the library."

"Good God." Crawford's expression was a medley of surprise, chagrin, and delight. "Damn—that's how he did it."

"Indeed." Sebastian gathered his reins and mounted. He settled in the saddle. "But there's something else that seemed contrived." He looked at Worthington, Filbury, and Wilson. "Did Connell read much?"

"Good God, no!" came from all three throats.

Then all three looked struck.

After a moment, Worthington slowly said, "I've never seen him with a book in his hand in all the time I've known him. And I've known him for a good ten years, ever since coming on the town."

"Well, that's that thread tied off." Crawford glanced around, noted McGibbin and Parrish trotting up, gathered his reins, and mounted. "Connell Boyne is our murderer."

"If you want a rationale for how and why he killed Cecilia," Antonia coolly said, "we've told you she was worried—even fearful—on that last night. She'd started to suspect something of what was behind Ennis's murder. I think she turned to Connell. He was Ennis's brother, and she trusted him—why wouldn't she? Her husband had. I think she might well have asked Connell to come to her room. When he did, she poured out her suspicions." Antonia looked at Filbury and Wilson. "Possibly, courtesy of that conversation you two had with her in the conservatory, she misinterpreted your concerns and suspected one or both of you. But Connell couldn't have Cecilia raising such concerns with the inspector or Sir Humphrey."

"So he killed her." Sir Humphrey's tone suggested there was no longer any question about that. The magistrate heaved himself into the saddle.

"All in cold blood." Crawford shook his head. "This is a bad business all around."

Sir Humphrey settled in his saddle and looked over the assembled company. "Right, then. We're all here." He swung his horse's head toward the stable arch. "So let's get after the blighter."

They clattered out of the stable yard and set course for Canterbury. When they reached the fields, Sir Humphrey directed them to spread out, and they galloped steadily on in pursuit of Connell Boyne.

\* \* \*

Antonia galloped on, holding the mare in position in the grim line between Sebastian and Hadley. The ground was damp, soft enough to hold tracks, and the inspector, Filbury, and Sebastian were all exceedingly good at picking them out.

That said, the afternoon light was waning, fading by degrees, and an autumnal mist was springing up, hanging low over the fields. Consequently, Sir Humphrey had ordered them to spread out in case Boyne swerved abruptly. The pace they were maintaining was moving them through the fields quickly, yet with little chance of missing any sudden diversion Boyne might have made.

They were still well within the estate when a riderless horse came galloping toward them.

Wilson—who had an excellent seat and hands and rode with instinctive confidence—diverted to intercept the beast, and Worthington and Parrish broke from the line and followed.

"Everyone else keep riding!" Sir Humphrey bellowed.

They did, all now peering ahead into the gathering gloom.

Three minutes later, Wilson, Worthington, and Parrish rejoined the line, with Wilson leading the other horse.

"Is it Boyne's?" the inspector called.

"We think so," Parrish replied. "It's from the Hall stables, and other than us, who else had a horse out?"

They all digested that.

Riding on Sebastian's other side, Sir Humphrey turned to him. "Any chance you more than winged him?"

Sebastian shook his head. "If I'd wounded him more severely, it would have slowed him down before he barreled out of the depths of the house. And the cavern where I shot him was just back from the shore—he'd covered a fair distance on foot in a reasonable time when he emerged, yet he made it to the stable, got on a horse, and rode off..." He paused, then grimaced. "It's possible the effort and the blood loss have caught up with him, and he's fallen off."

Sir Humphrey grunted. He settled back in his saddle and called to the company to keep their eyes peeled for a body on the ground.

Antonia hesitated, then leaned forward and called across Sebastian to Sir Humphrey, "Connell might have met someone with a carriage and turned the horse loose."

Sebastian grimaced.

Sir Humphrey looked disgusted. "That puts a different complexion on things." He raised his voice again. "Damn it—let's pick up the pace. We don't want to lose the beggar."

Sebastian and the inspector pulled a little ahead. Filbury joined them, all three keeping their gazes trained down, following the tracks imprinted on the grassy ground.

The group forged on. Connell hadn't leapt fences but had left gates swinging wide; although he'd detoured to go through the gates, he invariably returned to his northwesterly course. It became increasingly clear that he was making for the northwest corner of the estate. Antonia remembered the dense coppice that occupied that area. If one wanted to rendezvous with someone coming from elsewhere and be sure no one on the estate would see, that coppice was perfect in structure, location, and isolation.

Sure enough, Connell's horse's tracks led directly to the entrance to the narrow path meandering to the clearing in the center of the large coppice.

They all drew rein, dismounted, and tied their mounts to trees along the edge of the coppice.

Sebastian, Filbury, and Crawford were crouched just inside the edge of the trees, examining the surface of the path. They rose as, together with all the others, Antonia joined them.

The inspector met Sir Humphrey's gaze and tipped his head along the path. "He's gone striding in. No sign he's staggering." He'd kept his voice just above a whisper, but then looked down the path and humphed. "Chances are he's well on his way, but we'd better check."

The path was only wide enough for one. Crawford led the way, with

Sir Humphrey at his heels, with Sebastian, Antonia's hand again in his, behind the magistrate. The others followed Antonia in single file.

When they'd visited the coppice earlier in the day, by standing in his stirrups on the tall gray, Sebastian had been able to see through the largely bare branches into the clearing, but only well enough to discern that there was no building hidden within it. At ground level, the density of trunks and saplings restricted their view. It wasn't until, behind Sir Humphrey, Sebastian stepped into the clearing itself—obviously created to allow more effective access to the trees in the center of the unusually large coppice—that he could fully observe the enclosed space.

It was larger than he'd expected. Large enough that four trees had been allowed to grow in a clump in the clearing's center.

Connell Boyne was sitting on the ground, facing away from them, with his back against one of the central trees.

Crawford had checked at the sight of him. Now, he went forward cautiously. "Connell Boyne!"

Boyne didn't react.

Sebastian's imagination immediately provided a reason for Boyne's stillness, but he held the thought at bay and followed Sir Humphrey as, still moving slowly, the group split into two. Half followed Crawford clockwise around the trees, while the rest, including Sebastian and Antonia, followed Sir Humphrey in an anticlockwise direction.

Crawford was the first to look down on their quarry. The inspector's features set. Boyne sat slumped with his legs stretched out before him.

Sir Humphrey joined the inspector several paces back from Boyne's boots. The magistrate grimaced.

Sebastian and Antonia came up beside Sir Humphrey.

It was transparently clear that Connell Boyne was dead.

Quite aside from the bloody furrow above his left elbow that Mrs. Parrish had described, there was now a gaping, still sluggishly seeping hole in the left side of his chest.

Sebastian eased out a slow breath.

Antonia tightened her grip on his hand, and he squeezed her fingers.

All the other men joined them. Everyone stood silently looking down on what remained of Connell Boyne.

Then Antonia murmured, "He came here to meet someone—a meeting arranged beforehand. Connell expected to leave—to get away—with whoever he met—that's why he let his horse go." The other men glanced at her curiously; they didn't know anything about the motives behind the murders, about Connell's involvement in a serious plot.

"Yes." His expression like stone, Crawford nodded. "But whoever he met killed him instead."

A breeze stirred the last of the autumn leaves still clinging to the branches, setting up a dry, rustling susurration. The mist was thickening, lending a ghostly aura to the scene.

Sebastian stirred. "Dead men can't talk."

He glanced at Antonia, then at Sir Humphrey and Crawford. "Lady Antonia and I have to return to London."

# CHAPTER 15

*I*n what felt like an omen, the city's bells were tolling ten o'clock when Sebastian drew his grays to a stamping halt outside St. Ives House.

Wilkins leapt down to the pavement, rushed up the steps and plied the knocker, then returned to assist Beccy to the ground before running to hold the horses' heads.

Sebastian stepped down, surrendered the reins to the young groom in St. Ives livery who came pelting up the area steps, then went to the phaeton's side and handed Antonia down.

"Beccy." Safely on the pavement, Antonia turned to her maid. "We'll be spending the night at St. Ives House. The marquess and I have business to attend to which is likely to keep us out very late—you don't need to wait up."

Beccy bobbed a curtsy. "Yes, miss." As she straightened, she asked, "Should I unpack your things?"

"Just what I need for the night." Antonia glanced at Sebastian.

He briefly met her gaze, then looked over Beccy's head at Wilkins, who nodded. Despite the rush of leaving Pressingstoke Hall, Sebastian had found time to instruct Wilkins to tell the St. Ives housekeeper to put Antonia in the room next to his.

He reached for her arm, linked it with his, and turned her along the street. "Let's see if fortune has elected to favor us, and Drake's at home."

He—and, he felt sure, Antonia, too—fervently hoped Drake had returned from Ireland. To him, her, Sir Humphrey, and Inspector

Crawford, the manner of Connell Boyne's slaying had underscored the seriousness of the plot in which Boyne had—clearly—played his part. That, and ten hundredweight of gunpowder, tended to focus the mind wonderfully.

After finding Boyne dead, with Sir Humphrey's and Crawford's blessings, Sebastian and Antonia had immediately left the coppice and ridden hell for leather back to the house. They'd flung themselves into a flurry of packing, dallied only long enough for Antonia to farewell her friends and assure them that Hadley would explain all when he returned, then she and Sebastian had climbed into the phaeton, and he'd driven them back to town in record time.

Wolverstone House was a hundred yards farther along the north side of Grosvenor Square. Sebastian escorted Antonia up the steps, then wielded the knocker.

Light could be seen through the transom window; when the butler, Hamilton, opened the door, they saw the front hall was fully lit.

Hamilton recognized them instantly; before they could say anything, he bowed. "Lord Earith. My lady." He smoothly stepped back and waved them inside.

Surmising that Drake had mentioned they might arrive, with his hand at Antonia's back, Sebastian ushered her inside. Immediately Hamilton closed the door, Sebastian asked, "I take it the marquess is at home."

"Indeed, sir." Hamilton reached for Antonia's cloak. "He arrived not fifteen minutes ago and is presently bathing. He said you might call, and that if you did, the matter would be urgent." He relieved Antonia of her bonnet as well, then accepted the greatcoat Sebastian shrugged off. "I will inform his lordship of your arrival immediately."

"Thank you. Please confirm that the matter is, indeed, urgent. Oh, and Hamilton?"

"Yes, my lord?"

"Is there any chance of something to eat? We've driven direct from the Kent coast and haven't eaten since an early lunch."

Hamilton looked pleased; the man was known to thrive on domestic challenges. "Of course, my lord. If you and Lady Antonia will make yourselves comfortable in the drawing room, I will arrange for a suitable repast to be served momentarily."

Antonia added her thanks to Sebastian's, and they walked into the long, formal drawing room.

A cheery fire was crackling in the grate. Antonia led the way to one of the matching pair of sofas facing each other across the Aubusson rug spread before the fireplace and sank onto the silk damask with a sigh.

Sebastian followed and sat beside her. After a moment, he reached across, closed his hand about one of hers, then raised her fingers to his lips and pressed a kiss to her knuckles.

Then he lowered their linked hands to rest on his thigh, sat back, closed his eyes, and let the peace and stability, the tranquility of the house—and of her—wrap about him.

Ten minutes later—all of which they'd spent in blissful silence—Hamilton came to summon them to the smaller dining room, the one the family used. The table could seat twelve, and given the size of the current ducal couple's family, that was sometimes only just enough. Three places had been set at one end, with a plethora of dishes already arrayed before them.

Hamilton sat Antonia in the seat to the right of the carver, leaving Sebastian to claim the place beside her.

"The marquess requests that you make a start without him. He, too, hasn't yet dined and will join you as soon as he's able." Hamilton lifted the lid of a tureen. "I can recommend the oyster soup." A savory aroma emerged, carried on the steam.

Antonia nodded eagerly. Sebastian's mouth watered.

After serving them, being experienced in the ways of his masters, Hamilton filled their wine glasses, then retreated.

They were supping second servings of the delicious soup, when the door opened, and Drake entered.

Antonia lowered her soup spoon and blinked. "Good Lord."

Resplendent in a dark, multihued, silk-velvet dressing gown thrown over a shirt and soft trousers, Drake shut the door carefully, then strolled slowly forward. He waved languidly. "Pray excuse my déshabillé, Antonia."

She pointed at the carver. "For God's sake, sit, before you fall down." With a small, quite gentle smile, Drake moved to obey.

Antonia found herself staring at the dark circles around Drake's hooded eyes. His habitual languid drawl had sounded more drawly than usual, and the way he moved… She'd never seen the normally vigorous and virile Drake so drained and depleted. He looked as if he might collapse in a heap at any moment.

He made it into the chair, sinking into the embrace of the carver as if he was a much older man. But his golden eyes had already surveyed the dishes and their plates. "Is that oyster soup?"

"Yes." Antonia reached out and picked up the soup ladle. When Drake handed her his soup plate, she took it, added two ladlefuls of the creamy liquid, then handed it back. "Eat. You look like a shadow of your former self."

His long lips twitched. He exchanged a look with Sebastian. "I understand you've rushed up nonstop from Kent." He paused to take a mouthful of the soup. "Against that, I've been traveling for the past two days, some of it running. Literally."

Leaving him to eat—and hopefully recover his strength along with his usual incisive wits—Antonia set aside her emptied soup plate and served herself a helping of what appeared to be braised venison. She passed the dish to Sebastian, who handed her a dish of assorted boiled vegetables in return.

While they ate, she was aware of Drake's eagle's gaze assessing them—something that bothered neither her nor Sebastian. They'd long grown used to Drake's rather acute scrutiny; there was no real way to avoid it, and it was only an issue if one had something one wanted to hide.

Speaking of which…Antonia noticed the knuckles on Drake's right hand were scraped. She contemplated the sight, then glanced to her right, at Sebastian's hands. Looking again at Drake, she caught his eye and nodded at his hand. "You should have worn gloves."

Drake glanced at his knuckles and faintly winced. "Gloves wouldn't have fitted with the costume. I shouldn't have been there at all, but…" He shrugged.

"I mean," she persisted, "that if you want to pass for someone of lower station, you need to wear gloves. Your hands"—with her gaze, she directed his attention to Sebastian's—"are like his." Long fingered and elegant. "They immediately mark you for what you are."

Drake looked mildly taken aback. "Perhaps that was it…"

From which Antonia deduced he'd been playing one of his charades, had been found out, and had had to fight his way free.

Drake finished his soup and pushed aside his plate. After a moment, as if infused with renewed—renewing—energy, he sat straighter. As he helped himself to the venison, he murmured, "You both look rather rumpled—definitely not your usual debonair selves. I take it your day was eventful."

Sebastian had cleared his plate and was feeling human once more. He set down his cutlery, pushed aside the plate, reached for his wine glass, and leaned back in the chair. "Let's see—dealing with a Scotland Yard inspector and a magistrate, both engaged in investigating two murders, then riding out searching farmhouses, cottages, haysheds, barns, and the like for barrels of gunpowder, then scrambling down a cliff face, trudging through sand, following a tunnel into a dark cavern, finding evidence of ten barrels of gunpowder having been stored there, being shot at and having to take a dive, then racing back out to the beach, scrambling back up the cliff, riding like the wind across the estate, then riding out again in pursuit of the murderer—also the only one we knew of who could tell us about that gunpowder—only to find the man dead. Shot." Sebastian arched his brows. "Then we had to pack and drive up to town. So yes, eventful enough."

Drake had frozen in the act of skewering a potato. "Gunpowder." He stared at Sebastian, then looked at the potato, stabbed it, transferred it to his plate, then imperiously waved at them both. "Start at the beginning, and if at all possible, leave nothing crucial out."

Sebastian settled to relate all that had happened from the moment they'd arrived at Pressingstoke Hall. Antonia added her observations as appropriate.

When informed of Ennis's last words, Drake frowned. "Gunpowder here." After a moment, he shook his head. "At least you managed to find it."

"Unfortunately not—we only found where it had been." Sebastian continued describing all the pertinent events up to the point of them discovering the imprint of ten barrels in the cavern off the beach, and their deduction that the barrels had been moved during the previous night.

"So most likely into a wagon and most likely ferried up to London." Drake paused, then refocused on Sebastian. "And then?"

With several interjections from Antonia, Sebastian recounted how they'd been shot at by the man involved, who had proved to be Connell Boyne, how they'd missed catching him at the house and had given chase, and subsequently found him murdered in the coppice.

Drake had finished eating and, like Sebastian, was now sitting back in the carver and sipping wine. He grunted. "Dead men pass on no information." He sipped, then frowned. "But why was it necessary to kill him? Why not just spirit him away?"

Sebastian shrugged. "Too risky now the authorities knew who they were looking for?"

Drake's golden eyes narrowed. "Possibly." After several moments, he said, "The way I see this, Ennis, as well as his brother, Connell, had been secretly supporting the Young Irelander movement, but in Ennis's case, that support was by donation and encouragement, rather than by being actively involved. Connell, on the other hand, appears to have been seduced into actively working for the cause. Given he spent most of his time on the Ennis estate in Ireland, it's not hard to see how that might have come about."

"Possibly without Ennis knowing," Antonia said. She, too, was sitting back, cradling her glass, and listening avidly.

Drake inclined his head in agreement. He focused on the goblet he was slowly twirling between his long fingers. After a moment, his eyes hooded, he continued, "I was summoned to Ireland because my sources had heard whispers of some major plot being afoot. By the time I arrived in Dublin, they'd heard that the plot involved gunpowder. Subsequently, I learned that a group of Young Irelanders had secured a quantity of gunpowder—exactly how much, I didn't find out—and it had been dispatched to somewhere in England's south. The ship had already sailed from Limerick. The choice of port seemed odd at the time, but it might be explained by the Ennis estate lying in the countryside north of the town. Unsurprisingly, I decided we needed to know more about where the gunpowder was destined and for what purpose it was intended, so I worked my way deeper into the movement's hierarchy."

He frowned. "The strange—and to be truthful, troubling—fact was that no matter how high I went in the movement's upper ranks, no one seemed to know anything about this plot. No one was in charge of it, and it hadn't been discussed at any of the various inner council meetings."

"Did you reach deep enough—high enough—to be sure of that?" Sebastian asked.

Drake's expression hardened, and he glanced at his scraped knuckles. "Yes—that's what nearly broke my cover. I kept going higher in the organization. But I should have been following a solid trail from the foot soldiers who arranged the shipment—the Connell Boynes of the enterprise—to the upper echelons, but the moment I stepped away from the field, as it were, there was no trail—seemingly no connection whatsoever." Drake raised his lids, and his golden gaze met Sebastian's eyes. "And that makes me question whether this is, in fact, a Young Irelander plot at all."

It was Sebastian's turn to frown. "If not them, then"—he spread his hands—"who?"

"That, indeed, is the question." Drake drummed a finger on the table. "Someone over there in the higher ranks should have known about this plot, but no one did. Of that, I'm quite sure. While the Young Irelanders, like any movement of its kind, has its more militant arms, I've never heard of a scheme of this ilk being run purely by the lower ranks with no one in the upper echelons even being told of it. No well-organized movement encourages such things—renegade actions, those implemented without the knowledge or approval of the higher councils, risk said higher councils losing control of the movement."

Drake fell silent, then his finger stilled. After a moment, he murmured, "I wonder…could someone have seen the Young Irelander hotheads as potential hands to exploit?" Abandoning his sprawl, he leaned forward; with both forearms on the table, he cradled his goblet between his palms. His golden gaze was sharply intent and focused unseeing down the table. "Has someone been clever enough to manipulate a group of Young Irelander foot soldiers, including Connell Boyne, into thinking this plot is an officially sanctioned Young Irelander plot, even though it isn't?"

"That would certainly account for Ennis suddenly wanting to speak with you." Sebastian sipped, then lowered his goblet. "Consider this scenario—Connell, believing he's acting for the movement, arranges in secret for the gunpowder to be shipped, then comes to England to visit with Ennis at Pressingstoke Hall and discuss the harvest and other estate matters as he always does at this time of year—and while he's in Kent, to receive and hide the gunpowder, presumably directly off the ship, then to lead the men who arrive to take it on to London to the cavern. Either Ennis or Connell had to be there to show the ship's crew where the entrance to the cavern was and, later, to guide those who came with a wagon to take the barrels away."

"But," Antonia said, "Ennis knew nothing about the plot, not until Connell arrived at the Hall and told him of it."

Drake was nodding. "Do you know when Connell arrived in Kent?"

Sebastian exchanged a glance with Antonia. "I believe it was a week before the house party."

"Yes." Antonia said. "Cecilia confirmed that."

"The timing fits," Drake said. "Connell tells Ennis as soon as he arrives at the Hall. Assuming Ennis has been a supporter for years—and it's Ennis who has the money in the family—then Connell would have expected Ennis to be as committed to the plot as he himself was."

"Speaking of money"—Antonia glanced at Sebastian, then turned back to Drake—"we forgot to mention that we found a half-burned envelope in the grate in Ennis's study after he was murdered. On the envelope was written 'Three hundred pounds for'—but the rest had burned away."

Drake nodded. "And that fits, too. It would have fallen to Connell to pay the ship's captain for transporting the gunpowder, and so he had to tell Ennis all about the plot. Connell expected to have Ennis's full and unequivocal support. But Ennis saw the plot differently—he wasn't enthused at all. To his mind, such a plot would be a step too far—out of keeping with the movement's direction and very possibly not in its best interests. Open rebellion on home soil and protests in London and in parliament are one thing. But blowing up some building in London? Ennis was politician enough to know what that would lead to."

Sebastian snorted. "Even more heavy-handed repression."

"Indubitably." Drake paused, speculation growing in his golden gaze. After a moment, he went on, "I can imagine Ennis being prepared to give Connell the money to extricate Connell from this plot, even though Ennis intended subsequently to reveal all to the authorities—namely, to me."

Sebastian nodded. "That's why he insisted on meeting face-to-face. He would have demanded clemency, if not an outright amnesty, for his brother in return for revealing the details of the plot. Family loyalty—something to which we can all relate."

"Unfortunately," Antonia said, "in this instance, attempting to save his brother got Ennis—and his wife, too—killed."

Both Sebastian and Drake grimaced, but neither disagreed.

After a moment, Drake said, "For all their hotheadedness, the Young Irelander movement is not stupid enough to do something like this—not even their militant arms. As matters stand, there's no real benefit for them in it."

Sebastian concurred with a grunt.

A moment elapsed, then Sebastian looked at Drake. "That brings us back to your earlier supposition. Idealistic young men are notoriously easy to recruit and also to mislead—for instance, by someone who thinks like you. Or your father."

Drake swallowed a mouthful of wine. "There aren't, thank God, that many people in this world who think like His Grace." He quietly added, "It would be frightening if there were."

Antonia looked from one to the other. "Frightening or not, time, gentlemen, is getting on, and we have ten barrels of gunpowder that are presumably somewhere in London, in the hands of unknown plotters whose intentions we can't begin to guess. So what are we going to do?"

Drake looked at her, then looked at Sebastian and straightened in his chair. He set down his goblet. "Aptly put." He drummed the fingers of one hand on the table, then said, "I suggest we leave aside the question of exactly who is behind this, at least for now. Given that the only real use for ten barrels of gunpowder is to blow something up, the more pressing questions facing us are"—he raised his hands and ticked off each point on his fingers—"what are they planning to blow up, when, and where is the gunpowder now?"

"Arguably the most pertinent of those questions as of this moment," Sebastian said, "is how long we have before they act. How long do we have to stop them?"

"That," Antonia put in, "and how are we to approach answering Drake's three excellent and very pressing questions?"

All three of them looked from one to the other. Silence reigned, deep enough for them to hear the ticking of the long-case clock in the corner.

Then Drake grimaced. "I fear I'm not at my best at this moment, and, I suspect, neither are you. Despite the likely urgency, making decisions in a fuzzy-headed state is never wise." He glanced at the clock. "It's almost midnight. I suggest we reconvene tomorrow, after we've all had a decent night's sleep."

"An excellent idea." Sebastian pushed back his chair.

"Motion carried." Antonia waited until Sebastian and Drake rose, and Sebastian pulled out her chair.

As she got to her feet, Drake said, "We can meet here again—the parents are at Elveden, and my brothers will be out, so we'll have the house to ourselves."

Sebastian and Antonia nodded. With Drake, they walked slowly into the front hall, where Hamilton was hovering.

They strolled up the black-and-white tiles and halted before the front door. Hamilton retrieved their coats and Antonia's bonnet; after he'd assisted her to don her cloak, Antonia left him to help Sebastian while she turned to a large mirror and adjusted her bonnet.

When they were ready, Drake, who had been studying the floor, swung to face them, an amused light in his golden eyes. "As I take it you two have parents to see, arrangements to discuss, and announcements to make"—his smug expression made it clear that, without any word of it passing their lips, he'd guessed their intentions—"and I need to catch up on rather a lot of sleep, shall we say two o'clock?"

By ton schedules, that was still early in the day.

Antonia arched a haughty brow. "Two o'clock will suit admirably." She nodded to Hamilton, and he opened the door. With a dismissive, "Goodnight, Drake," she walked briskly out onto the porch.

Sebastian grinned, and he and Drake followed.

Drake halted on the threshold.

About to follow Antonia onto the porch, Sebastian halted and, curious, met Drake's eyes. "Aren't you going to wish us well?"

The light wasn't strong, but he would have sworn Drake faintly colored.

Drake glanced at Antonia, who was waiting, one brow arched expectantly, for his reply, then he looked back at Sebastian. "I would—I do." He looked uneasy—an odd look for Drake. "Except"—he grimaced—"once you make your announcement..." He met Sebastian's gaze. "I'm older than you."

Sebastian laughed and clapped Drake on the shoulder; he exchanged an amused look with Antonia, then murmured to Drake, "Perhaps it's time you faced the music, too."

Drake's expression turned genuinely horrified. "Thank you, but no." His features set, and he reached out and seized the door.

As, chuckling, Sebastian walked onto the porch, joining Antonia, Drake stepped back and firmly shut the door behind them.

Antonia laughed softly. She looped her arm in Sebastian's, and together, they descended the steps to the pavement. A wide smile on her lips, she murmured, "Poor Drake."

They set out to walk the short distance to St. Ives House, and Sebastian observed, "Matrimony appears to be one challenge our fearless Drake is in no hurry to face."

A few steps later, Antonia tilted her head; when Sebastian glanced her way, she caught his eyes.

The obvious yet critical question hovered between them.

*They* were ready to face what Drake still shied from, weren't they? The answer was there, in their eyes, clear enough for the other to see. Their expressions eased. As one, they faced forward. As one, they lengthened their stride.

# CHAPTER 16

*W*hether it was simply relief—to be home again, safe, with their part in the unfolding drama successfully played, at least to the end of this act—or welling exuberance over their triumph in having established a personal partnership that felt so very right, they were both smiling, and Antonia was actively reining in her delight, when she swept into Sebastian's room.

There'd been no staff downstairs to witness their entrance, just a lamp left burning low to light them up the grand staircase. In the gallery, his hand riding at the small of her back, Sebastian had guided her along the corridor into the east wing, then down another corridor to the room at the end.

Antonia walked confidently across the large room.

Over the years, she'd become familiar with much of St. Ives house, but she hadn't ventured into any bedchamber except for that of Sebastian's sister, Louisa, which was in the west wing. As it happened, Sebastian's room was the mirror of Louisa's in placement and size, with a wide bank of windows directly opposite the door through which they'd entered, and a secondary door in the wall to Antonia's right that she knew would lead to a large bathing chamber. The two doors on either side of the main door would each open into one of the rooms back along the corridor; one room would be Sebastian's dressing room, with the other the room—very likely rooms—reserved for his marchioness.

His wife.

The massive bed that stood against the wall to the right dominated the room. It was balanced by the huge fireplace in the opposite wall. As she crossed to the windows, she noted a pair of heavy tallboys against the other walls, a desk-cum-bureau against the wall between the windows and the fireplace, and four large, comfortable armchairs—one pair angled before the fireplace, the other pair placed to take advantage of the wide windows.

She reached the uncurtained windows and looked out.

Directly below, she glimpsed the edge of the terrace outside the family parlor; beyond it, silvered by moonlight, spread the lawns and neat shrubs of that section of the mansion's rear garden.

Curiosity welling, she turned and surveyed the room. Sconces set around the walls had been left turned low, shedding a warm glow throughout the chamber.

The decor was a reflection of Sebastian, of his personality. Expensive, yes, yet a touch austere, with a ripple of reined passion, of innate power, hidden beneath the smooth surface. The creamy ivory of the walls was offset by the richness of old oak, the warm patina glowing golden against the dark forest greens of upholstery and curtains. The frames—of the twin oval mirrors flanking the mantelpiece and of the paintings on the walls— were heavy and strong.

Wilkins would keep the place tidy, but there was a book on the side table beside the armchair before the fireplace, a bookmark jutting at an angle from between the pages, and a riding crop and a pair of riding gloves had been discarded on the low table between the chairs by the windows. The mantelpiece held an eclectic array of odds and ends— scrimshaw, a set of carved ivory figurines, a large ormolu clock, two dueling pistols mounted in a display case, and two lamps—and stuck into the frame of the large, restful landscape hanging above the fireplace were a selection of gilt-edged invitations.

Then there was the bed. Large and heavy—and sumptuously sensual with its forest-green silk coverlet and the mound of ivory-silk-encased pillows at its head.

Sebastian had paused in the doorway, watching her. As he stepped inside and shut the door, the clocks throughout the house struck twelve.

Midnight.

Despite the light cast by the sconces, it was primarily moonlight that lit his face, his long body, as he strolled slowly toward her.

He halted before her; the piercing quality of his gaze muted by the moonlight, he studied her face.

On the two previous occasions they'd come together, they'd been driven, not just by their newly discovered desires but also by a sense of, for one reason or another, needing to seize the moment. Tonight, there was no such blinding imperative; they both knew they could have each other—would have each other—time and again in the days, months, and years to come.

That, they'd already agreed, albeit without any declaration other than their passions.

So tonight, there was no need to rush, no sense of urgency to infuse their touch.

Not yet.

As if he could hear her thoughts—as if he shared them—he raised one hand and, with one fingertip, traced the line of her cheek from temple to jaw. Even as that single finger slid beneath her chin and nudged it upward, she was rising on her toes...

He bent his head and brushed his lips across hers. Once, then again, then his lips settled, and he kissed her.

Gently.

Yearningly.

With an invisible beckoning she felt tug at her soul.

She'd forgotten—overlooked—the fact he was a master, that in this sphere, he was openly classed as an expert.

As the warlock she'd sometimes thought him, with his strange, pale green eyes.

He wove a web of sensuality about her—slowly, with touches that mesmerized, with caresses that burned.

She followed his lead and returned the pleasure, and he allowed it. He proceeded slowly enough for her to take her own time managing their reins. Keeping them relaxed as they ambled along a road they'd already traveled, but this time, they went slowly enough to fully appreciate the landscape on both sides.

While their lips supped, tasting, exploring, reassuring, he drew off her bonnet, languidly tossed it on the nearby chair, then shrugged off his greatcoat and let it fall to the floor before he helped her shed her cloak.

Sometime later, he sank to his knees before her. "Lift your skirts."

The rumbling order was only just discernible; without rush, she obeyed. She gathered the folds of her carriage dress and ruffled petticoats and raised the hems—high enough for him to reach beneath, glide one palm up the back of her leg, then release her garter and roll her stocking down. He undid the laces of her half-boot and eased both boot and stocking from her foot. Then, still moving to that slow, regimented beat, he repeated the process with her other leg, baring it and leaving her standing barefoot.

Smoothly, he rose, and she let her skirts fall.

Practicing such restraint raised tension of a different sort, of a type she sensed would later break through their control and compel them, but for those moments in which they stood communing in the moonlight, that seemed an entirely reasonable toll to pay.

She pressed against him, her hands sliding up the wall of his chest to lightly grip his shoulders.

His arms closed around her, then crushed her to him.

Their lips met, and hunger leapt.

And she rejoiced.

And the kiss flared.

Hot.

Too hot.

As if both sensed the danger, the threat to their control, they drew back, and together, broke the kiss.

He trailed his lips to her ear, then down along her jaw, planting nibbling little kisses that distracted her senses and helped her to step back from the fiery lure.

Their breathing gradually steadied.

Determined to succeed in this novel endeavor, to maintain the measured tempo of this heady new dance, she drew in a slow, steadying breath and set her fingers to the folds of his cravat. She drew out the heavy gold pin with its large pale peridot, the gem the same color as his eyes. After anchoring the pin in his lapel, she eased the ends of the cravat free of his waistcoat and shirt.

While her fingers unraveled the simple knot, the winding folds, she felt his fingers sliding free the buttons that ran down the back of her carriage dress.

His lips were curved when, in the waning moonlight, they again brushed hers.

Again, left hers hungering.

Needing an anchor, a more definite distraction, and judging from the increasing tension gripping him that he might welcome the same, she murmured, "Once we break the news to our families, all hell will break loose, socially speaking."

"Mmm." His lips drifted to her temple, his breath a wash of heat across her cheek. "Do you think they'll be surprised?"

Wry cynicism colored the words.

She uttered a short laugh. "I doubt it will be any great shock." The last word turned breathless as his fingertips—just the tips—brushed her bare skin as the back of her tightly fitted carriage dress gaped.

This slowness, this lack of rush, this measured pace, was tensing her nerves and heightening sensation in a wholly novel way—on a plane of elevated intensity.

A fresh challenge.

She felt his lips trail down her throat. She tipped her head back and, in an effort to cling to control, gabbled the first thought that came to her. "And yet no one ever tried to steer me your way."

He raised his head. The moonlight etched his features as he caught her hands and drew them from his now-loosened cravat, then he reached for the shoulders of her dress and drew the bodice forward and down, sliding the sleeves down her arms.

She eased her hands from the tight sleeves, then pushed and sent the dress with its wide skirts slithering to pool in a heap about her feet.

She felt his gaze brush heat over her breasts, over her torso, screened though they still were by chemise and corset.

His voice had deepened and grown rougher when he said, "No one mentioned your name to me, either."

His gaze remained locked on her breasts. She heard him draw in a deeper breath—all but sensed him tighten his hold on his own reins— then he grasped her waist, spun her about, and set his fingers to the laces of her petticoats. A second later, he said, "It's curious, now I think of it, that none of the grandes dames we both know ever pushed me in your direction." He seemed to be concentrating on unraveling the laces, then he asked, "Did your mother or the others ever steer you toward...anyone?"

She frowned. "No. They always seemed to be waiting for me to choose...oh." She realized what he was suggesting. "You think that they knew all along, and we were the only ones who didn't?"

That thought wasn't comforting.

He grunted, and the waistband of her petticoats loosened. "Let's not think about that. The gloating will be enough to endure if and when it occurs."

"Indeed." Between them, they pushed down the froth of cotton and lace that was her multilayered petticoats. Taking her hand, he steadied her as she stepped free of the pile. She would have turned and walked into his arms, but his hands gripped her waist again, and he drew her back until her derriere met his thighs.

She leaned against him, her shoulders to his chest, and tipped her head back. He bent his, and their lips met again in a teasing temptation of a kiss.

Then he raised his head, and their lips parted. He didn't straighten, but through the shadows, studied her face, watched her reactions as he cruised his palms upward, then closed his hands about her breasts.

Her eyes locked with his. She drew in a slow, tense breath—then couldn't release it. She felt trapped in his gaze as he kneaded her flesh, then his artful fingers cruised the firm mounds, circling the puckered buds of her nipples, then closing, tightening...

Her lids fell, her spine arched, and she gasped and heard the sound hover in the dimness as if it came from someone else. He played, and her body bowed against his, her breasts pressing into his palms, an invitation he didn't refuse.

Yet still they danced to that slow, rousing—arousing—beat.

Power of a sort she hadn't encountered before, strange and compelling, rose and wreathed about them.

His hands possessed, then shaped the lines of her body, her hips, thighs, and derriere barely screened by the fine cotton of her chemise and drawers.

Her breathing had quickened, and her senses had come alive when he eased back an inch, steadied her, then withdrew his supporting hands and set his fingers to the laces of her corset.

Sebastian felt the power driving the desire that thudded, heavy and resounding, through his veins. Through his body, his mind, reaching into his soul. A compulsive beat that held him to its rigid cadence—slow, slow, slow.

The better to appreciate, to know and savor, the beauty before him. Not just the body, but the elemental being held within it.

The other half of him.

Where she was concerned, control was nothing more than an illusion, yet he wanted to give her this—this interlude, this engagement—one perfect moment encapsulating the promise before them.

His fingers were operating largely by rote, unpicking the laces of her lightly boned corset. A distraction seemed wise. He cleared his throat, then ventured, his voice gravelly with harnessed hunger, "When we're married..." He glanced briefly around and tried not to sound overly diffident as he continued, "We could buy a house somewhere else in town, if you prefer..."

Her head rose; he sensed her draw breath and swiftly scan the room. Then she glanced over her shoulder. He felt her gaze touch his face, but doubted she could read much through the dimness.

After a second, she faced forward. A second later, she murmured, distinctly breathlessly, "Let's leave such matters aside for now—we can deal with such things whenever we wish."

The last lace gave, and relief flowed through him. He grasped her corset, drew it from her, and tossed it to join her petticoats. "An excellent idea."

He closed the inch between them. His hands curving about her hips, he drew her flush against him, then skated his hands slowly upward, possessively reclaiming her curves; she all but purred as she instinctively arched against him.

They'd both, it seemed, accepted the imperative of clinging—for as long as they could—to that slow, rigid, compelling beat. It informed their every movement—their very breaths—as they continued to disrobe, there, in the moonlight before the windows.

She leaned back against him, her hands closing over his as his palms moved over her chemise-clad body, then he splayed one hand over the subtle curve of her belly and held her hips against his thighs as he reached down and, with the fingers of his other hand, found the slit in her drawers, and caressed her.

Her welcome flowed like molten honey over his fingertips. He reached further and slid one long finger into her scalding sheath. She tipped her head back against his shoulder and clutched the hand splayed over her belly with both her hands; her nails sank in as he probed, and she tensed, her body arching.

Slow, slow, slow.

He clung to the rhythm, heard her breathing fracture, felt her rise in his arms.

Then she cried out, the sound pure encouragement to his ears, her shuddering climax a goad to his libido he fought to suppress and ignore.

As she eased in his arms, he stripped the drawers from her, then, still constrained by that slow beat, he eased his hands under the fine material of her chemise and drew it—slowly, smoothly—up.

Her breasts heaving, she moved as if she was—as he felt—compelled by the invisible reins of their joint passion; she raised her arms and gracefully pirouetted as he drew the garment free of her upstretched arms.

Then she stood naked, facing him, bathed in the silver light of the moon as it poured through the windows behind him.

Her gaze was steady on his. There was not an ounce of uncertainty in her as she stepped forward to claim him.

And it was his turn to stand in apparent submission, in willing subjugation to their shared pleasure.

With her pale skin flushed with the warmth of spent passion, a rosy tint just detectable beneath the moon's pearlescent sheen, she moved like a nymph as she divested him of coat and waistcoat, tossing them aside to join the heap of fabric beside them. Then she drew the long strip of his cravat from about his neck with an artful lack of speed that demonstrated that she was as attuned to the music, to the magic of this moment, as he.

Then her features lighting with a sense of wonder over something that was still new to her—that still riveted and enthralled her—she unbuttoned his shirt, pushed the halves wide, and openly gloated.

Then she set her hands to his chest and—remembering at the last to cling to the beat—caressed.

He clenched his fists, locked his muscles—eventually clenched his jaw, closed his eyes, and tipped his head back—and endured.

The subtle and oh-so-pleasurable torture as she explored.

She stripped the shirt from him, then swiftly dealt with the buttons at his waist.

He sensed her pull up—and force herself to slow. To return to that compelling rhythm as, with sensuous gravity, she slid his trousers off his hips and down his long legs.

She crouched and, with his assistance, stripped away the trousers along with his stockings and shoes.

Then she rose.

He brought his head upright and opened his eyes in time to see raw passion light her gray eyes and infuse her face as her gaze locked on the evidence of his hunger for her. Released from the confines of his trousers, his erection tented his linen drawers.

As he watched, one of her hands darted to grasp the dangling cords; he saw her stop, almost swaying as she pulled on her own reins again. She found the beat again and forced her limbs, her eager fingers, to comply.

Slowly, to that rhythm both he and she could feel, she tugged and drew on the cord until the knot unraveled, and the garment sagged about his hips.

She set her palms to his sides, glanced once at his face, then she pushed the fine linen down, letting the drawers fall to his feet, fully exposing all of him to her now-very-avid gaze.

Also to her hands.

Greedy little hands she fought to restrain, to force to their accepted beat. Even so, he had to close his eyes, suck in a tortured breath, and, his head tipping back again, hold that breath while she played.

Not at all innocently.

But he held fast and gave her the moment, one she clearly wished for. One she transparently enjoyed.

Yet he knew his limits. Before she reached them, he straightened his head, opened his eyes, and set his hands to her body.

In short order, he reclaimed her attention, her senses.

When her hands, forgotten, went limp and eased from him, he stepped into her, and their lips met—in a kiss still slow and steady, but several orders of magnitude hotter. Hungrier.

Increasingly flavored with desperation and wanting.

He bent and swung her into his arms and carried her to the bed.

Kneeling on the covers, he shuffled forward, then laid her in the very center of the expanse, her long, lithe body gleaming like a pearl set on the dark silk of his counterpane.

He stretched out alongside her, set a hand to her curves, then bent his head and savored. He licked, laved, suckled, still moving to the increasingly heavy, increasingly compelling beat that drove them.

That beat might have escalated, yet it remained slow, still reverent.

Still slow enough to infuse every caress—his and hers—with a sense of worship.

Of giving thanks.

That they had this—that they'd found, seized, and could now claim this, their fated destiny.

They'd found their way through the drama, through the demands of the mission, and it was finally time—tonight was the time—for them to look into the face of what linked them, to bow their heads and acknowledge that power and rejoice in the glory it bestowed.

Tomorrow, the drama might well return, but tonight was their hiatus—their moment in the eye of the storm in which they could draw breath and freely evoke passion's mysteries.

He took her high again, with his tongue sent her soaring, and savored the satisfaction of feeling her tension—the tension he'd built in her—shatter and send her flying free.

Despite the rampant need thudding in his veins, he seized the moment to gloat, to delight in the sight of her sprawled bonelessly in his bed.

So wantonly abandoned—so very tempting.

She was watching him from beneath her lashes. Then she raised a hand and beckoned.

He was only too ready to move over her, but she caught his shoulder and surprised him by struggling up, lifting from the bed, and steadily pushing him back.

Wondering at her direction, he let her steer him back, back, until he was sitting on his ankles, and with a distracting sweep of her long legs, she came up on her knees and straddled him.

One hand gripping his shoulder for balance, she wrapped the other about his erection and, somewhat breathlessly, dictated, "This way."

Who was he to argue?

As she rose up, set his head at her entrance, then, in one long, excruciatingly slow slide, impaled herself on him and engulfed his throbbing erection in her gloriously scalding heat, arguing was far from his mind.

Breathless, well-nigh witless, Antonia struggled to absorb the pummeling tide of searing sensations battering her senses and setting fire to her nerves, all at the same time. The feel of him filling her was paramount, like a heated steel rod at her core, but the brush of his chest against the swollen fullness of her breasts, the abrasion of the sensitized peaks by the crinkly black hair that adorned the heavy muscle bands, and the sheer heat radiating off his large body all contributed to the sensual symphony.

And then there was the indescribable lust that flared when she raised up, then sank down—a sudden, driving, ungovernable impulse to seek completion. She wanted to—somehow needed to—go slow, to hold to some semblance of that earlier steady, relentless beat, but she teetered…she didn't think she could hold fast against the welling tide.

Then his hands clamped around her hips—hot, hard, possessive. The touch shocked her out of the swirling whirlpool that had threatened to sweep her away, and she steadied.

Determined, she grasped her own reins and held tight as she acceded to the urging of his hands and rose up again. Slid down again.

And gasped at the glory.

She had to admit that, in this sphere, control—exercising it—brought definite benefits.

Sebastian watched, guided, and let wave after wave of sensation wash through him. His focus on her, on her pleasure, on her direction, gave him the strength to hold his slavering demons at bay.

Gradually, she steadied, and the threat of her being overwhelmed faded. She mastered the moment and settled to a rhythm that satisfied, yet allowed their senses to expand, to seek, to explore.

From beneath her weighted lids, from under the fringe of her lashes, her gray gaze, now silvered with passion, met his eyes and held the contact.

Held to the connection, direct and open, their gazes merging even as their bodies did. Slow, steady, sending pleasure purling through them both, yet manageable. Controllable.

With nothing to immediately do other than follow her whim, he allowed his predator's mind to rise to the fore and, through his eyes, quietly study her.

At some level, he was very aware that, no matter what other words she'd uttered, no matter anything they'd done—no matter even this present engagement—she had yet to agree, to state unequivocally that she was his. That she would be his marchioness—his, forever.

At moments like this, the conquering nobleman was never far beneath his surface.

He picked his time. He waited until he sensed the tide of distracting sensation rising through them both, brushed his lips over hers—tasted her hunger as, instinctively, her lips followed his and for an instant clung—then he drew back enough to breathe over the swollen curves, "So when are we getting married?"

There were more ways than one of getting the answer he wanted.

Her breathing had gone ragged, but after several seconds, her lids rose, and at close quarters, her stormy eyes met his. For a second, she stared, then surprisingly calmly said, "You do know you haven't actually asked me to marry you." She rose up and slid down again. "Don't you?"

Damn female—was she truly challenging him? Now?

He was hanging onto control by his fingernails. As she rose and fell again, involuntarily, his fingertips sank into the lush flesh of her hips.

Trapped in her gaze, his jaw clenching, he managed to somewhat grimly say, "Very well. You perceive me on my knees."

Her head tipped back, and she nearly choked on a strangled laugh—and her sheath contracted powerfully about him; he thought he saw stars.

He lost his breath, almost lost his wits. In a rush of effort, he forced out, "Antonia Marguerite Rawlings—for God's sake, marry me and link your life with mine."

Having finally uttered the words, he suddenly felt free, as if some weight had lifted from him. He refocused on her, on her face. Gripping her hips, he thrust up and filled her.

To the hilt.

He leaned close, his forehead to hers, his lips a fraction of an inch from hers, and breathed—pleaded, "Marry me, Antonia."

She raised her lids just enough to meet his eyes. She rose and fell again, firmly sheathing him in her heat. Her breath mingled with his as she asked, "Why?"

He blinked. "You want reasons?" He nearly shook his head. Instead said, "At this juncture?" and powerfully thrust into her again.

She sucked in a breath and rode the wave of sensation. As it eased, she rose again—met his eyes again. "What better time?"

That had been his thinking, but he wasn't so sure of its wisdom now.

He tried to concentrate, but the lustful heat welling between them had built to the point where not even he could bring rational thought to bear. Somewhat to his surprise, he heard himself admit, "My mind isn't working all that well."

Despite all distractions, she was watching him closely. She had a death grip on his shoulders, her nails sinking in with every surge. She leaned forward and brushed his lips with hers—not in teasing, nor temptation, but in transparent encouragement. "That's why," she whispered, her voice sultry and low, drenched in sensuality and a bone-deep honesty, "this is the best time—the right time to ask." She paused, lids falling, fingers tightening as sensation spiked and rolled over them and played havoc with their wits. As the wave receded, her lids rose, and she locked her eyes with his again. "Just answer with the words that come to you. Who else is here to hear?"

He stared into her glorious silver-gray eyes. He'd reached the point where thought was beyond him, where the only words he could summon would be the truth as his inner self saw it. "Because we fit." He drew in a breath that shuddered. "Because you are and always have been the other half of me…and I don't think I can—or at least I don't want to—live without you."

She looked drunk on passion, and her lips curved. "See? You can manage the right words. So now…why?"

Exasperation flared—high enough to cut through the sensual fog that engulfed him. "Antonia—"

"No—just answer. Why do you feel that way about me?"

Enough self-protective instinct remained for him to clench his jaw and set his teeth—but then, aggrieved, he gritted out, "If this is some convoluted female test, I didn't read that textbook."

Antonia held his glare. She knew she was pressing him. Knew in her heart why—why she wanted, nay, *needed* to hear his answer to that most fundamental question. The textbook, did he but know it, was an oral one, crafted over centuries by women like her—those fated to mate with arrogant, commanding, irredeemably autocratic noblemen.

Even as, keeping to the now-tense rhythm of their joining, she rose on him again, and let him draw her down, a touch more forcefully as he thrust up and filled her again—deeply, completely—she accepted that she could not risk turning her back on the wisdom of generations. When dealing with men of his stripe, love was the only guarantee. But even if she knew—to the depths of her soul knew—that it existed in him, not even love could protect her—not unless he acknowledged and accepted it, at the very least between them.

Still holding his gaze, with the flames of their lovemaking rising between them, threatening to engulf them and sweep them away, she clung to the one thing strong enough to anchor her—her love for him.

"No." Her eyes locked with his, she paused to moisten her lips. Saw his eyes trace the movement of her tongue and accepted not even he could give them much more time. "I'm not teasing. The question—"

She broke off on a gasp. Her lids fluttered as he surged beneath her, into her, and she felt the last shreds of control thin. She forced her lids up, locked her gaze with his. "My question is important. To us both. I need to know, to hear you acknowledge it—to prove that you know the answer." She held his gaze and refused to let go. "Just once. That's all I need."

Sebastian felt his world shake. Quake. Fundamental instincts and the impulses they drove clashed inside him.

As always, his first impulse was to bury what his inner self regarded as a weakness, but she'd said the one word that bound him and irresistibly compelled him to the opposing tack.

Whatever she needed, truly needed…he would move heaven and earth to give her.

He looked into her gray eyes—felt himself balk on the cusp of the precipice and forced himself over. Knowingly, intentionally, he lowered the barrier he invariably kept between his feelings and his tongue and spoke as he very rarely did—without restraint. "You…are the world to me. I always knew there was something different about you. I told myself it was because you were a cousin-but-not—a slightly different species. But inside, I always knew there was something else there, something waiting to win free."

He dragged in a breath and surged with her, filling her—neither he nor she had let that rhythm lapse. Where they were—the point on the sensual road they'd reached—it was now too critical, a physical compulsion neither could or would deny.

He knew he hadn't yet said the words she needed to hear. He knew what those words were, knew they were an elemental truth. Yet getting them past his lips was still an effort. Briefly, he closed his eyes—drew breath, drew strength—then he raised his lids and locked his gaze with hers. "I love you. And I can't change that—I don't want to change that, even though I definitely do not appreciate some of the consequences." He drew in a deeper breath, felt his chest expand as if against some inner vise. "So there's your answer. I want you. I need you. But most important of all, I love you—so please be my wife, my marchioness, and stand by my side through all the years to come."

He ended one teeny tiny step away from glaring at her.

She held his gaze for an instant, then she smiled.

Just smiled. And it was as if every last screen in her gray eyes had whisked away, and he was looking unimpeded into her soul—into the glorious joy that reigned there.

In that instant, he decided to make the effort he just had more often; it would be worth every ounce of the struggle just to bask in that joy.

Then he remembered—and thrust deeper into her body, renewed lust buoyed on a surge of hope. "Yes," he prompted, his eyes almost crossing as she tightened in glorious welcome about him. "You're supposed to say yes."

"Yes." She tipped her head back as he surged inside her, and her fingers dug like claws into his shoulders. "Oh, God—yes!"

He huffed. It wasn't at all clear to what she was agreeing; had he left it too late?

But as if realizing her shortcomings, she hauled in a huge breath, straightened her head, and from beneath passion-weighted lids, her silver-gray eyes blazed into his. "Yes," she said, and there was no doubt of her certainty, of her commitment. "I'll marry you, Sebastian Cynster. And I fully intend to cleave to you for the rest of our lives."

For a split second, he exulted, then he pounced and seized.

She seized him back, and they plunged headlong into the raging inferno of ravenous, needy, rapacious passion they'd stoked, stoked, and yet held back.

The last rein snapped, and their joint passions roared over them.

Seized them, drove them to new and ever more desperate and devastating heights, then shattered and reforged them.

Finally, the tumult faded and left them wrung out and gasping in the battlefield of his bed—both victors, both triumphant.

Both utterly surrendered.

To the force that now bound them more irrevocably than any words.

To the love they'd always shared—the love they'd faced, acknowledged, and finally embraced.

* * *

Later, when dawn was streaking the sky outside the window, they woke in each other's arms, and after the storm of the night, reassured themselves that they could, indeed, be relatively civilized in their lovemaking.

Relatively being the operative word.

A new assurance had crept in on both their parts and now colored their caresses and the deeper intimacy of their joining.

A development neither regretted.

Later still, Antonia lay on her back, her head on Sebastian's chest as he lay beside her with his arms locked around her. They were comfortable, warm.

At peace.

After a moment, she raised a finger and prodded the heavy muscle in the arm that lay across her waist. "One thing we should discuss."

"The wedding?"

"No. Our biggest hurdle."

A wary silence held sway for a heartbeat, then he asked, "And what's that?"

She realized she needed to choose her words with care. "We've established that you love me and that I love you. I didn't say it, but I didn't have to—you already knew." He shifted fractionally, but didn't disagree. *Good.* "The point we need to discuss is what, for *both* of us, springs naturally from that love. From loving as we do."

She twisted her head and looked into his face. His impassive mask was well and truly in place, and his eyes had already narrowed. Undeterred, she went on, "Anyone you love, you protect—absolutely and without question." His brows started to lower. "And I have no issue whatsoever with that," she hurried to add. "But you have to accept that the converse is also true—that if you are threatened, then I will act to protect you."

He didn't like that. He opened his mouth—

"No." She narrowed her eyes and wriggled around so she faced him. "I spring from the same warrior caste as you—that's why we mesh so well together, as you phrased it, like two halves of one being. We are alike in many ways—and I will not sit meekly by while you go into danger." She locked her gaze with his. "For instance, what would have happened if, in Kent, I'd waited on the beach while you went into the passage and on to that cavern alone?"

Sebastian had already thought of that scenario—and had promptly buried the realization it had brought. He hadn't wanted to dwell on that then; he didn't now. But her words brought the memories flooding back in full force. "Those moments in the cavern will live blazoned in my mind forever."

Her gaze didn't waver. Somewhat coolly, she arched a brow. "And the reason you're alive to remember them at all..."

He exhaled through his teeth, slumped back on the pillows, and stared at the ceiling.

Inexorably, she went on, "If you hadn't been there, if I hadn't been there...one or possibly both of us would have died. But we were there together, and love, the desperation it brings, made me rush to push you out of harm's way—and for the very same reason, you changed direction in order to save me. Together, we won through. Singly, we wouldn't have."

Sadly, that was an inarguable truth.

He sighed. "I will never—*ever*—like, approve, or appreciate you being in danger." He raised his head and met her eyes. "Even if you're with me."

She held his gaze. "I know. And I'm not asking you to like it. I don't like, approve, or appreciate you being in danger, either. But I can't be your marchioness—we can't have the marriage we both want—unless you allow me to be me, to be the woman I truly am."

*Your equal.* She didn't say the words, but he heard them. And knew in his heart that she was right.

After a long, fraught moment, he eased his tense jaw enough to say, "I'll try."

She held his gaze for an instant, then inclined her head. "That will do."

Antonia knew she couldn't hope for any better outcome; she hadn't been sure she would gain even that much. From Sebastian, a Cynster, on that particular point, a commitment to try was a significant concession.

She felt his muscles ease beneath her. Keeping her satisfaction to herself, she turned and resettled in his arms, and he closed them about her once more.

After a moment, he murmured, "You can't expect me not to try to...avoid the issue."

"By keeping things from me?"

"By shielding you from circumstances that might...bother you."

She did smile at that, intently, even though he couldn't see. "Just as long as you aren't surprised if I refuse to be coddled."

She accepted she'd have to fight such battles through the rest of their days, but with men like him, that was only to be expected.

"About our wedding..."

She dutifully turned her thoughts in that direction. "I suspect we should speak with my parents as soon as possible." She glanced up at him. "Today?"

He nodded decisively. "I shudder to think of what will transpire if your father gets wind of you staying overnight before I make a formal offer for your hand—let's get that done this morning."

"As for the rest..." She settled, warm and secure, in his hold, and they ran through the immediate steps they needed to take—notifying his parents being the next highest on their list. "As to exactly when we should wed, I'm sure Mama will have thoughts on that head—best leave that until we speak with her."

He was silent for a moment, then murmured, "Given the season, if we time our announcements, we should be able to hold much of the ton and their sure-to-be-avid, not to say rabid, interest at bay." She felt him shift to look into her face and turned her head to meet his gaze. He searched her features, her eyes, then said, "At least until this mission of Drake's is over."

She nodded, entirely at one with that sentiment. "Yes. Let's keep the news under our hats for as long as possible, at least until the gunpowder has been found and made safe."

Sebastian was relieved she'd agreed. No matter the distraction, ten barrels of gunpowder and the havoc that could wreak in the heart of London was difficult to block from their minds.

# CHAPTER 17

"*A*m I allowed to say it's about time?"

Sebastian hid a wince. He'd just made formal application for Antonia's hand in marriage. "As you wish" didn't seem a wise response to make to the gentleman seated on the other side of the desk in the study of the Green Street house. Gyles Rawlings, Earl of Chillingworth and Antonia's father, was one of Sebastian's father's oldest friends.

"I suppose I should ask," Chillingworth continued, clearly unsurprised by Sebastian's silence, "what Antonia has to say to this."

"I've asked her, and she's agreed."

"Excellent." Sitting back in his chair, Chillingworth smiled. While Sebastian felt the earl was enjoying himself—thrilled to have a Cynster metaphorically at his mercy—he nevertheless appeared to be genuinely delighted. "A wise move on your part, and a highly satisfactory one on hers." He eyed Sebastian indulgently. "I suppose I should confess that your father and I long suspected it would come to this."

Understanding that Chillingworth was not inclined to even pretend to be averse to the union—not that Sebastian had anticipated rejection, but the earl could have made his approval much harder to gain—he tested the waters with a disgruntled grunt. "You—or he—might have warned me."

Chillingworth opened his eyes wide. "Where would be the fun in that?"

It was, Sebastian discovered, a touch disconcerting that Antonia had inherited her gray gaze from her father.

That gaze was currently fixed on him in a far-too-knowing fashion.

"Besides," the earl said, "we each of us have to find our own way into and out of the morass."

Sebastian nearly asked "Which morass?" but suspected he knew. Then it struck him that Chillingworth had to have faced many of the same issues—along with the same intense and rather fiery counter-response—he himself was now facing; it was widely acknowledged that Antonia had inherited both her black hair and the wilder, more dramatic side of her nature from her mother. "Apropos of that"—he rapidly searched for the right words, but in the end, settled for a man-to-man appeal—"as Antonia takes after the countess in many ways, do you have any helpful hints about how to manage the usual hurdles men of our ilk face?"

Chillingworth regarded him impassively, then, somewhat to Sebastian's surprise, the earl leaned forward, clasped his hands on the blotter, and fixed him with a serious look. "I'm sure your father would agree that the most critical aspect to understand in order to enjoy a long and happy marriage is to realize that power isn't entirely ours. Not with respect to wives—or at least not to our sort of wives. We might rule our roost, but only with their acquiescence. As long as we play by those rules and give them due deference, all goes smoothly. Try to lord it over them, and you will very quickly wish you hadn't—you really don't want to test them, or more to the point, plumb your own emotions, believe me. "

Sebastian considered that, then asked, "You mean that continues…forever?"

Chillingworth sent him a shark's grin. "To the grave. Ours, most likely."

The look Sebastian sent him clearly made the earl's day; Chillingworth laughed, then gestured to the door and made to stand.

Sebastian stayed him with an upraised hand. "One moment. There's something else you need to know."

Chillingworth sank back into his chair. There was nothing wrong with the earl's ability to read other men. His "What is it?" held a sharper edge.

Succinctly, Sebastian described Drake's mission, and how Antonia as well as he was now involved. "The intrigue is ongoing, and it's possible that I, and even Antonia, may have a further role to play."

Chillingworth didn't look thrilled. He stared at Sebastian for several seconds, then stated, "I can't order her out of it, any more than you can."

Sebastian grimaced. "So it seems."

Chillingworth studied him, then said, "Your father and I, and the others of our circle…when we were your age, we stepped into the fray when we needed to. When we were called on. We can hardly argue against you—and even Antonia—stepping up to the same mark in your time."

Sebastian held the earl's gaze, then arched a brow. "Like a baton being passed on?"

"Precisely." Chillingworth rose and waved him to his feet. "I could wish Antonia wasn't involved, but now she is..." He met Sebastian's gaze as Sebastian straightened to his full height. "I'll have to place my trust in your abilities to keep your marchioness-to-be safe."

Sebastian formally inclined his head. "You may be sure I'll accomplish that—come what may."

Chillingworth grinned and slapped him on the shoulder. "Excellent. Come. Let's find the ladies."

Together, they left the study. Chillingworth led the way to the back parlor.

When Sebastian and Antonia, with Beccy in attendance, had arrived nearly an hour ago as if they'd just returned from Kent, the earl and the countess had heard their voices in the front hall and had come to greet them. On learning that Sebastian wished to speak with the earl in private, the countess had blinked, then smiled delightedly. She'd linked her arm with Antonia's and had borne her daughter off to the back parlor, leaving the earl and Sebastian to confer in the study.

Sebastian followed the earl through the parlor door and saw Antonia seated on the sofa facing the long windows that gave onto the rear garden. The countess, Francesca, was perched on the window seat, her emerald eyes candidly and very shrewdly observing her daughter, her husband, and Sebastian.

Antonia swiveled to look at her father; she swiftly read the earl's expression, and her features eased, then she transferred her gaze to Sebastian.

He nodded to assure her all had gone well.

That short of the official announcement, they were now formally betrothed.

Francesca read that message in their faces. Her features lit with exuberant delight. She sprang to her feet and clapped her hands. "Wonderful! Champagne, Gyles—don't you think?"

"I do." Chillingworth walked to the bellpull. "Not every day one gets to set a ball and chain on a Cynster's leg."

"Papa!"

"Gyles, you will not say such things—especially not in front of Honoria!"

Having tugged the bellpull, the earl turned a bland gaze on his countess. "I do have some sense of self-preservation left to me."

The butler, Withers, appeared, and orders were given; while that worthy hurried to fulfill the request, Francesca congratulated her daughter and Sebastian warmly. As he'd known the countess from his earliest years, he wasn't taken aback by her ebullience; when she grew excited, her Italian upbringing tended to overwhelm her Englishness. Not that a proper English reserve had ever been a true part of Francesca's makeup; haughtiness was a façade she adopted only when it suited her.

Looking from mother to daughter, Sebastian accepted that the reserve expected of an earl's daughter that Antonia effortlessly maintained when in public was only a veneer, one barely thicker than her mother's.

He wasn't about to complain.

The champagne arrived, carried in by a beaming Withers; glasses were poured, and several toasts—some serious, others less so—were duly drunk.

Then Francesca called them to order. She resumed her position on the window seat. Sebastian joined Antonia on the sofa and stretched one arm along the sofa's back behind her shoulders, while the earl tugged an armchair to a spot between the end of the sofa and the window seat and sank into it.

"Now"—Francesca fixed her gaze on Sebastian—"I take it you have yet to inform your parents."

He nodded. "They're at Somersham, but I assume they'll be returning to town shortly." He glanced inquiringly at the earl.

Chillingworth stated, "Your father intended to be back for the next sitting of the Lords, so I'd expect them in a week or so."

Francesca waved dismissively. "They'll be back before that. Once Honoria hears your news, she'll be packing within the hour."

No one disagreed with that prediction.

"So," Francesca continued, "we should consider the where and when of your wedding. It will be a major affair, and with you both being who you are, I warn you there will be no way of avoiding that." She fixed a challenging look on Antonia and Sebastian. When they returned her regard meekly, Francesca humphed softly and continued, "As I have already mentioned to Antonia, a wedding at Lambourn Castle would be most appropriate. The castle is large and grand enough to do full justice to the event, the chapel there is lovely, and it is where Gyles and I married as well."

Sebastian glanced at Antonia, caught her gaze when she looked inquiringly at him, and deduced the plan met with her approval. He looked at Francesca and nodded. "That sounds...perfect." He was immensely relieved to be spared a full court wedding held in the bosom of the ton at St. George's in Hanover Square.

From the corner of his eye, he saw the earl's lips twitch mockingly; Antonia's father could very likely read his mind on that score.

But Francesca looked upon him with approval. "Good. You may leave the rest of the details to your mother and me to arrange."

"We wouldn't dream of doing otherwise," the earl murmured—and earned himself a narrow-eyed glance from his countess.

Then Francesca returned her gaze to Antonia and Sebastian. "With that settled, the only other point that, at this time, we need to discuss is the timing." The countess arched her brows. "When do you wish your wedding to be?"

The earl shifted and caught Sebastian's gaze. "I gather this intrigue of Drake's that these two were assisting with is still ongoing."

"It is?" Francesca's brows rose. "I'd forgotten about that." She looked at Sebastian. "Did you not deal with whatever it was down in Kent?"

"We did." Sebastian heard the grim note that had returned to his voice. He glanced at Antonia. "But the matter in Kent appears to have been only part of a greater whole, one with the potential to be a wider threat, possibly even to the country."

Francesca frowned. "How long will it take for this intrigue to be resolved?"

Ten barrels of gunpowder somewhere in London. Sebastian arched his brows. "Two—possibly three—weeks. I doubt it will drag on for much longer."

Francesca's face cleared. She waved dismissively. "Three or even four weeks is of no moment." She paused as if calculating, then focused on Antonia and Sebastian again. "Given the current season, you have a choice. You could be married in mid-November—not later than the third week, or we would risk early snows. But it's that, or late February or March next year."

That didn't sound like much of a choice to Sebastian. He glanced—hopefully—at Antonia.

She met his gaze, smiled easily, then turned to her mother and stated, "Mid-November."

"Excellent!" Francesca looked enthused. "Then that, too, is settled." Her emerald gaze fixed on Antonia. "But with the wedding so soon, we will need to start on your gown without delay."

Immediately, the conversation swung to consideration of the weights of various sorts of silks and the virtues of different types of beading and lace.

Sidelined, Sebastian glanced at Chillingworth.

The earl caught his eye and grinned. "You see? The first lesson you need to learn is that it's best to simply smile, surrender, and let them run."

Sebastian noted the contented expression on his soon-to-be father-in-law's face.

He looked at Antonia and her mother, both now animated to much the same degree. Knowing his father's counsel would be the same, he smiled, relaxed against the sofa, and followed the earl's advice.

If smiling, surrendering, and allowing them to run was another part of the price men like him had to pay to have women like Antonia, her mother, and his mother in their lives, so be it; in all matters social, it was a price he was entirely willing to pay.

* * *

In the parlor of a manor house deep in the quiet countryside, a man stood before a many-paned window. His upright posture that of the army officer he once had been, he looked out at the nearly leafless trees in the wood on the other side of a short stretch of poorly tended lawn, and in a deep, authoritative voice, succinctly reported on the progress of the mission he had agreed to undertake. "Boyne, most helpfully, stepped in and silenced his older brother, Lord Ennis, before Ennis could pass on anything of our plot to anyone."

From deeper in the room came a creak, and the old man seated in the Bath chair parked in the dimness into which the weak autumn light did not reach grunted. "By which you mean Boyne panicked and acted to save his own skin, as such men are wont to do. I did warn you he had overestimated his brother's commitment to the Young Irelander cause. Like many an Anglo-Irish peer, Ennis paid lip service to the notion of a free Ireland, and while he might have contributed to the cause's coffers, blowing up some government building in London would not have been something he would have condoned."

The man before the window frowned, safe in the knowledge that the older man couldn't see his expression. His lips compressed, then he relaxed them and said, "Regardless, Boyne got the money he needed from Ennis and was at the rendezvous to receive the gunpowder and pay off the captain." He hesitated, debating his next words, but the old man would probably hear of it anyway; his ability to learn of actions and details all the way down to minutiae despite being buried in the country and barely able to move from his chair was nothing short of miraculous. In an even tone, the ex-guardsman reported, "Boyne also killed his sister-in-law. He feared Ennis might have mentioned something to her, so he tied up that loose end for us, too."

The old man grunted again. "At least the man was thorough."

"He was, as you rightly guessed, panicked. But in the end, he played his part well enough—he did what we needed him to do."

A moment elapsed, then the old man asked, "Are you sure no one knows of the barrels?"

"Quite sure. As per your plan, we only left the barrels on the estate for a few days. We moved them out on the second night after they'd arrived, and no one was any the wiser. Boyne and I saw the barrels on the road to London, and I instructed him to ensure there was no evidence of any sort remaining of the barrels' existence." The ex-guardsman crossed his arms over his chest and settled, his feet apart, his legs braced. "When I met with Boyne yesterday afternoon, he confirmed he'd been to the cave, and that there were no traces there or elsewhere to alert anyone even to the existence of the barrels, much less of any plot."

"Excellent." Rich approval colored the old man's voice.

The ex-guardsman wasn't immune to the effect, even though he understood that that tone—and its effect—was one reason the old man had once been such an influential manipulator in the more rarefied circles of government.

The old man continued, "I take it you've eliminated Boyne."

"Yes." Again, the ex-guardsman hesitated, yet it wouldn't pay to step out of his role of subordinate, not at this point. "But he'd already been winged by someone and was desperate to drive off with me. I asked, and he said he was being chased over his brother's murder."

"By whom?"

"An inspector from Scotland Yard and the local magistrate."

The old man snorted derisively. "So no real threat to us, not now Boyne has been silenced." After a moment, he went on, "Given the circumstances, I assume you left his body where it would be found."

"Yes. If they were pursuing him, his trail would have led them to it."

"Good. The inspector and the magistrate will, in all likelihood, be grateful to be able to close the file on Lord Ennis's murder." The old man gave a dry chuckle. "It might even be said that you performed a civic service in killing Boyne and sparing the courts the trouble and expense of a trial."

The ex-guardsman allowed himself a thin smile.

"So the barrels are safely stored in London?"

"Yes." Unfolding his arms, the ex-guardsman turned away from the bleak view. He hunted in his coat pocket and drew out a piece of paper and a ring with two keys. He glanced at them, then crossed the room and offered them to the old man, who raised a partially palsied hand and took them. "That's the address of the warehouse and the foreman's keys. The barrels are sitting there, sweet as you please, and no one knows they're there."

His head bent, the old man studied the address, then he fumbled and folded the paper and slipped it along with the keys into the capacious pocket of his brown velvet smoking jacket. From beneath his shaggy white eyebrows, he shot a sharp look at the younger man's face. "What of the Young Irelander hotheads who transported the barrels and arranged their storage?"

The ex-guardsman's smile was cold. "They're in no condition to boast to anyone of their acts of defiance."

A smile split the old man's lined face, then he cackled. "This is proving to be far more entertaining than I'd expected. Not just using these idiotic fanatics to my own ends, but then simply removing them from this world... After all my years of having to deal with them politely, I'm sure you can comprehend that I find a certain satisfaction in that."

The ex-guardsman inclined his head.

The old man studied him.

The younger man remained as he was and showed no sign of being unnerved by the close scrutiny.

Then, slowly, the old man nodded his great head, which seemed almost too heavy to be supported by his emaciated neck. His expression eased into one of benevolent approval. "You've performed well. You can leave the matter with me for now. The next stage is not yours to run. I'll send word when next I need you."

The ex-guardsman half bowed. "I'll wait to hear from you." He stepped back, snapped off a deferential salute, then turned and strode for the door.

The old man sat, patient and still, and waited until he heard his visitor's horse's hoofbeats fade into the distance.

Then he reached out to the table beside his chair, picked up the brass bell that sat there, and rang it.

As the resounding clang died away, the old man smiled. He hadn't lost his touch. Everything was proceeding smoothly.

Inexorably.

"And now"—he pulled out the paper carrying the location of the gunpowder—"it's time for the next stage in my exquisitely orchestrated scheme."

THE END

Dear Reader,

As soon as I started working on Sebastian's story and discovered Lord Drake Varisey taking a hand, I knew the story would stretch to a trilogy and not just a single novel, and that made telling the three interconnected tales something of a challenge, intertwining the three consecutive romances and the evolving intrigue. I hope you've enjoyed the opening act of the Devil's Brood Trilogy and Sebastian's and Antonia's romance.

But now you've read the first installment, I know you'll be keen to learn what happens next – and as I didn't want to keep you in suspense (for too long) I have the next two works lined up and ready in the wings. Michael's story, AN IRRESISTIBLE ALLIANCE, and Louisa's romance, appropriately titled THE GREATEST CHALLENGE OF THEM ALL, will soon be here – see below for dates, preorder links, blurbs and links to excerpts.

In addition, as this storyline, of all my many works, draws on real events of those times, I've included an Author Note toward the end of this volume in which I detail the historical facts that feature or have influenced what is otherwise a work of fiction. If the question: How much of this is real? intrigues you, that Author Note is for you.

So we now know the problem Drake and his supporters face – stay tuned for the next exciting volume as Devil's three children meet their mates and save the realm to boot!

Stephanie.

For alerts as new books are released, plus information on upcoming books, exclusive sweepstakes and sneak peeks into upcoming novels, sign up for Stephanie's Private Email Newsletter http://www.stephanielaurens.com/newsletter-signup/

The ultimate source for detailed information on all Stephanie's published books, including covers, descriptions, and excerpts, is Stephanie's Website www.stephanielaurens.com

You can also follow Stephanie via her Amazon Author Page at http://tinyurl.com/zc3e9mp

Goodreads members can follow Stephanie via her author page https://www.goodreads.com/author/show/9241.Stephanie_Laurens

You can email Stephanie at stephanie@stephanielaurens.com

Or find her on Facebook https://www.facebook.com/AuthorStephanieLaurens/

# COMING NEXT

**The gripping continuation of the Devil's Brood Trilogy**
**AN IRRESISTIBLE ALLIANCE**
**May 11, 2017**

*A duke's second son with no responsibilities and a lady starved of the excitement her soul craves join forces to unravel a deadly, potentially catastrophic threat to the realm - that only continues to grow.*

With his older brother's betrothal announced, Lord Michael Cynster is freed from the pressure of familial expectations. However, the allure of his previous hedonistic pursuits has paled. Then he learns of the mission his brother, Sebastian, and Lady Antonia Rawlings have been assisting with and volunteers to assist by hunting down the hoard of gunpowder now secreted somewhere in London.

Michael sets out to trace the carters who transported the gunpowder from Kent to London. His quest leads him to the Hendon Shipping Company, where he discovers his sole source of information is the only daughter of Jack and Kit Hendon, Miss Cleome Hendon, who although a fetchingly attractive lady, firmly holds the reins of the office in her small hands.

Cleo has fought to achieve her position in the company. Initially, managing the office was a challenge, but she now conquers all in just a few hours a week. With her three brothers all adventuring in America, she's been driven to the realization that she craves adventure, too.

When Michael Cynster walks in and asks about carters, Cleo's instincts leap. She wrings from him the full tale of his mission—and offers him a bargain. She will lead him to the carters he seeks if he agrees to include her as an equal partner in the mission.

Horrified, Michael attempts to resist, but ultimately finds himself agreeing—a sequence of events he quickly learns is common around Cleo. Then she delivers on her part of the bargain, and he finds there are benefits to allowing her to continue to investigate beside him—not least being that if she's there, then he knows she's safe.

But the further they go in tracing the gunpowder, the more deaths they uncover. And when they finally locate the barrels, they find themselves tangled in a fight to the death—one that forces them to face what has grown between them, to seize and defend what they both see as their path to the greatest adventure of all. A shared life. A shared future. A shared love.

# COMING SOON

**The third and final volume in the Devil's Brood Trilogy**
**THE GREATEST CHALLENGE OF THEM ALL**
**July 13, 2017**

*A nobleman devoted to defending queen and country and a noblewoman wild enough to match his every step race to disrupt the plans of a malignant intelligence intent on shaking England to its very foundations.*

Lord Drake Varisey, Marquess of Winchelsea, eldest son and heir of the Duke of Wolverstone, must foil a plot that threatens to shake the foundations of the realm, but the very last lady—nay, noblewoman—he needs assisting him is Lady Louisa Cynster, known throughout the ton—for excellent reasons—as Lady Wild.

**AND MORE...**

**COMING LATER IN 2017**

**The first volume in**
**LADY OSBALDESTONE'S CHRISTMAS CHRONICLES:**
**LADY OSBALDESTONE'S CHRISTMAS GOOSE**

A short novel in which, with the aid of grandchildren and local villagers, Lady Osbaldestone discovers that Christmas can be a much more entertaining season than she'd thought.

# RECENTLY RELEASED

## THE ADVENTURER'S QUARTET

#1 New York Times bestselling author Stephanie Laurens brings you THE ADVENTURERS QUARTET, a thrilling blend of high seas adventure, a mystery shrouded in the heat of tropical jungles, and the passionate romances of four couples and their unexpected journeys into love.

THE ADVENTURERS QUARTET is a rollicking Regency-era adventure-romance quartet evolving from secondary characters encountered in THE LADY RISKS ALL, and also including some favorites from the Bastion Club and the Black Cobra novels.

The four volumes of THE ADVENTURERS QUARTET tell the story of four buccaneering brothers, who meet four adventurous ladies in four sultry romances while fighting to rescue others who have fallen prey to a band of villains in the deepest, darkest heart of Africa.

THE LADY'S COMMAND
A BUCCANEER AT HEART
THE DAREDEVIL SNARED
LORD OF THE PRIVATEERS

# AUTHOR'S NOTE

Readers often ask how much of what I write is based on fact. In general, the answer is: Not much. My characters and storylines are usually one hundred percent fictional, albeit based on prevailing mores and the probable occupations, interests, and activities of the relevant era. The one arena in which I try to be accurate to the time is in geography—in the placement of houses in the countryside, in the streets my characters walk in London, in the buildings of note they would see. In the main, I use historical fact as a backdrop—for color, for interest, for atmosphere. Where real historical figures appear in my works, they are usually restricted to the background—another element of historical color.

Occasionally, however, historical fact is just too perfect to pass up. In the case of the Devil's Brood Trilogy, a number of historical facts fitted the storyline too perfectly not to be incorporated into the work. So for those interested in such things, in this first volume, the historical facts woven into the story are:

*1) the Young Irelander movement and the unrest of 1848*
The Young Irelanders were a group of largely young Irishmen who actively supported the radical, post-union view of Irish Republicanism, which held that the use of force was necessary to found a secular Irish republic.

The Young Irelanders were inspired by the French Revolution and, most relevant to this story, emboldened by the wave of popular revolutions that swept Europe in 1848 in what became variously known as the "Springtime of the People," "the People's Spring," and "the Year of Revolution," during which governments and monarchies were overthrown. Countries affected included France, with the overthrow of King Louis-Phillipe and the establishment of the Second Republic, as well as the Germanic States, the Austrian Empire, the Kingdom of Hungary, Denmark, Wallachia, Poland, and the Netherlands, among others. The revolutions were democratic in nature, removing old feudal structures and creating independent national states, abolishing serfdom, ending absolute monarchies, and extending suffrage.

In July 1848, in response to the imposition of martial law by the English authorities, under the leadership of W.S. O'Brien, T.M. Meagher, and J.B. Dillon, the Young Irelanders launched a rebellion, sweeping through Co. Wexford, Co. Kilkenny, and into Co. Tipperary, culminating in a stand-off at the Widow McCormack's cottage in Ballingarry. The stand-off ultimately turned violent. English reinforcements arrived, and the

Young Irelander leaders were arrested, tried and convicted of sedition, and ultimately transported.

Although this broke the back of the Young Irelander movement, intermittent resistance continued to at least the end of 1849.

It is against this historical background that Drake and his political masters in Whitehall view and react to the rumors of a fresh Young Irelander plot.

*2) the manufacture, storage, and transport of gunpowder*
Gunpowder is composed of specific ratios of saltpeter (potassium nitrate), sulfur, and coal (charcoal). Each component is supplied as a powder and combined by being ground together under mill wheels, the resulting mass dampened, and later dried in small, grain-sized pellets. Gunpowder was manufactured in various mills; in England, these were concentrated in the southwest, the southeast around the Thames estuary, and in Cumbria. There were also gunpowder mills in Ireland, including a major one at Ballincollig, outside Cork. At the time of this story, almost all gunpowder mills in England and Ireland were in private hands. The government Board of Ordnance placed orders with many for supplies for the armed services. In addition, the gunpowder was used for explosives for mining and building, and for fireworks, as well as being exported.

The performance of gunpowder is highly susceptible to atmospheric moisture. The transport of gunpowder was usually by water as far as possible, but the issue of the gunpowder getting damp, and thus becoming useless, was a very real one (thus the many references to keeping your powder dry). Gunpowder barrels were usually made of oak by coopers trained to fit the staves especially tightly to prevent any degree of atmospheric seepage.

Where exactly in Ireland Connell Boyne got his ten barrels of gunpowder from is anyone's guess, but he could have got them from the Ballincollig Mill.
All goods brought into the Pool of London were scrutinized for excise, so ten barrels of gunpowder would have been noted and would have been traceable from that point had the barrels been brought into England by that route. In contrast, the coast of Kent was a well-known smugglers' coast and its limestone cliffs were indeed pocked with caves. It seems likely that Connell Boyne would have been chosen for his role in the plot most particularly because of his ability to arrange for the illicit barrels to be delivered to and stored in the cave beneath the Pressingstoke Hall estate.

To get the barrels into London without anyone in authority noticing, the barrels would have to be picked up by carters, about whom you will learn more in the next volume of this series.

*3) Wellington's presence at Walmer Castle*
In 1850, the Duke of Wellington, although a very old man, still held the position of Lord of the Cinque Ports, as well as that of Commander-in-Chief of the Army, among other titles. He was known to retire to Walmer Castle every autumn; he acknowledged it as his favorite residence.

Because of his long association with the corridors of power through his years in Parliament, ultimately serving as Prime Minister twice, Wellington was well acquainted with the various sources of political unrest. More, he was Anglo-Irish himself, had in his early career served in Ireland, was critically influential in getting the Catholic Emancipation Act through Parliament in 1829, and unquestionably retained a keen interest in that particular area. Wellington retired from public life in 1846, but returned in 1848, when he was involved in organizing a military force to protect London through that year of widespread political unrest. He was still privately abreast of politics in 1852.

So at the time of our story, Wellington was still well connected with all levels of government, and as he was at Walmer Castle at the time, it is reasonable to suppose that Sebastian Cynster, the heir to another duke with whom Wellington would have been acquainted since Waterloo, would have known Wellington was there, and given the situation, would have consulted him, hoping to pick his brains.

Walmer Castle is still standing and is essentially as described.

*4) the emergence of "the Press"*
Newspapers had evolved significantly from the news sheets of earlier decades. By 1850, there were literally dozens of newspapers published in London, and the proprietors of the many dailies were engaged in furious competition for readers. The coverage of crimes had already become a staple, one especially useful for driving circulation, and "newsmen," those we would now term reporters, were employed and sent out to cover the latest sensation (no, nothing much has changed!). Sebastian's prediction of having to run the gauntlet of a horde of pressmen at the gates in order to escape Pressingstoke Hall is all too likely to have been true. The lure of sensational murders at a country house party at a lordly estate would have brought the eager vultures of the press running—and the coast of Kent isn't far from London.

The second and third volumes of this trilogy also incorporate further historical facts. For your interest, I will continue to describe those in notes at the back of the relevant volumes.

Stephanie.

# ABOUT THE AUTHOR

#1 *New York Times* bestselling author Stephanie Laurens began writing romances as an escape from the dry world of professional science. Her hobby quickly became a career when her first novel was accepted for publication, and with entirely becoming alacrity, she gave up writing about facts in favor of writing fiction.

All Laurens's works to date are historical romances ranging from medieval times to the mid-1800s, and her settings range from Scotland to India. The majority of her works are set in the period of the British Regency. Laurens has published more than 60 works of historical romance, including 38 *New York Times* bestsellers and has sold more than 20 million print, audio, and e-books globally. All her works are continuously available in print and e-book formats in English worldwide, and have been translated into many other languages. An international bestseller, among other accolades, Laurens has received the Romance Writers of America® prestigious RITA® Award for Best Romance Novella 2008 for *The Fall of Rogue Gerrard*.

Laurens's continuing novels featuring the Cynster family are widely regarded as classics of the historical romance genre. Other series include the *Bastion Club Novels*, the *Black Cobra Quartet*, and the *Casebook of Barnaby Adair Novels*.

For information on all published novels and on upcoming releases and updates on novels yet to come, visit Stephanie's website: www.stephanielaurens.com

To sign up for Stephanie's Email Newsletter (a private list) for heads-up alerts as new books are released, exclusive sneak peeks into upcoming books, and exclusive sweepstakes contests, follow the prompts at Stephanie's Email Newsletter Sign-up Page.

Stephanie lives with her husband and two cats in the hills outside Melbourne, Australia. When she isn't writing, she's reading, and if she isn't reading, she'll be tending her garden.

CPSIA information can be obtained
at www.ICGtesting.com
Printed in the USA
LVQW13s0017170517
534728LV00012B/1156/P